B309 From Alphabears (Henry Holt & Co.) © 1984 Michael Hague

The Crocodile Bird

RUTH RENDELL

The Crocodile Bird

DOUBLEDAY CANADA LIMITED

Originally published in Great Britain by Random House UK in 1993.

Canadian Cataloguing in Publication Data

Rendell, Ruth, 1930–
The crocodile bird

ISBN 0-385-25429-6

I. Title.

PR6068.E63C7 1993 823'.914 093-094425-9

Printed and bound in the United States of America

Published in Canada by
Doubleday Canada Limited
105 Bond Street
Toronto, Ontario
M5B 1Y3

To Don, Simon, Donna, and Phillip

one

THE world began to fall apart at nine in the evening. Not at five when it happened, nor at half past six when the policemen came and Eve said to go into the little castle and not show herself, but at nine when all was quiet again and it was dark outside.

Liza hoped it was all over. She watched the car go down the lane toward the bridge and then she went back to the gatehouse and upstairs to watch it from her bedroom window, the red lights on its tail as it went over the bridge and its white lights when it faced her again as the road climbed and twisted among the hills. Only when she could see its lights no longer, could see no lights anywhere but a red moon and a handful of stars, did she feel they were saved.

Downstairs she found Eve, calmly waiting for her. They would talk now, but of course about other things, or read or listen to music. Eve smiled a very little, then composed her face. There was no book in her lap or piece of sewing in her hands. Liza saw that her hands were shaking and this frightened her. The first real fear she felt came from the sight of those small, normally steady hands, faintly trembling.

Eve said, "I have something very serious to say to you."

Liza knew what it was. It was Sean. Eve had found out about Sean and didn't like it. With a sense of shock she thought about what Eve did to men she didn't like or who interfered in her plans. An attempt would be made to separate her from Sean and if that failed, what would Eve do? She herself was safe, she always was, she was the bird who pecked at the jaws of death, but Sean was vulnerable and Sean, she saw quite clearly, might be the next candidate. She waited, tense.

It was about something quite different. "I know it'll be hard for you, Liza, but you're going to have to go away from here."

Again Liza got it wrong. She thought Eve meant both of them. After all, that particular threat had been hanging over them for days. This was a battle Eve hadn't been able to win, a conquest she couldn't make.

"When will we have to leave?"

"Not we. You. I've told the police you don't live here. They think you just come sometimes to visit me. I've given them your address." She stared hard at Liza. "Your address in London."

The falling apart of things started then, and the real fear. Liza understood that she had never really known what fear was until that moment, a minute or two after nine on an evening in late

August. She saw that Eve's hands had stopped shaking. They lay limp in her lap. She clenched her own.

"I haven't got an address in London."

"You have now."

Liza said in a jerky voice, "I don't understand."

"If they think you live here they'll ask you about what you saw and what you heard and perhaps—perhaps about the past. It's not only that I can't trust you"—Eve offered a grim little smile—"to tell lies as well as I can. It's for your own protection."

If Liza hadn't been so afraid she would have laughed. Hadn't Eve told her that saying things were for people's own protection was one way totalitarians justified secret police and lying propaganda? But she was too frightened, so frightened that she forgot she had been calling Eve by her first name for years and reverted to the childhood usage.

"I can't go away alone, Mother."

Eve noticed. She noticed everything. She winced as if that name had brought her a twinge of pain. "Yes, you can. You must. You'll be all right with Heather."

So that's whose address it was. "I can stay here. I can hide if they come back." Like a child, not someone of nearly seventeen. And then, "They won't come back." A sharp indrawing of breath, the voice not hers but a baby's. "Will they?"

"I think so. No, I know so. This time they will. In the morning probably."

Liza knew Eve wasn't going to explain anything, and she didn't want an explanation. She preferred her own knowledge to the horror of naked confession, admission, perhaps excuse. She said again, "I can't go."

"You must. And tonight, preferably." Eve looked at the dark out there. "Tomorrow morning, first thing." She closed her eyes for a moment, screwed them up, and made a face of agony. "I know I haven't brought you up for this, Lizzie. Perhaps I've been wrong. I can only say I had the best intentions."

Don't let her say that about my own protection again, Liza prayed. She whispered, "I'm scared to go."

"I know—oh, I know." A voice caressing yet wretched, a voice that somehow yearned, Eve's large dark eyes full of compassion. "But, listen, it won't be too hard if you do exactly what I say, and then you'll be with Heather. You always do what I say, don't you, Lizzie."

I don't. I used to once. Her fear held her rigid and silent.

"Heather lives in London. I've written the address down, this is the address. You must walk to where the bus stops. You know where that is, on the way to the village, between the bridge and the village, and when the bus comes—the first one comes at seven-thirty—you must get on it and tell the driver where you want to go. It's written down here. You must hold out your money and say, 'The station, please.' The bus will take you to the station, it stops outside the station, and you must go to the place where it says 'tickets' and buy a single ticket to London. 'A single to London,' is what you say. It's written down here: Paddington, London.

"I can't get in touch with Heather to say you're coming. If I go to the house to use the phone, Matt will see. Anyway, the police may be there. But Heather works at home, she'll be at home. At Paddington Station you must go to where it says 'taxis' and take a taxi to her house. You can show the taxi driver the piece of paper with her address. You can do all that, Lizzie, can't you?"

"Why can't you come with me?"

Eve was silent for a moment. She wasn't looking at Liza but at Bruno's painting on the wall, Shrove at sunset, purple and gold and dark bluish-green. "They told me not to go anywhere. You aren't planning on going anywhere, I hope, is what they said." She lifted her shoulders in that characteristic way, a tiny shrug. "You have to go alone, Liza. I'm going to give you some money."

Liza knew she would get it from the little castle. When Eve had gone she thought of the ordeal before her. It would be impossible. She saw herself lost as she sometimes was in dreams. Those were the kind of dreams she had, of wandering abandoned in a strange place, and weren't all places strange to her? She would be alone in some gray desolation of concrete and buildings, of empty tunnels and high windowless walls. Her imagination created it out of well-remembered Victorian fiction and half-forgotten monochrome television scenes, a rats' alley from Dickens or a film studio. But it was impossible. She would die first.

The money was a hundred pounds in notes and some more in coins. Eve put it into her hands, closing her fingers around it, thinking no doubt that Liza had never touched money before, not knowing that she had done so once when she found the iron box.

The coins were for the bus, the exact fare. What would she say to the driver? How would she ask? Eve began explaining. She sat beside Liza and went through the instructions she had written down.

Liza said, "What's going to happen to you?"

"Perhaps nothing, and then you can come back and everything will be like it used to be. But we must face it. The chances are they'll arrest me and I'll have to appear in the magistrates' court and then—and then a bigger court. Even then, it may not be too bad, it may only be a year or two. They aren't like they used to be about these things, not like"—even now she could be reassuring, joky—"in the history books. No torture, Lizzie, no dungeons, no shutting up in a cell forever. But we have to face it, it may be—for a while."

"You haven't taught me to face anything," Liza said.

It was as if she had slapped Eve's face. Eve winced, though Liza had spoken gently, had spoken despairingly.

"I know. I did it for the best. I never thought it would come to this."

"What did you think?" Liza asked, but she didn't wait for an answer. She went upstairs to her room.

Eve came in to say good night.

She was cheerful, as if nothing had happened. She was smiling and at ease. These mood swings made Liza more frightened than ever. She thought it likely Eve would fall asleep at once and sleep soundly. Eve kissed her good night and said to be off in the morning early, to take a few things with her, but not to bother with too much, Heather had cupboards full of clothes. Smiling radiantly, she said it sounded terrible to say it, but in a strange way she felt free at last.

"The worst has happened, you see, Lizzie, it's rather liberating."

The last thing Liza noticed before her mother left the room was that she was wearing Bruno's gold earrings.

She had meant not to sleep at all, but she was young and sleep came. The sound of a train woke her. She sat up in the dark, understanding at once it had been a dream. No train had run along the valley for years, not since she was a child. Without the trains the silence had been deeper than ever.

Fear came back before the memory of what there was to be

afraid of. A vague unformulated terror loomed, a great black cloud, that split into the constituents of her dread, the initial departure, the bus—suppose it didn't come?—the terrible train, in her mind a hundred times the size of the valley train with its toy engine, and Heather, whom she recalled as tall, strange, remote, and full of secrets to be whispered to Eve behind a guarding hand.

In all of it Liza had forgotten Sean. How could she let Sean know? The load of bewilderment and despair cast her down among the bedclothes again and she lay there with her face buried and her ears covered. But the birds' singing wouldn't let her lie quiet. The birds were sometimes the only things down here to make a sound from morning till night. The dawn chorus broke with a whistling call, then came a single trill and soon a hundred birds were singing in as many trees.

She sat up fully this time. The gatehouse was silent. Outside all but the birds seemed quiet, for the wind had dropped. The curtains at the window were wide apart as they always were, since the only lights ever to be seen were those of Shrove. She knelt up on the bed in front of the window.

Some demarcation was visible between the brow of the high wooded hills and the dark but clear and glowing sky. There, in the east, a line of red would appear, a gleaming red sash of light unraveled. Meanwhile, something could be seen, the outline of the house, a single light in the stable block, a dense black shapelessness of woodland.

Knowledge of what was out there began to give the prospect form, or else the cold glow that comes just before dawn had started to lift the countryside out of darkness into morning twilight. The water meadows showed themselves pale as clouds and the double line of alders on either side of the river seemed to step out of the surrounding dark. Now Liza could see the shape of the high hills beyond, though not yet their greenness, nor the road that banded them halfway up like a white belt.

She got off the bed, opened the door very quietly, and listened. Eve, who never rested by day, who was always alert, attentive, watchful, uncannily observant, slept by night like the dead. She was going to be arrested today but still she slept. The uneasy feeling came to Liza, as it had come before, that her mother was strange, was odd inside her head, but how would she really know? She had no standard of comparison.

If she didn't think about what she was going to do but kept her mind on practical things, if she didn't *think,* it wasn't so bad. These moments had to be lived through, not the future. She went downstairs to the bathroom, came back and dressed. She wasn't hungry, she thought she would never eat again. The thought of food, of eating a piece of bread, of drinking milk, made her feel sick. She put on the cotton trousers Eve had made, a T-shirt from the reject shop, her trainers, Eve's old brown parka, the hundred pounds divided between its two pockets.

Did Eve mean her to say good-bye?

Opening her mother's door, she thought how this was the first time she had done so without knocking while Eve was inside since Bruno came, or earlier even, since the first Jonathan days. Eve lay asleep on her back. She wore a decorous white nightdress, high at the neck, and her thick dark brown hair was spread all over the pillows. In her deep sleep she was smiling as if she dreamed of lovely pleasurable things. That smile made Liza shiver and she shut the door quickly.

It was no longer dark. Clouds were lifting away from the thin red girdle that lay along the tops of trees, dark blue feathers of cloud being drawn away up into a brightening sky. Birdsong filled up past silence with its loud yet strangely remote music. Liza was thinking again, she couldn't help it. Opening the front door and going outside and closing it behind her was the hardest thing she had ever done. It exhausted her and she leaned on the gate for a moment. Perhaps nothing would seem so hard again. She had taken her key with her, why she couldn't tell.

The chill of daybreak touched her face like a cool damp hand. It brought back the feeling of sickness and she breathed deeply. Where would she be this time tomorrow? Better not think of it. She began to walk along the lane, slowly at first, then faster, trying to calculate the time. Neither she nor Eve had ever possessed a watch. It must be somewhere between six-thirty and seven.

Too light for cars to have their lights on, yet these had, the two of them that she could see in the far distance coming along the winding road toward the bridge. She sensed that they were together because both had lights, one following the other, aiming for a certain goal.

By now she was in that part of the lane that was the approach to the bridge and where no tall trees grew. She could see the flash the morning light made on the river and see too the tunnel mouth on the other side where once the train had plunged into the hillside. Suddenly the car lights were switched off, both sets. Liza couldn't even see the cars anymore, but she knew they were coming this way. There was nowhere else for them to go.

If she got onto the bridge they would have to pass her, only they wouldn't pass her, they would stop. She climbed up the bank and hid herself among the late-summer tangle of hawthorn and bramble and wayfarer's tree. The cars glided up silently. One of them had a blue lamp on its roof, but the lamp wasn't lit.

Liza had been holding her breath all the time and now she expelled it in a long sigh. They would come back—they would bring Eve back—and in doing so pass the bus stop. She scrambled down the bank and ran onto the bridge. The river was wide and deep and glassy, not gulping at boulders and rippling between them until much farther up. On the bridge Liza did what it was unwise to do, she stopped and turned and looked back.

It might be that she would never see it again, any of it. She would never return, so she stopped and looked back like the woman in the picture at Shrove had done, the tall sad woman in white draperies who Eve told her was Lot's wife and her forsaken home the Cities of the Plain. But instead of those desolate and wicked places, she saw between the trees that rose out of the misty water meadows, the alders and the balsams and the lombardy poplars, the gracious outlines of Shrove House.

The sun that had risen in a golden dazzlement shed a pale amber light on its stone facade, the central pediment that held a coat of arms of unknown provenance, its broad terrace approached by flights of steps on both sides, its narrow door below and wide, noble door above. This was the garden front, identical to the front that faced the gates in all but that aspect's gracious portico. All its windows were blanked by this light that lay on them like a skin. The house looked as immovable as the landscape in which it rested, as natural and as serene.

From nowhere else could you see Shrove as from here. Trees hid it from spectators on the high hills. They knew how to conceal their homes from view, those old builders of great houses, Eve had said. Liza said a silent good-bye to it, ran across the bridge and out onto the road. The place where the bus stopped was a couple of hundred yards up on the left. Whatever Eve might think, she knew it well, she had often walked this way, had seen the bus, a green bus that she had never once been tempted to board.

What time was it now? A quarter past seven? When would the next bus come if she missed this one? In an hour? Two hours? Insurmountable difficulties once more built themselves up before her. Ramparts of difficulties reared up in her path, impossible to scale. She couldn't wait for that bus out in the open and risk the police cars passing her.

For all that, she kept on walking toward the bus stop, shifting the bag onto her other shoulder, now wondering about the train. There might not be another train to London for a long time. The train that had once run along the valley had passed quite seldom, only four times a day in each direction. How would she know if the train she got into was the one for London?

The sound of a car made her turn, but it wasn't one of their cars. It was red with a top made of cloth and it rattled. As it passed it left behind a smell she wasn't used to, metallic, acrid, smoky.

One other person waited at the stop. An old woman. Liza had no idea who she was or where she came from. There were no houses until the village was reached. She felt vulnerable, exposed, the focus of invisible watching eyes as she came up to the stop. The woman looked at her and quickly looked away as if angry or disgusted.

It took only one more car to pass for Liza to know she couldn't wait there, she couldn't stand on the verge and wait for the bus. What was she to do there? Stand and stare? Think of what? She couldn't bear her thoughts and her fear was like a mouthful of something too hot to swallow. If she waited here by the old woman with the downcast eyes, she would fall down or scream or cast herself onto the grassy bank and weep.

An impulse to run came to her and she obeyed it. Without looking to see if anything was coming, she ran across the road and plunged in among the trees on the other side. The old woman stared after her. Liza hung on to the trunk of a tree. She hugged it, laying her face against the cool smooth bark. Why hadn't she thought of this before? It had come to her suddenly what she must do. If she had thought of this last evening, how happy the night would have been! Except that if she had, she would have left last night, gone when Eve first told her to go, fled in the darkness across the fields.

A footpath ran close by here and through the pass. You couldn't really call it a pass, a pass was for mountains, but she had read the word and liked it. First of all she had to scramble up a hundred yards of hillside. The rumble of the bus, whose engine made a different noise from a car's, made her look down. Somehow she guessed it had arrived exactly on time. The old woman got on it and the bus moved off. Liza went on climbing. She didn't want to be there still when the cars came by. The footpath signpost found, she climbed the stile and took the path that ran close under the hedge. The sun was up now and feeling warm.

It was a relief to be far from the road, to know that when they came back they would be down there below her. When the path came to an end she would find herself in a web of lanes, buried in banks, sheltered by hedges, far from thoroughfares that went anywhere. The nearest town was seven miles off. It ought not to take her more than half an hour from here and she would be with him soon after eight. She wouldn't let herself think he might have gone, he might have moved on, that, angry with her, he had abandoned her and fled.

The birds had stopped singing. All was still and silent, her own footfalls soundless on the sandy track. The white and gold faces of chamomile flowers had appeared everywhere amid the grass and the old man's beard that had been clematis clung to the hedges in cascades of curly gray hair. She encountered her first animals, half a dozen red cows and two gray donkeys cropping the lush grass. A ginger cat, going home from a night's hunting, gave her a suspicious look. She had seen few cats, most of them in pictures, and the sight of this one was as pleasing as that of some exotic wild creature might be.

With the bright morning and her marvelous decision, fear was fast ebbing away. She had only one isolated fear left, that he wouldn't be there. The path came to an end with another stile and she was out in a lane so narrow that if she had lain down and stretched her arms beyond her head, her hands might have touched one side and her feet the other. A small car could have got along it, tunneling between the steep, almost vertical banks, green ramparts hung with the long leaves of plants whose flowers had bloomed and faded. The tree branches met and closed overhead.

It was flat, even a little downhill, and she began to run. She ran from youth and an increasing sense of freedom but from hope and anxiety too. If he had gone, meaning to let her know tomorrow or the next day . . . Her hands in her pockets closed over and crushed the notes, two thin fistfuls—a lot or a little?

She ran on through the green tunnel and a rabbit ran across ahead of her. A cock pheasant squawked and flapped, teetered across the lane, a poor walker and a worse flier, its two hens following it, scrabbling for the shelter of the bank. She knew about things like that, knew far better she suspected than most people, but would it suffice? Would it do until she could learn about the other things?

The lane met another and another at a fork with a tiny triangle of green in the midst of it. She took the right-hand branch where the land began to fall still farther, but she had to go past one bend and then another before she saw the caravan below her. Her heart leapt. It was all right. He was there.

It was parked, as it had been for the past few weeks, since midsummer, on a sandy space from which a bridlepath opened and followed the boundary between field and wood. Horses were supposed to use it, but Liza had never seen a horse or a rider on that path. She had never seen anyone there but Sean. His old Triumph Dolomite, like a car from a sixties film, was parked where it always was. The curtains were drawn at the caravan windows. He only got up early for work. She had been running, but she walked this last bit, she walked quite slowly up to the caravan, mounted the two steps, and taking her right hand from her pocket and the notes it had still been enclosing, brought it to the smooth surface of the door.

Her hand poised, she hesitated. She drew in her breath. Knowing nothing but natural history and scraps of information from Victorian books, she nevertheless knew that love is unreliable, love is chancy, love lets you down. It came to her, this knowledge, from romantic dramas and love poetry, the sighs of the forsaken, the bitterness of the rejected, but from instinct too. Innocence is never ignorant of this, except in those nineteenth-century novels, and then only sometimes. She thought of how he could kill her with the wrong word or the abstracted look, and then she expelled her breath and knocked on the door.

His voice came from in there. "Yes? Who is it?"

"Sean, it's me."

"Liza?"

Only amazed, only incredulous. He had the door open very quickly. He was naked, a blanket from the bed tied around him. Blinking at the light, he stared at her. If she saw a sign of dismay in his eyes, if he asked her what she was doing there, she would die, it would kill her.

He said nothing. He took hold of her and pulled her inside, into the stuffy warm interior that smelled of man, and put his arms around her. It wasn't an ordinary hug but an all-enveloping embrace. He folded himself around her and held her inside himself as a hand might enfold a fruit or a cone, softly but intensely, sensuously appreciating.

She had been going to explain everything and had foreseen herself telling her long tale, culminating in what had happened yesterday. It was a justification she had had in mind and a defense. But he gave her no chance to speak. Somehow, without words, he had made plain to her his great happiness at her untoward unexpected arrival and that he wanted her without explanation. As his arms relaxed their hold she lifted up her face to him, to look at his beautiful face, the eyes that changed his whole appearance when they grew soft with desire. But she was deprived of that too by his kiss, by his bringing his mouth to hers, so sweet-tasting and warm, blinding and silencing her.

When the bed was pulled down out of the wall the caravan was all bed. Her face still joined to his, she wriggled out of her clothes, dropped them garment by garment onto the floor, stepped out of the tracksuit pants, kicked off her trainers. She put her arms up again to hold him as he had held her. He let her pull him down onto the bed. It was warm where he had left it. They lay side by side, her breasts soft and full against his chest, hip to hip, their legs entwined. He began to kiss her with the tip of his tongue, lightly, quickly. She laughed, turned her face.

"I've run away! I've come to you for good."

"You're a marvel," he said. "You're the greatest," and then, "What about her?"

"I don't know. The police came, they came in two cars, they'll have taken her away." She appreciated his look of amazement, his interest. "I'd gone by then. Are you pleased?"

"Am I *pleased?* I'm over the moon. But what d'you mean, the police? What police?"

"I don't know. The police from the town."

"What's she done?"

She put her lips close to his ear. "Shall I tell you about it?"

"Tell me the lot, but not now."

He ran his hands down her body, down her back in a long slow sweep, and drew it close to him in a delicate arch. Without looking, she sensed him viewing her, appreciating her smoothness, her whiteness, her warmth. His hip touched hers, his thigh pressed against hers, warmth to warmth and skin to skin.

"Don't talk now, sweetheart," he said. "Let's have this now."

two

SHE slept for a long time. She was very tired. Relief had come too and a reprieve. When she woke up, Sean was sitting on the bed, looking down at her. She put out her hand and took hold of his, clutching it tightly.

Sean was wonderful to look at. She hadn't much to judge by, the painted man at Shrove, grainy monochrome images of actors in old movies, the postman, the oilman, Jonathan and Bruno, Matt, and a few others. His face was pale, the shape of the features sharply cut, his nose straight, his mouth red and full for a man's, dark eyes where she fancied she saw dreams and hopes, and eyebrows like the strokes of a Chinese painter's brush. She had seen a painting in the drawing room at Shrove with willow leaves and pink-breasted birds, a strange flower Eve said was a lotus, and letters made up of black curves like Sean's eyebrows. His hair was black as coal. Liza had read that, for as far as she knew she had never seen coal.

"You've been asleep for six hours." He said it admiringly, as one acclaiming another for some particular prowess.

"For a minute, when I woke up, I didn't know where I was. I've never been to sleep anywhere but in the gatehouse."

"You're kidding," he said.

"No, why would I? I've never slept away from home." She marveled at it. "This is my home now."

"You're the greatest," he said. "I'm lucky to have you, don't think I don't know it. I never thought you'd come, I thought, she'll never come and stay and *be* with me, she'll go and I'll lose her. Don't laugh, I know I'm a fool."

"I wouldn't laugh, Sean. I love you. Do you love me?"

"You know I do."

"Say it, then."

"I love you. There, is that okay? Haven't I proved I love you? I'd like to prove it all the time. Let me come in there with you, love, let's do it again, shall we? D'you know what I'd like best? To do it to you all the time, we wouldn't eat or sleep or watch TV or any of those things, we'd just do it forever and ever till we died. Wouldn't that be a lovely death?"

For answer she jumped up, eluding his grasp, and shifted to the far corner of the bed. He had laid her clothes there, the garments shaken and carefully placed side by side, like Eve might. Quickly she pushed her legs into the tracksuit, pulled the top over her head.

She said gravely, "I don't want to die. Not that way or any other." A thought came that she had never considered before.

"You wouldn't ever do it to me without me wanting it, would you, Sean?"

He was angry for a moment. "Why d'you say things like that? Why did you ask me that? I don't understand you sometimes."

"Never mind. It was just an idea. Don't you ever have nasty ideas?"

He shrugged, the light and the desire gone out of his face. "I'm going to make us a cup of tea. Or d'you fancy a Coke? I've got Coke and that's about all I have got. I haven't got nothing to eat, we shall have to go down to the shop."

Anything, she thought. *I haven't got anything to eat.* She wouldn't tell him this time. "Sean," she said, up in the corner, her back to the wall. "Sean, we'll have to *go*. I mean, leave here. We ought to put a good many miles between us and her."

"Your mum?"

"Why do you think the police came? I told you they came." As she spoke she knew he hadn't thought, he hadn't listened. Probably he hadn't heard her say that about the police. He had been consumed by desire, mad for her, closed to everything else. She knew how that felt, to be nothing but a deaf, blind, senseless *thing*, swollen and thick with it, breathless and faint. "I told you the police came."

"Did you? I don't know. What did they come for?"

"Can I have that Coke?" She hesitated and made the hesitation long. "I'm supposed to have gone to her friend Heather. That's where she thought she'd sent me. But I came to you."

"Tell me what she's done."

His expression was a bit incredulous and a bit—well, indulgent, she thought the word was. He was going to get a surprise. It wasn't going to be what he thought—she searched her imagination—stealing something or doing things against the law with money. He sat down where he had sat before and became intent on her. That pleased her, his total absorption.

"She killed someone," she said. "The day before yesterday. That's why they came and took her away and I'm afraid they'll want me, they'll want me to be a witness or something. They'll want to ask me questions and then maybe they'll try to put me somewhere to have people look after me. I've heard about that. I'm so young, I won't be seventeen till January."

She had been wrong about his absorption. He hadn't been listening. Again he hadn't heard her, but for a different reason. He was staring at her with his mouth slightly open. As she noted this he curled his upper lip as people do when confronted by a horror.

"What did you say?"

"About what? My age? Being a witness?"

He hesitated, seemed to swallow. "About her killing someone."

"It was yesterday, after I came back from meeting you in the wood. Or I think so. I mean I didn't actually see it, but I know she killed him."

"Come on, love." An awkward grin. "I don't believe you."

It left her helpless, she had no idea how to respond to this. She drank a few mouthfuls out of the open triangle in the top of the can. Eve had once told her that when a cat is in doubt how to act, it waves the tip of its tail. She felt like a cat but with no tail to wave. He must make the next move, for she couldn't.

He got up and took a few steps away. The caravan was too small for more than a few steps to be taken. She drank some more of her Coke, watching him.

"Why did you say that," he said, "about her killing somebody? Was you kidding? Was you trying to be funny?"

"It's true."

"It *can't* be."

"Look, Sean, I didn't make it up. It's why I came away. I

didn't want them to take me and shut me up, make me live somewhere. I knew they'd come this time. This time they'd find out and it wouldn't take long. I was expecting them all night."

His naturally pale face had gone whiter. She noticed and wondered why. "You mean she killed someone by accident, don't you?"

"I don't understand what that means." It was a sentence she was often obliged to utter since she had been with him.

"She was shooting birds and she shot someone by mistake, is that it? You told me she wouldn't never kill birds or rabbits, you told me that when we first met."

Only the last four words really registered with her. They made her smile, remembering. She slithered down the bed, jumped off, and put her arms around him. "Wasn't it lovely that I met you and you met me? It was the best thing that ever happened to me."

This time it was he who pulled away from the embrace. "Yes, love, okay, it was great. But you've got to tell me. About this killing, this is serious, right? What happened? Was it some guy poaching?"

"No," she said, "no, you don't understand."

"Too bloody right I don't and I won't if you don't tell me."

"I'll try." She sat down and he sat down and she held his hand. "She murdered him, Sean. People do do that, you know." It seemed a wild and curious statement for her to be making. "She murdered him because she wanted to be rid of him. She wanted him out of the way, it doesn't matter why, it's not important now."

This time he didn't say he disbelieved her but, "I *can't* credit it."

What had Eve said? "Then you must just accept."

"Who did she murder?"

She could tell from his tone that he still thought she was lying. That made her impatient.

"It doesn't matter. A man. No one you know. Sean, it's the truth, you have to believe me." She was learning truths of her own. "I can't be with someone who thinks I'm telling him lies." From delighted laughter, she was near to tears. She sought for a way out. "I can't prove it. What can I do to make you believe it?"

He said in a low voice, "I sort of do believe you—now."

"I'll tell you all about it." She was eager. She took hold of his shoulders and brought her face close up to his. "I'll tell you everything, if you like, from when I was small, from when I can first remember."

He kissed her. When her face was as close to his as that, he couldn't resist kissing her. His tongue tasted of the caramel sweetness of Coke as she supposed hers must. They were on the bed, that was where you sat in the caravan, and her body grew soft, sliding backward, sinking into the mattress, she was wanting him as much as she had when she first arrived that morning. He pulled her up, grasping her hands.

"I want you to tell me, Liza. I want to know everything about you. But not now. Now tell me what your mum did."

Being frustrated made her sulky. "What's the good? You won't believe it."

"I will, I've said so."

"I think we ought to leave, we ought to be on our way, not sitting here talking."

"Don't you worry yourself about that, I'll see to all that. You tell me about your mum and this man." She saw it in his eyes as the idea came to him. "Did he try raping her, was that it?"

"He was teaching her to shoot pigeons with a shotgun. He was out there shooting and she said, show me how."

"You've got to be joking."

"It's the truth. If you're going to say that, I won't tell you."

"Right, then. Go on."

"I hate shooting birds. I hate people shooting anything, rabbits, squirrels, anything, it's *wrong.* And I thought Eve—my mother—I thought she did too. She said so, she taught me to think like that. But she told him the pigeons were eating her vegetables and she asked him to show her how and he said he would. You see, I think he'd have done anything she asked, Sean."

"She's an attractive woman."

"More attractive than I am?"

"Don't be bloody ridiculous. Was you watching all this?"

"I'd been in the wood with you," Liza said. "They didn't see me. I came up through the garden and they were on the grass where the new trees are. Sound carries terrific distances there, you know. Even when people are speaking softly you can hear them. I saw the two of them with just the one gun and I thought she must be telling him not to shoot the pigeons. He was allowed to, you know, because though pheasant shooting doesn't start till October you can shoot pigeons when you like. Poor things! What did it matter to him, he wasn't a farmer, they weren't his cabbages they were eating, and even if they were, the pigeons have got to live, haven't they?

"I thought, good for her, she's going to stop him, but she didn't. She was out there with him for a shooting lesson. I'd heard her talking about it with him, but I didn't think she was serious. When I saw them I asked myself, what on earth is she doing? He started showing her things about the gun and she was looking and then he handed it to her.

"I didn't want to see the birds killed. I started to go back toward the gatehouse. Then the shot came and immediately afterward this screaming choking noise. So I turned around and ran across the lawn and there she was looking at him where he lay. She wasn't holding the gun, she'd dropped it, she was looking down at him and all the blood on him."

Sean had put up his hand to cover his mouth. His eyes had grown very big. He took his hand away, pushing at his cheek in a curious wiping movement. "What did you do?" he said in a small voice.

"I didn't do anything. I went home. She didn't tell the police and I didn't, so I think Matt must have. You know Matt?"

"Of course I do."

"He was there, up by the house. Only I don't think he saw any more than I did. He guessed."

"But you said the police had only just come, they were coming when you left—when? A couple of hours ago?"

"They came last evening. They didn't see me. You see, they didn't come to the gatehouse, not then. First of all, cars came and a black van to take away the body. I watched it all from my bedroom window. Eve told me to stay there and not come out, not to let anyone see me. I didn't want them to see me. She went up to Shrove and I think the policemen talked to her there. They talked to her and they talked to Matt and Matt's wife.

"She knew they'd come back, so she said I must go. For my own protection, she said. I ran away to you. That's it."

"That's all of it?"

"Not *all,* Sean. It'll take me a long time to tell you all of it."

"I'll get the van fixed up to the tow bar," he said.

She went outside with him. The day was warm and sultry, two in the afternoon, and the sun a puddle of light in a white sky. Watching him, she picked blackberries off the hedge and ate them by the handful. She was enormously hungry.

The battered Dolomite shifted the caravan with the slow weary competence of an old carthorse. It groaned a bit and expelled a lot of black exhaust. Liza got into the passenger seat and banged the door. Car and caravan lurched off the grass verge onto the harder surface of the lane.

"Where shall we go?"

"We have to go where they'll let me park the van. Before you come I was thinking of trying Vanner's. They're wanting pickers for the Coxes. We could both of us do that."

"Coxes won't be ready till the third week of September," she said, always glad to show off something she knew and he might not. "Anyway, how far is it?"

"Twenty-five miles, thirty. Far enough for you?"

"I don't know. What else can you do?"

He laughed. "Electrical work, sort of, put washers on taps, grind knives, I'm halfway to a motor mechanic, wash your car, do your garden—as *you* should know—clean windows, most things, you name it."

"Why apples, then?"

"Apples make a change. I reckon I always do pick apples in September and cherries in July."

"I'm hungry," she said, "I'm so *bloody* hungry."

"Don't swear, Liza."

"You do. Who d'you think I got it from?"

"It's different for me. You're a woman. I don't like to hear a woman swear."

She lifted her shoulders, the way Eve did. "I'm tremendously hungry. Can we buy some food?"

"Yeah, we can get takeaway." He looked at her, remembered and explained, "Stuff they've cooked for you in a shop, right? Or we'll find a caff, maybe a Little Chef if there's one on the A road."

She was no longer afraid. Fear might not be canceled, but it was postponed. The prospect of going into a café excited her. And she'd be with Sean. Shops she had been in, one or two over the years, but a real restaurant, if that was the word, that was very different. She remembered what she had taken with her when she left the gatehouse.

"I've got money. I've got a hundred pounds."

"For Christ's sake," he said.

"It's in the van, in my coat."

"Did you nick it?" His tone was stern.

"Of course not. Eve gave it to me."

He said nothing. She looked out of the window at the passing countryside, all of it new, all uncharted for her. They drove through a village as the church clock struck three, and ten minutes later they were in a sizable town with parking in the marketplace.

On either side of the carpark the roads that enclosed it were lined with shops. She had seen something like this before, though not here, the dry cleaner's, the building society, the estate agent, the Chinese restaurant, the Oxfam shop, the sandwich bar, the building society, the insurance company, the Tandoori House, the bank, the pub, the card shop, the estate agent. An arch, in pink glass and gold metal, led into a deserted hall of shops. Perhaps all towns were like this, all the same inside, perhaps it was a rule.

Sean's practiced eye quickly summed up the situation. "The caffs are closed, it's too late. Pubs are meant to stay open till all hours, but they don't never seem to. I can go get us pie and chips or whatever."

Her hunger was greater than her disappointment. "Whatever you like. Do you want some money?"

She said it cheerfully, trying to strike the right note, having never said it before. Yet for some reason he was offended. "I hope I'll never see the day when I've got to live off my girlfriend."

Once he had gone she got out of the car. She stretched her arms above her head, tasting freedom. It was heady stuff, for something was making her shiver and it couldn't be the day, which was as warm as high summer. She had never felt like this before, dizzy, faint was perhaps the word, as if she might fall.

She opened the door of the caravan and clambered up inside. Five minutes' sitting down and a few deep breaths and she felt better. The bed was stowed away in the wall, the sheets and blankets folded, and the table down, ready for a meal by the time Sean came back. The packages he was carrying had grease seeping through the wrapping paper and gave off a pungent smell of deep frying.

She had been so hungry and the smell from the chips and Cornish pasties he unwrapped was so enticing, but she couldn't help herself. Without warning to herself or him she burst into violent tears. He held her in his arms close to him, stroking her hair while she sobbed. Her body shook and her heart was pounding.

"It's all right, it's all right, sweetheart. You've had a shock, it's delayed shock, you'll be okay. I'll look after you."

He soothed her. He stroked her hair and when she was just crying, not sobbing and shrieking anymore, wiped her eyes with his fingers, as gently as a woman, as gently as Eve when she was being gentle. As she quietened he did something she loved him to do, began combing her hair with his own comb, which had thick blunt teeth. The comb ran smoothly through the length of her long dark hair, from crown to tip, and as he paused she felt his fingers just touch and then linger on her neck and the lobe of her ear. She shivered, not this time from shock or strangeness.

"Give us a kiss," he said.

It was more enthusiastic than he had bargained for, a deep sensuous kiss full of controlled energy now released. He laughed at her. "Let's eat. I thought you was hungry."

"Oh, I am. I'm starving."

"You could've fooled me."

This was her first Cornish pasty. She had no means of knowing whether it was a good one or passable or bad, but she liked it. In the past she had never been allowed to eat with her fingers. There had been many gently enforced rules and much benevolent constraint.

"When we get wherever we're going," she said, "I'll tell you the story of my life."

"Right."

"I don't *know,* but I don't think there've been many lives like mine."

"You've got a long way to go with it yet, like maybe seventy years."

"Can I have the last chip? I'll tell you from back as far as I can remember. That's when I was four and that's when she killed the first one."

She pulled a length from the toilet roll he kept by the bed to use as tissues and wiped her mouth. When she turned back to him to say she was ready, they could be off as soon as he liked, she saw that he was staring at her and the look on his face was aghast.

three

ONE of the first things she could remember was the train. It was summer and she and Mother had gone for a walk in the fields when they heard the train whistle. The single track ran down there in the valley between the river and lower slopes of the high hills. It was a small branch line and later on, when she was older, Mother told her it was the most beautiful train journey in the British Isles. Her eyes shone when she said it.

But on that afternoon when Liza was four there were not many passengers and those there were couldn't have been looking out to appreciate the view, or else they were all looking out the other side at the high hills, for when Mother waved and she waved no one waved back. The train jogged along not very fast and disappeared into the round black tunnel that pierced the hillside.

Liza suspected that she and Mother hadn't been there very long the day she saw her first train. If they had been, she would have seen a train before. It was possible they had been at the gatehouse for only a few days. Where they had come from before that she had had no idea then nor for a long time to come. She could remember nothing from before that day, not a face nor a place, a voice nor a touch.

There was only Mother.

There was only the gatehouse where they lived and the arched gateway with the tiny one-roomed house on the other side and Shrove House in the distance. It was half-concealed by tall and beautiful trees, its walls glimpsed mysteriously and enticingly between their trunks. When Mother read stories to her and there was a palace in them, as there often was, she would say, "Like Shrove, that's what a palace is, a house like Shrove." But all Liza had seen of the real Shrove until she was nearly five and the leaves had turned brown and blown off the trees, were a dreamy grayness, a sheet of glittering glass, a gleam of sun-touched slate.

Later on she saw it in its entirety, the stone baluster that crowned it, broken by a crest-filled pediment, the many windows, the soaring steps, and the statues that stood in its alcoves. She was aware even then of the way it seemed to bask, to sit and smile as if pleased with itself, to recline smiling in the sun.

Nearly every day Mother went up to the house that was like a palace in a fairy tale, sometimes for several hours, sometimes for no more than ten minutes, and when she went she locked Liza up in her bedroom.

The gatehouse was the lodge of Shrove House. Later on,

when Liza was older, Mother told her it was built in the Gothic style and not nearly so old as the house itself. It was supposed to look as if it dated from the Middle Ages and had a turret with crenellations around its top and a tall peaked gable. Out of the side of the gable came the arch, which went over the top of a pair of gates and came down on the other side to join up with the little house that looked like a miniature castle with its slit windows and studded door.

The gates were of iron, were always kept open, and had SHROVE HOUSE written on them in curly letters. The gatehouse and the arch and the little castle were made of small red bricks, the dark russet color of rosehips. Liza and Mother had two bedrooms upstairs, a living room and a kitchen downstairs, and an outside lavatory. That was all. Liza's was the bedroom in the turret with a view over their garden and the wood and Shrove park and everything beyond. She disliked being locked in her bedroom, but she wasn't frightened, and as far as she could remember she didn't protest.

Mother gave her things to do. She had started teaching Liza to read, so she gave her rag books with big letters printed on the cloth pages. She also gave her paper and two pencils and a book to rest on. Liza had a baby bottle with orange juice in it because if she had had a glass or a cup she would have spilled the juice on the floor. Sometimes she had two biscuits, just two, or an apple.

Liza didn't know then what Mother did in Shrove House, but later on she found out because Mother began taking her too and she was no longer locked in her bedroom—or only when Mother went shopping. But that was more than six months later, after it had all happened and the winter had come, when snow covered the hillsides and the only trees to keep their leaves were the huge blue cedars and the tall black firs.

Before that, in the summertime, the dogs came. Except in pictures Liza had never seen a dog or a cat or a horse or any animals but wild ones. She thought these two came the day after she and Mother had walked in the fields and seen the first train, but it may have been some other day, a week or even a month later. It wasn't easy to remember time spans from so far back.

The dogs belonged to Mr. Tobias. It wasn't he who brought them but another man. Liza had never seen Mr. Tobias but only heard about him, and she wasn't to see him for a long, long time. The man who brought the dogs came in a kind of small truck with a barrier like a white wire fence across the back inside to keep the dogs off the front seats. His name was Matt. He was a short, squarish man with big shoulders who looked very strong and his hair grew up from his broad red forehead like the bristles on a brush.

"They are Doberman pinschers," Mother said. She always explained everything slowly and carefully. "In Germany, which is another country a long way away, they used to be trained as police dogs. But these are pets." She said to Matt, who was staring at her in a strange way, "What are their names?"

"This one's Heidi and he's Rudi."

"Are they nice, friendly dogs?"

"They'll be okay with you and the kiddy. They'll never attack women, they've been trained that way. I'd be up the nearest tree myself if someone called out 'Kill!' when they're around."

"Really? Mr. Tobias didn't say."

"Thought you might say no to looking after them, I daresay." He gazed around him, stared at the high hills beyond the valley as if they were the Himalayas. "Bit isolated down here, aren't you? Not what you'd call much life going on."

"It's what I like."

"It takes all sorts, I suppose, though I'd have thought a smashing-looking girl like yourself'd want something a bit more lively. Bright lights, eh, bit of dancing and the movies? You wouldn't have such a thing as a cup of tea going, I daresay?"

"No, I wouldn't," said Mother and she took the dog leashes in one hand and Liza's hand in the other, went into the gatehouse, and shut the door. The man outside on the step said something Liza couldn't catch but which Mother said was a dirty word and never to say it. They heard his van start up with a roar as if it was angry.

The dogs started licking Liza, they licked her hands, and when she stroked them, they licked her face. Their coats felt like nothing she had ever touched before, shiny as leather, soft as fur, smooth as the crown of her own head when Mother had just washed her hair.

She said to Mother, "Heidi and Rudi are black lined with brown," and Mother had laughed and said that was right, that was just how they looked.

"You can't remember all those things your mum and him said word for word, can you?" said Sean.

"Not really. But it was *like* that. I know all the kinds of things she says and ever could say. I know her so well, you see, it's as if I know her perfectly because I don't know anyone else."

"How about me? You know me."

She could tell she had hurt him and tried to make amends. "I know you *now*. I didn't then."

"Go on, then. What happened with the dogs?"

"Eve was looking after them for Mr. Tobias. He had to go away, he went to see his mother in France, and he couldn't take the dogs for some reason."

"Quarantine."

"What?"

"When he come back in he'd have to put the pair of them in quarantine for six months. That means they'd be in like kennels. It's the law."

"I expect that was it."

"Why couldn't this Matt look after them wherever it was he lived?"

"In the Lake District. He had a job, he was working all day. He couldn't take them out for exercise—or wouldn't. Anyway, Eve wanted to do this for Mr. Tobias, she wanted to please him.

"We were supposed to have them for two or three weeks, I can't exactly remember. I loved them, I wanted us to have a dog after they'd gone back, but Eve wouldn't. She said Mr. Tobias wouldn't like it."

"So it wasn't them she killed?"

"I told you, it was a person, a man."

Liza never knew who he was or what it was he had tried to do. Now that twelve years had passed and she was grown up, doing the thing that grown-ups did herself, she could guess.

It was she who saw him first. Mother was down at Shrove and she was locked up in her bedroom. Where the dogs were she didn't know. Probably in the little castle where they slept at night or even at Shrove, for in a sort of way it was *their* house. It belonged to Mr. Tobias, who owned them.

Mother had been gone a long time. Who could say now how long those long times actually were? It's different when you're four. Half an hour? An hour? Or only ten minutes? She had read the letters in the rag book and made them into words, "dog," "cat," "bed," "cot." The baby bottle had been sucked dry and the pencil had scribbled over every single sheet of paper.

She climbed upon the bed and crawled on all fours over to the window. The room had six sides and three windows but was too small for the bed to be anywhere but pushed against the wall with the window that had the best view. The sun was shining, sparkling on the river, and the wind was blowing the clouds and making their shadows run across the slopes of the high hills. A train whistled from somewhere out of sight and came into her view from out of the tunnel. She climbed onto a chair to look out of the window that overlooked the gateway and the little castle.

There was never anyone there. There was never anyone to be seen but Mother, the milkman and the postman in the morning, and Mr. Frost on his tractor on certain afternoons. Sometimes a car came down on its way to the bridge. Mostly the lane was empty and all that showed its face in the barn on the other side was the white owl, so seeing the man made her jump. He was holding on to one of the gates and looking toward Shrove, a tall man in blue jeans and a pullover and brown leather jacket and with a canvas bag on his back.

Suddenly he looked up in the direction of her window and saw her there between the curtains. She knew he saw her and it frightened her. She couldn't have said why it did, but it was something to do with his face, not a nice face, not the kind she had ever seen before. It was masked in yellow-brown hair all over it, great bushes of curly hair from which eyes stared and the nose poked out. Later she wondered if she had thought the face not nice because of the beard, which was new to her. She never saw another until the day Bruno and Mother took her shopping in the town.

She was afraid he was coming to the gatehouse and would get in and come to get her. Ducking down from the window and wriggling across the floor and hiding under the bed couldn't stop that and she knew it. She knew it even then. Under the bed she didn't feel safe, only a bit saf*er,* and she thought it might be a little while before he found her. Mother had locked the door of her room and the front door of the gatehouse, but that didn't make Liza think the man wouldn't be able to find her.

A long time went by and Mother came back. She pulled Liza out and hugged her and said she hadn't seen any man and if there was one he was probably harmless. If he wasn't she'd set Heidi and Rudi on him.

"How will you know?" Liza said.

"I know everything."

Liza believed that was true.

Late that afternoon there was a knock at the front door and when Mother went to answer it the man with the beard was on the step, asking for a glass of water. Liza thought Mother would say no, she hung on to Mother's skirt, peering around her until Mother said to let go, not to be so stupid. The man said he hoped he wasn't a nuisance.

"Go and fetch some water, please, Liza," Mother said. "Not a glass, a mug. You know how to do it."

Liza knew. In some ways Mother had brought her up to be independent. Only in some, of course. For a long while she had fetched her own water when she wanted a drink, climbing up onto the chair by the sink, taking a mug from the shelf, turning on the tap, and filling the mug and then being very careful to turn the tap off again. She did this now, filling the mug that had a picture on it of a lady in a crown, and carrying it back to the front door. Some of it spilled on the way, but she couldn't help that.

The man drank the water. She saw so few people she noticed everything about the ones she did see. He held the mug in his left hand, not his right like Liza and Mother did, and on the third finger of that hand was a wide gold ring. That was the first time she had ever seen a ring on anyone's hand, for Mother wore none.

He said to Liza, "Thank you, darling," and gave her back the mug. "Is there anywhere around here doing B and B?" he said to Mother.

"Doing what?"

"B and B. Bed and breakfast."

"There's nowhere around here doing anything," Mother said, sounding glad to say it. She took a step outside, making him step backward, and spread out her arms. "What you see is what you get."

"Best press on, then."

Mother made no answer. She did what Liza didn't like her doing to *her.* It was a way she had of lifting her shoulders and dropping them again while looking hard into the other person's eyes, but not smiling or showing anything. Until then Liza hadn't seen Eve do it to anyone but herself.

From an upstairs window, the one in Mother's room in the gable which overlooked the lane this time, they watched the man go. It was only from here that you could see where the lane ran along past the wood on its way to the bridge in one direction, and in the other to peter out into first a track and then a footpath. The man walked slowly, as if his pack felt heavier with each step he took. At the point where the lane wound and narrowed he paused and looked back in the direction of Shrove or perhaps just at the high hills.

They lost him among the trees, but they went on watching and after a little while saw him again, by now a small figure plodding along the footpath under the maple hedge. After that it became a game between the two of them, each claiming to be able to see him still. But when Liza got excited, Mother lifted her down from the window and they went downstairs to get on with Liza's reading lesson. An hour every afternoon was spent on teaching her to read and an hour every morning teaching her writing. The lessons were soon to get much longer, with sums as well and drawing, but at the time the man with the beard came they lasted just two hours each day.

Every morning very early, long before the writing lesson, they took the dogs out. Heidi and Rudi had been used to living indoors, so couldn't have kennels outside, which Mother would have thought best, but slept in the little castle. Liza had never been in there before the dogs came, but Mother had a key and took her in with her and she saw a room shaped like her bedroom with six sides and narrow windows with arched tops, only these had no glass in them. The floor was of stone with straw on it and two old blankets and two old cushions for the dogs. Rudi and Heidi bounded about and nuzzled her and licked her face, making noises of relief and bliss at being released.

Liza had thought how horrible it would be if they met the man with the beard while they were out in the water meadows. But they met no one, they hardly ever did, only a vixen going home with a rabbit in her mouth. Mother ordered the dogs to sit, to be still, and they obeyed her. She told Liza about foxes, how they lived and raised their young in earths, how people hunted them, and that this was wrong.

That might have been the morning she saw her first kingfisher. It was about that time, she couldn't be sure. Mother said kingfishers were not common and when you saw one you should phone up and tell the County Kingfisher Trust. So it must have been that morning, for after they got home and the dogs were back in the house next door, Mother locked her in her bedroom and went over to Shrove to phone.

Liza read the words in the rag book and drew a picture of

Mother on one of the sheets of paper. It might have been another day she did that, but she thought it was the Day of the Kingfisher. From about that time she got it into her head that all men had fair hair and all women dark. The man who delivered the oil was fair and so were the postman and Matt and the man with the beard, but Mother and she were dark. She drew a picture of Mother with her long dark hair down her back and her long colored skirt and her sandals.

It was just finished when Mother unlocked the door and let her out. There was something different in the living room, Liza spotted it at once. It was hanging up on the wall over the fireplace, a long dark brown tube with a wooden handle. She had never seen anything like it before, but she knew Mother must have brought it back from Shrove.

"It was a gun," said Sean.

"A shotgun. There were a lot of guns at Shrove. I began thinking about it later—I mean years later—and I think that man had really frightened her. Frightened is probably not the word, she doesn't get frightened. Let's say, alerted her to danger."

"Yeah, maybe she reckoned she should never have said that about what you see is what you get. I mean, like, you know, not being no one else around for miles."

"I expect so."

"But he'd gone, hadn't he?"

"He came back."

It stayed light in the evenings until nearly ten, but Liza was put to bed at seven. She had her tea, always wholemeal bread with an egg or a piece of cheese. Cake and sweets were not allowed, and years passed before she found out what they were. After the bread she had fruit, as much as she wanted, and a glass of milk. The milkman came three times a week, another man with fair hair.

Mother read her a story when tea was over: Hans Andersen or Charles Kingsley, books borrowed from the library at Shrove. Then came her bath. They had a bath in the kitchen with a wooden lid on it. She wasn't locked in her bedroom at night, she was never locked in except when Mother went to Shrove or shopping in the town. When Liza couldn't get to sleep she knew it was useless calling out or crying, for Mother took no notice, and if she came downstairs Mother would shrug at her and give her one of those wordless looks before taking her back up again.

So all she could do was wander about upstairs, looking out of the windows, hoping to see something, though she hardly ever did. If Mother knew Liza went into her room and played with her things, she gave no sign of it. Mother read books in the evenings, Liza knew that, or listened to music coming into her ears through wires from a little square black box.

In Mother's room she opened the cupboard door and examined all the long bright-colored skirts that Mother wore and the other things she never wore, long scarves, a couple of big straw hats, a yellow gown with a flounce around the hem. She looked in her jewel case, which was kept in the dressing table drawer, and could have told anyone precisely what the case held: a long string of green beads, two pairs of earrings, a hair comb made of brown mottled stuff with brilliant shiny bits set in it, a brooch of carved wood and another of mother-of-pearl. Mother had told her that was what it was when she wore the brooch just as she told her the beads were jade and the two pairs of earrings made of gold.

That evening the green beads and one pair of earrings were missing because Mother was wearing them. Liza closed the box, went back to her own room, and knelt upon the bed, looking out of the window. The gatehouse garden, in which Mother later on grew peas and beans and lettuces, soft fruit on bushes and strawberries under nets, was mostly bare earth at that time. Mother had been working on it that day, digging it over with a fork. There was just one tree, a single cherry tree, growing out of the soft red-brown soil, and two long grass paths.

Liza shifted her gaze upward, waiting for the last southbound train, which would go through a bit after eight-thirty. She hadn't known about north and south and eight-thirty then, though Mother was teaching her to tell the time and to understand a map, but she knew the last train would come out from the tunnel while it was still light but after sunset. The sky was red all over, though you couldn't see where the sun went down from her room. Once it had set, the high hills went gray and the woods changed from green to a soft dark blue.

The train whistled at the tunnel mouth and came chugging down. Lights were on inside, though there was a lot of light outside still. It would stop at the station, at Ring Valley Halt, but you couldn't see the station from here. In the distance, the train grew very small, long and wriggling like one of the millipedes that lived near the back door. After it was gone there would be nothing more to be seen from this window. Liza scrambled off the bed and went on tiptoe back across the landing to Mother's room.

From here, you could see the bats that lived in the barn roof on the other side of the lane and swooped after moths and gnats. Sometimes she saw the great cream-colored owl with a face like a cat's in a book. She had never seen a real cat. It was a little too early for owls this evening. Down below her, in the little patch of front garden, as twilight came, the color began to fade from the red and pink geraniums and the tobacco flowers began to gleam more whitely. If the window had been open she could have smelled them, for their scent came out at dusk.

Just as Liza was thinking nothing would happen, it would get dark without anything happening, the front door opened and

Mother came out in her green and purple and blue skirt and purple top, her green beads and gold earrings, with a black shawl wrapped around her. She opened the gate in the wall that ran around the garden, unlocked the door of the little castle, and the dogs came rushing out. Mother said, "Quiet. Sit," and they sat, though trembling and quivering, Liza could see, hating this enforced stillness.

Mother said, "Off you go," and the pair of them began gamboling about, jumping up and trying to lick her, leaving off when she didn't respond. She walked around the side of the gatehouse out of sight, the dogs following, but Liza knew she wouldn't go far because she never did in the evenings.

Liza ran back into her own bedroom, climbed onto the bed, and pressed her face against the window. Outside a bat swooped, so close that she jerked her face back, though she knew the glass was there. Rudi and Heidi were in the back garden playing, grappling with each other and making mock growling noises and rolling over and over. Mother wasn't with them, Mother must have come back into the house.

Back on the landing, Liza listened, but she couldn't hear Mother down there. She ran into Mother's room and up to the window. Mother was sitting on the wall, listening to the music coming out of the band around her head and holding the little black box in her hands.

Where were the dogs? No longer in the back garden, she discovered as she bounced back onto her own bed. They must have gone out through the opening in the fence and into the wood, as they sometimes did. But they were well-trained, they always came back at a call.

It would get dull now if nothing more happened than Mother sitting on the wall, waiting for the dogs to finish their play. Liza never considered getting back into bed and trying to sleep as an alternative to this roving from room to room. Either she fell asleep when she happened to be on her own bed or Mother found her asleep on the landing floor or in the chair by the front bedroom window. She always woke in her own bed in the mornings. But she didn't want to be there now, she wasn't tired.

Perhaps Mother had decided to do something different. Liza ran back to check. Mother was still there, still listening. It was nearly dark but not too dark to see the man with the beard come along the lane from the bridge direction. The man looked just the same except that this time he hadn't got his backpack with him.

His footsteps made no sound on the sandy floor. Mother wouldn't have heard them if they had with that thing on her head and the music that was called Wagner flowing into her ears. Liza began to be frightened. Mother had said the dogs would protect them but the dogs weren't there, the dogs were a long way away in the wood.

Liza couldn't look.

Why hadn't she banged on the window to warn Mother? She hadn't thought of that till afterward. The first time the man came she had got under the bed, the second time she had fetched him a drink of water. This time she put her hands over her eyes. They were talking, she could hear their voices but not what they said. Very cautiously she parted her fingers and peeped through them, but they had gone, Mother and the man, they had come too near the gatehouse for her to see or else they had walked around the back. She ran to the back and as she jumped on her bed, Mother screamed.

"What was he doing to her?" Sean said.

"She never told me, she never said a word about it, not then and not later. I know now, of course I do. When she screamed I was so frightened I covered up my ears, but I could still hear, the window was open. I thought the man would catch her and—oh, make her his prisoner or something—and then come and get me."

"You were only a little kid."

"And there was no one else for miles and miles. You know that. There never was. If there had been it couldn't have happened, none of it could."

It wasn't dark but the beginning of the long midsummer twilight. When Mother's scream died away she heard the man laugh but she couldn't hear what it was he whispered. She looked out of the window, she had to look, and Mother was on the grass path and the man was on top of her. He was trying to hold her there with one hand and with the other he was undoing his jeans.

Liza was so frightened she couldn't make a sound or do anything. But Mother could. Mother twisted her head around under the man's arm that pinned her neck and bit his hand. He jumped and pulled up his hand, shouting that word Matt had used on the doorstep, and Mother screamed out, "Heidi, Rudi! Kill! Kill!"

The dogs came out of the wood. They came running as if they had been waiting for the summons, as if they had been sitting among the trees listening for just that command. In the half-dark they no longer looked like nice friendly dogs that licked your face but hounds of hell, though that was before Liza had ever heard of hounds of hell.

They didn't jump at the man, they flew at him. All eight powerful black legs took off and they were airborne. Their mouths gaped open and Liza could see their white shining teeth. The man had started to get to his feet, but he fell over on his back when the dogs came at him. He covered his face with his hands and rolled this way and that. Heidi had half his great yellow beard in her jaws and Rudi was on him biting his neck. The dogs made a noise, a rough, grumbling, snorting sound.

Mother jumped up lightly as if nothing had happened and dusted down her skirt with her hands. She stood in that way she had, with her hands on her hips, the shawl hanging loose from her shoulders, and she watched them calmly, the dogs savaging the man and the man screaming and cursing.

Then, after a little while, she said, "All right, dogs, that'll do. Quiet now. Still."

They obeyed her at once. It was clever the way they stopped the moment she spoke. Rudi had some of the man's blood on his face and Heidi a mouthful of beard. The man rolled over again, his head on his arms, but he had stopped screaming, he didn't make a sound. Mother bent over him, looking closely, she didn't touch him with her hands but prodded him with one small, delicate foot.

Liza made a little sound to herself up in her bedroom, a whimper like a dog whining behind a closed door.

Sean said hoarsely, "Was he dead?"

"Oh, no, he wasn't *dead.*"

"What did she do?"

"Nothing. She just looked at him."

"Didn't she get help? There was a phone in Shrove House, you said."

"Of course she didn't get help," Liza said impatiently.

Mother took hold of the dogs by their collars and put them in the little castle for the night. Liza saw her do that from the other window and heard her come into their own house and shut the front door after her. She went out onto the landing and listened. In the sitting room Mother was moving a chair about and it sounded as if she had climbed on the chair and jumped off it. Liza scrambled across the bed to have another look at the man on the grass. He was still there but not lying face-downward anymore.

It was really dark now, too dark to see much but the shape of the man sitting there with his head on his knees and his arms up around his head. Soon he would get up and go away and leave them and they'd be safe. She peered out through the dark, hoping for that to happen.

Suddenly she could see the man very clearly in a big oblong of light. The back door was open and light was coming from the kitchen. She wrinkled up her nose and made a face because the man's face and beard were a mass of blood. Her knees had looked like that when she fell over and hurt herself on the gravel.

Mother walked out into the light and pointed something she had in her arms and there was a tremendous explosion. The man tumbled over backward and jerked a bit and shuddered and lay still. In the little castle the dogs set up a wild barking. Mother came back into the house and shut the door and the light went out.

f o u r

IN the late afternoon, going by the lanes instead of the A road, Sean and Liza reached Vanner's fruit farm. This was orchard country, acre after acre of close-pruned stubby apple trees in long lines and then acre after acre of Comice pears and Louise Bonnes. The big wooden crates that would take the apples were stacked on top of one another in the corners of orchards. Liza saw women mounted on steps picking the big green Comice. Very few of the pears had been left to fall, but the apple crop, Discovery and Jonagold, had been a heavy one, and under the trees the ground was scarlet with abandoned fruit.

Sean took the left-hand turn into Vanner's land. He had been there before and knew where to go. The long straight macadamized roadway was bounded on either side by lines of alders, neat quick-growing trees to make high hedges. He had to pull in to let a car with its soft top down go past in the other direction, coming from the farm shop. A woman was driving. She had shiny blond hair and red lipstick on, gold earrings and red varnish on her nails, and Liza stared at her, fascinated.

"You're not still thinking women are all dark and men are all fair, are you, love?"

"Of course I'm not. I was only *four.*"

"Because there's other ways of telling the difference." He put his hand in her lap and moved the fingers into her crotch. "Bet you can't talk while I'm doing that. Go on, try. I bet you can't."

"I can do that too," said Liza, reaching for him. "It'll be worse for you, you won't be able to drive."

He laughed and gasped and grabbed her hand. "Better leave off till we get there or I'll have to stop the van and we'll cause an obstruction."

The parking place for caravans was in a remote spot where the orchards ended and the strawberry fields began. The strawberries were long over, the people who came to pick their own departed, and the fields a desolate waste of brown tendrils and dying leaves. A line of extremely tall Lombardy poplars on a high bank divided these fields from the Discovery orchard, and under the shadow of the poplars, on a rutted area of dried mud and scrubby grass, stood a sign that said: PICKERS' VANS PARK HERE. Beside the sign was a water tap, and an arrow spraypainted on cardboard pointed to the waste disposal.

Other pickers there might be, but there was only one caravan. It was parked at the far end up against the bank and looked as if no one was living in it or had lived in it for a long time. Its door and windows were shut and its blinds down. Just the same, Sean parked his car and van as far away from it as he could.

He didn't uncouple the van from the car or get the generator going or fill the water tanks. He and Liza, without a word, with scarcely an exchanged glance, got out of the car, went into the van, and made love. They delayed for just the time it took to pull the bed down.

"I tell you what," said Sean, when it was finished and she was lying in his arms, warm and damp and sighing with pleasure. "Now we're here and got a base, you can get yourself to the family planning or whatever and go on the Pill. Then I won't have to keep on using these things, I hate them."

She looked up at him, uncomprehending. When he had explained she said, "You'll have to come with me, then. I won't know what to do."

"Haven't you never been to the doctor's?"

He would be hurt if she said, "Haven't you *ever* been," so she didn't say it. "Eve took me a couple of times. It's lucky I'm healthy. She said I had my injections when I was a baby."

"Yeah, okay, but injections won't stop you getting yourself pregnant."

"You getting me pregnant," she said.

He laughed. He liked her being a bit sharp with him. Hugging her tight, he said, "D'you mind talking about it or is this the wrong time? I mean, you know, what happened after your mum shot the guy with the beard."

"Why would I mind?"

She couldn't see why she would. Eve said people liked talking about themselves better than anything and now, savoring the pleasure of it for the first time, she understood this was right. Thinking about it, going over it all, picking the bits to tell him and the bits not to, she enjoyed very much. It was her life and she was beginning to see what an extraordinary one it had so far been.

"I started crying, I couldn't help it. I lay on the bed sobbing and screaming."

"I'm not surprised."

"No, well, Eve came up and hugged me. She got me a drink of water and told me not to cry, not to worry, everything was going to be all right. The man had gone away, she'd blown him away."

"Christ."

"She didn't mean me to think she'd killed him. She didn't know I'd been watching. I didn't tell her. I was only four but somehow I knew not to tell her. All she knew was that I'd seen the man come and heard the shot. She got into bed with me and I liked that. I was always wanting to sleep in the same bed with her but she'd never let me. She was so nice and warm and *young*. D'you know how old she is now?"

"About thirty-five?"

"She's thirty-eight. But that's young, isn't it? I mean, it's not young to us but people would call it young, wouldn't they?"

"I reckon," said Sean, who was twenty-one. "How did she come to have a funny name like Eve?"

"It's Eva, really. It's German. Her father was German. I didn't know what her name was till I heard Mr. Tobias call her Eve. She was just Mother. And then when Bruno was always calling her Eve I started doing it too and she didn't mind."

"Who's Bruno?"

"Just a man. He doesn't come into it for years and years. I'll tell you about him when we get there. We'd got this other man lying dead on our grass, or Eve had, it wasn't really much to do with me. The thing was no one ever came near us then, no one at all but the milkman and the oilman and the man who read the electric meter at the cottage and at Shrove. And they didn't go in the back garden or ask any questions.

"The milkman was strange. I noticed more when I was older. I never knew any children so I don't know if he talked like a child but Eve said he had a mental age of eight. He used to say things about the weather and the trains and that was all he ever said. 'Here comes the train,' he'd say and, 'We're in for a cloudburst.' He never noticed things. That man's dead body could have been lying on our doorstep and he'd have just stepped over it."

"What about it, then?" said Sean. "The dead body."

She didn't know exactly. Real events got mixed up with dreams at this point. She'd had awful dreams that night, had woken screaming and found Eve gone, back to her own bed. But she had come and comforted her and stayed, as far as Liza knew, for the rest of the night.

But she couldn't have, Liza realized that later, for in the morning when she looked out of the window, the man was gone. What does death mean to a child of four? It hadn't really registered with her the night before, that the man wouldn't ever get up again, wouldn't ever speak again or laugh or walk about. She had just been terribly frightened. When he was gone she thought he had gone of his own volition. He had mended and got well and walked away.

It was years afterward when she was much older, piecing memories together and comparing them with similar contemporary events, that she understood he was dead and Eve had killed him with Mr. Tobias's shotgun. Not only had Eve killed him but had taken his body away.

Eve was a small woman with a tiny waist and slender elegant legs. She had small hands with long tapering fingers. Her face was wide at the cheekbones and narrow at the chin, her forehead high, her upper lip short, and her mouth full and lovely. Slightly tilted, her pretty nose was a little too small for her face. She had large hazel-green eyes and black eyebrows like Chinese brush-strokes, not unlike Sean's, and her thick, shiny dark hair reached to the middle of her back. But she was very small, no more than five feet or five feet one at best. Liza didn't know her weight, they had no scales, but when she was sixteen Eve estimated seven and a half stone for herself and eight stone and a bit for Liza and that was probably right. Yet this tiny woman had somehow moved a man one and a half times her weight and nearly six feet tall.

And put him where? Somewhere in the wood, Liza decided when she thought about it around that sixteenth birthday. She put the body in the wheelbarrow and took it through the gap in the fence and buried it in the wood. During the night while Liza slept and before she woke up screaming. Or after she had held her and soothed her and she had slept again, Mother had gone down and worked silently in the dark.

The first thing she saw from the window that morning—even before she saw the man was gone—was Matt opening the door of the little castle and letting the dogs out. He wasn't due till mid-morning, Mother said, running into the room. She sounded cross and upset. Liza went to the other window. The dogs had made straight for the place where the man had lain and ran about sniffing the grass in a frenzied way and pushing their noses into the earth.

"There's something fascinating them," Matt said when Liza and Mother went outside. "They been burying bones?"

"Do you know what time it is?" Mother said. "It's six-thirty in the morning."

"So it is. Dear, oh, dear. I'd some business down this way yesterday, so I stopped the night and come over here first thing. Not got you girls out of bed, I hope."

Mother ignored this. "Has Mr. Tobias come back from France?"

"Coming back tonight. He wants his dogs there when he gets home. They're all the company he's got, I reckon. It wouldn't suit me, I like a bit of action myself, but it takes all sorts to make a world."

"It certainly does," said Mother, not very pleasantly.

"You'd think he'd get himself a girl—well, he does, but nothing permanent." Matt spoke as if Mother didn't know it all already. "Of course he's loaded, got his own place and this here and the London one and there's girls falling over themselves to get him, but to be perfectly honest with you he's just not interested." He winked incomprehensibly at Liza. "Not in settling down, I mean."

In spite of what had happened, Liza wasn't afraid to put her arms around each dog's neck and place a tender kiss on each glossy black skull. She cried a bit when they had gone. She asked Mother if they could have a dog of their own.

"No, absolutely not. Don't ask me."

"Why couldn't we, Mother, why couldn't we? I do want a dog, I love Heidi and Rudi, I do want one of my own."

"Then you must want." Mother smiled when she said it, she wasn't angry, and she called Liza Lizzie, which she sometimes did when she was pleased with her or not too disappointed in her. "Listen, Lizzie, suppose Mr. Tobias came to live at Shrove? He might, it's his house—one of his houses. Then Heidi and Rudi would come with him and what would happen to our dog? They don't like other dogs, they'd attack it. They'd hurt it."

Like they hurt the man, Liza felt like saying but she didn't say it. Instead, she said, "Is he going to come? I'd like him to come because then we'd have *his* dogs and we wouldn't have to have our own. Is he going to come?"

Mother said nothing for a moment. Then she put her arm around Liza and pulled her close against her skirts and said, "I hope so, Lizzie, I hope he will," but she wasn't smiling and she gave a heavy sigh.

Next day was Mother's day for going shopping. She went once a fortnight to get the things the milkman wouldn't bring. He brought butter and eggs and porridge oats and orange juice and bread and yogurt as well as milk, but he never brought meat or fish. Until they grew their own, Mother had to buy vegetables. She had to buy fruit and cheese. The bus that went to the shops—to town, that is—ran four times a day and Mother had to walk down the lane and go over the river bridge and a hundred yards along the road to the bus stop. When Mother went to town she never took Liza with her. Liza was locked up in her bedroom.

She was used to it and she accepted, but not this time. At first she gave in, sat on the bed with the rag book and the pencils, sucked at her orange juice bottle. Mother had given her an apple as well for a treat, a Golden Delicious because there were no English ones in July. She knelt on the bed and watched Mother go along the lane toward the main road. Then she shifted her gaze from the distance to the foreground and saw where the man had been and the dogs and the explosion had happened. She began to scream.

Probably she couldn't have screamed for the whole hour and a half Mother was away. Halfway through she may have fallen asleep. But she was screaming when Mother came back. Mother said, "I won't leave you again," and she didn't for a long while but of course she did again one day.

It might have been that evening or an evening days or weeks later, at any rate it was after the dogs had gone, that Liza was playing her roving-between-the-bedrooms game after bedtime. She tried on Mother's straw hats, the golden one with the white band and the brown one with the cream scarf tied around it, and she stroked Mother's suede shoes, that had things inexplicably called trees thrust into them. When she was tired of that she looked inside the jewel case.

Mother was wearing one set of earrings and the mother-of-pearl brooch, so of course those things weren't in there. Liza hung the jade beads around her own neck, put the comb with the shiny bits on it into her hair, and admired the result in the mirror. She picked up the wooden brooch and found lying underneath it a gold ring.

Whose could it be? She had never seen it before, she had never seen any ring on Mother's hand. Examining it with great interest, she saw that there was some writing on the inside of the ring, but she was only four then and she couldn't read very well. Nor did she at that time connect the ring with the man with the beard.

~

"It was his ring?" said Sean.

"It must have been. I looked at it again later, when I could read. The writing said: TMH AND EHH, MARCH 3, 1974. I didn't know what it meant then, but now I think it was his wedding ring. Victoria had a wedding ring. Do men have them?"

"I reckon there's some as do."

"Those were his initials and his wife's and that was the date they got married, don't you think?"

"She must have took it off him, off his hand," said Sean, making a face.

"I don't know why she did unless she thought she might sell it one day. Or maybe she thought if she buried it with him someone might dig it up."

"Why did she do it?"

"Do what? Shoot that man?"

"Why didn't she get an ambulance, have him taken to the hospital? You said he could sit up, he'd have got all right. It wasn't her fault, no one'd have put the blame on her, not if she said he'd been going to rape her."

"I never knew quite why," Liza said, "but it might have been something like this. Later on someone told me a story about a child being attacked by dogs and I put two and two together. It was Bruno, as a matter of fact, he told me. You see, the man would have told them at the hospital and they'd have told the police. About the dogs, I mean. And the dogs would have been killed."

"Destroyed."

"Yes, I expect that's the word. The dogs would have been destroyed like the ones in Bruno's story. Mr. Tobias loved his dogs and he'd have blamed Eve and given her the sack and turned us out of the gatehouse. Or that's what she thought. Maybe he would and maybe he wouldn't, but she thought he would and that was the important thing. She couldn't leave Shrove, you see, she couldn't, that was the most important thing in the world to her, Shrove, more important even than me. Well, Mr. Tobias was important to her too but only in a special sort of way."

Sean was looking bewildered. "You've lost me."

"Never mind. That's really all there was to it. If the dogs had killed the man she wouldn't have had to kill him. I expect that's the way she thought. But they hadn't killed him, so she had to, or else he'd have told the police. She shut the dogs up and went into the house and got the gun and shot him."

"Just for that? Just so Tobias wouldn't get mad at her?"

Liza looked at him doubtfully. "I don't know. Now you put it like that, I really don't know. Perhaps there was more to it. Perhaps she had some other reason, something to make her hate him, but we're never going to know that, are we?"

She watched Sean as he got up and washed at the sink. He put his jeans back on again and found himself a clean T-shirt. It occurred to her that she hadn't any clothes except the ones lying in a heap on the floor. She'd have to wear his, or those of his that would fit her, and when she'd made some money picking apples . . . The hundred pounds, she had forgotten the hundred pounds.

"I want to drive into town, wherever that is," she said, "and go and eat in a real restaurant. Can we?"

" 'Course we can. Why not? We can go and have a Chinese."

Liza washed her knickers and her socks at the sink. She had to put her jeans on over nothing but that didn't much matter. Her jeans were a cause of great pride, not least because it had been such a struggle getting Eve to let her have them. She'd managed to get two pairs, these and a pair she'd left behind. Eve hated trousers and had never worn jeans in all her life. Liza borrowed a long-sleeved check shirt with a collar from Sean and thought a little about Eve, wondering where she was now and what was happening to her.

Sean had been thinking the same thing. "We ought to get a paper tomorrow. You haven't never seen a paper, I suppose? A newspaper, I mean."

"Oh, yes, I have." She was a bit huffy. Once, in a magazine rack at Shrove, she had found a newspaper called *The Times* and the date on it was the year before she was born. Eve had taken it away before she could read much of it. "What we ought to get is television."

"Now there's something you've never seen, telly, I bet."

She answered him in quite a lofty way. "I used to watch it at Shrove every single day. Eve never knew, she'd have stopped it but I didn't tell her. It was a secret thing I did."

"Like me," said Sean.

"Not really like you. You're much better. But I didn't know you then. I watched it for *years* till the set broke and Jonathan wouldn't have it mended." The expression on his face made her laugh. "Could we have one in here? Would your generator work it?"

"Hopefully," he said. " 'Course it would."

"Then I'm going to buy one." A thought struck her. "Only, I don't know—is a hundred pounds a lot of money, Sean?"

He said rather bitterly, "It's a lot for us, love," and then, "Hopefully it'd buy a little portable telly but I don't know about color."

Her eyes grew wide. "Does it come in color? Does it really?"

When they went outside to the car they saw that the other van, the camper, wasn't unoccupied as they had at first thought. A light was on inside it and the blind was raised in the window nearest to the roadway. They had to pass it to get out. Inside, a fiercer, bluer glow than the overhead lamp indicated the presence of a television screen, and as they passed within a few feet Liza saw the little rectangle filled with dazzling color, emerald-green grass, yellow-spotted leaves, and an orange-and-black tiger prowling.

"What a lot I've got to catch up with," she said.

Life at the gatehouse had been of the simplest. Much of it would seem dull to Sean, incredible. There was a good deal she wouldn't tell him but keep locked in her memory. For instance, how, because Eve wouldn't leave her alone in the cottage anymore even with the doors locked, couldn't bring herself to do that when she screamed so piteously, she had been obliged to take Liza with her.

And that was how she came to enter Shrove House for the first time. The palace, the house of pictures and secrets, dolls and keys, books and shadows. Sean would never see it quite like that, no one would but herself and Eve. Most of all Eve.

f i v e

THEY walked up the drive between the trees, the hornbeams that were nearly round in shape and the larches that were pointed, the silver birches whose leaves trembled in the breeze and the swamp cypresses that came from Louisiana but grew happily here because it was damp by the river. There were giant cedars and even taller Douglas firs and Wellingtonias taller than that, black trees you saw as dark green only when you were close up underneath them. The trees parted and she saw the house for the first time and to her then it was no more than a big house with an enormous lot of windows.

A man was mowing the grass, sitting up in a high chair on

wheels. She had seen him once or twice before and was often to see him again. His name was Mr. Frost, he wasn't a young man, but had wrinkles and white hair, and he came on his bicycle from the village on the other side of the river. White hair was only another kind of fair hair and his confirmed Liza's belief. He raised one hand to Mother and Mother nodded but they didn't speak.

Steps went up one side to the front door of Shrove and then there was a kind of platform before the stairs ran down the other side. The stairs had railings like theirs at the gatehouse but the rails here were made of stone with a broad stone shelf running along the tops of them. On the shelf were stone vases from which ivy hung and between the vases stone people stood looking toward the trees.

Liza and Mother went up the flight on the left and Liza held on to the stone railings. Everything was very large and this made her feel smaller than usual. She looked up, as Mother told her, to see the coat of arms, the sword, the shield, the lions. The house towered, its windows shiny sheets, its roof lost in the sky. Mother unlocked the front door and they went in.

"You will not rush about, Liza," Mother said, "and you will not climb on the furniture. Do you understand? Let me see your hands."

Liza held them out. They were very clean because Mother had made her wash them before they came out and she had held Mother's hand all the way.

"All right. You can't get them dirty in here. Now, remember, *walk,* don't run."

The carpets were soft and thick underfoot and the ceilings were very high. None of the ceilings was white but done in gold and black squares or painted like a blue sky with white clouds and people with wings flying across it, trailing scarves and ribbons and bunches of flowers. The lamps were like raindrops when it is raining very hard and some of the walls had things like thin carpets hanging on them. A huge painting covered one entire wall. Mother called it *The Birthday of Achilles* and it showed a lot of men in helmets and women in white robes all rushing to pick up a golden apple while a woman in green with flowers stood by holding a fat naked baby.

Mother took her through the drawing room and showed her the fireplace with the lady's face on it, the screen painted with flowers, and the tables that were of shiny wood with shiny metal bits on it and some with mother-of-pearl like mother's brooch. The tall glass doors were framed in mahogany, Mother said, and they were more than two hundred years old but as good as new. Liza and Mother went through the doorway out onto the terrace at the back, and when Liza ran down the steps and stood on the lawn and looked up at Mother, she was frightened for a moment because the back of the house was the same as the front, the same coat of arms, sword, shield, and lion, the same railing around the roof and up the stairs, the same windows and the same statues standing in the alcoves.

Mother called out to her that it was all right, it was supposed to be that way, but that if she looked closely she would see it wasn't quite the same. The statues were women, not men, there was no front door, and instead of ivy, small dark pointed trees grew in the stone urns on the terrace.

So Liza ran up again and she and Mother made their way to the kitchen. Mother unhooked an apron from behind a cupboard door, a big ugly brown apron, and wrapped it around herself, covering up her white cotton blouse and and long, full green-and-blue skirt. She took a clean yellow duster from a pile and tied her head up so that you couldn't see her hair, she trundled out a vacuum cleaner and found a large, deep tin of mauve polish that smelled of lavender.

For the next three hours they remained in Shrove House while Mother cleaned the carpets with the vacuum cleaner, dusted the surfaces and the ornaments, and polished the tables. She couldn't get it all done today, she said, and she explained to Liza how she did a bit one day and another bit two days later and so on, but she hadn't been in there for two weeks because, as she put it, of one thing and another. She had been afraid of Liza being a nuisance or of breaking something, but Liza had been as good as gold.

Remembering not to run, she had walked through all the rooms, looking at everything, at a table with a glass top and little oval pictures in frames inside, at a small green statue of a man on a horse, at a green jar with black birds and pink flowers on it that was taller than she was. One room was full of books, they were all over the walls where other rooms had paint or paneling. Another, instead of books, had those things hanging up like the one Mother had that made the explosion. She didn't stay in there for long.

A cabinet in one room was full of dolls in different dresses and she would have loved to touch, to get them out, she *longed* to, but she did what Mother told her, or if she didn't she made sure Mother couldn't find out. But mostly she did as she was told because as well as loving Mother so much, she was afraid of her.

The door to a room opening out of that one was shut. Liza tried the handle and it turned, but the door wouldn't open. It was locked, as her bedroom door used to be locked when Mother went out, and the key gone. Of course she very much wanted to get into that room, as much as anything because the door was locked. She rattled the handle, which did no good.

There were three staircases. By this time she had learned to count up to three—well, to six, in fact. She went up the biggest staircase and down the smallest, having been in every bedroom, and climbed onto one of the window seats—Mother wouldn't find out, the vacuum cleaner could be heard howling downstairs—and looked across the flat green valley floor to watch a train go by.

If not, then, conscious of beauty, she was aware of light, of how radiantly light the house was everywhere inside. There wasn't a dark corner or a dim passage. Even when the sun wasn't shining, as it wasn't that day, a clear pearly light lit every room and the things inside the rooms gleamed, the glass and the porcelain, the silver and brass and the gilt on the moldings and cornices. The biggest staircase had flowers and fruit carved on the wood on each side of it and the carving gleamed with a deep rich glow, but all she could think of then was how much she would like to slide down the polished banister.

They left at four o'clock, in time to get home for Liza's reading lesson.

"Doesn't Mr. Tobias ever live there?" she asked, taking Mother's hand.

"He never has. His mother did for a while and his grandfather lived there all the time, it was his only home." She gave Liza a thoughtful glance, as if she was pondering whether the time had come to tell her. "My mother, who was your grandmother, was his housekeeper. And then his nurse. We lived in the gatehouse ourselves, my mother, my father, and I." Mother squeezed Liza's hand. "You're too young for this, Lizzie. Look up in the ash tree, see the green woodpecker? On the trunk, picking insects out with his beak?"

So if the day the man with the beard came was called the Day of the Kingfisher, this was the Day of the Woodpecker, the day of the first visit to Shrove.

After that Liza always went with Mother to Shrove and now, when Mother went to town on the bus, instead of locking Liza in her bedroom in the cottage, she put her in one of the Shrove bedrooms. Mostly it was the one called the Venetian Room because the four-poster bed had its posts made out of the poles used by gondoliers in Venice, Mother said. Liza could read quite well by the time she was five and had a real book in the room with her. She wasn't in the least frightened of being shut up in the Venetian Room at Shrove, she wouldn't have been frightened of being in her own room anymore, but she did ask Mother why Shrove and not at home.

"Because Shrove has central heating and we don't. I can be sure you're warm enough. They have to keep the heating on all winter because of the damp, even though no one lives there. If it was allowed to get damp the furniture might be spoiled."

"Why is the little room next to the morning room always locked up?"

"Is it?" said Mother. "I seem to have mislaid the key."

Shrove was to become her library and her picture gallery. More than that, for the paintings were a guide to her and a catalog of people's faces. To them she ran when she needed to identify a new person or when confirmation was required. They were her standard of comparison and her secondhand portrait of the outside world. This was how other people looked, this what they wore, these the chairs they sat on, the other countries they lived in, the things their eyes saw.

In the cold depths of winter, a very cold one when the river froze over and the water meadows disappeared under snow for a whole month, a black car with chains on its tires slid slowly down the lane and parked in the deep snow outside the gatehouse. There were two men inside. One stayed in the car and the other one came to the front door and rang the bell. He was a fat man with no hair at all but for a fairish fringe surrounding the great shiny pale egg that was his head.

By chance, Liza and Mother had been sitting side by side at Mother's bedroom window, watching the birds feeding from the nut feeders they had hung on the branches of the balsam tree. They saw the car come and the man come to the door.

"If he talks to you you are not to say anything but 'I don't know,'" said Mother, "and you can cry a bit if you like. You might like that, it might amuse you."

Liza never found out who the man was. Of course she guessed later on. He said he was looking for a missing person, a man called Hugh something. She had forgotten his other name but Hugh she remembered.

Hugh came from Swansea, was around these parts last July on a walking holiday, but left the B and B he was stopping at without paying for his two nights. The fat man talked a lot more about Hugh and why they were looking for him and what was making them look six months later, but Liza didn't understand any of it. He described Hugh, which she did understand, she remembered his fair beard, she remembered tufts of it in Rudi's mouth.

"We are very quiet down here, Inspector," Mother said. "We see hardly anyone."

"A lonely life."

"It depends what suits you."

"And you never saw this man?" He showed Mother something in the palm of his hand and Mother looked at it, shaking her head. "You didn't see him in the lane or walking the footpath?"

"I'm afraid not."

Mother lifted her face and looked deep into the fat man's

eyes when she said this. Although it meant nothing at the time, when she was older, thinking back and comparing her own personal experience, Liza understood how Mother's look must have affected him. Her full red lips were slightly parted, her eyes large and lustrous, her skin creamy and her expression oh so winsome and trusting. About her shoulders her glorious hair, a rich, dark shining brown, hung like a silk cape. She had one small white finger pressed against her lower lip.

"It was just a possibility," the fat man said, unable to take his eyes off her, but having to, having to drag his eyes away and speak to Liza. "I don't suppose this young lady saw him."

She was shown the photograph. Apart from prints on the fronts of Mother's books, it was the first she had ever seen, but she didn't say so. She looked at the face which had frightened her and which Heidi and Rudi had ruined with their teeth, looked at it and said, "I don't know."

This made him eager. "So you might have?"

"I don't know."

"Have another look, my love, look closely and try to remember."

Liza was growing frightened. She was letting Mother down, she was obeying Mother but letting her down just the same. The man's face was horrible, the bearded man called Hugh, cruel and sneering, and who knew what he would have done if Mother hadn't . . .

She didn't have to pretend to cry. "I don't know, I don't know, I don't know," she screamed and burst into tears.

The fat man went away, apologizing to Mother, shaking hands with her and holding her hand a long time, and when he had gone Mother roared with laughter. She said Liza had been excellent, quite excellent, and she hugged her, laughing into her hair. For all that she loved Liza and cared for her, she hadn't understood that she had been really frightened, really shy of people, really bewildered.

It took the driver a long time to get the car started and an even longer time to pull it out of the snow without its wheels spinning. Liza calmed down and began to enjoy herself. She and Mother watched the driver's struggles from the bedroom window with great interest.

The snow went away and the spring came. Most of the trees that were coniferous looked just the same, always the same greenish black or light smoky blue, but the larches and the swamp cypresses grew new leaves like clumps of fur of an exquisite pale and delicate green. Mother explained that larches too were deciduous conifers and the only ones native to the British Isles.

Primroses with sunny round faces appeared under the hedges and clusters of velvety purple violets close by the boles of trees. Wood anemones, that were also called windflowers and had petals like tissue paper, grew in the clearings of the wood. Mother told Liza to be careful never to pronounce them an-enomies, as so many people did who ought to know better. Liza hardly talked to anyone but Mother, so was unlikely to hear the wrong pronunciation.

Except the postman, though they didn't discuss botany. And the milkman, who noticed nothing but the trains and the signs of changes in the weather, and the oilman who came to fill Shrove's heating tank in March, and Mr. Frost, the gardener who mowed the grass and trimmed the hedges and sometimes pulled out the weeds.

Mr. Frost went on never speaking. They saw him ride past the gatehouse on his bicycle and if he saw them he waved. He waved from his mowing machine if he happened to be there when they walked up the drive to Shrove. The oilman only came twice a year, in September and again in March. Liza had never talked to him, though Mother did for about five minutes, or listened rather, and listened impatiently, while he told her about his flat in Spain and how he had found a cut-rate flight to Malaga that was so reasonable you wouldn't believe. Liza didn't know what that meant, so Mother explained how he went across the sea in one of those things that flew overhead sometimes and made a buzzing noise about it, unlike birds.

The milkman said, "It feels like spring," which was silly because it *was* spring, and "Here comes the train," that he needn't have bothered to say because anyone could see and hear it.

They got very few letters. Liza never got any. Letters came for Mother sometimes, from someone called her aunt, though she never explained what an aunt was, from her friend Heather in London, and one regularly once a month from Mr. Tobias. This one had a piece of pink paper in it, which Mother said was a check. When next she went to the shops she took the pink paper with her and took it to a bank and they turned it into money. Like a good fairy waving a wand, suggested Liza, who was much into fairy tales at that time, but Mother said, no, not like that, and explained that this was money which she had earned for cleaning Mr. Tobias's house and looking after it and seeing it came to no harm.

In April the dogs came again to stay. Matt brought them and told Mother that Mr. Tobias had gone to somewhere called the Caribbean this time, not France. Liza hugged Heidi and Rudi, who knew her at once and were overjoyed to see her. Had they forgotten the man with the beard called Hugh? Had they forgotten how they attacked him? Liza wondered if they would attack Matt if she called out, "Kill!"

"Why doesn't Mr. Tobias ever come himself?" Liza asked Mother while they were out in the meadows with the dogs.

"I don't know, Lizzie," Mother said and she sighed.

"Doesn't he like it here?"

"He seems to like it better in the Dordogne and Moçambique and Montagu Square and the horrible old Lake District," said Mother incomprehensibly. "But perhaps he will come one day. Of course he'll come one day, you'll see."

Instead of coming himself, he sent a postcard. It had a picture on it of silver sand and palm trees and a blue, blue sea. On the back Mr. Tobias had written: *This is a wonderful place. It's good to get away from cold, gray England in the cruelest month, though I hardly suppose you would agree. Say hallo to Heidi and Rudi for me and to your daughter, of course. Ever, J.T.*

Liza couldn't read joined-up writing, even the beautiful curvy large kind like Mr. Tobias's, so Mother read it to her. Mother made a face and said she didn't like him putting his dogs before her daughter but Liza didn't mind.

"I know what T's for," she said, "but what's his name that starts with J?"

"Jonathan," said Mother.

By the time the summer came, Liza could read Beatrix Potter and the Andrew Lang fairy books if the print was large enough. She could write her name and address and simple sentences, printing of course, and she could tell the time and count to twenty and add up easy sums. Mother took her into the library at Shrove and said that when she was older she would be welcome to read all the books in there she wanted. Mr. Tobias had told *her* to help herself to any books she fancied reading, he knew she loved reading, and of course that invitation extended to her daughter.

"Jonathan," said Liza.

"Yes, Jonathan, but you must call him Mr. Tobias."

There were history books and geography books and books about languages and philosophy and religion. Liza noted the words without understanding their meaning. Mother said there were also a great many books that were stories, which meant made-up things, not things that had really happened, they were novels. Most of them had been written a long time ago, more than a hundred years ago, which wasn't surprising since they had belonged to Mr. Tobias's grandfather's father, who had bought the house when he got rich in 1862. The books were rather old-fashioned now, Mother said, but perhaps that was no bad thing, and she looked at Liza with her head to one side.

It grew hot that summer and one day Liza went with Mother to a part of the river that was very deep, a pool below the rapids that came rushing over the stones, and Mother began teaching her to swim. Mother was a good strong swimmer and Liza felt safe with her, even where the water was so deep that even Mother's feet couldn't touch the bottom. The second or third time they had been down there they were coming back up the lane—Mother said afterward she wished they'd come through the Shrove grounds as they usually did—when they had to flatten themselves against the hedge to let a car go by. It didn't go by, it stopped, and a lady put her head out of the window.

That was when Liza had to revise her ideas on her hair-color–sex-linkage theory, for the lady's hair was blond. It was not otherwise much like hair at all but seemed to be carved out of some pale yellow translucent substance, a kind of lemon jelly perhaps, and then varnished. The lady had a face like the monkey in the illustrations to Liza's *Jungle Book* and hands with ropes under the skin on the backs of them and a brown paper dress Mother said afterward was called linen and made from a plant with blue flowers that grew in the fields like grass.

The lady said, "Oh, my dear, I haven't seen you for an age. Don't you ever come down to the village anymore? I must say I've expected to see you in church. Your mother was such a regular at St. Philip's."

"I am not my mother," said Mother, very coldly.

"No, of *course* not. And this is your little girl?"

"This is Eliza, yes."

"She will be going to school soon, I suppose. I don't know how you're going to get her there with no car, but I suppose the school bus will come. At least it will come to where the lane joins the main road."

Mother said in the voice that frightened Liza when it was used to her, which was seldom, "Eliza will be educated privately," and she walked away without waiting for the lady to put her head in and her window up.

That was the first time Liza heard school mentioned. She didn't know what it was. At that time no school or schoolchildren figured in the books she read. But she didn't ask Mother, only what the name of the lady was and Mother said Mrs. Hayden, Diana Hayden, whom Liza would probably never have to see again.

They had the dogs back for a fortnight in October and again six months later. When the time came for Matt to come with the van to collect them he didn't turn up. Something must have gone wrong, Mother said. There was no means of letting her know, as they had no phone and it was impossible to send telegrams anymore.

But when he didn't come on the following day she got it into her head this was because Mr. Tobias would come himself. He had told the man to leave it to him this time, he would collect the dogs when he got back. But he wasn't due back till today. After he had had a good night's sleep and got over his jet lag he would get in his car, or more likely the estate car, and drive down here from Ullswater, where he lived but had no one willing to look after his dogs. Mother was sure he would come. She and Liza went over to Shrove early in the morning and Mother gave it a special clean.

At home she had a bath in their kitchen bath and washed her hair. That was the next day, in the morning. She put on one of her long bright-colored skirts and her tight black top, the green beads around her neck and the gold hoops in her ears. It took her half an hour to plait her hair in the special way she had and pin it to the back of her head. And she did all this because Mr. Tobias was coming.

He didn't come. Matt did. He drove up in the afternoon and pushed past Mother into the gatehouse before she could stop him.

"I've been down with one of them viruses that's going about," he said, "or I'd have been here before."

"Where is Mr. Tobias?"

"He rung up from Mozam-whatsit, said he'd be home today. Didn't he never let you know? Dear, oh, dear. Never mind, there's no harm done, is there?"

No harm done! Mother went up to her bedroom after Matt had gone and lay on her bed and cried. Liza heard her crying and went up and got into bed with her and hugged her and said to stop, not to cry, it was going to be all right.

And so it was. In the month of June, when all the wild roses were out and flowers were on the elder trees and the nightingales sang in the wood, Mr. Tobias came to Shrove in his dark green shiny Range Rover and, with the dogs at his heels, ran up the cottage garden path and banged on their door, calling, "Eve, Eve, where are you?"

That was how Liza learned what Mother's first name was.

She called the day gone by the Day of the Nightingale because the nightingales had sung from morning till night and beyond. People who didn't know, Mother said, believed nightingales only sang by night but that was false, for they sang all around the clock.

six

MY real name's Eliza. I've sometimes thought she called me after Eliza Doolittle in *Pygmalion.*"

"Come again?" said Sean.

"Because she intended to do the same thing with me as Pygmalion did with Galatea and as Professor Higgins did with Eliza Doolittle, he remade her to be the way he wanted her, or let's say he had an ideal and he tried to turn her into that."

Sean frowned while he concentrated. "Sounds like *My Fair Lady* to me."

"She said she didn't, anyway, when I asked her. She just liked the name." Liza finished her strawberry milkshake and wiped her mouth. "Sean, can I have a burger? D'you know I've never had one."

" 'Course you can. We'll both have a burger and chips."

"Isn't it funny? I was so afraid to leave the gatehouse and *her,* I thought I'd die of fright."

"You're always dying of something, you are."

"Only I never do really, do I? I was so frightened and now I'm out in the world—that's how I see it, out in the world—I really like it. Or perhaps it's just you I like. I wouldn't have liked Heather."

"You might've. You don't know her."

"Oh, yes, I do. I *did.* She came to stay. But not then, not till after Mr. Tobias had been."

They were in the town, Liza wary of the crowded pavements but liking the shops and the big green with a few old people sitting on wooden seats and children feeding ducks on a pond. Sean wouldn't take her money, he had a bit saved up, and when they had had lunch he bought two bottles of wine and sixty cigarettes, something else she had never tried before. Sean lit a cigarette as soon as he was in the car.

"Eve said they kill you."

"She's not the only one says that. But I reckon it's just the same old thing, them trying to stop you having a bit of pleasure. I mean, look at it this way, my grandad, he's eighty-seven, he's smoked forty a day since he went out to work at fourteen and there's not a thing wrong with him, spry as a cricket he is."

"What's a cricket, Sean?"

"There's the game cricket, you know, test matches and whatever, there's that, but it's not that, is it? I reckon I don't know what it is, to tell you the honest truth."

"You shouldn't use words if you don't know what they mean."

Sean laughed. "Sorry, teacher."

He wanted her to try a cigarette, so she did. It made her cough and then it made her feel sick, but Sean said it was always like that the first time and you had to persist.

They called in at the farm shop on the way back to the caravan and saw Mr. Vanner in the office. He was short of pickers for the Emile pears and took them both on to start next day. On the way out Liza helped herself to a James Grieve from the basket with the notice that said: *Help yourself and enjoy a great taste.*

She'd taken a big bite out of it when Mrs. Vanner behind the counter said in a nasty tone, "Those apples are intended for our paying customers, if you don't mind."

No one had ever spoken to her in that rude way before. Sean squeezed her arm to stop her answering back, though she wouldn't have done that, she was too shocked.

"What a horrible woman," she said the moment the door closed behind them.

"Mean old bitch," said Sean.

Another camper had arrived at the caravan park. Whoever owned it had already put up a washing line with washing on it and tied a black terrier up to the steps. Liza glanced at the other camper, the one who was there before they came, and saw the blue glow of the screen under the raised blind.

"D'you know what we forgot, Sean? We forgot to buy the television set."

"I can think of better things to do than watch telly," said Sean, putting his arm on her shoulders and stroking her neck with his fingertips.

"And something to read," she said as if he hadn't spoken. "I'll need books to read. How can I get books?"

"I don't know." He wasn't interested.

"I can't exist without books."

But she went into his arms very willingly when they were inside the caravan and the door was shut. She was soon pulling off her clothes and climbing across the bed to where he waited for her. They hadn't bothered to put the bed back in the wall that morning, knowing they would be sure to need it again soon.

Mother said, "This is Mr. Tobias, Lizzie, that you've heard so much about," and to Mr. Tobias she said, "I'd like you to meet my daughter Eliza, Jonathan."

It was a new experience for Liza to shake hands with someone. Mr. Tobias's hand was warm and dry and his handshake very firm. He got down on his haunches so that their eyes were on a level. His were dark brown and his hair light brown, lighter than his skin, which was very deeply tanned. Of all the men that Liza had ever seen—the milkman, the postman, and the oilman, Mr. Frost, Mr. Tobias's man who brought the dogs, and that other one who had a beard—of all of them, Mr. Tobias had the nicest hands. They were thin and brown with long fingers and square nails.

And he had a lovely voice. Instead of sounding like Matt or the oilman or the man with the beard or the milkman, who all sounded different from each other, his voice was more like Mother's but deeper of course and somehow softer. It was the sort of voice you'd like to read you a story before you went to sleep.

"She's very like you, Eve," he said. "She is you in little. A clone, perhaps?"

"I'm afraid not," Mother said. "But I'm glad she looks like me."

Liza was very surprised to see a bottle produced and two glasses, a bottle with brown liquid in it, and orange juice for her.

Mr. Tobias was very tall and had to bend his head to get under the doorway into their living room. He wasn't wearing jeans like most of the other men she had seen or the bottom part of a suit like Mr. Frost, but trousers in pale fawn stuff like the ribbing on a sweater and a white shirt with an open neck and a brown velvet jacket. Eve told her afterward that it was velvet. It looked, and she imagined felt, like the mole she had seen come out of an earth mountain on the Shrove lawn.

She was very shy of him. While he talked to her in his bedtime-story voice, she could only stare at him with her eyes very wide open. He asked her what she did all day long and if she could read and would she draw something for him. While she was drawing a picture of Shrove with the river behind and the high hills and Heidi and Rudi running about on the grass, he said he expected she would be going to school soon. Mother said briskly that there was time enough for that and changed the subject. She wished he had let her know he was coming, she would have got some food in and given the house a special clean.

"*You* would? You're supposed to get a woman in from the village to do that."

"I know, but they aren't reliable and they'd have to have a car. It's easier to do it myself. I prefer to do it myself, Jonathan."

"I thought it was odd when I went through the accounts with Matt and there was no provision made for a daily."

Mother said again, "I prefer to do it myself." She looked down in rather a meek way, her long eyelashes brushing her cheek. "You pay me so generously that, really, I feel it's my duty."

"My idea when you came here was that you would be a kind of estate manager. You had the cottage and a—well, a salary, to run the place."

"Dear Jonathan, there's nothing to run but Mr. Frost and the oilman," said Mother and they both laughed.

Liza finished her drawing and showed it to Mr. Tobias, who pronounced it very good and said she must sign it. So she wrote Eliza Beck in the bottom right-hand corner and wondered why Mr. Tobias gave her signature such a strange long look before turning to Mother with one eyebrow up and a funny little crooked smile.

The dogs were not to sleep in the little castle this time but over at Shrove with Mr. Tobias. Liza played with them until it was her suppertime, and then she and Mother took them halfway up the Shrove drive and released them. She stood under the tallest Wellingtonia and called to them to run home, to run and find the master. Mr. Tobias came to the front door of Shrove and down the steps and waved to them.

He had something hanging around his neck on a strap. Liza couldn't see very well from that distance, but as they came closer she thought it looked rather like the thing Mother had that made music. He beckoned and put the thing up to his face, holding it in both hands. Mother went on walking toward him, telling her not to be shy, Mr. Tobias was only taking a photograph of them. But Liza *was* shy, she hid behind a tree, so Mother got into the picture by herself.

By this time she had almost grown out of that baby game she used to play after she was put to bed, running from one room and one window to the other, but that night, for some reason, she felt like playing it again. Perhaps the reason was that Mother had come upstairs to check that she was asleep. Liza dived under the covers and lay with her eyes shut, breathing steadily.

She half opened an eye as Mother tiptoed out and saw that she had changed into her best skirt, the one she made herself from a piece of blue and purple and red material she had bought when she went to town. Mother wore the new skirt, which was very full and long, nearly to her ankles, a tight black top, and a shiny black belt around her little waist. Her hair was done in the way Liza loved and which took half an hour to do, drawn back from her face and done in a fat plait that started at the crown of her head and was tucked under at the nape of her neck.

Liza thought she heard the front door close. She jumped out of bed and ran across to Mother's room and the window. Mother was letting herself out by the front gate. It was a warm evening, still daylight, but the sun was low in the faded blue sky. Mother hadn't a coat or a shawl. She was going toward the gateway. Liza ran back into her own room, the turret room, stood on the chair, and watched Mother passing through the open gateway and starting up the drive to Shrove.

Liza had never been left alone before, unless she was locked in and safe. Mother was walking under the trees, through the park and up to the house; she had never gone so far before. Fear sprang within her and, as it does when one is a small child, touched off immediate tears. In a moment she would have screamed and sobbed but in that moment, while her breath was held, Mr. Tobias came strolling out from the back of Shrove House. He stopped and held out both hands and he and Mother looked at each other.

Somehow, Mr. Tobias being there, knowing that all Mother was doing was meeting him, made everything all right. Mother took both his hands in her hands and said something and laughed. He walked around her, looking her up and down, nodded, touched the beautiful shiny plait with one finger. Then he took her hand and hooked it over his arm and they went on toward the house, walking very closely side by side. Liza no longer much minded Mother going because they were together and would only be at Shrove.

She minded a very little bit because she wasn't there with them, she felt left out. But not afraid anymore. She ran back into Mother's room to see if anything was going on at the front, even if it was only rabbits feeding on the grass verges. There were always rabbits in the evening, that wasn't exciting. They couldn't get at Mother's vegetables because most things were covered in nets, the lettuces, the cabbages, the peas, and the carrots, but not the beans and the strawberries because rabbits never ate them.

The sun was setting behind the woods, turning the trees black and the sky almost too dazzling a gold to look at. She watched it dip and sink until all the gold was drained away and the sky turned from yellow to pink to red. Once the sun went the bats came out. Mother had explained how they can hunt for insects in the dark, by their squeaks, which humans can't hear, bouncing off flying objects and echoing back at them.

A moth flew up to the window and Liza identified it as a privet hawk, though its body was yellow and brown instead of pink and brown and its lower wings were yellowish. Perhaps it was just a common yellow underwing. Mother had brought her a moth book from the library at Shrove as well as *Frohawk's Complete British Butterflies.* She ran downstairs and fetched the book. Perhaps she would have an apple too, but there were no apples at this time of the year. Instead she ate some of the strawberries she and Mother had picked before Mr. Tobias came.

She couldn't find the moth, or a picture she could be sure was of the one outside the window, and she must have fallen asleep when she got back into bed, for she remembered nothing else from that night and it was the following evening or the next that she looked out of Mother's room much later, in the dusk, and saw them at the gateway of Shrove, standing close up against the wall of the little castle. Mr. Tobias had his arms around Mother and he was kissing her in a way Liza had never seen anyone kiss anyone before, on the mouth.

The truth was that she had never *seen* anyone kiss anyone ever except Mother kissing her, which wasn't the same thing. Mr. Tobias let Mother go and Mother came into the house. Liza crept very quietly across the landing on her way back to her own room and as she passed the top of the stairs she heard Mother singing down there. Not very loudly but as if she was enjoying singing. And Liza knew the song and that it was something called Mozart, for she had often heard Mother play the record where the lady sang how she would make her lover better with the medicine she kept in her heart.

When the weekend came, so did a lot of visitors to Shrove. They were all friends of Mr. Tobias, Mother said, two men and three ladies, and they came along the lane and past the gatehouse and right in through the gates of Shrove up to the house. Liza said, could they go up there, she and Mother, and see the people, but Mother said, no, she wouldn't be going there again till Monday and Liza certainly would not.

"Why?" said Liza.

"Because I said no," said Mother. "Mr. Tobias invited us but I said no, not this time."

"Why?"

"I think it best, Liza."

On the Saturday evening she saw all the people coming back from a walk. She was at Mother's window and she saw them all very clearly, passing the gatehouse garden. One of the ladies had stopped to admire Mother's big stone tub that was full of geraniums and fuchsias and abutilon in full bloom.

The men were just men, nothing special, though one of them had bare skin instead of hair on top of his head, and the ladies were nice-looking but not one of them as pretty as Mother. Perhaps Mr. Tobias thought so too, for he turned his head as they passed and gave the gatehouse a long look. Liza didn't think he was looking at the flowers. But still, there was something special about the ladies, they looked different from anyone Liza had ever seen before, smoother somehow and cleaner, their hair cut as trimly and evenly as Mr. Frost cut the edge of the lawn where the flower border began. All three wore jeans like the milkman and Hugh, but one had a jacket like Mother's best shoes, the suede ones with the trees in them that Liza liked to stroke, and a silk scarf with a rope and shield pattern, one a wondrous sweater with flowers knitted into the pattern and her face painted like Diana Hayden's and the third a shirt like a man's but long and made of bright green silk.

Half an hour later one of their cars came down the drive from Shrove House—well, from the stable block, really, where cars were kept—with Mr. Tobias's Range Rover ahead of it to show the way, and in the morning Mother told her they had all gone out to dinner in a hotel somewhere. By Monday they had gone away and she and Mother went up to Shrove to change the beds and clear up the mess. Or Mother did. Liza talked to Mr. Tobias and he showed her his holiday pictures. He took her into the library and said she must have any book from it she wanted to read. They took the dogs down to the river and waved to the train and when they got back Mother had finished.

"I'm not at all happy about you doing this, Eve," Mr. Tobias said and he didn't *look* happy.

"Perhaps I will try to get someone," Mother said.

Liza thought she seemed quite weary and no wonder, the house had been an awful mess, Mother had said nothing when they first arrived, but Liza had stared wide-eyed at the sticky glasses, the cups and plates standing about everywhere, the powdery gray stuff mixed up with burned paper tubes in the little glass trays, and the big brown stain on the drawing room carpet.

"I should have cleared up myself," said Mr. Tobias, which, for some reason, made Mother laugh. "Come out with me tonight? We'll go somewhere for dinner."

"I can't do that, Jonathan. I have Eliza, remember?"

"Bring her too."

Mother just laughed again, but in a way that somehow made it clear they weren't going out for dinner and that it was an absurd suggestion.

"Then you can cook my dinner. At the gatehouse. It's a poky little place and I'm going to have it done up for you from top to bottom, but if we haven't a choice, the gatehouse it must be. Needs must when the devil drives. You're a bit of a devil, you know, Eve, and you know how to drive a man, but you shall cook my dinner. If you're not too tired, that is?"

"I'm not too tired," said Mother.

Liza didn't expect to be allowed to stay up with them. It was a nice surprise when Mother said she could, though she must go to bed straight after. Mr. Tobias came at seven with a bottle of something that looked like fizzy lemonade but had its top wired on and a bottle of something the color of Mother's homemade raspberry vinegar. The top came out of the lemonade bottle with a loud pop and a lot of foam. They had a salad and a roast chicken and strawberries, and when Liza had eaten up the last strawberry she had to go to bed. Oddly enough, she went straight to sleep.

Next morning she did what she always did in the mornings, ran into Mother's room for her cuddle. Mother had always been alone in her big bed but she wasn't alone this time. Mr. Tobias was in the bed with her, lying on the side nearest to the window.

Liza stood and stared.

"Go outside a moment, please, Liza," Mother said.

A moment always meant counting to twenty. Liza counted to twenty and went back into the room. Mr. Tobias had got up and done his best to get his broad shoulders and long body inside Mother's brown wool dressing gown. He muttered something, grabbed his clothes from the chair, and went downstairs to the kitchen. Liza got into bed with Mother and hugged her, she hugged her so tight that Mother had to say to let go, she was hurting. The bed smelled different than usual, it didn't smell of clean sheets and Mother and her soap, but a bit like the river in a season of drought, a bit like the dead fishes washed up on the sand, and like water with a lot of salt in it for cooking.

Mr. Tobias came back, washed and dressed, saying it was terrible they hadn't got a bathroom, he would have a bathroom put in as a priority. And why on earth didn't Eve have a phone? Everyone had a phone. He went away after breakfast but came back in the afternoon with a present for Liza. It was a doll. Liza had very few toys and what she had had been Eve's—a rag doll, a celluloid one, a dog on wheels you pulled along with a piece of string, a box of wooden bricks.

The doll that Mr. Tobias had bought her wasn't a baby but a little girl with dark hair like her own that you could wash and legs and arms and face that felt like real skin and a wardrobe of clothes for her to put on when the dress she was wearing had to be washed.

Unable to speak, Liza stared mutely.

"Say thank you to Mr. Tobias, Lizzie," said Mother, but she didn't seem very pleased and she said, "You really shouldn't, Jonathan. She will get all sorts of ideas."

"Why not? Harmless ideas, I'm sure."

"Well, I'm not. I don't wish her to have those ideas. But you are very kind, you are very generous."

"What shall you call her, Liza?" Mr. Tobias said in his softest sweetest voice.

"Jonathan," said Liza.

That made them both laugh.

"Jonathan is a man's name, Lizzie, and she's a girl. Think again."

"I don't know any girls' names. What were the ladies called who stayed with you?"

"Last weekend? They were called Annabel and Victoria and Claire."

"I shall call her Annabel," said Liza.

After that Mr. Tobias slept in Mother's bed most nights. Liza slept with Annabel and brought her into Mother's bed in the morning, knocking on the door first as instructed to give Mr. Tobias a chance to get up. He stayed at Shrove for three weeks, then four, and the dogs with him, but no more people were invited for the weekends.

Mother was very happy. She was quite different and she sang a lot. She washed her hair every day and made herself another new skirt. Every day they were either up at Shrove or Mr. Tobias was with them at the gatehouse, and if anything was wrong it was only that when Mr. Tobias wanted to take them out in the Range Rover, Mother always said no. Liza very much wanted to go to the seaside and the suggestion was made, but Mother said no. All right, said Mr. Tobias, come to London with me for the weekend, come to Montagu Place, but Mother said that would be worse than the seaside.

"You like it here, Jonathan, don't you? It's the most wonderful place in the world, nowhere is more beautiful."

"I like a change sometimes."

"Have a change, then. That's probably the best thing. Have a change and then come back here to us. I can't believe the Ullswater house is more beautiful than this."

"Come and see. We'll all go up for the weekend and you shall judge."

"I don't want to go from here ever and Liza doesn't. I thought"—Mother turned her face away and spoke quietly—"I thought it might be attractive to you now because I am here."

"It is. You know it is, Eve. But I'm young and, frankly, I'm rich. You know my father left me very well-off. I don't want to settle down in one place for the rest of my life and see nothing of the world. That doesn't mean I don't want you to see the world with me."

Mother said she didn't want to see the world. She had seen enough of it for a lifetime, enough forever, it was all horrible. Nor did she want the gatehouse done up and a bathroom put in. She didn't want him wasting his money on her. Luxuries of that kind meant nothing to her and Liza. If he must go away and she could tell he wanted to, he must leave the dogs with her and that way he would come back.

"I don't need a reason to come back. Matt can look after the dogs."

"Leave them with me and then I'll know you have to come. You must always leave them with me."

He slept in Mother's bed that last night and went back to Shrove in the morning. Later on he came to the cottage in the Range Rover and said good-bye. He hugged Mother and kissed her and kissed Liza, and Liza said Annabel would miss him. They waved after the Range Rover as it went down the lane and Liza ran upstairs to watch it go over the bridge. When it was out of sight she and Mother put the dogs in the little castle and Mother said they might as well go up to Shrove to tidy up and put things to rights.

Mr. Tobias had left a lot of mess, though for the past three weeks he hadn't been there much. While Mother was running the vacuum cleaner over the bedroom carpets, Liza went into the morning room and looked at the door that was always locked. She tried the handle just in case it was, for once, unlocked. It wasn't. Squatting down because she was quite tall by then, she put one eye to the keyhole and closed the other. She was surprised to find she could see quite a lot, a piece of the red upholstery of a chair and the braid on its arm, the corner of a kind of table with drawers in it, the bright-colored spines, blue and green and orange, of books on a shelf. What could there be in there she wasn't allowed to see?

Liza now wished she had told Mr. Tobias about the locked room on the several occasions he and she had been together in the house while Mother was cleaning upstairs or in the kitchen. But of course they had never been in the morning room, it wasn't much used and there was no reason why it should be when there were a drawing room, a dining room, and a library as well. Liza was convinced that if she had asked Mr. Tobias he would have fetched the key and opened the door at once.

Next time he came she would ask him. When he came back to fetch the dogs. But the weeks went by and he didn't come. He didn't write, not even a postcard, and after nearly a month Matt came in the Range Rover and took the dogs away. Mother happened to see the Range Rover coming across the bridge. It was the right color, though she couldn't see the number, she was sure it was Mr. Tobias himself coming and even more sure when she saw it in the lane. Mr. Tobias had never before sent Matt in the Range Rover but he had this time, and when Matt had gone and Heidi and Rudi with him, Mother went into her bedroom and cried.

Liza had never told anyone about that. Well, she had had no one to tell until now, but she didn't tell Sean, she kept it locked up and secret inside her head. And when Sean said, this guy Tobias, the one that Shrove House belongs to, did he ever come, she said only, yes, he did, but he didn't stay long.

"And didn't you never go to school?"

"No, I never did. Mother taught me herself at home."

"It's against the law, that."

"I expect it is. But you know where Shrove is, the back of beyond, far away from just about everywhere. Who would know? Eve told lies about it. She was very open with me. She said it was important not to tell lies unless you had to, but if you had to the important thing was to know they were lies. She told some of the people that asked that I went to the village school and the other people that I went to a private school. We met Diana Hayden in the lane and Eve told her we were in a hurry because she was taking me to catch the bus for school. You have to remember there weren't many people. I mean, basically, there were just the milkman, the postman, the man who read the meter, Mr. Frost, and the oilman, and they weren't going to ask. None of them was there for more than five minutes except for Mr. Frost and he never spoke."

"Didn't you want to go to school? I mean, you know, kids want friends."

"I had Eve," Liza said simply, and then, "I didn't want anyone else. Well, I had Annabel, my doll. She was my imaginary friend and I used to talk to her and discuss things with her. I used to ask her advice and I don't think I minded when she didn't answer. I didn't *know,* you see. I didn't know life could be different.

"When I could read, I mean really read, Eve started teaching me French. I *think* I speak quite good French. We did history and geography on Mondays and Wednesdays and arithmetic on Tuesdays. She started me on Latin when I was nine and that was on Fridays, but before that we did poetry reading on Thursdays and Fridays and music appreciation."

Sean was staring at her aghast. "What a life!"

"I really didn't need to go to school. We talked all day long, Eve and me. We walked all over the countryside. In the evenings we played cards or did jigsaws or read."

"You poor kid. Bloody awful childhood you had."

Liza wasn't having that. She said hotly, "I had a wonderful childhood. You mustn't think anything else. I collected things, the gatehouse was full of my pressed flowers and pine cones and bowls with tadpoles in and caddises and water beetles. I never had to dress up. I never ate food that was bad for me. I never quarreled with other children or fought or got hurt."

He interrupted her and said perspicaciously, "But you know about those things."

"Yes, I know about them. I'll tell you how, but not now, not this minute. Now I just want you to know my childhood was all right, it was fine. She's not to blame for anything that happened to *me,* she was a wonderful mother to me."

Again his face wore that incredulous expression and he shook his head faintly. She was silent and gently she took his hand. She wasn't going to tell him—or not yet—that things had changed, that the happiness was not perpetual.

Eve told her the myth of Adam and Eve, insisting as she did so that it was only that, a myth. They read the passage on the creation in Genesis, and then the expulsion from the Garden in Milton, so she knew about the serpent in paradise and later imagined it was Eve and herself who hand in hand through Eden took their solitary way.

But all she told Sean of the months before her seventh birthday was that Mr. Tobias came back once, for a day and a night, a night he didn't spend at the gatehouse with Eve but in his own bed at Shrove. Then he went away, if not forever, for a very long time.

s e v e n

AT first Sean was better at picking pears than she was. He knew how to lift each fruit from the twig on which it grew and bend it gently backward until it came away in his hand. Liza just pulled. The pears got bruised and sometimes her fingernail went through the mottled green skin, wounding the white flesh beneath. Mr. Vanner would dock her pay, Sean said, if she damaged his fruit, so she tried to be more careful. She was used to being told, it wasn't something she had learned to resent.

They picked the pears before they were ripe, before the outside turned yellow with a red blush and while the inside was still firm and waxy. Since they came to Vanner's, the sun was always shining. Each morning they woke to a pale blue sky, a stillness and a white mist lying on the fields. Over the farm buildings the Russian vine spread snowy clouds of blossom and Mrs. Vanner's garden was overgrown with yellow and orange nasturtiums. They began picking before it grew hot and took a couple of hours off from noon till two. At that time they had lunch, packets of crisps and a pork pie, cans of Coke and Mars bars, sticky from being kept in a hot pocket.

The pear fields were a long way from the caravan, so mostly they didn't bother to go back but ate their food sitting on the bank under the quickthorn hedge. At first they were nervous about being seen by the other pickers, but no one was interested in them, no one came their way, and on the second day they slipped into the little sheltered place where the elders made a tent of branches and made love on the warm dry grass. Both knew they would make love that evening and when they went to bed but it seemed too long to wait.

Afterward Sean fell asleep, stretched out full-length, his head buried in his arms. Liza lay awake beside him, her cheek resting on his shoulder and her arm around his waist. She liked looking at the way his dark hair grew on the nape of his neck, in two points like the legs of an M, and she thought for the first time that it was also the way Mr. Tobias's hair grew.

Mother hadn't told her the history of *her* mother and the Tobiases until she was older. She must have been about ten when she learned about her grandmother Gracie Beck and old Mr. Tobias, also called Jonathan, and the will; old Mr. Tobias's daughter, Caroline, who was Mr. Tobias's (that is, Jonathan's) mother, and her enormously rich husband, who left her because she was so awful. When she was seven all Liza knew was that Mother and Mr. Tobias had known each other since he was a big child and she a small one and that somehow or other Shrove House ought to have belonged to Mother and not been Mr. Tobias's at all.

Oh, and that Mother loved Mr. Tobias and he loved her. Mother told her that one evening in the winter when they were sitting by the big log fire and Liza had the doll called Annabel on her lap. Liza had noticed that Annabel often brought Mr. Tobias into Mother's mind.

"The difficulty is," Mother said, "that Mr. Tobias is a restless man and wants to see the world, while I intend to remain here for the whole of my life *and never go away.*" She said that last bit quite fiercely, looking into Liza's eyes. "Because there is nowhere in the world like this place. This place is the nearest thing to heaven there is. If you have found heaven, why should you want to see anywhere else?"

"Have you seen everywhere in the world?" Liza asked, carefully combing Annabel's hair.

"Near enough," Mother said mysteriously. "I have seen more than enough of people. Most people are bad. The world would be a better place if half the population were to perish in a huge earthquake. I have seen more than enough places. Most places are horrible, I can tell you. You have no idea how horrible and I'm glad you haven't. That is the way I want it to be. One day, when you have grown up the way I want you to, you can go out and have a peep at the world. I guarantee you'll come running back here, thankful to be restored to heaven."

Liza was uninterested in any of that, she didn't know what it meant. "Mr. Tobias doesn't think other places are horrible."

"He'll learn. It's only a matter of time, you'll see. When he has traveled about for long enough and seen enough, he'll come back here. It just takes him longer than it took me."

"Why does it?"

"Perhaps because I have seen more dreadful things than he has or just that I'm wiser."

In the spring of that year Heather came to stay. Mother said nothing about it until the day before she arrived, and then all she said was, "You'll be sleeping in my room with me for the next week, Liza. Miss Sawyer is coming and will have your room."

Liza knew who Miss Sawyer was from the letters Mother got. She was the same person as Heather.

"For heaven's sake don't call me that, child," said Heather five minutes after she got there. "My name is Heather. 'Miss Sawyer' sounds like a headmistress. What's your headmistress called?"

Liza, who had understood almost nothing of what was said, simply gazed at her, her extreme thinness, her height, her small head and sleek red hair.

"Head teacher, then? I can't keep pace with all these new terms."

Mother changed the subject. She explained to Liza that she and Heather had met while they were at college and Heather knew Mr. Tobias.

"Is he still around?"

"Shrove is *his* house, Heather. Surely you remember that?"

That was when Heather first began whispering to Mother behind her hand. She gave Liza a glance, then quickly turned, put up her hand, and began the whispering. "Wishy, wishy, wishy," was how it sounded to Liza.

After she had been upstairs and seen her room, Heather said she had never before stayed in a house without a bathroom. She didn't know houses without bathrooms existed anymore. But no, of course she wasn't going to allow Mother to carry hot water upstairs for her, which Mother had offered to do. She would use the bath in the kitchen like they did, only it was going to be very awkward.

Another awkwardness was what she called "lack of TV." Liza didn't understand that either and wasn't very interested. The weather was fine, so they went out for many long walks and Heather went for a ride in the train from Ring Valley Halt. She had to go alone. Mother said she had been too many times to want to go again, so Liza couldn't go either.

There was no car to go out in—Heather had come by taxi from some distant station—no record player, hardly any books published later than 1890, no phone, and no restaurants nearer than eight miles away. The village where Mr. Frost came from had something called a pub, Mother said, but they couldn't go there because pubs didn't like children and wouldn't let them in.

"Wishy, wishy, wishy," whispered Heather behind her hand.

"Oh, do speak out, Heather," said Mother. "You are creating mysteries where none need exist."

So Heather stopped whispering and said boldly, the night before she was due to go, "You'll go mad here, Eve."

"No, I shall go sane," said Mother.

"Oh, dear, how epigrammatic!"

"All right. I mean I shall become normal again. I might even be happy. I shall recapture the old-fashioned values and bring up a daughter who has been kept clean of the hideous pressures of our world."

"It all sounds very high-flown and unnatural to me. Anyway, you won't be able to. Her contemporaries will see to that. When you get tired of being a noble savage, remember I've always got a couple of spare rooms."

Eve must have remembered those words when she was finding somewhere for Liza to seek sanctuary. Or else Heather wrote it in a letter, for she never came back and that was the only time Liza ever saw her.

Mother left Liza to her own devices while she swept the bedroom carpets at Shrove with the vacuum cleaner ("You must never say 'hoovered,' Lizzie") and at those times Liza explored the library. One of the books she found was of fairy stories and the tale of Bluebeard was in it. After she had read it she began to associate the locked room with Bluebeard and wondered fearfully if it might contain dead brides. She thought perhaps old Mr. Tobias had married several women, killed them all, and left them to molder behind that locked door.

Even when Mother showed her old Mr. Tobias's portrait, a big painting that hung in the upstairs hall of a man with a proud expression and gray hair but no beard, blue or otherwise, she still wondered. She wanted to know what that thing was sticking out of his mouth, a stick with a little pot on the end of it. Mother said it was called a pipe, something you put ground-up leaves in and lit with a match, but Liza, remembering that Mother claimed to be a good liar, for the first time disbelieved her.

In a much more prideful place, where the light was bright and no eye could fail to be drawn to it, hung a portrait of the lady called Caroline. She wore the kind of dress Liza had never seen on an actual woman, ankle-length, flowing, low-cut, and of silk the same red as her mouth. Her hair was chestnut-colored, her skin like the petals of the magnolia even now blooming in the Shrove gardens, and her eyes fierce. Liza spent a long time looking at all the pictures in the house that were of real people, alive or long dead. There was no portrait of Mr. Tobias and none of the rich man who had run away from Caroline.

Heather wrote Mother a thank-you letter and after that weeks went by without the postman ever coming to their door. The milkman came and said, "The ten-thirty is late" and "This sunshine is a real treat," but they never saw the postman until one day he brought an envelope with a little paper book in it. Liza managed to get a fascinated look at this book, which was full of pictures of irons and hair dryers and towels and sheets and dresses and shoes, before Mother came and took it away from her. A log fire was burning in the grate and Mother got rid of the book by tearing it into pieces and putting the pieces on the fire.

After that there was no post for weeks, nothing from Mr. Tobias until a postcard came, a plain one, not even a picture, with just a few lines on the back asking them to have the dogs.

"Not if it's a nuisance," he wrote. "Matt will willingly have them. It is only for two weeks while I go to France to see my mother."

"Caroline," Liza said.

Mother said nothing.

"Does she live in the house in the place called Dordogne?" Liza had spent a long time studying the large maps of France in the library atlas. "Does she live there by herself? Is she called Mrs. Tobias?" She remembered the fierce eyes and the red, mouth-colored dress.

"She is now. She is called Caroline Tobias. When she was married she was called Lady Ellison, but our Mr. Tobias was always called Jonathan Tobias because that was his grandfather's wish. She lives in a house in the Dordogne her husband gave her when they were divorced." Mother gave Liza a speculative look as if she was considering explaining something, but she must have thought better of it. "Mostly, she lives by herself. Mr. Tobias goes to see her."

"We can have the dogs, can't we?" said Liza. "Even if Matt really wants them, we can have them, can't we?"

"Of course we shall have the dogs."

So that Mr. Tobias would be sure to come. Liza knew that only in retrospect, not at the time.

It was the day of her first French lesson *("Voici la table, les livres, la plume, le cahier")* that Matt came with the dogs. She was pursing her lips, trying to make that funny sound which is halfway between an E and a U, when they heard the van coming and then the knock at the door. It was rather a cold day even for April, she remembered, and the old electric heater was switched on.

The dogs were pleased to see her, as they always were, jumping up and licking her face and wagging the bit at the end of their backs where their tails had been chopped off. But Rudi was less violent in his affections than in the past, his breath smelled, and his muzzle was going gray. Dogs had seven years to every year of ours, Matt said, and that made Rudi over seventy. Heidi, of course, was only six, or forty-two.

"Will he die?" Liza said.

Matt's hair was much longer than last time, hanging down in greasy hanks. "Don't you worry yourself about that," he said. "That's a long way off."

But Mother said, "Yes, he'll die this year or next. Dobermans don't live much past eleven."

Liza knew her tables. "Or seventy-seven."

It had the effect of making Matt ask her why she wasn't at school. Before she could reply Mother said coldly, "It's Easter. The schools have broken up for Easter."

Some years went by before Liza realized a vital fact about that statement, though she knew there was something odd about it at the time. Mother hadn't told a lie, it *was* the Easter holidays, but just the same the impression she had given Matt was a false one. Later on she observed other instances of Mother doing this and learned how to do it herself.

Mother asked Matt how long they were to have the dogs this time and he said two or three weeks, he couldn't be more precise. But they'd let her know.

"Still haven't got no phone, I see."

"And never shall have."

"It'll have to be a postcard, then."

"I think we can leave that to Mr. Tobias," Mother said in the very cold way she sometimes had, and then, less coldly, almost as if she was asking for something she didn't want to have to ask for, "Will he come for them himself?"

Liza didn't like the look Matt gave Mother. He wasn't smiling but it was as if he was laughing inside. "Like you said, we'll have to leave that to him." With one of his winks, he added, "It'll depend on what Miss Fastley has to say."

Liza had never heard of Miss Fastley, but Mother looked as if she had, though she said nothing.

"When him and her get back from France," Matt said.

As soon as he had gone, Liza thought they would return to the French lesson but Mother said that was enough for today and to take the dogs down to the river. They wrapped up warmly and went down through the Shrove garden. A couple of trains had very likely passed by, Liza couldn't remember details like that, but it was probable at that hour. Likely too that she had waved to the train and one or two passengers waved back. There were never more than a few to wave back.

Mother stood looking across the valley and up to the high hills where the white road ran around among the greening trees. The woods were white with cherry blossom and primroses grew under the hedges.

"It's so beautiful, it's so beautiful!" she cried, spreading out her arms. "Isn't it beautiful, Lizzie?"

Liza nodded, she never knew what to say. There was something about the way Mother looked and the breathy edge to her voice that made her feel awkward.

"I don't mind the trains, I think in a way the trains make it better, it's something to do with all the people being able to sit inside and see how beautiful it is."

And she told Liza a story about a man called George Borrow who sold Bibles, wrote books, and lived in Norfolk, and who moved away and lived away for years because he couldn't bear it when they built a railway through the countryside he loved.

"Who's Miss Fastley?" Liza said on the way back.

Mother can't have heard her that first time because she had to say it again.

"She is one of the ladies who came to stay at Shrove for the weekend last year. She is the one called Victoria."

"Annabel had the sweater with flowers on," said Liza, "and Claire had the jacket like your shoes, so Victoria must have been the one in the green silk shirt."

"Yes, I believe she was."

They didn't put the dogs straight into the little castle but had them in with them for the evening. Rudi lay in front of the electric heater and slept. He was tired after his walk, Mother said they had taken him too far. Liza sat on one side of the fireplace and Mother on the other side. Liza was reading *Winnie the Pooh* by A. A. Milne and Mother was reading *Eothen* by A. W. Kinglake. They sometimes read bits aloud to each other and *Winnie the Pooh* was so funny there were a lot of bits Liza would have liked to read aloud but when she looked up she saw that Mother wasn't reading but gazing sadly at the hearth rug and she had tears on her face.

Liza didn't offer to read aloud but went silently back to her book. She thought Mother was crying because Rudi was old and would soon die.

~

The money they earned Liza wanted to save up. Eve had set her an example of thrift. There had been the bank account and the tin in the kitchen. And, of course, the secret box in the little castle. Strict accounts had been kept of what Eve earned and what they spent and these were consulted and referred back to before a length of material was bought to make a dress for Liza or a new skirt for Eve. The biggest expenditure Liza remembered was on the tape player Eve bought so that Liza could learn about music and get used to hearing the works of the great composers. She was nearly eight when that happened.

Sean appreciated her economies. He said that being sensible about money was one thing she *could* teach him. They might have Cornish pasties or pork pies and crisps for lunch with chocolate bars afterward, but it would be wiser not to go into town so much in the evenings for a meal at the Burger King or even Mr. Gupta's Tandoori. One evening Sean saw a notice in the window of the new supermarket that they wanted assistants. It would be only for sticking labels on packets and putting cans on shelves, but he said he was going to apply for it. The money would be at least twice what he earned at Vanner's, maybe three times as much.

"I will too, then."

"I don't reckon you can, love. They'll want your insurance number and you haven't got none."

"Can't I get one?"

"Not without giving your name you can't."

They found the family planning clinic too—Liza gave Sean's name and called herself Elizabeth Holford—and a notice board in a newsagent's window on which five people were advertising for domestic help. Liza studied it thoughtfully. Housework was something she could do.

When they got back, the man with the black dog put his head around the door of his camper, said hi and how about a cup of tea?

Liza could see Sean didn't want to, but it was rude to say no, so they went into the man's camper, the kitchen part, where the black dog was sitting on a counter, watching television. Instead of tea the man, who said his name was Kevin, produced a bottle of whiskey and three glasses, which Liza could see made Sean feel a lot better about going in there.

The little glowing screen fascinated her, the picture was so clear and the colors so bright. But at first she was half-afraid to look in case a policeman appeared describing her own appearance or even Eve herself. There was no need to worry. This was a program about small mammals in some distant part of the world, ratlike creatures and squirrellike creatures, which perhaps accounted for the dog's absorption.

He was much smaller than Rudi and Heidi, less sleek and with a real tail, which thumped on the counter when the squirrels jumped about, but just the same he reminded her of Mr. Tobias's dogs, now long dead. She and Mother had looked after them for three weeks, not two, on that occasion and at the end of that time, without warning, Matt appeared to take them away. When Mother saw his van stop outside and saw him get out of it, his hair longer than ever and tied back now, all the color went out of her face and she grew very white.

Liza thought she would be bound to ask him where Mr. Tobias was but she didn't, she hardly spoke to him. The dogs were handed over, Liza having hugged them both and kissed the tops of their heads, and somehow she knew as she watched the van depart that they would never come again, or not both of them, or not in the way they had before. She didn't know how she knew this, for Mother said not a word about it, didn't even look out of the window but set the French book in front of Liza and told her quite sharply to begin reading.

That evening Mother said they must go over to Shrove House, which surprised Liza because they never did. They never went there after about three in the afternoon. It was just after six when they walked across the parkland between the tall trees. There were cowslips in the grass and against the hedges cow parsley and yellow Alexanders. But this time Mother said nothing about how beautiful it was. They walked in silence, hand in hand.

Mother took her into the library and set her a task: to find the French books, to count them and then to see if she could find one called *Émile* by Jean-Jacques Rousseau. It took Liza no time at all. There weren't many French books, she could count only twenty-two, *Émile* among them. She took it down from the shelf, a very old book bound in blue with gilt letters, and went to look for Mother.

She was in the drawing room, talking into the telephone. Liza had never before seen anyone do that. Of course she had seen the telephone and more or less knew what it was, Mr. Tobias had told her, and on that occasion she remembered, while he was explaining, Mother had frowned and shaken her head. It was Mother using it now. Liza kept very still, listening.

She heard Mother say, "I've said I'm sorry, Jonathan. I've never phoned you before." Her voice went very low so that Liza could hardly hear. "I had to phone. I had to know."

Somehow Liza had expected to hear Mr. Tobias's voice

coming out of the other end of the receiver, but there was silence, though she could tell Mother could hear him.

"Why do you say there's nothing to know? If there was nothing, you would have come."

Liza had never heard Mother speak like that, in a ragged, pleading, almost frightened voice, and she didn't like it. Mother was always in control of things, all knowing, all powerful, but that wasn't how she sounded now.

"Then, will you come? Will you come, Jonathan, please? If I ask you, *please* to come."

Even Liza could tell he wasn't going to come, that he was saying, no, I can't, or, no, I won't. She saw Mother's shoulders hunch and her head dip down and heard her say in her cold voice, not unlike the one she used to Matt, "I'm sorry to have troubled you. I do hope I haven't interrupted anything. Goodbye."

Liza went up to her then and put out her hand. She showed her the blue book called *Émile* but Mother seemed to have forgotten what she had asked her to do and everything about it. Mother's face was as pale as a wax candle and as stiff. . . .

"You lost in a dream, love?" Sean said. "I offered you a penny for them and you never heard a word I said. Kevin wants to know if you'd like a glass of his Riseling?"

Liza said, yes, thanks, she'd love some, and when she saw the wine box and read the name she somehow managed to stop herself telling them it was pronounced "reesling," she thought their feelings might be hurt. Kevin was a small man with a nut-brown face and black hair, though not much of that was left. He might be thirty or he might be forty-five. Liza couldn't tell, she wasn't much good at guessing ages, and no wonder.

The men talked about football and then about the dog that Kevin said was a good little ratter. It had started to rain, Liza could hear it drumming on the roof of the camper. What would become of them if it rained? Mr. Vanner wouldn't pay them if they couldn't pick. She suddenly thought, with a fierce hunger, not altogether unlike the desire she often had for Sean, that if she didn't soon have a book in her hands, if she couldn't soon read a book, she'd die.

She asked Kevin how much his TV cost and could tell at once from Sean's expression that she shouldn't have. But Kevin didn't seem to mind. He said he didn't know, he hadn't a clue, because it was one of the things he'd brought with him from their household when he and his wife split up and he reckoned it was she who bought it in the first place.

"Not thinking of getting married, are you?" he said when she and Sean were going. "Only you want to think twice. Hang on to your freedom while you can."

"Of course we're not thinking of getting married," said Liza, and she laughed at the very idea, but Sean didn't laugh.

She hadn't said much to Sean at all about Eve and Mr. Tobias, it had all been in her head, all memories. It was he who brought the subject up next day, he must have been thinking about it, she didn't know why. They were still in bed, though it was quite late in the morning, but there was no point in trying to go out and pick with the rain pouring down.

When she first woke she had been quite disorientated, not knowing where she was but imagining she must be in the gatehouse. The rain made it unnaturally dark. Half-asleep still, she had looked for the book that should have been open and face-downward on the bedside cabinet. But there was no bedside cabinet and no book, and when she turned over she rolled into the warm eager arms of Sean. Instead of reading she cajoled and kissed him into making love to her—never a hard task—which he would have said was better any day, and often she would agree.

Suddenly he said, "This guy Tobias, he slept with your mum? I mean, they was in the same bed?"

"They were lovers, they were like us."

"That wasn't right," Sean said very seriously, "not with you in the house, not with a little kid."

"Why not?"

She didn't know what he meant and she could tell he found it hard to explain.

"Well, it's just not. Everyone knows that. They wasn't married. Your mum should have known better, an educated woman like her. It's one thing just the two of them, but not with a little kid in the house. You got to have principles, you know, love."

She said, no, she didn't know, but he took no notice. "D'you reckon she thought he'd marry her?"

"She hoped he would."

"Yeah, she must have been lonely. It wasn't right, him taking advantage of her like that."

Liza told him about the phone call and how Eve had been afterward, quiet and preoccupied and sometimes as if she was frightened.

"Well, she was in love, wasn't she?" Romantic Sean pressed his lips into her neck. He stroked her hair. "She loved him and she thought she'd lost him, you got to pity her."

"I don't know about being in love," Liza said. "Maybe a bit. She wanted Shrove House, that was what all that was about. She wanted Shrove House for herself, to make sure she'd never be parted from it. That was the only way. If she married Mr. Tobias it'd have been hers."

He was shocked. "That's not right."

"I can't help it. It's the way it was. It was always like that. She wanted that place, to be there all the time and to be sure she could be, more than anything in the world. It was all she wanted."

"It sounds crazy to me." She could feel him shaking his head as it lay on the pillow beside hers. "Whatever happened, then?"

"He married someone else," said Liza. "He married Victoria."

e i g h t

LIZA was eight years old and for as long as she could remember she had never been away from Shrove. Once a week Mother went on the bus into town to do the shopping, but Liza had never asked if she could come. Now, when she thought about it, she couldn't imagine why she had never said, "Can I come?" Locked up in her bedroom or else locked up in one of the rooms at Shrove, she had been content or she had accepted.

"That was wrong." Sean was in censorious mood. "Suppose something had happened to you."

"It didn't."

"Maybe not. Just as well for her. You might have hurt yourself or the place caught on fire."

She thought but didn't say that the place burning down would have been a bigger tragedy for Eve. Shrove on fire would be worse than Liza dying in it.

"If they'd found out what was going on they could have took you away and put you in care."

"They didn't know, whoever they are."

"Wasn't you scared?"

"No, I don't think I was, not ever. Well, for a bit after the man with the beard, but I saw what she did about that, you see. It showed me she'd always look after me. I liked being locked up in the library at Shrove best, there or in the morning room. It was so warm."

"What d'you mean, warm? The place was empty, wasn't it?"

"The heating was always on from October to May."

"He must be rolling in it," Sean said disapprovingly. "Central heating blasting away when no one lived there and there's poor buggers sleeping rough on the streets."

She wasn't interested, she hardly knew what he meant. "I used to read the books. Of course there were lots I didn't begin to understand, they were years and years too old for me. Eve said to me once, I just wonder what people would say, the ones who think you ought to have gone to school, if they could have seen you trying to read Ruskin and Matthew Arnold at seven-and-a-half."

Sean had no comment to make on that.

"Anyway, I was never left for more than two hours. Then Eve would come for me and she'd always have something nice, some treat, colored pencils to draw with or a new pair of socks or a painted egg. I remember once she came home with a pineapple,

I'd never seen one before. Then one day she brought a picture."

It was a painting of Shrove House. Mother had to tell her what it was or she might not have known, the painting was so strange, the colors so strong and the house not looking the way she had ever seen it. But when Mother explained that this was just one man's, the painter's, view of it, that he had chosen to paint it at sunset and after a storm, that he saw it as a symbol of wealth and power and had therefore accentuated all the yellows to express gold and the dark purples to reveal strength, then she began to understand. Mother had seen the painting in the window of a place she called a gallery and had bought it "on an impulse." It was cheap, she said, for what it was.

"Besides, we've got quite a lot of money," Mother said, and proudly, "We don't fritter money away."

She hung the painting on the wall in their living room where the gun had once been. When Liza climbed up on a stool to look more closely at it she saw that the words Bruno Drummond were written in red in the bottom right-hand corner with the date 1982.

It was the next morning, or perhaps the morning after next, that the postman came and brought with him the letter from Mr. Tobias. Mother tore open the envelope and read it. She threw the envelope into the rubbish bin, read the letter a second time, and folded it up. She said a strange thing, she said it in an intense concentrated way while she stared at the folded letter in her hand.

"In ancient times they used to kill a messenger who was a bearer of bad news. It's fortunate for that postman that things have changed."

Liza could hear his van going back up the lane. She waited for Mother to tell her what Mr. Tobias had written, but Mother didn't tell her and there was something in her face that stopped her asking. There were more lessons than usual that week and sometimes they went on into the evening. That was one of the signs that something had happened to upset Mother, an increase in lessons.

On the Saturday morning, while Liza was eating her breakfast, Mother said, "Mr. Tobias is getting married today. This is his wedding day."

"What's wedding?" said Liza.

So Mother explained about getting married. She turned it into a lesson. She talked about marriage customs in different parts of the world, how in some countries, for instance, a man could have several wives, but not here, here people could be married only one at a time. It was called monogamy. She told Liza about Islam and about the Mormons, about Christian brides in white dresses being married in churches and Jewish people under canopies stamping on glass. Then she read out something from the Book of Common Prayer about marriage being forever until the two people were parted by death. Mr. Tobias wouldn't be married like that, however, but in an office by a registrar.

"Were you ever married?" Liza asked.

"No, I never was," said Mother.

At a quarter past twelve she said it must all be over now and they were man and wife. Liza said, wasn't he a man before, and Mother said she was quite right, it was just an expression and not a very good one. They were *husband* and wife.

"Will they come and live here?" said Liza.

Mother didn't answer and Liza was going to repeat the question, but she didn't because Mother had gone a dark red color and clenched her fists. Liza thought it best to say no more about it. She married Annabel to the rag doll in a ceremony of her own invention but she did it upstairs in the privacy of her bedroom.

And of course Mr. and Mrs. Tobias never did come to live

at Shrove, though they stayed there from time to time, the first time being a fortnight after the wedding. Another letter came first. Mother read it, screwed it up, and looked cross.

"What does he mean, get a woman in to get the place ready? He knows I'll never do that. He knows I clean it and that I'll clean it ready for his wife." And she said those final two words again. "His wife."

She and Liza spent the afternoon at Shrove. Mr. Tobias would no longer be sleeping in his old bedroom but in the one that had been Caroline Ellison's in the four-poster with yellow silk curtains. With Victoria, Liza thought, though Mother hadn't said so. The four-poster was quite different from the Venetian one and made of dark brown carved wood with a carved wood roof Mother called a tester. She said that in olden times before there was glass in windows and when ceilings were very high, birds used to fly in and roost in the rafters on cold nights. You needed a roof on your bed to protect you from owl and hawk droppings.

While Mother put clean white sheets on the four-poster and mats of yellow silk and white lace out on the dressing table, Liza tried the handle of the door to the locked room on the off-chance of its not being locked for once. But it was, it always was.

Mother had said she must start writing compositions—well, stories really—and asked her to do one about getting married. Liza was already working it out in her head. She was going to have a girl called Annabel get married to a man called Bruno who brought her home to his big house in the country by a river. Annabel found the locked room while Bruno was out riding on his horse and then she found the key to the door in the pocket of his dressing gown. Next time he went out she unlocked the door and inside she found the dead bodies of three women that he'd killed before he married her because only Moslems could have more than one wife. Liza didn't know what would happen next but she'd think of something.

She expected Mr. Tobias to come running to their door as he had in the past, the dogs at his heels. Mother was busy sewing, her back to the window, her feet working the treadle on the machine faster than usual and her hands guiding the cloth, but Liza sat on the step outside, waiting for him. It was October but warm and sunny, the leaves on the balsam tree still green, the blackberries and the elderberries over and the holly berries turning from green to gold. The morning had been misty but now the air was clear, the sky blue, and everything very still.

They were late. Liza was almost at the point of giving up and going indoors when at last the car came, not the Range Rover but the Mercedes. Later on Liza was to learn to identify many makes of cars, but at that time she only knew a Range Rover, a Ford Transit van, a Mercedes, and whatever kind it was the police used. The Mercedes was going quite fast, it was going to sweep straight in through the open gates, but Mr. Tobias did see Liza, and he stuck his arm out of the window and waved. Of course he was on the near side of the car, the side nearest to her. On the other side sat the lady who had worn the green shirt. Victoria. Mrs. Tobias.

It was a pity because Liza couldn't see her very well. She wasn't wearing a green shirt this time but a fawn sweater with a neck that came right up to her chin and then folded over. Her hair was fair, a pale blond, it was exactly the same color as the jumper but silky instead of woolly and rough. Her face wasn't visible. Liza supposed the dogs must be in the back, though she couldn't see them. She waved and waved until they were out of sight and then she went in to give Mother all the details. That evening she expected them to come or him to come, best of all she would have liked him to come alone, and she sat in the window with Annabel, as if Annabel would draw him in some magic way.

"It must have been like turning a knife in the wound," she said to Sean, "the way I went on and on about him. When was he coming? Could we go up there? Poor Eve! But I didn't know any better. I was only a child."

"I shouldn't worry. You said yourself, she only wanted him for that place of his."

"Things aren't so simple," said Liza. "Anyway, they came next day, both of them."

Mrs. Tobias was tall and slim. ("Quite elegant, I suppose," Mother said.) Her fair hair, the color of newly sawn wood, was cut very short like a man's, but her face was painted in a way Liza had never seen before, not in the least like Diana Hayden's. The effect was more like a wonderful picture or a piece of jewelry. Her mouth reminded Liza of a fuchsia bud and her eyelids were crocus purple. She had fuchsia bud nails and on one finger were Mr. Tobias's rings, gold and diamonds flashing brilliantly.

She was very nice and polite to Mother, thanking her for making the house so clean and beautiful and telling her what Mr. Tobias was always saying, how she must, she just must, get a woman in to do all this cleaning. Either she found someone or she, Mrs. Tobias, would absolutely have to find someone herself.

All the while Mr. Tobias was looking rather strange, rubbing his hands together, walking up and down, then studying their old chromium electric heater as if he was passionately interested in things like that.

Liza said, "Where are Rudi and Heidi?"

"I'm afraid Rudi's dead," he said.

He looked more awkward than ever and tried to explain it away, as if it wasn't important, a dog dying. Rudi was old, he lost his appetite, he'd got a thing called a tumor growing inside him, and the kindest thing was for him to die a peaceful death.

"Did you shoot him with a gun?" Liza asked.

Mrs. Tobias screamed out when she said that. "Oh, my God, where does the child get these ideas!"

"I took him to the vet," Mr. Tobias said, "and he was very quiet and peaceful and happy. The vet gave him an injection and he went to sleep with his head on my lap."

"He never woke up again, he died," said Mother, getting a very strange look from Mrs. Tobias, who curled back her upper lip and showed her little white top teeth. "What about Heidi?"

Mr. Tobias said Matt had her with him in Cumbria. Heidi lived with him now, in his council house. "Victoria's allergic to dogs."

"It isn't something I can help," Mrs. Tobias said. "Of course I adore them but just having one near me can bring on these horrendous attacks of asthma."

After that they saw Mr. and Mrs. Tobias only in the distance. From her bedroom window, one evening, Liza saw them come walking out of the wood with their arms around each other. She heard the car go past several times and when they had been there nearly a week she heard shots.

"Mr. Tobias never used to shoot things," she said to Mother. "Why's he doing it now?"

"I expect it's his wife's influence."

"What is he shooting?"

Mother shrugged. "Pheasants, partridges—rabbits, perhaps."

Mr. Tobias called on them and brought a couple of dead pheasants. A brace, he called it. He came alone. Mrs. Tobias had a pain in her back and wasn't feeling well. Liza didn't think she would be able to eat things she had seen in the meadows, such beautiful birds, as beautiful as the peacocks she had seen in pictures, but when it came to it and Mother had roasted them she found that she could. When she ate the soft brown meat that seemed to melt in her mouth, she forgot about the shining blue and gold feathers and the bright beady eyes.

The Day of the Pheasant, she called it. She wrote the composition about marriage for Mother and had it given back with just a red tick on the bottom but otherwise no comment. That was the week Mother smacked her, the first and the last time this happened. Mother found her playing with the husband and wife dolls and came upon her just as the rag doll was killing Annabel with a gun made from a twig.

It was as if she didn't stop to think but lifted up her hand and smacked Liza on the bottom. Afterward she said she was sorry and that she shouldn't have done that.

The weather got cold very suddenly, the night frosts so heavy that in the morning it looked as if snow had fallen. The frost drove the Tobiases away. They called at the gatehouse as they were leaving, and Mrs. Tobias, who was wearing a wonderful coat of white sheepskin, said it was shocking having no bathroom at the gatehouse and one must be put in as a matter of priority. Mr. Tobias had used those very words himself but done nothing about it, Liza remembered. His wife urged Mother once more to get a cleaner. After all, if she knew Mother was doing it on her own she would have to tidy up herself, her conscience would make her.

"Please, Eve," said Mr. Tobias, looking more uncomfortable than ever. "And we'll see about that bathroom."

The car had disappeared up the lane for no more than ten minutes before Mother and she were on their way to Shrove House to clear up the mess.

But there was no mess. Everything was clean and tidy and someone had washed the dishes and done the dusting Liza couldn't tell how she knew this but she sensed that Mother, curiously, would have preferred a mess. While Mother was stripping the bed and putting the sheets in the washing machine, Liza made another attempt on the locked door. This time, for the first time ever, it wasn't locked. She turned the handle and the door came open.

There were no bodies, no dead brides. She found herself in a small sitting room in which was a writing desk, a pair of occasional tables, three armchairs, and a sofa. On the walls, in frames of polished wood, were the kind of dull gray pictures Mother said were called etchings and a pair of vases with Chinese people on them that held bunches of dried red roses. Facing the sofa and the chairs, on a cabinet made of a rather bright golden wood with a complicated curly grain, stood a large brown, box-shaped thing with a kind of mirror on the front of it. She could see herself in the mirror, but not very clearly, rather in the way she could in a window with dark curtains drawn behind the glass.

"What was it?" Sean asked. "A TV?"

"Yes, but I didn't know that then. I couldn't think what it was. The extraordinary thing was that I wasn't very interested in it. I was *disappointed.* You see I'd given that room such a terrific buildup in my mind, I thought there'd be at least some amazing wild animal in there or a box of jewels, treasure, really, or even a skeleton. I'd seen a picture of a skeleton in one of the books in the library. And all there was was this box thing with a mirror that didn't even work like mirrors are supposed to."

"But you switched it on."

"No, I didn't. Not then, not for ages. I wouldn't have given it another thought, I'd probably never have gone back there, if Mother hadn't come in. It was her coming in and being so obviously, well, taken aback that I'd got in there and found the thing that made me so anxious to know what it was."

"Kids are like that," said Sean sagely.

"Are they? I don't know. I only knew me. She wasn't cross. It was more as if she was worried. It's hard to describe, I have to find an expression, sort of knocked sideways, the wind taken out of her sails. She took my hand and led me out of there and got the key and locked the door again."

"But why?"

"That was the point of the whole thing, wasn't it? The whole way I was being brought up. The world had treated her so badly, it was so awful out there, that I wasn't to be allowed to go through any of that. I was to be sheltered from the world, hence no school and no visits to the town, no meeting other people, other people kept down to the minimum, a totally protected childhood and youth."

"She taught you to express yourself all right, didn't she?" he said admiringly and he lit a cigarette as if he needed it.

Liza wished he wouldn't. The caravan quickly filled with smoke, it was so small, and it made her cough. She sighed a little before going on. "Television would have undone a lot of her work. Once I'd seen that, I'd know about the world out there, I wouldn't only want to see it, I'd start talking like the people on TV and learning the sort of ways she thought were bad."

"You said the world had treated her bad. I mean, like what? What had it done to her?"

"You won't believe this, but I don't know. That is, I don't know the details. She'd had me without a husband, there was that, she hadn't got Shrove when she thought she was going to, she told me a lot more about that later, but she never told me what made her, well, bury herself and me down there. When she took me out of that room and locked the door again I hadn't any idea why and she didn't explain. I only knew it had something to do with the box with the glass front."

"You said she got the key. Where did she get it from?"

That had been the most interesting thing. Mother had looked around her for the key and clicked her tongue when she saw it lying on top of the glass-fronted cabinet that was full of dolls. She locked the door and then, in Liza's presence, not bothering to hide from her what she was doing, she climbed onto a chair and from the chair onto the top of a dresser in which was kept breakfast china and cutlery. The top of the dresser was on a level with Liza's head.

On the wall above hung a large picture Liza was to learn was called a still life. This one was by Johann Baptist Drechsler and was of a bunch of roses with dew on them and fritillaries and morning glory. The painter had put a Painted Lady butterfly on a blade of grass and on the top left-hand side a moth with brown forewings and yellow underwings and a strange pattern on its back. The picture was in a thick gilt frame that stuck out six inches from the wall. Mother put the key on top of the frame, over to the right-hand side, and while she did so she explained to Liza that the moth was called the death's-head hawk moth because the pattern on its back looked like a skull, or the bones inside a person's head. If this was designed to distract Liza's attention from the key and the locked room, it failed to do so.

Liza knew she had about as much chance of getting up there as she had of owning a dog. But she wanted to get up there. Soon it became the thing she most wanted to do in all the world. She thought about it a lot and she thought that in that little book that had once come in the post and she had managed to study for five minutes before it was taken away and torn up, in there had been a picture of just such a box as was in the locked room at Shrove House.

When it was winter and Mother went shopping she was always locked up at Shrove because of the warmth there. Sometimes in the morning room, sometimes in the library, sometimes in one of the bedrooms. When it was the morning room she had been in the habit of spending a lot of the time just gazing at the dolls in the cabinet. The dolls were of historical personages, Mother had said and had named some of them, Queen Elizabeth I, Mary Queen of Scots, a man called Beau Brummel and another called Louis Quatorze, Florence Nightingale and Lord Nelson. But now instead she stood staring at the picture of the flowers, the butterfly, and the moth with the skull on its back, knowing the key was lying there on the top of the frame, though she couldn't see it even if she stood on a chair.

Her ninth birthday came and went. It was very cold and the grounds of Shrove lay under six inches of snow. A partial thaw came but the half-melted snow froze again, and the house, the stables and coachhouse, the gatehouse, the little castle, and the owl barn were hung with icicles. Hoar frost turned all the trees into pyramids and cascades and towers of silver lace. The lane was blocked with snow drifts and Mother couldn't get out to catch the bus for town. When she did, at last, she left Liza in the library.

Reading books, playing with the terrestrial globe, looking out of one window after another at the birds in the snow, Liza came to the far end where it was always rather dark, the darkest place in that light house, and saw, resting against the wall, something long-familiar yet forgotten, the library steps.

There were eight steps, enough to get even a small person up to the topmost bookshelf. But Liza was locked in the library. Anyway, she thought the steps would be too heavy for her, they looked heavy, they were made of dull gray metal. She touched them, she put both hands to them and clasped the rails that enclosed the treads. She tried to raise them as if they would be heavy and they flew up in her hands. The steps were light, they were nearly as light as if made of cardboard, a little child could lift them, she could lift them with one hand.

But she was locked in. Mother came for her soon afterward and they went back to the gatehouse through the snow. It snowed even more heavily that night and they spent next morning digging themselves out and the afternoon making cakes of dripping and bread for the bird feeders. Two weeks, three, went by before Mother could go to town again. It was soon after that, in March probably, when the snow had gone but for patches of it left in shady places, that the postman brought the letter that was to change their lives.

"Tobias again?" said Sean.

"No, we never heard from him. Well, Eve got her money all right and Mrs. Tobias sent a postcard from Aspen in America that they went skiing, but there was never a thing from him. This letter was from Bruno Drummond."

"The artist guy."

"Yes. The Phoenix Gallery had told him about Eve buying his painting, I don't think he sold many paintings—well, I know he didn't. He said he'd wanted to phone her but he couldn't find her number in the book. Not surprising, was it, since she'd no more have a phone than she would a television. He said the painting ought to be varnished and if she'd bring it to him he'd do it. He told her where he lived and said it was easy to park her car outside!

"Of course she didn't answer. She said if the painting needed varnishing she was capable of doing that herself. And she was very annoyed with the gallery for giving him her address. She kept saying, 'Is nothing sacred? Is there no privacy?' "

In February the Latin lessons began. *Puella, puella, puellam, puellae, puellae, puella.* And *Puella pulchra est.*

"The girl is beautiful," said Mother, but it was herself that she looked at in the mirror.

Liza enjoyed learning Latin because it was like doing a hard jigsaw puzzle. Mother said it would stretch her brain and she read aloud from Caesar's *Invasion of Britain* for Liza to get accustomed to the sound of it.

In March she began her collection of pressed wildflowers. Mother bought her a big album to keep them in. To the left-hand page she attached the pressed flower and on the right-hand one she painted a picture of it in watercolor. A snowdrop was the first one she put in and next a coltsfoot. Mother let her borrow *Wild Flowers* by Gilmour and Walters from the library at Shrove so that she could identify the flowers and find their Latin names.

The weather grew warmer and in April Mr. and Mrs. Tobias came down to Shrove to stay, bringing four other people with them. Claire and Annabel and a man Liza had never seen before and Mr. Tobias's mother, Lady Ellison.

"Caroline," said Liza.

"Yes," said Mother, "but you mustn't call her that."

As it turned out, Liza didn't get the chance to call her anything.

Before they came, Mrs. (not Mr.) Tobias had written to Mother and said some more about a cleaning woman.

"Can you imagine having such a person here?" Mother was calm but Liza could tell she was angry. "She would come in a car and we should have that noise and dirt. I would have to let her in, I couldn't trust anyone with a key, and then teach her what to do and, just as important, what *not* to do. Why can't Victoria Tobias leave it alone? Why can't she just leave me to do it?"

Liza couldn't answer that. Mother thought about it all day, she *worried* about it, she kept saying she didn't want any more intruders, Mr. Frost was bad enough, not to mention the postman *and* the milkman *and* the man who read the meters *and* the one who serviced the Shrove central heating, there was no end to it.

"You could do it yourself and pretend you'd got a lady to do it."

At first Mother said, no, she couldn't, and, how about the money, and then she said, why not? It wouldn't be dishonest to take the money so long as the work was done, so Mother invented a woman and she and Liza thought up a name for her. They laughed until they almost cried at some of the names Liza thought up. She got them from the wildflower book, Sweet Cicely Pearlwort and Mrs. Sowthistle and Fritillaria Twayblade. But Mother said it mustn't be funny, it must sound like a real name, so in the end they called her Mrs. Cooper, Dorothy Cooper.

Mother wrote to Mr. (not Mrs.) Tobias and said she'd found a cleaning woman called Dorothy Cooper who would come once a week and if he sent the money to her she would pay her. In the week before Easter, Mother gave Shrove House a tremendous spring clean while Liza sat in the library reading *Jane Eyre.* That is, for most of the time she read *Jane Eyre.* She also carried the steps out of the library and into the morning room.

At the morning room windows hung long heavy curtains of slate-gray velvet. Even when you pulled the cords that drew them across the windows they still covered about two feet of the gray-and-white wall on either side. Liza put the steps up against the wall on the right-hand side of the right-hand window. The curtains covered them, you couldn't see they were there.

It was just as well she hadn't used them to get the key down and open the door because, when she had finished upstairs, Mother came into the morning room, climbed onto a chair and then onto the sideboard, and reached up for the key on top of the picture frame. Liza crept out of the library and watched her from the morning room doorway. Mother unlocked the door and went into the secret room, pulling the vacuum cleaner behind her.

She was in there for half an hour. Liza kept dodging from the library to the morning room door to check on her. When she heard the howl of the vacuum cleaner from the morning room she went to the door and said she was hungry and could they go home and have lunch?

The key was in the lock of the door to the secret room. It had to be, of course it did, because Mr. and Mrs. Tobias and their friends were coming. Liza and Mother had their lunch in the Shrove kitchen and all the time Liza was thinking, perhaps the key will still be in that lock after they have gone away again.

It wasn't. Liza thought Mother had probably gone over there and put it back on the picture before she was even up. She had seen very little of Mr. and Mrs. Tobias and their friends, just the Mercedes going by once or twice with the other car following behind and once caught a glimpse of Claire and a tall old woman in a tweed skirt down on the Shrove lawn with golf clubs. Could it be Caroline? Could *that* be the Caroline of the plump white shoulders and the lipstick-colored dress? But one evening, after she had gone to bed, she heard someone come to their front door. There was a low murmur of voices, a man's and Mother's.

She was almost but not quite sure the other voice was Mr. Tobias's. They were downstairs in the living room, talking, and she crept out of bed to listen at the top of the stairs. But Mother must have heard her because she came out and called up to Liza to go back to bed at once.

The murmur went on and on, then she heard the front door close and Mother come up to bed. If Mother had been crying it wouldn't have surprised her, she didn't know why, but instead Mother was talking out loud to herself. It was uncanny and rather frightening.

"It's all over," Mother was saying. "You have to get it into your head that it's all over. You have to start again. Tomorrow to fresh woods and pastures new."

Did that mean they were going away?

"Tomorrow to fresh woods and pastures new," Mother murmured and closed her bedroom door.

"No, of course we're not leaving," Mother said in the morning. "What on earth gave you that idea? Mr. and Mrs. Tobias are leaving and goodness knows when they'll come back again."

Liza saw the cars come down the drive from Shrove House, the Mercedes with Mr. Tobias driving and Mrs. Tobias beside him and Claire in the back. A minute later along came the other car with the man driving and Caroline Ellison beside him. It stopped outside the gatehouse and the man sounded his horn. Liza didn't know what he meant by it but Mother did. Mother was furious. I'm not going out there, I'm not being summoned in that way, she was fuming, it's like the Royal Family stopping outside some keeper's house. But she did go out and talked to Lady Ellison.

This enabled Liza to get a good look at Mr. Tobias's mother, who had actually got out of the car. She was so tall she made Mother look child-sized. And Mother made her look like a giantess as well as uglier than ever. Liza thought her hands were like a hawk's claws that had been dipped in some poor small animal's blood.

Mother came back into the house making terrible faces of rage and disgust, which the people in the cars couldn't see because her back was to them. The cars were hardly out of sight before she and Liza were up at Shrove House, where there was an awful mess to be cleared up. No doubt, Mrs. Tobias thought Dorothy Cooper would be clearing it up. That was when Liza found the secret room door locked and the key, so far as she knew, back on top of the picture.

It was May now but not very warm, though beautiful to look at, as Mother kept saying. The new leaves were a sharp fresh green and the cream and red flowers on the broom were out, sweet smelling and covered with bees. Last autumn Mr. Frost had planted hundreds of wallflowers. Like folds of multicolored velvet they were, red and amber and gold and chestnut brown, spread across a whole sweep of land with not a blade of green to be seen between them. Liza picked speedwell for her wildflower collection and Mother said she could take one, but just one, cowslip.

They had lunch at home. The afternoon was for Latin, arithmetic, and geography. Liza was doing long division when the doorbell rang. Because the doorbell hardly ever rang it was always a shock when it did.

"That will be Mr. Frost wanting something," Mother said, though he hardly ever did want anything.

She opened the door. A man was standing there. His car, which was the orange color of a satsuma and looked as if made of painted cardboard, was parked outside their gate. He was quite a young man with curly brown hair long enough to reach his shoulders and very big blue eyes with long lashes like a girl's. Well, like hers or Mother's. There were little brown dots, which Mother later explained were freckles, sprinkled on his small straight nose. His lips were red and his small teeth very white. He wore blue jeans and a denim jacket over a check shirt and a gold ornament hanging from a chain around his neck. Liza stared fascinated at the earrings he wore, two gold rings both in the same ear. He was carrying a bag made out of a carpet. It looked as if it was made from one of the Persian rugs at Shrove.

"Oh, hi," he said. "This really is the end of the world, isn't it? I'm amazed that I've found you. Let me introduce myself. My name is Bruno Drummond."

nine

LIZA said she was like Scheherazade, telling her man stories every night. Only Sean wouldn't chop her head off in the morning, would he, if one night she was so worn out she couldn't collect her thoughts? Sean said, who was that then, that She-whatever, but Liza was too tired to explain.

They were both exhausted, picking Coxes. The crop was a particularly big one this year. They picked from first thing in the morning until sunset, which was as long as Mr. Vanner would let them. He said he'd have to take on extra labor to cope with the crop and they wanted to stop him, they wanted to earn all the money that was going, but it was a losing battle. On the third morning a troop of women moved in to help, housewives from the village that was a mile away.

Sean wanted to hear more about Bruno, but Liza was too tired to tell him, too tired to watch the little colored television set she'd finally bought with the hundred pounds and some apple money, too tired for everything but making love, and they only managed that because it happened in bed and they fell asleep straight afterward.

The news was something Liza had seldom been able to watch on television even if she had wanted to. It is rarely transmitted between two and five in the afternoon. Now she learned it was for mornings and evenings, so she watched it at breakfast time and, once the women had come and there was no point in working so hard, at six o'clock and nine. She was looking for something about Eve. But there never was anything.

"That's because they've had her in court," Sean said, "and now she's on what-d-you-call-it, remand, that's it, remand, and the papers and the telly can't have anything on about her until she comes up in court again."

This was very much what Eve herself had told her. She admired him for knowing it. Feeling very pleased that he knew about this legal matter, she realized she had begun accepting that she knew much more than he did about almost everything but the absolutely practical things. Of course he *thought* he knew more than she, but she could tell that mostly he didn't. When it was books and music and nature and art and history, she knew it all and he knew nothing, so she was pleasantly surprised.

"When will that happen, Eve coming up in court?" she asked him.

"Not for weeks, maybe months."

She was disappointed. "Where do they do it, this remand?"

"In prison."

Her knowledge of that had its base on her reading of fiction, *A Tale of Two Cities* and *The Count of Monte Cristo.* She saw Victorian hellholes, she saw dungeons with a tiny barred window up in the wall.

"What do you care?" he said. "You ran away, you got out of that and quite right too."

"I'm tired, Sean. I've got to go to sleep."

She crept into his arms, her naked body close up against his. The nights were starting to get cold. He slid his mouth over hers and entered her smoothly as if it were the natural next step. They were like that, locked together, when she woke up in the deep night and moved her body gently to arouse him again. He said sleepily that he loved her and she said, I love you too, Sean.

Next day wasn't the last one for picking the Coxes but Friday would be. Kevin said he was moving on before the end of the week and why didn't they follow him? They were advertising for unskilled hands at the Styrofoam packings works on an industrial estate ten miles away. Kevin thought he'd give it a go.

But Sean wasn't interested. He knocked off early, spruced himself up, put on a clean shirt and jeans, and went into town to apply for the supermarket job. Liza wasn't a bit surprised to hear he'd got it. They asked Kevin in to share a couple of bottles of wine. Kevin said his telly wasn't a patch on hers, it was wonderful, really, the way the colors came up so bright and the picture so sharp on a screen that size.

Liza said good-bye to the dog. She put her arms around it and its cold nose nuzzled her neck. It was a gentle mild creature. The feel of the fine skull and sleek black pelt under her lips reminded her once more of Heidi. It still made her indignant, thinking of how Mr. Tobias had simply ditched Heidi when he married Victoria, handed her over to Matt as if she were a piece of furniture he didn't need anymore.

She had still liked Mr. Tobias, but her affection for him had been shaken by his treatment of Heidi. To handle that she had blamed the changes in him on Victoria, as she guessed her mother did. It was Victoria who made him shoot things and Victoria who kept him away from Shrove.

Perhaps Victoria would die. Dogs died, so why not people? It was about this time that she began fantasizing how life would be if Mr. Tobias married Eve and they both went to live at Shrove House. Like children in books, she would have a father as well as a mother.

Sean was to start his job on Monday. They'd have to find somewhere else to put the caravan but before that he was going to take advantage of being on Vanner's land.

He often called her Teacher when she imparted information. This time, he said, he was going to teach her something. He'd teach her to drive.

She wouldn't be old enough to get a license till she was seventeen, which would be in January, but she could drive on the tracks around the orchards, that was private land. They picked the last row of trees on Friday morning and collected the last pay they would get. Then Sean got her up in the driving seat of the Dolomite and taught her how to start it and use the gears. It wasn't difficult.

"Like a duck to water," Sean said, very pleased.

She wanted to drive out onto the road and take them to wherever the new place they were going to park would be, but Sean said no. It wasn't worth the risk. They couldn't afford to pay fines. Reluctantly, Liza agreed.

"I suppose I can't risk the police getting hold of me."

"Anyway, it's against the law," Sean said very seriously.

She sat in the passenger seat next to him, eating Coxes. She'd filled a cardboard box with apples she'd picked up. Vanner was so mean he didn't even like the pickers taking home windfalls.

"You mind he don't put the fuzz on you," Sean said, but he laughed and she knew he was joking. Then he said, out of the blue, "Your mum, she ever try to get this Tobias away from his wife?"

"What made you suddenly ask that?"

"I reckon I was thinking about the cops and about them catching her and remembering you never said if he come back again after he had all them people there for the weekend."

"Well, she never did, no. At least, so far as I know she didn't. She didn't get a chance, did she, with him so far away and then we hadn't a phone or a car, we were trapped down there in a way."

"But wasn't that what she wanted?"

"Oh, yes, it was what she wanted. She wanted to be at Shrove and be undisturbed and isolated, but what she'd wanted most was to *own* Shrove. I think she gave up that idea when he got married. I mean, she gave it up for a while. It was very hard for her, she'd counted on it for so long, but she had to give it up. Of course, I don't know what went on in her mind, I was only a child, but I think she regretted a lot of things, she had bitter recriminations."

"Come again?"

"I mean she was sorry she hadn't behaved differently. You see, maybe if we'd gone to London with him when he first asked or gone traveling with him, he'd have got so close to her he'd have thought he couldn't live without her. It might only have been for a year or two and then we could have all come back to Shrove together. He and she were mad about each other then, I'm sure they were, like you and I are."

"That's true anyway," said Sean with a smile, looking pleased that she'd said it.

"But she wouldn't because of me. She was determined to bring me up without—well, the contamination of the world. I wasn't to be allowed to suffer as she'd suffered. If she'd gone to London with Mr. Tobias she'd have had to send me to school there and I'd have met other children and seen all sorts of things, I suppose. You could say she put me first or perhaps she just put Shrove first. The irony was that she lost Mr. Tobias because she put his house first. As for me, I'd have loved to live at Shrove House and have Jonathan Tobias for my father. You'll laugh but I used to think that if I lived there and it was mine I could get into that room."

Sean did laugh. "But he married someone else and that was the end of her love life."

"Oh, no, you could say it was the beginning of it. That was when Bruno came. Now that I'm grown up, I think I know what went through her mind. She thought, I've lost Jonathan, I can't waste my whole life mooning over him, so I might as well cut my losses and have a new lover. She was only a bit over thirty, Sean, she was young. She couldn't give up everything."

"How about that bathroom? Did he have it done?"

"In the end. Not for years. He forgot about it the minute Shrove was out of sight. He meant to do it but he just forgot, he was very thoughtless. When I think about it all now I really believe that when Shrove was out of sight he forgot about Eve too. She'd come into his mind once or twice a year and then he'd send her a postcard."

The place they found to park the caravan was a piece of waste ground at the point where a bridle path turned off a lane. No one used it much. People on horseback might notice they were there, but it could be weeks before whoever owned the land did. Law-abiding Sean had tried to find out who that was but had failed. The difficulty was that there was no water supply apart from the stream that tumbled over rocks under the stone bridge a little way up the lane. That was all right to drink, Liza told the dubious Sean. Mostly they'd boil it, anyway. They could get washed in the public swimming pool next to the supermarket he'd be working at. She was full of plans. Of much of the world she might be ignorant, but she knew how to *manage.*

The day he started she was left alone. Winter was coming and it had started to get cold. They heated the caravan with bottled gas and an oil heater, so that was all right, but for the first time in her life she had nothing to do.

It was rainy and cold out there, but she went out and walked along the public footpath down to the stream and over the bridge close by the ford. The leaves were falling now, gently and sadly dropping from the boughs because there was no wind. They floated down to make another layer on the wet slippery mass underfoot. Leaves coated the surface of the sluggish stream. The sky was gray and of a uniform unbroken cloudiness. She walked for miles along woodland paths and meadow edges, keeping the church tower always in sight so that she would know how to find her way back.

Once or twice she crossed a road, but she saw no one and no traffic passed her. A muntjac stag appeared under the trees, showed her his top-heavy antlers, and fled through the bracken. Jays called to one another to warn of her approach. She gathered all kinds of fungus but, in spite of her knowledge, feared to cook them and shed a trail of agarics and lepiotas as she walked. When it was about noon, according to her haphazard but usually accurate calculations, she made for home.

There, with no prospect of Sean coming home for four hours,

she was at a loss. Never before had she been without something to read. There was no paper in the caravan and nothing to write with, no means of playing music, no collections to pore over, no needles or thread to sew with. At last she turned on the television. An old Powell and Pressburger film with Wendy Hiller in it mystified her as such films had when the Shrove House set was available to her. Had such people ever existed, talked like that, dressed in those clothes? Or was it as much a fairy tale as Sheherezade?

When Sean came back she had fallen asleep. The television was still on and he got cross, saying she was wasting power. Next day she went with him into the town and applied for the job with Mrs. Spurdell.

Liza said she was eighteen. She had no references because she had never worked for anyone before, but she knew all about housework. She had watched Eve and later on helped Eve.

The house in Aspen Close was a little like the house Bruno had wanted them all to live in. But inside was different. She had never before seen anything like this large, dull, ugly room carpeted and curtained in beige, with no pictures on the walls and no mirrors and, as far as she could see, no books. Flowers that could not be real, artificial white peonies and blue delphiniums and pink crysanthemums filled beige pottery bowls. Across the middle of a table and along the top of a cabinet lay pale green lace runners.

Mrs. Spurdell was the same color, except that her hair was white. Her fat body was squeezed into a pale green wool dress and underneath that, Liza thought, must be some kind of controlling rubber garment that made her shape so smooth, yet segmented and undulant. Like a plump caterpillar shortly to become a crysalis. The shoes she wore, shiny beige with high heels, looked as if they hurt her ankles, which bulged over the sides of them.

Liza was shy at first. If Mrs. Spurdell had been kind and friendly she might have found things easier, but this fat old woman with the surly expression made her speak abruptly and perhaps too precisely.

"You don't sound the sort of person I was looking for," Mrs. Spurdell was moved to say. "Frankly, you sound more as if you'd be off to university than looking for a daily's job."

Liza thought about that one. It gave her ideas but of course she didn't voice them. She said, "If I can work for you I'd do it properly."

Mrs. Spurdell sighed. "You'd better see the rest of the house. It might be too much for you."

"No, it wouldn't."

But Liza went upstairs with Mrs. Spurdell, walking behind her. The caterpillar waist and hips and the wobbly fat legs threatened to made her giggle, so she made herself think about sad things. The saddest thing she could contemplate was Eve in prison. Her thoughts flew to Eve and she experienced a moment or two of sharp fear.

Mrs. Spurdell's bedroom was all in pink. A white fluffy rabbit sat in the middle of the pink satin bed. Another bedroom was blue and a third a kind of peach color. Liza began to hope and hope she would get the job because there were so many things here she longed to look at more closely, to study and speculate about. Then Mrs. Spurdell took her into a room she said was Mr. Spurdell's study and Liza saw the books. There was a whole bookcase full of them. There was a box full of white paper on the desk and pens and pencils in a jar made of some kind of green-veined stone.

She saw a few more books in the gloomy chamber Mrs. Spurdell called the dining room, about twenty of them on a shelf. At once Liza began to feel differently about the house. It was no longer simply grotesque and ridiculous. It was a place with books in it and paper and pencils.

"I can keep this clean," she said. "It won't be too much for me."

"I'll start you on a trial basis. You look very young."

But not so young as I am, Liza thought. The amount Mrs. Spurdell offered her seemed very low indeed. Even to her, ignorant as she was, it seemed low. She would have to be strong and speak up. To her surprise she heard herself say very firmly to Mrs. Spurdell that two pounds fifty an hour wouldn't be enough, she wanted three pounds. Mrs. Spurdell said certainly not, she wouldn't consider it, and that left Liza at a loss. There seemed nothing for it except to go, but when she got up, having no idea that this was bargaining or even what bargaining was, Mrs. Spurdell said to wait a minute and all right, but to remember it was on a trial basis. Two mornings a week and one afternoon and she could start next week. Tomorrow, please, said Liza.

"Goodness me," said Mrs. Spurdell in a voice that implied Liza would fail in her undertaking, "you are keen."

For the rest of the day she wandered about the town, doing all sorts of adventurous things, going into a pub and then a cinema. Some of them made her heart beat faster, but she did them. They served her in the pub, though somewhat suspiciously. It seemed she could just pass for eighteen. The film she saw shocked her deeply. She was also electrified by it. Were there such places? Were there huge cities of stone buildings taller than any tall tree, where the streets were gleaming loops on stilts, where a million cars went to and fro and chased each other and men made violent assaults on women? But she took it calmly when a man screamed and died, his blood spraying onto the wall behind him. After all, she had seen the real thing.

The rest of it she found hard to believe. Reluctantly, she decided it must belong in a genre of entertainment Eve had mentioned in their English literature lessons: science fiction. H. G. Wells, she thought vaguely, and John Wyndham, whose names she had heard but whose works she had never read.

If she had access to Eve she could have asked. She asked Sean instead while they were going home in the car.

"That's Miami."

"What do you mean, that's Miami? What's Miami?"

He was never much good at explaining. "It's a place, isn't it? In America. You seen it on TV."

"No." One day she'd tell him why she hadn't. "Have you been there?"

"Me? Come on, love, you know I never been there."

"Then you don't know, do you? They might have made it up. They might have built it in a—in a studio. Like toys."

"Them guys firing guns, they wasn't toys."

"No, they were actors. They didn't really die, it wasn't real blood, it couldn't be, so how d'you know the rest wasn't made up too?"

He had no answer for that. He could only keep saying, " 'Course it's real, everyone knows it's real."

As they were going up into the caravan, she said, "If it's real I'd like to go there, I'd like to see."

"Chance'd be a fine thing," said Sean.

Because life is like that—you see or hear something new to

you early in the day and then later the same information comes up again in quite another context—Miami was on the television that evening. Not Miami, L.A., said Sean, but it looked the same to her. Probably, then, such places existed just as, in another program, the great castle called Caernarvon and the place called Oxford.

"Eve was there," she said, answering the bell that rang in her head.

"What was she doing there?"

"She was at a school. It's called a university. Mrs. Spurdell thought I was going to one, she said so."

"Your mum was at Oxford University?"

She was genuinely puzzled. "Why not?"

"Come on, love, she was having you on."

"No, I don't think so. She had to leave it, I don't know why, something to do with me being born."

Sean didn't say anymore, but she had the impression he wanted to, that he was struggling to say something but didn't know how to put it. At last he said, "I don't want to upset you."

"You won't."

"Well, then, d'you know who your dad was?"

Liza shook her head.

"Okay, sorry I asked."

"No, it's all right. It's just that she doesn't know, Eve doesn't know."

She could see that she had shocked him. The spraying bullets on the screen and the spurting blood didn't affect him, nor did the violated women or the bombs that flattened a city, but that Eve was ignorant of the identity of her child's father, that shook him to the core. He was bereft of speech. She put her arm around him and held him close.

"That's what she said, anyway." She tried to reassure him. "I've got my own ideas, though. I think I know who it was, whatever she said."

"Not that Bruno?"

"Oh, Sean. She didn't know Bruno till I was nine. Shall I go on telling you about him?"

"If you want." He said it gruffly.

"Well, then. He stayed and varnished the picture. He'd brought all the stuff with him in his bag. I didn't think Eve would let him do it but she did. I didn't think she'd speak to him but I was wrong there too. She asked him how he'd ever come to paint Shrove House and he said he'd seen it from the train.

"Not with the sun setting behind it you didn't, she said, you must have been looking eastward. Ah, but I could tell how wonderful it would be from the other side, he said, so I came down here one summer evening and made a start. I was here a good many summer evenings. I didn't see you, Eve said, and he said, I didn't see *you.* If I had I'd have been back sooner."

It was as if Sean hadn't heard a word since she said that about not knowing who her father was. "She must have had one bloke after another," he said, "one one night and another the next or even the same day. That's really disgusting. That's a terrible what-d'you-call-it to bring a child up in, especially a girl."

"Environment," she said. "Why especially a girl?"

"Oh, come on, Liza, it's obvious."

"Not to me," she said, and then, "Don't you want to hear about Bruno Drummond?"

ten

THE second time he came, the important time, was the day Liza saw the death's-head moth. It was June.

He was thirty-one and lived in the town, in rooms over Mullins the greengrocer's. His father was dead but his mother was still alive up in Cheshire. Once he had had a wife but she had left him and was living in somewhere called Gateshead with a dentist.

Liza, who was listening to this, said, "What's a dentist?"

Bruno Drummond gave her the sort of look that meant he thought she was teasing him and said something about expecting she'd been to one of those a few times. But Mother said, "A kind of doctor who looks after your teeth."

The reason for his visit, he said, was to paint the valley with the train, and perhaps he had done some painting earlier, but he called at the gatehouse soon after ten in the morning, stayed to lunch, and was still there in the evening. Instead of a chair he sat on the floor. He related the story of his life.

"I should never have married," he said. "I don't believe in marriage but I allowed myself to be persuaded. Marriage is really the first step in getting swallowed up in the killing machine."

"What do you mean, the killing machine?" said Mother.

"Society, slavery, conformity, the poor ox that treads out the corn, walking round and round all day long, and muzzled too, most likely. I'm an anarchist. Now you'll say, what sort of an anarchist is it that marries and gets a civil service job to pay the mortgage? Not exactly a card-carrying one. My defense is that I got out of it after three years of hell."

"Were you really a civil servant?"

"On a low rung. Of course I'd been to art school. As a matter of fact, I was at the Royal College. When I was married I worked in the DSS benefit office in Shrewsbury."

"So how do you live now?"

"I paint, that's what I always wanted to do, but it's not lucrative. Then I paint houses too, rooms, that is. I'll tell you how I got into that. Someone, a woman, asked me what I did and I said, I paint, so she said, would you come and paint my dining room? I'd like to have spat in her face, the fool. But then I thought, well, why not? Beggars can't be choosers. And I've been doing it on a regular basis ever since—more or less, I'm opposed to regularity of any kind. I don't pay tax, I don't pay National Insurance. I suppose somewhere someone's got a record of me and keeps sending me demands to my old address. But they don't know where I am, no one does but my mother, even my ex-wife doesn't. That's freedom and the price I pay is relatively small."

"What price is that?" said Mother.

"Never having any money."

"Yes, that's freedom," said Mother. "Some would call it a very high price."

"Not me. I'm different."

Bruno played his guitar after that and sang the Johnny Cash song about finding freedom on the open road and men refusing to do what they were told. Liza could tell Mother liked him, she was looking at him the way she had sometimes looked at Mr. Tobias. Perhaps she liked his voice and the way he pronounced words, unlike the way anyone else did. Liza remembered Hugh with the beard, his fuzzy cheeks and upper lips. Bruno looked as if no hair had ever or could ever grow on his smooth girlish face.

In the summer the solanum plant that climbed over the back of the gatehouse showed its blue flowers at Liza's window. Mother called it the flowering potato because it and potatoes and tomatoes all belonged to the same family. When she came up to bed that evening Liza knelt on the bed up at the window and saw, a few inches from her eyes, the death's-head moth, immobile and with its wings spread flat, on one of the solanum leaves.

The moth book had told her *Acherontia atropos* likes to feed on potato leaves. It also told her how rare a visitor to the British Isles this moth is. But she was in no doubt about it, this was no Privet Hawk. No other moth had that clear picture of a skull on its back between its forewings, a pale yellowish death's-head with black eyeholes and a domed forehead. This was the moth Drechsler had put into his painting, the one at Shrove on whose frame the key was kept.

She knew Mother would want to see it too. Mother might be quite cross, at the very least disappointed, if she didn't tell her about *Acherontia* outside the window. She went down and opened the door. Bruno was softly twanging his guitar and they each had a glass of red wine. They didn't look very busy, but Mother said she couldn't come now, Liza ought to be in bed, and if it really was a death's-head moth it would no doubt reappear the next day.

But the next morning it was gone, never to be seen again. Because she had found Mr. Tobias in Mother's bed after just such an evening, with wine and food and enjoyment, she expected to see Bruno there in the morning. She was older now, she approached the door more tentatively and pushed it open with care. Mother was alone and when Liza went to the window she saw that the little orange car was gone.

The day gone by, the first time Mother had been indifferent to the things she cared for, she called the Day of the Death's-head.

It was over a week before they saw Bruno again and that was the day Mother went into the town on the bus. She had a list with her, and most of the items on it were the kind of things you bought at a fruit and vegetable shop. Liza had seen pictures in a baby's book when she was little. A greengrocer's was the correct word, Mother said.

"Can I come?"

Mother shook her head.

"All right, but I don't want to be left here in my bedroom. It's boring."

"You can go in the library or the morning room at Shrove if you prefer that. It's up to you."

"The morning room."

Because it was much lighter and from the windows you could see the trains go by, Mother must have thought. Or because the famous people from history were there in their glass case. Perhaps, though, she was thinking about Bruno Drummond, and not about Liza at all.

After Mother had gone and she had seen a train going south and had studied once more the wedding photograph of Mr. Tobias in a sleek dark suit and Mrs. Tobias in a large hat and spotted dress, she drew aside the curtain to reveal the stepladder. It was just as she had left it.

She carried it across the room and set it up close beside the picture of the flowers and the death's-head moth. She took great care to press down the top step, which would lock the ladder and make it safe. It was possible, of course, that the key was no longer there. Mother had been in this room many times since Liza had seen her place it on top of the picture frame and it was a wonder she had never come upon the hidden steps. Climb up and find out.

The key was there. Liza jumped down, unlocked the door, and opened it. She stood in front of the box thing with the window on the front and studied it. There were knobs and switches underneath the window, rather like the knobs and switches on Mother's electric stove. Liza pressed or turned them one after another but nothing happened.

She understood about electricity. Their old heater wouldn't work unless it was plugged into the point and the switch pressed down. Here the plug was in but the point not switched on. She pressed the switch down. Still nothing. Try the routine of pressing or turning all those knobs and switches.

When she turned the largest knob nothing happened but

when she pushed it in a buzzing sound came out of the box and, to her extreme astonishment, a point of light appeared in the window. The light expanded, shivering, and gradually a picture began to form, gray and white and dark gray, the colors of the etchings on the morning room walls, but recognizably a picture.

And not a still picture, as an etching was, but moving and happening, like life. There were people, of about her own age, not speaking but dancing to music. Liza had heard the music before, she could even have said what it was, something called *Swan Lake* by Tchaikovsky.

Briefly, she was afraid. The people moved, they danced, they threw their legs high in the air, they were manifestly real, yet not real. She had taken a step backward, then another, but now she came closer. The children continued to dance. One girl came to the center of the stage and danced alone, spinning around with one leg held out high behind her. Liza looked around the back of the box. It was just a box, black with ridges and holes and more switches.

A lot of print, white on black and gray, came up on the window, then a face, then—most alarming of all—a voice. The first words Liza ever heard come out of a television set she could never remember. She was too overawed by the very idea of a person being in there and speaking. She was very nearly stunned.

But that feeling gradually passed. She was afraid, she was shocked, she was filled with wonder, then she was pleased, gratified, she began to *enjoy* it. She sat down cross-legged on the floor and gazed, enraptured. An old man and a dog were going for a walk in a countryside very like the one she knew. Sometimes the old man stopped and talked and his face got very large so that she could see all the furrows in his face and his white whiskers. Next there was a woman teaching another woman to cook something. They mixed things up in a bowl, eggs and sugar and flour and butter, and no more than two minutes later, when the first woman opened the oven door, she lifted out the baked cake, all dark and shiny and risen high. It was magic. It was the magic Liza had read about in fairy stories.

She watched for an hour. After the cooking came a dog driving sheep about on a hillside, then a man with a lot of glass bottles and tubes and a chart on the wall, not one word of which she could understand. She went into the morning room to look at the clock. Mother couldn't get back before five and it was ten past four now. Liza sat down on the floor again and watched a lot of drawings like book illustrations moving about, a cat and a mouse and a bear in the woods. She watched a man telling people the names of the stars in the sky and another one talking to a boy who had built a train engine. If it had been possible, she could have watched all night. But if Mother came back and caught her she would never be able to watch it again, for she had intuited that the door was kept locked because Mother didn't want her to watch it at all.

At five minutes to five, most reluctantly, she turned off the set by pulling toward her the knob she had pushed in and switched off the plug at the point. She locked the door and climbed up the steps to put the key back on the top of the picture frame. It was just as well she started when she did. Carrying the steps back to hide them behind the curtains, she saw through the first window Mother coming up the drive toward the house and Bruno Drummond with her.

They were early because he had brought Mother back in his car. Liza wasn't much interested in him that evening. Her head was full of what she had seen on, or through or by means of, the window on that box. She wondered what it was, how it did what it did, and if there was only one like it in the world, the one at Shrove, or if there were others. For instance, did Mr. and Mrs. Tobias have one in London? Did Caroline have one in France and Claire have one wherever it was she lived? Did Matt and Heidi, Mr. Frost and the builders? Did *everyone?*

There was nobody to ask. Why was it bad for her to see? Would it hurt her? Her eyes, her ears? They felt all right. It was strange to think of Mother knowing all about this magic and never saying, to think of Bruno Drummond knowing too, very probably having one of his own at home over the greengrocer's shop.

Why didn't they have one in the gatehouse? There was no one she could ask. She was so quiet that evening, hardly saying a word throughout the meal—which Bruno stayed for—that Mother asked her if she was feeling all right.

After she had gone to bed, she heard them go out of the front door. She got up and looked out of the window she used only to be able to reach by standing on a chair. She didn't need the chair now. They were going into the little castle. Mother unlocked the front door and they went inside. It reminded her of the dogs and when they used to live in there and she was suddenly sad. She would much rather have had Heidi and Rudi in there than Bruno Drummond. Without knowing why, she didn't like him much.

They didn't stay long in the little castle and soon she heard Bruno's car depart, but he was back next day with paints and canvas and brushes and a thing he called an easel. The easel he set up on the edge of the water meadow and began painting a picture of the bridge. Liza stood watching him while Mother did her cleaning at Shrove.

He disliked her being there, she could sense that, she could sense waves of coldness coming at her. Bruno looked sweet and gentle, he looked kind, but she guessed he wasn't really like that. People might not always be the way their faces proclaimed them to be.

Mother was watching her from the window, "keeping an eye on you," and she smiled and waved, so Liza didn't see why she shouldn't watch *him* as he mixed up his colors from those interesting tubes of paint and then laid thick white and blue all over the canvas. She came quite close till she was nearly touching his arm. The cold waves got very strong. Bruno stirred his brush round and round in swirls through the whitish-blue mixture and said, "Don't you have anything to play with?"

"I'm too old to play," said Liza.

"That's a matter of opinion. You can't be more than nine. Don't you have a doll?" His voice was like the voices that came out of the box in the locked room.

"If you don't want me looking at you I'll go and read my French book."

She went into Shrove House but, instead of reading her book, made her way upstairs to the Venetian Room, where there was a picture she thought might look like Bruno. Or he look like it. And she had been right. It was a pious saint in the painting, kneeling in some rocky desert place, his hands clasped in prayer, a gold halo around his head. Liza sat on the gondolier's bed and stared at the picture. Bruno was just like that saint, even to his long silky brown hair, his eyelashes, and his folded lips that had a holy look. The saint's rapt eyes were fixed on something invisible in the clouds above his head.

Bruno wore two gold earrings in one ear and the saint none. That was the only difference between them as far as appearance went. Liza took her book of fairy tales onto the terrace on the garden front and sat reading it in the sunshine.

He was much nicer to her when Mother was there. She soon noticed that. They all had lunch together and he said it was amazing, seeing her reading French fairy tales. "Like a native," he said. "You've got a bright one there, Mother. What do they say about her at school?"

Mother passed over that one and said nothing about Bruno calling her "Mother." They talked about the possibility of Bruno having his studio in the little castle and Mother explained what a studio was. Liza wasn't sure she liked the idea of Bruno being next door all day long.

"It belongs to Mr. Tobias," she said.

"I shall write to Mr. Tobias," Mother said, "and ask if Bruno can become his tenant."

But whether Mr. Tobias said yes or no, Liza never discovered, for it was into their house, the gatehouse, that Bruno moved. It happened no more than a fortnight later. He moved into the gatehouse and went to sleep in Mother's bedroom.

Unlike Heather, he never complained about the lack of a bathroom. Washing, he said, was bourgeois. Liza looked up the word in Dr. Johnson's dictionary, which was the only dictionary in the Shrove library, but there was nothing between "bounce" and "to bouse," which meant to drink too much. Guesswork told her that "bourgeois" was probably the opposite of "anarchist."

The little castle had a north light, which Bruno said was good for artists. Good or not, he never seemed to go in there very much, though he filled it up with his things, stacks and stacks of canvases and frames as well as brushes and jars and dirty paint rags. And he never went to town, painting people's houses.

It was at this time that Liza stopped going into Mother's

bedroom in the morning. Once she had gone in, having first knocked on the door, but even so had found Bruno on top of Mother, kissing her mouth, his long brown curly hair hiding her face. Liza felt heat run up into her face and burn her cheeks, she didn't know why. She retreated in silence.

Her life had changed. She was never again to be quite as happy as she had been in those early years. A cloud had come halfway across her sun and partially eclipsed it. Until Bruno came she had sometimes been alone and enjoyed aloneness, but now she knew what it was to be lonely.

Her consolation was the television set at Shrove. She found out what it was called from Bruno. Not that she told him what she watched up at the house whenever she got the chance. It was he who asked Mother why they hadn't got one.

"I can bring mine over from the flat," he said. "The flat" meant his rooms over the greengrocer's.

Mother said, no thank you very much, that was something they could happily do without. He could go home and watch his own, if that was what he wanted. You know what I want, he said, looking at Mother as the saint looked at the clouds.

More often alone and often lonely, Liza found it easy to go to Shrove more or less when she liked. She grew adept at climbing up for the key and hiding the steps. But—and she had no idea why—Mother had grown reluctant to lock her in anywhere since Bruno came. She had the run of the house now and carried the steps back and forth between the library and the morning room. Aged ten, she discovered to her astonishment and pleasure that she no longer needed the steps. She had grown. Like Mother, she could reach the key by mounting a chair and standing on the cabinet.

When Mother sat by Bruno while he painted, she watched

television. On the rare occasions that Bruno took Mother out in the car, she watched television. From the television she began to learn about the world out there.

It was Bruno who put into her head the idea that it was time she saw the reality for herself.

She sat in the back of the little orange car. Mother was in the passenger seat next to Bruno, and Liza could tell by the rigidity of her shoulders and the stiffness of her neck how deeply opposed to this outing she still was. She had allowed Bruno and Liza herself to win her over.

Bruno had said, "I'm being quite selfish about this, Mother. Maybe you'll think I'm being brutally honest but the fact is I want to take you out and about and to do that we have to take the kid with us." He always called her "the kid" just as he always called Mother "Mother" when Liza was being discussed. "Taking her into town'll be a start. Get her into that and next we can all have a day out." He whispered the next bit but Liza heard. "I'm not saying I wouldn't rather be on our own if there's any option."

"I can't keep going out, anyway," Mother said. "I haven't got time. For one thing, Liza has to have her lessons."

"That kid ought to go to school."

"I thought you were an anarchist," said Mother.

"Anarchists aren't against education. They're all in favor of the right sort of education."

"Liza is getting the right sort. If you set her beside other children of her age, she'd be so far ahead, she would be years in advance of them, it would be laughable."

"She ought to be in school for social reasons. How's she going to learn to interact with other people?"

"My mother interacted with other people and she died a miserable disappointed woman in a rented room in her sister's house. I interacted with other people and look what happened to me. I want Liza kept pure, I want her untouched, and most of all I want her *happy*. 'A violet by a mossy stone, half-hidden from the eye.' "

Bruno made a face. "I ask myself what's going to happen to that kid. How's she going to earn her living? Who's she going to have relationships with?"

"I earn my living," said Mother. "*I* have what you call 'relationships,' horrid word. She will be me, but without the pain and the damage. She will be me as I might have been, happy and innocent and good, if I had been allowed to stay here."

"All that aside," said Bruno, who liked arguments only when he was winning them, "I still think she ought to come into town with us, Mother, for her own good."

And eventually Mother had agreed. Just for this once. She could come for once.

Nothing happened for a while that Liza hadn't expected. There was the lane and then the bridge, the village, and at last the bigger road. Cars passed them and once they overtook a car, a very slow one because Bruno's orange cardboard car couldn't go fast. Most of the things Liza saw she had seen before or else seen them on television, if not in color. It was different in the town, mainly because there were so many people. The number of people staggered her so, she was afraid.

Bruno put the car in a car park where hundreds were already parked. Liza couldn't believe there were so many cars in the world. She walked along in silence between Mother and Bruno and, to her own surprise, scarcely aware of doing it, she took Mother's hand. The people clogged the pavement, they were everywhere: walking fast, dawdling, chatting to each other, standing still in conversation, running, dragging along small children or pushing them in chairs on wheels. You had to take care not to bump into them. Some smoked cigarettes, like on the television, and you smelled them as they passed. Quite a lot were eating things out of bags.

Liza stared. She would have liked to sit on the low wall outside that building Mother said was a church and just watch the people. Most of them in her eyes were ugly and awkward, fat or crooked, grotesque or semisavage. They compelled her gaze, but as a toad might or a frightening picture in a book, with horrified fascination.

"How beauteous mankind is!" said Mother in the special voice she put on when she was saying something from a book. "O, brave new world that has such people in it." The laugh she gave was a nasty one as if she hadn't meant those words seriously.

As for a brave new world, Liza thought most of the shops nasty and boring. There were clothes in one window, magazines in another. The flowers in the flower shop weren't as nice as those at Shrove. The places that interested her most were the shop with four boxes like the one in the locked room at Shrove in its window, four blank screens, and the one that was full of books, but new ones with bright pictures on their covers.

She wanted to go in that shop but Mother wouldn't let her, nor was she allowed inside the one that sold newspapers, though Bruno was sent in there to buy a tape of Mozart's horn concertos. They went to the greengrocer's and bought fruit, then through a side door and upstairs to where Bruno used to live. It smelled so nasty in there, like the kitchen at Shrove after the Tobiases and their guests had gone and as if things had been left to go bad, that Liza started to cough.

Mother opened the windows. They collected some stuff of Bruno's, which he packed into a case, and then he picked up off the doormat the heap of letters that had come for him while he was away. For a man whose whereabouts no one knew he got a lot of letters.

Looking about her, Liza began to understand what Mother had meant when she said those things about most places being horrible. She wrinkled up her nose. Bruno's flat was very horrible, dirty and uncomfortable, with nothing in it that looked as if it had been cared for, every piece of furniture bruised or broken, the windows blue-filmed and with dead flies squashed against the panes. The only books were on the floor, in disorderly heaps.

She was glad to get out again, and said so, even though being out meant once more avoiding bumping into people. There seemed more of them than ever and a good many were of her own age or a bit older. They had come out of school, said Bruno with a meaningful look at Mother, school stopped each day at three-thirty.

Liza had never seen children before. Well, except on the television, that is. She had never seen a real person who was less than in his or her twenties. She took back what she had thought about all mankind being ugly. These people weren't. There was a boy with a black face and a girl she thought might be Indian with deep-set dark eyes and a long black pigtail. She wondered how it would be to talk to them.

Then a boy walking along in front of her stuck out his leg and tripped up the boy beside him so that the second one staggered and nearly fell into the road in front of an oncoming car and a girl screamed and another one started shouting. Liza felt herself shrink back against Mother and hold on to her hand more tightly. She had realized what was making her feel dizzy: the noise.

Once she had turned up the sound on the television by mistake. It was like that here, a continuous meaningless roar of sound, interspersed with the squeals of brakes, music that wasn't real music strumming out of car windows, the peep-peep-peep of the pedestrian signal at a traffic light crossing, the revving up of engines. As they made their way back to the car park, a siren started up. Bruno told her it was the siren on a police car and he said the sound it made was supposed to imitate a woman screaming.

"Oh, it can't be, Bruno," Mother said. "Where on earth did you get that from?"

"It's a fact. You ask anyone. They invented it in the States and we copied it. That's supposed to be the sound that most gets under people's skins, a woman screaming."

"Well, don't talk about it to me, please," Mother said, so loudly and sharply, that one of the ugly people turned to stare at her. "I don't want to hear. It just expresses the worst side of men."

"All right, all right," said Bruno. "Sorry I spoke. Please excuse me for living. Will madam condescend to accept a lift home, her and her charming, courteous offspring?"

As soon as she was in the car Liza fell asleep. She was exhausted. The people and the noise and the newness of it all had worn her out. At home she lay on the sofa and slept, though not so deeply that she failed to hear Mother tell Bruno she had told him so, Liza hadn't liked it, it had been too much for her and no wonder. Wasn't it a horrible place, a travesty of what a country town should be and once had been, noisy, dirty, and tawdry?

"She wouldn't feel that way if you hadn't sheltered her from everything the way you have."

"I feel it and God knows I haven't been sheltered."

"You know what you'll do, don't you, Mother? You'll turn the kid psychotic. Or maybe schizophrenic, one of those what-d'you-call-its."

"Talk about what you understand, Bruno, why don't you?"

With half an eye open, she thought they would start quarreling again. They were always quarreling. But instead they did what often impeded or ended their quarrels. Their eyes met, they reached for each other and began kissing, the kind of kissing that soon got out of hand, so that they were grappling and climbing all over each other, grunting and moaning. Liza turned over and squeezed her eyes tightly shut.

In the days that followed she felt unwell, what Bruno called "under the weather," something unusual for her. She remembered the town and its people not with longing or nostalgia, but with revulsion. The peace of Shrove and its lands was more than usually pleasurable. She lay in the long grass and the cow parsley, watching the insect life moving among the mysterious green stems and the nodding seed heads, saw a raspberry-winged cinnabar moth climbing a ragwort stalk. There was no sound but the occasional heavy hum of a bumble bee passing overhead.

A week after their day out in the town she became ill with chicken pox.

e l e v e n

HADN'T you had any of those things, measles and whatever?"

"I'd had some immunizations when I was a baby. I got chicken pox because I hadn't built up any natural immunity. I'd never been with people."

"Did the doctor come?"

"Eve phoned him from Shrove. He said he'd come if I got worse but otherwise there was nothing to be done but let it take its course. I wasn't very bad. Eve was strict about scratching. She said if I scratched my face she'd tie my hands up, so I didn't except for one awful big spot on my forehead."

Liza pulled back a lock of dark hair and showed him the small round hole on her left temple. "She was afraid of me getting those all over."

"I know you didn't," said Sean, giving her a sidelong sexy look.

"No, nothing like that. All that happened was that I gave Bruno shingles."

"You what?"

"The virus or whatever you call it, it makes chicken pox in children and shingles in grown-ups. It's the same thing. Eve didn't catch anything, but Bruno caught shingles."

"My grandma had that. She had it around her middle and she was dead scared because if it meets around your waist you die. That's a fact."

Liza doubted it but she didn't say so. "He got it on the side of his face and down the back of his neck. He was quite ill and he looked quite ugly with all that red on his face. I thought he disliked me because I gave him shingles, that was the way I reasoned when I was ten. But if he hadn't made me go into town with them I wouldn't have caught chicken pox and couldn't have given him shingles, so it was his fault, really. That was how I saw it. Of course now I know it wasn't that at all. I was in the way, I was a nuisance, I came between him and Eve."

Now she was more or less grown-up herself and sexually involved, Liza could understand what had held Eve and Bruno together. She hadn't understood at the time. It puzzled her and made her increasingly uneasy that two people could quarrel so much, could behave as if they hated each other, but still seem to need each other's company in a hungry way.

She was aware too of something else. There was something Bruno wanted to do with her mother that he couldn't do unless Liza wasn't there. It was to do with the kissing and struggling and lying on top of Mother. Liza knew and had known for some time the facts of human and animal reproduction, Eve had taken care to educate her in these matters, but for some reason she never connected them with what Bruno wanted to do with Mother. And what, though less urgently, Mother wanted to do with Bruno. She didn't understand and she shied away from understanding. All she knew was that Bruno wanted her out of the house as much as she could feasibly be out of it and that Mother to some lesser extent went along with this.

Without saying a word as to her destination, she went up to Shrove and watched the television in the once-locked room. It was always in late mornings and early afternoons that she watched it. Old films were what she saw and nature programs, productions for schools and the Open University, chat shows and quiz games. Some of the programs came from America. They taught her that Bruno was an Englishman who for some reason put on a half-American voice.

When he was well again things got worse. It was late summer and fine weather and he took Mother out in the car every day. Liza could have gone with them, Mother was always suggesting it now as enthusiastically as she had once vetoed it, but Liza wouldn't. She remembered the day in town with a kind of horror, as if the experience had been inextricably entangled with police sirens and scratching and chicken pox. So Mother and Bruno went and she stayed behind alone, often doing no more than sitting outside on the gatehouse wall or lying in the grass wondering what would happen to her if Bruno prevailed and she was sent away.

More than once he had mentioned sending her to something called boarding school. Mother said she had a lot of money when she bought his picture but now, she said, she had none and boarding schools cost a lot. Liza clung to this. Mother had no money and Bruno had no money and no prospect of getting any. Bruno himself would never go, she was sure of that with the pessimism of a ten-year-old who believes that good things never last and bad things go on forever. He was a bad thing that would never change, he was the hated third in their household, with as permanent a place in their lives as the balsam tree and the train.

Two things happened that autumn. Bruno's mother fell ill, very ill, and Mother heard on her radio that British Rail intended to stop running the train through the valley.

~

The first time Mrs. Spurdell went out, Liza took the opportunity to have a bath. It was ten o'clock in the morning. The bath was a muddy beige color and the bathroom carpet grass-green and beige in little squares, but the water was hot. The soap smelled of sweet peas. When she had finished she cleaned the bathroom thoroughly, washing down and polishing all the tilework.

Mrs. Spurdell had been rather reluctant to leave the house. Liza hadn't much experience of human behavior, but even she could tell Mrs. Spurdell thought she would come back and find her cleaner gone and the video, microwave, and silver with her. She nearly laughed out loud at Mrs. Spurdell's face when her employer came in the back door to find her sitting at the kitchen table polishing that same silver. That was the first occasion on which Liza got a cup of coffee in the house in Aspen Close.

While they were together Mrs. Spurdell talked most of the time. Her conversation was primarily concerned with demonstrating her superiority and that of her husband and grown-up daughters to almost everyone else, but particularly to her employee. This was an ascendancy in the areas of social distinction, intellect, wordly success, and money, but principally of material possessions. Mrs. Spurdell's possessions were more expensive and of better quality than those of other people, more had been paid for them initially, and they lasted longer. This applied to her engagement ring, a massive stack of diamonds, the allegedly Georgian silver, the Wilton carpets, the Colefax and Fowler curtains, and the Parker-Knoll armchairs, among many other things. Liza had to be taught these names, shown these objects, and instructed in how to examine them for evidence of their worth. She was adjured to be very careful of all of them, with the exception of the engagement ring, which never left Mrs. Spurdell's finger. The finger was so grossly swollen above and below the ring that Liza doubted if it would come off.

The husband and the children couldn't be demonstrated, but they could be talked about and photographs produced. After that first cup of coffee, reward for not decamping with the precious artifacts, a mid-morning refreshment session became the regular thing. Liza was told about Jane, who was an educationalist after having got several degrees, and about Philippa, a solicitor married to a solicitor, and erstwhile top law student of her year, now mother of twins so beautiful that she was constantly approached by companies making television commercials for the chance of using their faces in advertising, offers which she indignantly refused. Liza listened, memorizing the unfamiliar expressions.

Mr. Spurdell, said his wife, was a schoolmaster. Liza thought they were called teachers, that was what Bruno had called them and Sean called them, but Mrs. Spurdell said her husband was a schoolmaster and a head of department, whatever that was.

"At an independent school," she explained, "not one of these comprehensives, I wouldn't want you to think that."

Liza, who was incapable of thinking anything about schools, merely smiled. She never said much. She was learning.

"He could have been a headmaster many times over but he

isn't one for the limelight. Of course there is family money, otherwise he might have been forced to take a higher position."

A fresh set of photographs came out, Jane in gown and mortarboard, Philippa with the twins. The impression was subtly conveyed that their mother was prouder—and fonder—of Philippa because she had a husband and children. Liza preferred Jane, who hadn't any lipstick on and wasn't simpering. She was longing for Mrs. Spurdell to get up and say she was going out so that she could have another bath. It wasn't easy managing in the caravan, and the swimming pool was expensive besides leaving you smelling of chlorine.

At last Mrs. Spurdell put the photographs away and prepared to go out. The weather was colder today and it was a different coat she had put on, of a thick hairy stone-colored cloth with lapels and cuffs of glossy brown fur. Liza was told that this coat had been bought twenty years ago—"in the days when no one had these ridiculous ideas about not wearing fur"—and had cost the then-enormous sum of sixty pounds. She had to feel the quality of the cloth and stroke the fur. It simply refused to wear out, said Mrs. Spurdell with a little laugh, tying her white hair up in a scarf with "Hermès" written all over it. Liza wondered what a silk scarf had to do with the Messenger of the Gods.

She went without her bath. On her way to run it she paused at the doorway of Mr. Spurdell's study. This was a room she wasn't supposed to touch beyond vacuum cleaning the floor, for his books were sacred, never to be dusted, and the papers on his desk inviolate. But Liza was alone in the house now and Mrs. Spurdell would no more know she had been in there than she knew the purpose for which her hot water was often used.

Once or twice she had taken fleeting looks at the bookshelves while pushing the vacuum cleaner about, but she had never examined them thoroughly. Now she did. They were of a very different kind from those in the library at Shrove. Here were no eighteenth-century works on travel and exploration, no theology, philosophy, or history, no essays from the eighteen-hundreds, no poetry of a century before that, no tomes of Darwin and Lyell, and no Victorian literature. Mr. Spurdell's fiction came in the form of paperbacks.

These shelves carried the kind of books Liza had never seen before. Accounts of people's lives, they seemed to be, and she recognized the names of some of their subjects: Oscar Wilde, Tolstoy, Elizabeth Barrett Browning. But who was Virginia Woolf and who was Orwell? Apart from these, there were books about how writers wrote what they wrote, or as far as she could gather they were about that, one called *The Common Pursuit* and another *The Unquiet Grave.* Liza sat down at Mr. Spurdell's desk and leafed through his books, wondering how it was that she understood so little of what she read yet passionately wanted to understand.

Time passed quickly when she was occupied like this. It always went very fast while Mrs. Spurdell was out, but this time it seemed to fly by. Reluctantly, she had to stop reading because she needed at least ten minutes to look at the papers on the desk and there was no chance of Mrs. Spurdell being out for more than an hour and a half. It was lucky she could do the housework in half the time allowed for it.

The papers were essays. She could tell that much. They had names written along the tops of the first pages, of their authors presumably. It took the minimum of detective work to infer that these were pupils of Mr. Spurdell's. He had gone through the pages with a red pen, correcting the spelling and making acid comments. Some of these made Liza laugh. What interested her most, though, were the pieces of yellow paper he had stuck to the first page of each. These were small paper squares of a kind she had never seen before and which had a sticky area on them that you could nevertheless peel off. She tried this carefully and then to her satisfaction re-stuck it.

Each yellow square had something different written on it in Mr. Spurdell's writing. One said, "Should get at least an A and a B," another, "Doubtful university material," and a third, "Oxbridge?" Liza had heard of Oxford and of Cambridge but not of that place. She had to stop at this point, it would be awful to jeopardize her future chances by letting Mrs. Spurdell catch her snooping. The papers replaced exactly as she had found them, she grabbed the vacuum cleaner and was removing white hairs from the master bedroom carpet when the front door opened and closed.

In a little while Mrs. Spurdell came lumbering up the stairs and into the bedroom to hang up the precious coat. Liza moved along, back into the study, only to clean the carpet of course, but while she was there she wondered if she dared borrow a book. Would he know if one was missing? If one was missing for just two days? She would very much like to read the life of Elizabeth Barrett Browning. When she first met Sean she had read the "Sonnets from the Portuguese" and memorized several of them. ("How do I love thee? Let me count the ways.") Putting herself into Mr. Spurdell's shoes—a pair of them, slippers really, sat side by side under the desk—she decided that, yes, she would know if a book of hers was missing. If she had any books, if only she had.

Mrs. Spurdell paid her for her morning's work. She always did this grudgingly and very slowly, choosing from the wad in her handbag the oldest and most crumpled five-pound notes, never handing over a ten. The rest of the sum she made up in small change, twenty- and ten-pence coins and even twos. This time she was worse than ever, giving Liza a whole seven pounds in fifty pees and tens and fives and keeping her waiting while she went off somewhere to hunt for a fiver. Eventually she came back with it, a worn and withered note that had been torn in half and stuck together with tape.

The secondhand bookshop took it. Liza had been worried they wouldn't when she handed it over in payment for three shabby paperbacks she had found among a row of others on a trestle outside. The real bookshop, the proper one in which everything sold was new, was far beyond her means.

It was nearly five-thirty and Superway would be closing. She walked along the High Street and across the marketplace. Soon it would get dark, they would soon put the clocks back, and the chill of evening was already apparent. Was it cold in prison? She thought about Eve in the prison, she often did, she thought about her every day, but she never said any of this to Sean.

He was waiting for her outside the main entrance with a carrier bag full of food. Superway encouraged employees to buy the products that had reached their sell-by date and at a very reduced price. Liza and Sean walked together to the car. He told her what he'd got for their supper and then he wanted to know what was in her bag. She showed him *Middlemarch,* a *Life of Mary Wollstonecraft,* and Aubrey's *Brief Lives,* and saw at once the displeasure in his face.

"We can't afford to spend money on books."

"It's my money," she said. "I earned it."

"I wonder what you'd say, Liza, if I said that when you wanted me to get your food."

She was silent. He had spoken reproachfully and like a middle-aged person. Mr. Spurdell would talk like that, she thought.

"You've got telly," he said. "I don't know why you need books as well."

She got his supper and while he watched his favorite serial, she started reading *Middlemarch.* A good many Victorian girls must have lived very much as she had, being educated at home, knowing no one but the nearest neighbors, sheltered from everything. With Dorothea Brooke she could identify, though society wouldn't have allowed Dorothea a Sean.

Now that his program was over, she was aware that he kept glancing uneasily at her. He would have to get used to it, she thought. He would have to get used to her being more and more preoccupied with books. It came back to her, as her concentration weakened under his gaze, that Bruno had never much liked her mother reading. He had done all kinds of things to capture her attention, walking about, pacing the room, even whistling. Sometimes he had sat down beside her and taken her hand or stroked the side of her face. Liza remembered her mother jumping up on one of these occasions, shaking him off, and shouting at him to leave her alone.

It was soon after this that Bruno had gone away to be with his sick mother. He had gone on the day the last train ran through the valley.

Liza hadn't known it would be the last train. How could she? She never saw a newspaper and she could never watch television at the times the news was on. It was a fine warm day in October, just over six years ago and a year before the hurricane. The blackberries were over and the crabapples were ripe. Liza went down through the meadows and along the hedges looking for crabapples to make into jelly. You boiled the apples, then strained them through a cloth tied to the four legs of an upturned stool before adding the sugar. She had seen Mother do it many times and thought it was time she tried.

Before she had picked a single apple, before she had even found a tree, she saw the people lined up along the railway line. She thought she was dreaming, she closed her eyes and opened them again. Never in her life had she seen so many people all at once except on television and that didn't count. There must have been hundreds. They stood along the railway embankment, on both sides of the line, between the boundary of the Shrove land and the little station that was called Ring Valley Halt, and each one of them was holding a big placard.

From where she was Liza couldn't read what was on the placards. She forgot about crabapples and jelly, stuffed the big plastic bag she was carrying into her pocket, and ran down the field path toward the river.

Some of the placards said, SAVE OUR RAILWAY, and others, FOR BR READ USSR and LAST TRAIN TO CHAOS. On the far side a group of people were holding a long banner with WILL BR CARE WHEN WE MISS THE TRAIN? on it. Liza sensed something was going to happen, though she couldn't tell what. Besides, the sight of so many people fascinated her, there were more than on that day in town, there were more than in the film she'd seen about Ancient Rome.

Reserved by conditioning if not by nature, she considered concealing herself in the bushes to watch. She didn't want to talk to anyone, talking to strangers was something she was beginning to find hard, she met so few. It had been a dry autumn and the river was low, at this point just a broad sheet of shallow water trickling and splashing over boulders. While on this side she couldn't talk to anyone, but even as she thought that, she had her shoes and socks off and was wading across.

It was too late to hide. They all seemed to be looking at her. Before she could pretend to be merely taking a walk, a woman had grabbed her by the arm and, evidently mistaking her for some other child, asked where on earth she had been and to take hold of this banner at once.

It was a replica of the one on the other side and it took four people to hold it up. Liza did as she was told and held on to the bit above the letters BR. A man was to the left of her and a boy to the right. Both of them said hi and the boy said, did she live around here? Up in one of the cottages, Liza said, you couldn't quite see from here, but only half a mile away.

"On your own doorstep, then," the man said. "Your family use the train a lot, do they? Or should I say, did they?"

"Every day," Liza said.

It wasn't the first lie she had ever told. She'd been telling lies regularly to Mother about where she'd been when she'd really been watching television.

"They take it for granted everyone's got a car," the man said. "Has your dad got a car?"

The woman on the other side of him said, "Sexist. Why not ask if her mum's got one? Women are allowed to drive here, you know. We're not talking about Saudi Arabia."

Liza was just saying they hadn't got a car—she didn't count Bruno's—and thinking of saying she hadn't got a dad, when the train whistle sounded on the far side of the tunnel. It always whistled going into the tunnel and coming out of it, it was a single-line track and maybe there was a remote possibility of another train meeting it in the dark and going headlong into it. There wouldn't be any more such possibilities, however.

"The last train ever," the man said. "The last poor bloody train."

When it came out of the tunnel and whistled again some of the people cheered. Liza could hardly believe her eyes when the four people holding the banner on the other side and three others with placards all began climbing down the embankment toward the line. The seven, four men and three women, took up their positions right across the line, in the path of the oncoming train, holding their banner and their placards aloft. The train could now be seen in the distance, heading this way.

What if it didn't stop? What if it came right on, ploughing the people down, as Liza had seen in a television film about the Wild West? She held on tight to the banner, clenching her fists around the cloth, making white knuckles.

"Look at them," shouted the woman who had seized her arm. "The Magnificent Seven!"

As the train came on the crowd began to sing. They sang, "We Shall Overcome." Liza had never heard it before but the tune was easy, she soon caught on and began singing it too. "We shall overcome one da-a-a-ay. Deep in my heart, I do believe that we shall overcome one day!"

The engine driver saw them in plenty of time. You could hear him applying the brakes, a long, low howl like a dog baying. The train came slowly on and ground to a halt a good hundred yards from where the Magnificent Seven held their banner and placards aloft. The crowd started singing "Jerusalem." The engine driver and another man in the same kind of uniform got down from the train and came marching up the track to argue with the protestors. All the train doors and windows opened and passengers stuck their heads out. Then they too began getting out and pouring along the line.

It was more than ever like a Western film when the Indians came or the mob of robbers from Dodge City. Liza and her fellow banner-carriers moved closer to the line to get involved in the arguments. There was a lot of shouting and threatening and one man had to be restrained from punching the engine driver. It wasn't his fault, anyway. Liza thought it most unfair. But she enjoyed every minute of it, she hadn't enjoyed anything so much since before Bruno came. In fact, thinking about it afterward, she understood she hadn't enjoyed anything since the coming of Bruno.

She stayed with the protestors right over lunch and well into the afternoon. They gave her sandwiches and biscuits from their lunches, all of them believing her parents were down by the station and she had somehow got detached from them. The train people went on arguing. The Magnificent Seven stood firm. After a while some British Rail officials arrived, there was talk of the police, the protestors on the embankments sat on the grass, and a couple of people fell asleep. Liza listened to a discussion about nuclear power, destruction of the environment, and the betrayal of democracy. She noted all the words, stored them in her memory without understanding anything that was said, until at last, growing bored, she wandered away.

She was still barefoot, her shoes tied to her belt with the socks stuffed inside them. From the position of the sun and the feel of the air she calculated it must be at least three-thirty. She sat down on the grass to put her socks on. As she was tying her shoelaces, she heard the train start and turned around to watch it.

The protestors must have been persuaded, cajoled, or threatened into leaving the line. Gradually the train gathered speed, passed between the rows of the defeated demonstrators, and came to the station. Liza saw it leave again and finally disappear into the curve that the hills swallowed, the last train forever.

She went home by way of the Shrove garden, across the smooth lawn cut by Mr. Frost that morning. Mother was sitting on the wall in front of the cottage, eating an apple. The orange car wasn't there.

"Where have you been? I was worried when you didn't come home for lunch."

Lies were easier and safer. "I took my lunch with me. I made sandwiches."

Mother wouldn't have known. She'd been in bed with Bruno. Where was he, anyway?

Before she could ask, Mother said, "Bruno's gone up to Cheshire to be with his mother. His mother's very ill."

Nothing could have been better, more calculated to make her happy, nothing except to hear he wasn't coming back.

"He may be gone a long time," said Mother.

She took Liza into the house and when they were inside and the door was closed she put her arms around her and said, "I'm sorry, Liza. I've been neglecting you, I haven't been a good mother to you lately. I can't explain, but you'll understand one day. I promise things will be like they used to be now we're alone again. Will you forgive me?"

Mother had never apologized to her before. She hadn't had to until Bruno came. Liza would have forgiven her anything now Bruno was gone.

It had been the Day of the Last Train.

Sean said gruffly, "Did he ever do anything to you, this Bruno guy?"

"Hit me, d'you mean?"

Sean said, no, not that, and explained what he did mean.

"I never heard of that," Liza said. "Do men really do that?"

"Some do."

"Well, he didn't. I told you, he hated me. He wanted to be alone with Eve and I got in his way. It wasn't always like that, he quite liked me at first, he painted that portrait of me, the one I told you about. He was always painting pictures of Eve and then he said he'd do one of me. I sat on a chair inside the little castle and he painted me. He was very kind then. I had to sit still for a long time and he bought cranberry juice for me, I'd never had that before, and biscuits with icing on that Eve wouldn't let me have. He used to buy lots of things for me when they went shopping. When I look back, I think he was just trying to ingratiate himself with Eve."

"Do what?"

"Ingratiate himself. Make her like him more. But then he must have realized he didn't have to do that, she liked him enough. And he changed. When he was ill and he realized he couldn't persuade Eve even to send me to a day school, that was when he changed. I can't tell you how relieved I was when I knew he'd gone, I was so happy."

Sean turned off the television. It was a concession, Liza realized that and closed her book. He put his arm around her.

"Who was that woman you were talking about, the one who told her husband stories?"

He'd remembered, Liza thought, pleased. "Scheherazade. She was an Eastern woman, an Arab, I suppose. Her husband was a king who used to marry women and have them executed the morning after their wedding nights. He'd have their heads chopped off."

"Why did he?"

"I don't know, I don't remember. Scheherazade was determined not to have hers chopped off. On their wedding night she started telling him a story, a very long one that she couldn't finish, but he longed to know the end so much that he said he'd keep her alive until the morning after the next night so that he could hear the end. But it didn't end or she started another, and so it went on until he got sort of addicted to her stories and couldn't have her killed, and in the end he fell in love with her and they lived happily ever after."

"What about all the other poor women he'd killed?"

"Too bad for them," said Liza. "I don't suppose that bothered her. Why did you ask about Scheherazade?"

"I don't know. I wanted you to tell me a bit more about what happened. You've stopped telling me."

"Lucky to be alive, then, am I?" She laughed but he didn't. "What happened next, after Bruno'd gone that is, is that Mr. and Mrs. Tobias came down. It was the first time for about a year. Mr. Tobias said he wanted to meet Bruno, and Eve had to tell him where Bruno had gone. Seeing his paintings was the next best thing, Mr. Tobias said, so Eve took him and Mrs. Tobias into the little castle and the first thing they saw was the portrait of me.

"Of course they saw other pictures, too, and Mrs. Tobias, Victoria, said she'd like to buy one. She wanted one he'd done of Shrove by moonlight. 'Oh, I adore it,' she said and she clapped her hands, and when Eve said four hundred pounds she didn't even flinch. Mr. Tobias—Jonathan, why do I keep on calling him that, like a child?—he wrote a check for it there and then and gave it to Eve."

"Didn't she wait to ask Bruno?"

"I suppose she knew he wanted to sell them. Anyway, she didn't wait. She was very pleased about getting money for him. Next day Jonathan started shooting and Victoria did too. There was a pair of partridges used to strut about, I'd got fond of them, red legs they were and a beautiful pattern on their backs. She shot them both. I wish I'd had a gun, I'd have shot *her*. When they'd shot all the birds they wanted they went back to London and as soon as they'd gone Eve sat down with me and told me the whole story of old Mr. Tobias and Caroline and *her* mother and why she never got Shrove for herself."

t w e l v e

EVE'S parents had gone to work for old Mr. Tobias and his wife when Eve was five and Jonathan was nine. Jonathan didn't live at Shrove at that time, but he came down for the holidays with his mother and father, Caroline, who was Lady Ellison, and her husband, Sir Nicholas Ellison. Then Sir Nicholas left Caroline and Caroline went back home to her parents.

Eve's father was a German called Rainer Beck, he'd been a prisoner of war in this country and after the war was over he didn't go back to Germany but stayed on and married Gracie, the daughter of the farmer he worked for. They were married for ages without having any children and Gracie had given up hope.

She couldn't believe it when, after ten years, she became pregnant. The baby was a girl and they called her Eva, after Rainer's mother in Hildesheim.

Agricultural laborers were nearly the worst paid of all workers and, in any case, as farms became mechanized and hundreds of acres could be run with only a couple of men, they weren't much needed. Gracie saw the housekeeper and handyman's jobs advertised in *The Lady* magazine while she was at the dentist's, so they applied for it and got it. One of the inducements was that a house went with the job.

Old Mr. and Mrs. Tobias interviewed Gracie and offered her the job at once. Rainer was too hard for them to pronounce, so they called him Ray.

The Tobiases liked making people change their names. Jonathan had been christened Jonathan Tobias Ellison but at his grandfather's suggestion he dropped the Ellison and became Jonathan Tobias. He went away to his public school but he was at Shrove during the holidays, and he and Eve grew up together. That was the way she put it, grew up together. They were inseparable, they were best friends.

Old Mrs. Tobias was ill. She died when Gracie and Rainer had been there a year, and soon after that Caroline went off with a man she'd met on holiday in Barbados. Jonathan remained at Shrove. Sometimes he went to stay with his father, but mostly he was at Shrove telling Eve he was going to marry her when he grew up. He and she would marry and live together at Shrove forever until death parted them.

Ray wasn't a gardener or a butler but a handyman. Mr. Frost, who was quite young then, came up from the village on his bicycle—the same bicycle, Eve said—to do the garden. There wasn't enough work for Ray to do full-time. By a great stroke of luck he got a job in the village working for a builder as a bricklayer, the job he'd been trained for all those years ago in Germany. Ray put in a few hours every week at Shrove, cleaning the windows and the cars. It was Gracie who was the important one. But for Gracie the place would have fallen apart. With Mr. Frost's daughter to help her three times a week, she kept Shrove clean and did all the cooking. She did the washing and ironing, ordered the groceries, made jam and pickles, acted as secretary to Mr. Tobias and, increasingly, as his nurse. She was indispensable.

Eve went first to the village school, then to the school in town where you had to pay fees. Mr. Tobias paid her fees. She was very bright, brighter than Jonathan, Mr. Tobias said, and he adored Jonathan. Gracie thought he was going soft in the head, maybe it was the onset of Alzheimer's, when he said Eve would very likely get to Oxford. Gracie's sister had had nine months at a secretarial college and she looked on that as the summit of academic ambition.

Mr. Tobias didn't have Alzheimer's but a very slow growing cancer. He was eighty and malignant growths proceed slowly in people of that age. He could get up and walk about, go out in the car with Ray to drive him, and lead quite a normal life. But sometimes he had to go into hospital for radiotherapy and then, when he came home, he was very ill for a while. There was plenty of money and he could easily have afforded private nursing, but he didn't want anyone near him but Gracie.

The doctors at the hospital—they were called oncologists, Eve explained—called him their longest surviving cancer patient. The primary cancer had been detected nine years before and still he lived on. It wasn't Mr. Tobias who died but Rainer Beck. The planning authority had given permission for some "in-filling" in the village and Ray's employer was putting up a house on the site between the row of cottages and the village hall.

While Ray was laying bricks for the front wall he keeled over and died of a heart attack with his trowel still in his hand.

"He was clutching on to it and the cement got hard," said Liza. "The cement stuck it onto his dead hand and they had to prise it open. They had to break his fingers. It was either that or burying him with that trowel in his hand."

Sean turned his mouth down. "Yuck. Do you mind?"

"I'm only telling you how it was."

"You don't have to go into details."

When Ray was dead Gracie began worrying about her future. One week she had a husband's income to depend on and the next week she hadn't. She never would have again. She had no home of her own, a sixteen-year-old daughter dependent on her, and an employer who might die and leave her jobless at any moment. Caroline occasionally reappeared at Shrove, beautifully dressed, arriving in a big new car, still not divorced, still married to Sir Nicholas and supported by him, but often with a man friend in tow. She had never liked Gracie, disapproved of the friendship between her son and "the housekeeper's girl," and made it plain Gracie wouldn't last there a week after her husband was dead.

Gracie laid her troubles before Mr. Tobias. She was young enough to get a job if she left now. Her sister was a travel agent with a small business in Coventry, from which her partner had just pulled out. If Gracie would join her, learn the business, and take the partner's place, she'd help her with a mortgage on a flat. But it would have to be now, not next year or in five years' time when Gracie would be well over fifty.

It happened that she said all this just at the time the doctors had discovered another lump on Mr. Tobias's spine. Once it was removed, he'd have more radiotherapy and be convalescent for weeks. He begged Gracie not to leave him. Caroline had gone off again. Not that she ever did a hand's turn in the house and moreover she was too squeamish, she said, to be a nurse. Jonathan was up at Oxford. If Gracie left he would have to resort to private nurses and that would kill him.

Gracie told her sister she would need awhile longer to make up her mind. Meanwhile Mr. Tobias went into hospital and the growth on his back was surgically removed. He became extremely ill.

"I expect she hoped he'd die," said Liza.

"Come on, Liza, the poor old fellow. He was all on his own with no one giving a bugger what happened to him. It's only natural he didn't want her to go."

"She had to think of her future. Rich people like him just use people like my grandmother, Eve said. It wasn't as if he couldn't afford to pay nurses."

"Money never brings happiness," said Sean with a sigh.

"How do you know? Have you ever known any rich people? I have. Jonathan was ever so rich all the time I knew him and he was happy for years and years."

Mr. Tobias came home and Gracie nursed him. She moved herself and Eve out of the gatehouse and up to Shrove. For a whole two weeks before he could get up she had to give him bed pans and dress the wound on his back, which started suppurating. The doctor came every day and said she was wonderful. Meanwhile Eve sat for her O-Levels and passed in eleven subjects. Mr. Tobias called her into his bedroom to congratulate her and gave her fifty pounds "to buy some dresses."

What about me, said Gracie when he was up and about again, what's going to become of me? My sister's starting to get impatient. Mr. Tobias had been thinking about it and he told her the decision he'd come to.

If she would guarantee to stay with him until he died, having sole care of him and nursing him—she could have any help in the house she wanted—if she'd do all that, he would leave her Shrove House in his will. He knew she loved it, he knew how she appreciated this beautiful place.

It's my daughter that loves it, said Gracie, so shocked by what he'd said that she couldn't think of any other answer to make. It's Eve who couldn't bear the thought of leaving. This had held her back from agreeing to her sister's proposition nearly as much as Mr. Tobias's dependency on her. Eve worked so hard and did so well at school, was such a happy girl, because she loved Shrove and its surroundings and the whole lovely valley. And being with Jonathan whenever he was at home, thought Gracie, though not saying this aloud. She hadn't dared tell Eve there was a chance they might leave and go up to Coventry.

So what do you think of my idea? Mr. Tobias had perhaps expected more enthusiasm. It came. Gracie was stunned, Gracie couldn't believe what he'd said. Did he really mean it? What about Caroline? Wasn't it Caroline's by right?

Caroline hates the place, said Mr. Tobias, confirming what Gracie had long known. She couldn't wait to get away. Besides, she may not have lived with Nicholas for the past ten years but he's still mad about her and he'll leave her everything he's got, you'll see. He's not a well man, poor Nicholas, he'll not last as long as I will, and when he goes Caroline will be a rich woman, even allowing for the bulk of his fortune going to Jonathan.

It took Gracie five minutes to say yes. Yes, she'd stay. Then you can phone my solicitor and ask him to pop in sometime next week, said Mr. Tobias.

The new will was made and Mr. Frost and Mr. Tobias's doctor witnessed it. In the presence of the testator and of each other, Eve explained. That was the law.

Mr. Tobias made a quick recovery after that. Making sure

that Gracie would stay spurred him on to get better. He was up and actually walking about the garden by the time Jonathan came home for the long vacation. Gracie's sister took a friend of hers into the travel agent's business, a woman who had been secretary to the managing director of a domestic airline.

Having no secrets from her daughter, Gracie told Eve about the will. It made Eve feel as if Shrove was already hers. She had always felt about Mr. Tobias as if he were her grandfather and now she saw herself inheriting the place as his natural heir. It was true what her mother said that she loved it. All she wanted, at age seventeen, was to live there forever. With Jonathan, of course. Jonathan could come and live there with her.

Eve got three A-Levels to A and went to Oxford. Jonathan was still there, though he had his degree, and they saw a lot of each other.

"What does that mean?" said Sean. "D'you mean they was lovers?"

"I suppose. Yes, I'm sure they were. Eve didn't actually say. Well, she wouldn't then. Not to me. I was only ten."

"Old enough to see her in bed with one man after another."

Liza shrugged. There was no answer to that. Eve and Jonathan must have been lovers. What was there to stop them? Besides, Liza had her own very personal reasons for knowing they were. Back at Shrove, Mr. Tobias lived on. He often had setbacks and once he had a bad fall trying to get down the steps from the terrace, his arm was broken, and while they X-rayed it they found cancer in the bone. Gracie nursed him through it all.

At the end of her first year at Oxford Eve came home for July and August and September and Jonathan with her. They spent all their time together. But when Eve went back Jonathan didn't go with her. He stayed behind to be with his grandfather, who everyone said was really dying now. There were no audio books in those days and Jonathan spent hours every day reading aloud to Mr. Tobias.

Jonathan was going to be "something in the City." That was what Eve had said. Liza didn't know what it meant and Sean had only a hazy idea.

"In a bank maybe," he said, "or a stockbroker."

"What's that?"

"Don't know really. It's like doing stuff with shares."

"Anyway, he didn't. He didn't have to because his father died and left him everything, all his money, which was millions—well, a million or two—and the house in London and the place in the Lake District. He got to be something called a 'name' at Lloyds, whatever that is, but it wasn't work. Caroline got the house in France and something called a life interest in a lot more money. Only no one knew."

"What d'you mean, no one knew?"

No one at Shrove knew. Gracie and old Mr. Tobias knew Sir Nicholas Ellison was dead, of course they did, Gracie sent a wreath from Mr. Tobias to the funeral, but they thought all the property had gone to Caroline. Eve knew. Jonathan had written to her at Oxford and told her, but it didn't occur to her to tell her mother, it didn't interest her much who got the money, Jonathan or Caroline, one of them was bound to have done.

Mr. Tobias must have assumed it was all Caroline's. After all, he had forecast it would be. There was so much money, you see, Liza, Eve said. These people, they don't know how much money they have got. People like us, we always know, down to the last pound, maybe the last fifty pee, but the Tobiases and the Ellisons of this world, they could have two million or three or something in between, they don't exactly know. It's all in different places, making more, accumulating, and they lose count of now much there is.

There was money slurping around, lots of it, more and more, some coming from here and some from there. Maybe Mr. Tobias didn't even care, didn't worry about it, didn't *think* about it. He was very old and very ill and very rich and the last thing he was going to get precisely sorted out in his mind was who had what when it came to money.

Something unexpected happened next. Eve had been two years at Oxford; Jonathan divided his time between visiting her and visiting his grandfather; Mr. Tobias at eighty-four was very feeble and needing constant attention but not in danger. It was autumn. Gracie, who had been fit all her life, suddenly had alarming symptoms. They did tests and told her she had cancer of the womb. She was rushed to hospital for a hysterectomy.

There was nothing for it but nurses, a nurse for the day and a nurse for the night. Jonathan couldn't manage the bedpans and the blanket baths. The nurses were there all the time, a rota of nurses coming and going. Jonathan sat with his grandfather, wrote letters to Eve, shot pheasants. What else happened while Gracie was in hospital became clear after Mr. Tobias was dead.

He bitterly resented her leaving him. It was impossible to make him understand that she had had no choice, that it was her life that was threatened. Perhaps she should have explained to him more carefully what was happening to her. But she was afraid. For once, she was thinking of no one but herself.

As for him, it was as if he refused to admit that anyone but himself could have a life-endangering disease. He spoke to her in the tone of a disappointed father whose daughter has let him down by behaving immorally or in some criminal way. He constantly alluded to "the time you left me on my own."

Gracie took over the care of him once more. The nurses left. Jonathan left for France and his mother. Gracie had been told not to lift heavy weights for six months, and Mr. Tobias, though so old and thin, was very heavy. When she couldn't lift him up in bed properly and prop him on pillows, he grumbled and reproached her.

Eve came home at Christmas, and returned to Oxford in January. She was expected to get a first.

"What's that?" said Sean.

"The best kind of degree. Like getting a first prize."

By the time the spring came, Mr. Tobias couldn't be at home anymore, he was too ill. He was taken to a nursing home, where he went into a coma, lingered for a few weeks, and died in May. Gracie was sad in a way, but he had been so unkind to her those past months that she had lost most of her affection for him. She knew Shrove was hers now, when she woke up on the morning after Mr. Tobias's death, she had gone outside and laid her hands on the brickwork of the wall, saying, "You're mine, you're mine." But she thought she should phone the solicitor to ask when she could legally take possession.

He told her his client had left everything to Jonathan Tobias Ellison, known as Jonathan Tobias. Well, not quite everything. There was a legacy for her of a thousand pounds.

"He had made a new will while she was in hospital," said Liza. "He got Jonathan to send for the solicitor and the nurses were witnesses. In the presence of the testator and of each other."

"You mean Jonathan fixed it."

"Eve says not. She says he told his grandfather he didn't need Shrove, he had what his father left him. But Mr. Tobias didn't understand or didn't want to. He told him he wouldn't leave it to 'that woman who's deserted me.' "

"What did your grandma do?"

"What could she do? Eve didn't mind too much, not then. It would be all the same to her in the end because she and Jonathan were going to get married."

Jonathan asked Gracie to stay on at the gatehouse. He might live at Shrove one day but not yet. All she would have to do would be a kind of caretaker. No nursing, no cooking, it would be almost the same as if it were actually hers. Gracie wouldn't, she was too humiliated. As for Eve, it made her furious. Where was she supposed to go on the holidays until she and Jonathan were married? Gracie was adamant. She went off to Coventry and rented her sister's spare bedroom.

That was nearly the end. Eve didn't come into the story for a while and when she reappeared she had no degree, first or otherwise, but she did have a baby.

"Me," said Liza.

"Is that all you know?"

"She said she'd tell me when I was older."

Eve knew Jonathan was going to South America. He had already started going to places "just to see what it was like." "Come too," he said, but of course she couldn't go to Brazil or Peru or wherever it was at the start of the university term. They quarreled a bit about that and didn't see each other for a fortnight, but the day he went to catch his plane for Rio, Eve went to Heathrow with him to see him off.

He was expected back after three months, after six months, but he didn't come back, he stayed and stayed. Eve had to leave Oxford because she was going to have a baby. In a Coventry hospital Gracie was dying. She hadn't had the hysterectomy soon enough.

After she was dead, Eve and Liza stayed with Eve's aunt. She made it plain she didn't want a niece and a great-niece in her little house, she didn't like babies, but she meant to do her duty. Eve had a hard time making ends meet. For one thing, she was in a bad psychological state. She'd never got over what happened before Liza was born, though she never wished she'd had an abortion. She'd never considered it, she wanted Liza to know that.

"Fine thing to tell a kid of ten," said Sean.

"Okay, I know what you think of her. You don't have to go on and on."

Heather got in touch with her and said, come and live with me. Eve was so unhappy with her aunt that she accepted, though Heather's flat in Birmingham was tiny with only one bedroom. They all three lived there as best they could. Heather found Eve a job teaching in a private school where they would take on staff who weren't qualified. She put Liza with a baby-minder, but that wasn't very satisfactory. When she went to pick her up in the afternoon she found the babies, all six of them, strapped into push-chairs that were stuck in front of the television.

"So I had seen television before, when I was one, but I couldn't remember."

It made Eve determined never to let her child watch television. And that started a train of other ideas about bringing up her child. If only she had somewhere to live, but there was only one place in the world she really wanted that to be.

Jonathan didn't know where she was. She'd changed her job twice and the baby-minder three times before he found her.

Liza was three and Eve had had a job handing out freebie magazines in the street, another trying to be a secretary and learning to type at the same time, and Liza had fallen over at the baby-minder's and cut her head. Jonathan had found a letter at Shrove with the aunt's address on it and, thinking it worth a try, came to find her. One evening he rang the bell at Heather's flat.

When he said he'd a proposal to put before her she thought

for one mad moment he was going to ask her to marry him, even now, even after all that had happened. He was friendly but cool. Would she like to live in the gatehouse at Shrove in exchange for keeping an eye on the house? That was the expression he used, "keeping an eye on." He would pay her a salary, a handsome one, as it turned out.

She accepted. She really had no choice.

"It got her back there, you see. It got her to the one place in the world she wanted to be, even though in the gatehouse she was like the Peri outside the gates of paradise."

"The *what?*"

"Peris were superhuman beings in Persian mythology, sometimes called Pairikas. They were bad spirits, though they hid their badness under a charming appearance, but of course they couldn't get into paradise."

"Of course not," Sean said sarcastically.

"And that was it, you see. That was how we came to live there and it all began."

thirteen

BRUNO was gone and life went back to what it had once been. Lessons resumed. It was just as well Liza liked learning, because she seldom had a chance in his absence to get up to Shrove and watch television. Mother taught her relentlessly. Sometimes the way she instructed and lectured was almost ferocious in its intensity.

Winter came and with it the sunless days and long nights. Every morning the two of them went walking, but they were gone for only an hour and the rest of the day was spent with Liza's books. Occasionally Mother would insist that they spoke only French, so breakfast, lunch, and supper were eaten in

French and their discussions of other subjects were in French. She set Liza an examination in English, history, and Latin. Liza learned whole pages of poetry by heart and in the evenings she and Mother read plays aloud, Mother taking all the male parts and she the female. They read *Peter Pan* and *Where the Rainbow Ends* and *The Blue Bird.*

Bruno was never mentioned. If letters came from him, Mother never said so. Now that Liza was older she didn't get up so early, Mother was always up before her, so Liza wouldn't have known if letters had come. She knew Heather sometimes wrote, her letters were left about. The Tobiases sent a Christmas card, as did Heather and the aunt. Did we send them cards? Liza wanted to know. Mother said no, certainly not. It was absurd celebrating Christmas if you didn't believe in the Christian God, or indeed any god at all, but she gave Liza a lesson on the Christian religion just as she taught her about Judaism and Islam and Buddhism.

One day, shortly before Liza's eleventh birthday, she was looking through Mother's desk for a pad of lined paper Mother said was in the middle section, when she came upon a letter in Bruno's writing. She recognized the writing at once. Without ever having been told, she somehow knew that reading other people's private correspondence was wrong. It must have come from all the highly moral Victorian books she read from the Shrove library, the works among others of Charlotte M. Yonge and Frances Hodgson Burnett. She read it just the same.

Mother had gone upstairs. She could hear her moving about overhead. Liza read the address, which was somewhere called Cheadle, and the date, which was the previous week, and the first page of the letter. It started, "My darling lovely Eve." Liza wrinkled up her nose but read on. "I miss you a lot. I wish I could call you, it's crazy us not being able to call each other in this day and age. *Please* ring me. You can call me collect if you're afraid of J.T. getting his knickers in a twist. Now my ma is dead I'm not poor anymore, do you realize that? It won't be much longer now, I've just got all this stuff to see to, inevitable really, and I must grin and bear it. Just to hear your voice would—"

She had to stop there because she heard Mother's footsteps on the stairs. She didn't dare turn the page over. Much of what she had read about "calling" and "collect" was incomprehensible, but not "it won't be much longer now." He was coming back. For a moment she wondered why his mother's dying stopped him being poor, but then she remembered the tale of Shrove and old Mr. Tobias and understood.

It was a hard winter. A little snow fell before Christmas, but the first heavy fall came in early January. It lay in deep drifts, masking the demarcations between the road surface and the grass verge, then piling up to hide the ditch and spreading a thick concealing cloak over the hedgerow. And when it melted a little it froze again, more fiercely than ever, so that the thawed snow, falling in drops and trickles, turned into icicles, pointed as needles and sharp as knives.

Icicles hung around the eaves of the gatehouse like fringe on a canopy. A crust of ice lay on top of the thick snow. It had been two days since a car had been able to get down the lane. The council, Mother said, hadn't bothered to snowplow it because they were the only ones living there and they hadn't a car.

The postman stopped coming, which pleased Liza because it meant no more letters from Bruno. While the lane was blocked like this, Bruno couldn't come. The little orange car would never get through where the post van failed. And still the snow fell, day after day, adding more and more layers to the deep quilt of crisp whiteness that covered everything.

They fed the birds. They had a bird table for bread crumbs,

two bird feeders made of wire mesh to fill with nuts, and they hung up pieces of fat on string. One morning Liza saw a woodpecker at one of the wire feeders and a tree creeper hanging on its tail, both pecking at the nuts. Remembering Jonathan taking photographs, she said she wished they had a camera, but Mother said, no, your own mind is the best recording instrument, let your memory photograph it.

And then she said the bird was like Trochilus, a kind of hummingbird. So Liza looked Trochilus up in the encyclopedia and she thought she saw what Mother meant, for its other name was the crocodile bird, so called because it is the only creature that can enter with impunity the mouth of a crocodile and pick its teeth. It also cries out to warn the crocodile of an impending foe.

Liza loved the snow. She was too old to make snowmen, but she made them. She made herself an igloo. When it was finished she sat inside her igloo, eating a picnic of Marmite sandwiches and Nice biscuits and rejoicing in the snow that would keep Bruno away, wishing as hard as she could that more and more snow would fall, that it would lie heavy and impenetrable in the lane until March, until April. Mother had told her about a very bad winter when she was a little girl, even before she and Gracie and Ray came to Shrove, when the snow started in January and lasted for seven weeks and all the water pipes froze. It was a bad winter, but to herself Liza called it a "good" winter.

Mother had a cold that she must have caught in town the last time she went there before the snow came. Coughing kept her awake at night so she lay down to rest in the afternoons, and when she did Liza made her way up to Shrove for an hour or two of television. She had missed the old films and school programs and quiz shows. She was beginning to understand too, in a vague, puzzled way, that the small square screen was her window to a world of which she otherwise knew very little.

The second time she went up there she saw the snowplow as she came out of the cottage gate. It was clearing the lane. The big shovel on the front of it was heaving up piles of snow, spotted like currant pudding by the gravel lodged in it, and casting it up on the verges. Liza felt sure this would somehow open the way for Bruno. It was as if he had been waiting on the other side of the bridge in his orange car for the snowplow to come and make a smooth, clean road for him.

But when she returned there was no car and no Bruno. She should have asked Mother, she knew that, she should have said to Mother, "Is Bruno coming back?" but she couldn't bring herself to do this. She was afraid of being told yes and of being given a definite time. Doubt was better than knowing for sure.

The snow thawed and he hadn't come. All that was left of the snow were small piles of it lying in the coldest shady places, map-shaped patches of snow on the green grass. Mother's cold went when the snow did, so there was no more television but plenty of lessons. In February, on a freak warm day, Liza went up into the wood to see if the aconites were out, and when she got back a car was parked outside the cottage, a dark brown car of a shape and make she had never seen before. Instead of a letter of the alphabet at the start of the registration number there was one at the end. She had never seen that before either. The car was called a Lancia.

The Tobiases, she thought, having long dropped the respectful Mr. and Mrs. They were always getting new cars. She went warily into the house, preparing to say a cool hallo before going upstairs. The memory of the partridges remained with her and now the story of Gracie and the grandfather too.

She saw Bruno before he saw her, she moved so quietly. He was sitting on the sofa beside Mother, holding both her hands in his and looking into her eyes. Liza stood quite still. He was unchanged, except that his long, soft wavy hair was longer and his freckles had faded. He still wore denim jeans and a leather jacket and the two gold earrings in the lobe of one ear.

Perhaps there was some truth in the theory she had read that you can sense when someone is staring very intently at you, for although she hadn't moved or made a sound Bruno suddenly raised his head and met her eyes. For a moment, a very brief instant of time, there came into his face a look of such deep hatred and loathing that she felt a shiver run straight down her back. She had never seen such a look before, but she knew it at once for what it was. Bruno hated her.

Almost immediately the terrible expression had passed and a look of bland resignation replaced it. Mother also looked around, dropping Bruno's hands. Mother said, "Goodness, Lizzie, you're as quiet as a little mouse."

Bruno said, "Hi, Liza, how've you been?"

That was the way he talked. Not like an English person and not like an American person—she had heard plenty of them on television—but as if he lived midway between the two countries, which was impossible because it would have been the Atlantic Ocean. She noticed a red blush on Mother's face. Mother hadn't told her he was coming. She must have known. Why hadn't she told her?

"What d'you reckon to my new jalopy, then?"

"He means his car," said Mother.

"It's okay," Liza said, a television expression that made Mother frown. "I liked the orange one."

"The orange one, as you call it, has gone to where all bad old cars go when they die, the breakers' yard."

"Where do the good ones go, Bruno?" said Mother.

"They go to people like me, my sweet. The one outside's

what I mean by a good one. It was my ma's, still is, as a matter of fact, I've never transferred it. She had it for ten years and only did seven thousand miles on it."

Mother was laughing. Liza thought, she didn't tell me because she knows I hate him. I wonder if she knows he hates me? In that moment she lost some of her respect for Mother, though not her love. That was the evening when, as soon as she could get Mother alone, she asked if she could start calling her Eve.

"Why do you want to?"

"Everyone else does."

If Mother thought "everyone" a bit thin on the ground, she didn't say so. "You can if you like," she said, though not in a happy voice.

Liza had been wrong when she thought Bruno hadn't changed. She would have understood that he had even if Eve hadn't pointed it out, if Eve hadn't said while they were having their dinner, "You never used to care about money, you used to be indifferent to it."

He had been talking about all the things "they" could do now he had his mother's house to sell.

"You'd better wait till you've sold it," said Eve in the dry voice she sometimes used.

"I've practically done that small thing," Bruno said in his twangy tone. "I've got a buyer who's even keener to buy it than I am to sell."

That was in the boom time of five and a half years ago. Eve said she understood you could sell anything these days, a remark that went down less than well with Bruno, who started insisting on how lovely his mother's house was, how he *and* she would have been delighted to live in it if only it hadn't been in the north.

"You can leave me out of it," said Eve. "I live here and I'm going to live here for the rest of my life."

He wasn't an anarchist anymore. He had forgotten about money and property being unimportant. Having a big house to sell and a proper car and some thousands of pounds in the bank had gone to his head.

"I didn't even have a bank last time I was here, Eve."

"Aren't we going to talk about anything but money?" said Eve.

She was so rough with him, "scathing" was the word, that Liza really expected him to go off somewhere for the night. But the guitar music went on playing softly and persistently downstairs, sometimes Bruno sang in his Johnny Cash or his Merle Haggard voices, and she wasn't really surprised when, hours later, their footfalls on the stairs woke her and she heard them go into Eve's bedroom together.

The only good that came of Bruno's return was free afternoons for watching television. Lessons didn't stop, but once more they became few and far between. Bruno was almost always there and when he was he sneered at Eve's teaching methods, picked on her for not being a qualified teacher, and went on and on about how "the kid" ought to be at school.

"Why ought she?" Mother said at last.

"Come on, Mother, she's not getting a proper education."

"Don't call me 'Mother,' you're only two years younger than I am. How many children of eleven have you come across that can read, write, and talk French, can do a Latin unseen, recite *Lycidas,* and give you a thoroughly good precis of at least four Shakespeare plays?"

"She doesn't know any science and she doesn't know any maths."

"Of course she doesn't. She's only eleven."

"That's the age they're supposed to start these things, remember?"

"You teach her, then. You were good at maths, you're always saying."

"I'm not a teacher," Bruno said. "I'm not like you, I know my limitations. She needs real teachers. I bet that kid couldn't do a simple sum. I'm not talking about calculus and logarithms and all that, I'm talking about, say, long division. Come on, Liza, you've got a bit of paper there. Divide eight hundred and twenty-four by forty-two."

Eve snatched the paper away. "Nobody needs to divide eight hundred and twenty-four by forty-two on paper anymore. Even I know that, out of the world as I am. You have calculators to do that for you."

"Calculators can't do algebra," said Bruno.

And so it went on. Liza knew very well—though Eve didn't seem to—that Bruno only wanted her to go to school to be rid of her, to get her out of the way. He didn't care whether she learned algebra or got to know about biology. He just didn't want her there when he was there. She understood now, because Bruno had told her, that Eve was breaking the law in not sending her to school. Bruno made a lot of that, he was always saying how Eve broke the law, though he was breaking it himself not buying a new Road Fund license for his car.

But for all the fault he found with Eve, Bruno wanted to be with her, he wanted her to be with him. When his mother's house was sold, he wanted to buy a new one for him and Eve to live in. It could be near Shrove, only in the town, for instance, or in one of the villages on the other side of the valley. He liked it around here, he was happy enough to stay around here, knowing how Eve loved it.

"I thought you wanted to be free," Eve said. "That's what you always used to say, how you loved freedom, how you didn't want to be tied down."

"I've changed. Becoming a property owner changes you. You start to understand the meaning of responsibility."

"Oh, really, Bruno, you'll be asking me to marry you next."

"I can't. I'm already married, you know that. But I do want to live with you for the rest of my life."

"Really?" said Eve. "I don't know what I want to do for the rest of my life except stay here."

"But that's what I'm saying. We'll stay here. You *can* stay here. You'll only be four or five miles away."

"I mean here. *Here.* On this spot. You may as well make up your mind to it, Bruno. You can buy a house if you want, I'll even drop in sometimes if you ask me, but I'm staying here."

Bruno never said anything about Liza living in the house he was proposing to buy. She wanted to ask Eve what was really going to happen. Did she mean it when she said she wouldn't leave here in any circumstances? Was she definite about not living in Bruno's house? And what about Liza? Would Eve give in to Bruno and send her away to school? Liza longed to ask Eve for the truth, she desperately wanted to know, but she was never alone with Eve, Bruno was always there.

In March, when the weather got a bit warmer, he and Eve started going for a lot of drives in the brown car with the out-of-date Road Fund license that had been Bruno's mother's. Eve tried to get Liza to come with them, but Liza wouldn't. She went up to Shrove instead and watched television. Bruno had said, and Eve hadn't denied it, that they went on trips looking at houses that were for sale.

"If I did come with you," Eve said one evening when they were all sitting around the fire in the cottage, "if I did, which I wouldn't dream of, but if I did, what would we live on? Have you thought of that? Your mother's bit of money won't last forever. It won't last for *long*. While you're here, you live off me, in case you need reminding, but if I left here my money would stop. I get paid for being here, have you forgotten that?"

"I'm a painter. If I don't make much it's because I refuse to compromise, you know that. But things are looking up. You know what they say, nothing succeeds like success. Those Tobiases bought my painting, didn't they? Or we could start up in business, you and me, we could be interior decorators, for instance." Something she had said seemed to strike him for the first time. "What d'you mean, you wouldn't dream of it? Why've you been coming to look at all these houses with me if you wouldn't dream of it?"

"I've told you," she said, "I've told you a hundred times. You buy a house, go on, if you want to, I'll go with you and look at it, but I'm not living in it. I'm living here in this house, at Shrove. Is that clear?"

They had this conversation every evening, or one very like it, until Liza didn't listen anymore. She sat reading her book or went up to bed while they argued. But one evening things took a different turn. It had been a bad day, a day on which a nasty, frightening thing happened, something quite unforeseen.

The weather was perfect, the kind of April day that might have been June, but clearer and fresher than June would be. Bruno was out painting somewhere. This meant that Liza could have her Latin lesson without fear of interruption, which might be a sarcastic comment or derive simply from his presence, silent, looming, his eyes sometimes cast upward.

If Liza had been able to express it in words, she would have said Bruno was taking them over, controling them, setting the pace, or calling the tune. But she knew none of these expressions, only that where Eve had ruled he was fast becoming the ruler. Eve was sharp with him or scathing but she resisted him less and less. She was gradually ceasing to give Liza lessons because of his disapproval.

They could have this one because he wasn't there. As if it was something wrong or against the law, they had to do it in secret. The French lesson had to be outside in the garden. This, Liza suspected, was because if he came back sooner than he had said, he would think they had gone out somewhere, he wouldn't look for them down there under the cherry tree.

The cherry blossoms were out everywhere and the woods were white, not sprinkled with white as when the blackthorn flowered in March, but a pure, clean white like a fallen cloud. When the lesson was over, Liza and Eve went out walking to look at all the cherry trees because Eve said, quoting a poet, you could see it only once a year, which meant that at her age she probably only had forty more chances. They went to the woods down by the bridge and to their own wood, and after that Eve went home in case Bruno was already there.

Liza wandered off on her own. She crossed the bridge and began walking along the old railway line, disused for six months now, but the rails and sleepers still there. If you followed the line, just walking along it and through the quarter mile of tunnel, out the other side into another valley, eventually you'd come to the town and then another town and at last to the big city. Not yet, but perhaps one day, she would do that.

It was six o'clock in the evening but not yet sunset. The warmth had lasted and there was no wind. She walked along the line the other way, toward the station at Ring Valley Halt. Would they have taken the station name away? And what had become of the building, red brick with a canopy and a gingerbread trim, with windowboxes and tubs of flowers, which had also been the signalman's house?

She didn't see Bruno until she was no more than a few feet from him, until she couldn't avoid him or hide. The station house looked just the same from a distance, but as she came closer she saw that the curtains upstairs were gone and the door marked PRIVATE stood open. Instead of flowers in the windowboxes and the beds that ran along the backs of both platforms, weeds had sprung up. Where last year there had been daffodils and grape hyacinths grew dandelions. Liza climbed up onto the platform and made her way through the door marked EXIT into the room where people had bought tickets, through that room and, suspecting nothing, out of the main door onto the sandy lane that had been the station approach.

Bruno was sitting there, not on his camp stool but on the low wall with his easel in front of him. He was holding up a brush loaded with gamboge and he was staring straight at her.

Of course, what he had really been staring at was the station entrance from which she had come. She went closer, she went right up to him, because retreat was impossible. The picture he was painting was of what could be seen through those open doors, the empty line, the deserted platform, paint peeling off the gingerbread fringe on the canopy, the sunflower faces of the dandelions.

When Eve wasn't there he didn't bother with any of that "hi, and how are you?" He cast up his eyes, the way he often did when he saw her. She was at a loss, suddenly frightened with no real reason to feel fear. Could she just pass on? Was it possible to ignore him and go on up the sandy path until she was out of his sight?

The brush approached the canvas, touched it, painted in the

dandelion petals. His box of paints, the heap of paint-stained rags, the jar of sticky brushes were on the wall beside him. He drew the brush away and began wiping it on a strip of cloth, which she saw had been torn from an old skirt of Eve's, a skirt she remembered her wearing years before, when first they came to Shrove.

He spoke in a tone that was at first mild and conversational. "You're old enough to realize what's being done to you. She's denying you your birthright—well, what's the birthright of kids living in civilized countries. We're not talking about the Third World. This is the United Kingdom in the nineteen-eighties, in case she hasn't noticed."

Liza said nothing.

"She's crippling you. She might as well have chopped off one of your legs or arms. In another way she's buried you. You're not dead, but she's buried you just the same. In one of the remotest parts of England. She's cut you off. You're not much better than one of those poor devils that get lost as babies and bears or wolves raise them."

"Romulus and Remus," said Liza.

"There you are, you see. That's just it. You know all that stuff, that god-awful useless crap, but I bet you can't tell me who the president of the United States is."

Liza shrugged, the way Eve did.

"You're so like your goddamn mother you might be her clone, not her daughter. Maybe you are, eh? Only you don't know what a clone is, any more than you know what H_2O is or pi or anything that's not Shakespeare or fucking Virgil."

The word was new to her. Strange, then, that she sensed he shouldn't have used it, it shouldn't be uttered in her presence. A blush climbed up her neck and made her face hot.

"I'm gonna say just one more thing to you and then you can

go home to her and tell tales out of school. That's a laugh, isn't it? Out of school is right. I'm gonna say one more thing and it's this: If you don't get yourself sent to school right now, in the next six months at the very outside, if you don't you won't have a chance of life, you'll be lost forever. All that learning'll be wasted. It's all very well her saying education doesn't have a purpose, it's not *for* anything, it's all very well her quoting fucking Aristotle or Plato or whoever and saying it's for turning the soul's eye toward the light or some shit like that, but you try telling that tale when you want to go to college, when you want a job, when you haven't got any qualifications, not even O-Levels. Who's going to give a shit about your French and your Romulus and Remus then?"

"I hate you," Liza said softly.

"Big deal. I'm not surprised. I've been telling you this in your best interests and maybe you'll realize it one day. When it's too late. The best thing you can do is go home and tell her you want to go to school. The term starts next week. You go and tell her that."

Liza did go then. She walked until she was sure he could no longer see her and then she ran. She was shaking inside and something she called her heart felt as if it had swelled up until it was too big for her chest, until it must burst.

If she had met Eve at that moment, as she was running along the footpath by the maple hedge, if Eve had come out to look for her and they had met, she would have thrown herself into her mother's arms and told her everything he had said. But she didn't. Eve was at home making the dinner. And by the time Liza reached the gatehouse she had slowed her pace to catch her breath, she had collected her thoughts.

The awful knowledge had come to her that whatever she told Eve of the things Bruno had said, it would make no difference.

Eve was somehow conquered by him, in ways beyond Liza's understanding. It was as if she didn't really like Bruno any more than Liza did herself, but still she wanted him there and she wanted him to like her. Rude to him she might be, but she wanted him to look at her in that way he had, as if she were an angel in the clouds.

She even dressed in a different way to please him, with her hair loose down her back, the jade beads around her neck, and sashes and scarves and chains decorating her, things he'd bought her on their outings. The two of them clattered around in beads and chains, their hair shaggy, barefoot or wearing boots. He talked his mid-Atlantic language, and sometimes Eve, precise, pedantic Eve, echoed his expressions. Why then did Liza have this rooted idea that though Eve would never tell him to go, she would be just as happy as Liza if he were gone?

Calling out to Eve in the kitchen that she was back, she went upstairs and looked hard at her own face in the mirror. She had never noticed it before but now she could see that what he had said was true in at least one respect, she did look like Eve, she was exactly a younger version of Eve, same features, same golden-brown flushed skin, clear water-brown eyes, and golden-gleaming dark brown hair, exactly as curly and exactly as long.

That day, when she remembered the weeds' sun-shaped faces and the yellow paint on the brush tip, she thought of as the Day of the Dandelions but she was growing out of giving names to special days and she only ever named one more.

After a little while she heard Bruno come in. His arrival was followed by utter silence. She hoped for something, though she hardly knew what. Perhaps she hoped that Eve, without being told, would somehow guess her unhappiness and the reason for it. She would guess and make things right again, as she had used to do when Liza was miserable. Bruno being reprimanded over her, really reprimanded, was something she longed to see. She could bear Bruno if Bruno were changed, were made nicer.

As silent as they were themselves, she tiptoed down the stairs.

The two of them were on the sofa, embracing, wound around each other, devouring each other, so closely locked it looked as if it must hurt. At that sight, Liza's sense of isolation, even of rejection, was so great as to amount to panic. A sound escaped her, she couldn't help herself, a whimper of pain. They were too preoccupied with each other to hear her.

Or Mother was. Bruno's blue angelic eye appeared above Mother's curved cheek. It stared at Liza coldly, unblinking. The worst thing was that it went on staring while Bruno's mouth kept sucking Mother's mouth and Bruno's hands clutched and pummeled her back.

Liza turned and ran. She remembered the Andrew Lang fairy stories from long ago and thought he had put Mother under an evil spell.

fourteen

MAGIC spells," Sean said indulgently, "they don't happen in this day and age."

"This one did."

"What did you do, make a wax what-d'you-call-it and stick pins in him?"

She didn't understand. "I didn't have to do anything. He did it himself. I could have told him there were things meant more to her than he did. Well, two things."

"Shrove and you."

"Shrove, anyway. I mattered, but not as much." She hesitated. "I can't help wondering now how much I matter, Sean. I know she's in prison but it's as she said, it's not a dungeon, it's not the Tower of London. They'd let her try to get in touch, wouldn't they? She doesn't know where I am, she thinks I'm with Heather, but she can't have checked or she'd know I'm not. And then wouldn't they have the police look for me?"

"You can't have it both ways, love. You can't not want them to look for you and want them to."

"No, you're right. But still I think it's that she loved me when I was a child and she could sort of remake me, shape me the way she wanted, but when I grew up she lost interest. I could *feel* her losing interest."

"You've got me now."

"I know. I'll go on about Bruno and breaking the spell, shall I? He must have been very stupid to threaten her and not see it wouldn't work. I see that now but I didn't then, I was too young. I thought she'd send me away and leave the place and if that happened I thought I'd die."

Bruno kept on and on at Eve to come and live with him in this house he wanted to buy. He'd found somewhere he liked but he wouldn't make the vendor an offer until he got a promise out of Eve. His mother's house was sold by then and he'd got far more for it than it was worth, as often happened in the late eighties. The place he'd found was a big house built fifty years before on the edge of the village where Eve went to catch the bus for town.

Even Liza had been to see it. They took her with them in the car. She thought it very ugly with the dark wooden strips on the yellow plaster, done to look like houses she'd seen in pictures of when Elizabeth I was on the throne of England, the red roof and the windows made of hundreds of tiny diamond-shaped panes.

The garden was very big, which Bruno kept saying Eve would like, and surrounded on three sides by enormously tall hedges of the cypress Liza knew was called leylandii. The ugliest tree in the world, Eve had once said. They drove through the village and Eve pointed out the place where Rainer Beck had fallen down dead while building the wall of bricks. Someone else must have finished building the house between the row of cottages and the village hall, for there it stood, looking quite old, as if it had been there for a hundred years.

Almost into town, on the outskirts, they called at a supermarket that looked a bit like Bruno's new house, but fifteen times as big and only on one floor. It was another first time for Liza, going in there, and she enjoyed it tremendously. She walked slowly past the shelves, counting how many kinds of fruit juice there were, how many sorts of canned vegetables. The different varieties of biscuits numbered over a hundred. There were dozens of types of food she didn't recognize, that she wouldn't have known were food at all. The soaps and sprays and cleansers fascinated her. She could happily have spent the rest of the day there but Eve got fidgety and made her leave as soon as they had bought their fruit and cornflakes. Liza was being exposed to just the kind of thing Eve most dreaded.

It was that evening, when they were quarreling again about the house, when Liza was curled up in an armchair reading *Kim* in the crimson and gold Shrove library edition, that Bruno suddenly said, "Does Mr. Jonathan Tobias, your liege lord and master, by any chance know that kid doesn't go to school? That she's never been to school?"

The question distracted Liza from Kim Rishti Ke and the Eye of Beauty and she looked up. The truth was that Jonathan Tobias didn't know. Even she knew that, or guessed it. Of course she was always at home when the Tobiases came to Shrove, but they didn't come often and always came on the school holidays or at half-term. If Jonathan Tobias had ever asked Eve how she was getting on at school she no doubt lied to him. Liza hadn't actually heard her do so but she wouldn't have been surprised.

"He doesn't know, does he?"

"It's no business of his," Eve said.

"It's everyone's business in the community. If he knew, I doubt if he'd let you stay here. It's not just the not going to school, it's all the rest of it. Keeping her isolated here, not employing a woman to clean because you don't want any more prying eyes, keeping the money yourself you're supposed to pay to this nonexistent woman, not to mention letting the kid run wild at Shrove, taking what she wants out of the library. Look at her now. That's probably a first edition she's got there. A first edition in the hands of an eleven-year-old who's never even been to school!"

"I didn't keep her isolated enough," Eve said quietly. "I didn't keep myself isolated the way I promised myself I would. I've been weak, I've been a fool. The biggest mistake I made was letting you in."

He said to Liza, "Go to bed. It's nearly nine o'clock at night and you've no business down here."

"Don't you dare speak to her like that!" Eve stood up, facing him. "This is Liza's home, she can do as she likes. Do you really think threatening me is likely to make me come and live with you in that mock-Tudor monstrosity? Don't you know anything about human beings?"

He flinched from the flash of her eyes. "I thought you liked the house," he said sulkily. "I thought you did. You didn't say anything about it being a monstrosity."

"And you who called property-owners bourgeois! Truly money is the root of all evil if it changes people the way it's changed you."

Liza got up, took her book, and said she was going to bed. She got halfway up the stairs and stopped, listening. They were off again. Did she want to hear what was said or didn't she? She couldn't be sure. If he made Eve believe he'd tell the Tobiases, wouldn't she have to give in? Wouldn't she have to send Liza to school and go and live with him, whatever she said about not being forced by threats? Would school be like the school in *Jane Eyre*?

She crept down again and listened.

"I don't have to tell Tobias, Eve." Bruno had stopped calling Eve "Mother." "I only have to contact the County Education Authority. No, it's not spite, it's not revenge, it's my duty. It would be anyone's duty."

Eve said in a wheedling voice, the kind of tone Liza had never heard her use, "And if I agree, that is if I go and live in that house with you, you'll keep silent about this?"

"More or less. Hopefully, I'd persuade you that what you're doing is wrong, but I wouldn't take any direct action. Not for a while, anyway."

"I think you're right when you say they would take her into care. I also think it probable I should lose this house and my job. Without this place I really don't know what would become of us."

Liza came closer to the door.

"There's no point in being so goddamned sarcastic."

"I'm not being sarcastic. I mean it. I'm simply being frank about the facts. Without this place I don't know what would become of us. There's nowhere I could go and keep Liza."

"There is a place you can go. A real home. A far better home than this antiquated little dump. A hovel without a bathroom!"

Liza heard Eve's little laugh. "And you called yourself an anarchist. You were a free spirit."

"All right. I can be frank too. Have you ever heard of an

anarchist with money or a free spirit with a hefty bank balance? Can't you see it's for the best, Eve? Can't you face up to it and go the whole hog, come and live with me and give up this whole crazy project? Let the kid go to school and lead a normal life like other kids. I could afford fees for boarding school, you know, a good *co-ed* private school. She could come home at weekends."

There was silence. Liza held her breath. The door was suddenly flung open and Liza saw the wild face Bruno wasn't allowed to see, the dilated eyes and curled lip, the nostrils narrowed like a cat's.

"Go to bed at once! How dare you listen at doors! Perhaps you *should* go away to school, perhaps I've been wrong all these years. I haven't just sheltered you, I've spoiled you. Go to bed now."

Liza seldom cried but she did that night. She wept until she slept, woke again at the sound of Eve and Bruno coming up to bed together, whispering tenderly, no longer angry, reconciled, content with each other.

Years later, three or four years, she went back to look at the house Bruno had wanted to buy.

It was on the other side of the valley, about two miles away by road or one as the crow flies and as she walked, wading through the river where the water was low, and crossing the disused railway line. By this time the rails and sleepers had been taken away and the line was a grassy track between embankments overgrown with gorse and wildflowers. Climbing the slope, she looked back at the station house where on the frightening occasion she had encountered Bruno painting. The painting he had done Eve had liked and had hung it up in the cottage living room. Every time Liza looked at the dandelion faces in the foreground she remembered the gamboge on his raised brush as he spat out those harsh words to her.

She climbed the hillside, took the footpath, then went across the fields that were private land yet where no one ever came but the sheep that grazed there. It was scarcely a village, just a church, a meeting hall and a green with a few old houses and the four newer ones built around a half-moon-shaped road. The people who had bought the house she called Bruno's, though it never had been his, though he had never even made that offer for it, had cut down all the Leyland cypresses and painted the walls pink. A child's climbing frame stood in the middle of the lawn. Lying down asleep inside a wire enclosure was a big yellow dog with a feathery tail and long ears.

She might have lived there herself. But perhaps not, perhaps there had never really been a chance of that. She sat on the green for a while, then lay face-downward in the sun, the prickly scented grass pressing into her skin. When she got up she could feel with her fingertips the ridges the grass had made on her cheek, like wrinkles.

This time, for a change, she went back through the woods, though it was a longer way around. There were still great spaces in there where giant trees had fallen and no new ones yet been planted. Rocky outcrop appeared all over this hillside, among the trees as well as on the open heathland. It was very pale gray rock that sometimes looked white, like bones lying among the brown beech leaves and the gnarled dark tree roots. You might fancy you saw a skull, but when you approached more closely you could see it was only a bowl-shaped lump of rock, just as the bone-white strips among the brambles were limestone, not a weathered femur or humerus.

"Did she give in to him, then?" said Sean.

"I don't know. I don't exactly know what happened. I never saw him again."

Sean put up his eyebrows. "What, you mean you never saw him after that night?"

"I told you, I didn't get up very early. I came downstairs at about nine and Eve said he'd gone out painting. It was midsummer, you see, and sometimes the light was best for painting very early in the morning. He often went out early. Now he didn't need to, he painted all the time. We had our lessons. We'd got into the way of having them while he was out of the house. I can't remember but I think it was French that morning and maybe history. Yes, it was history because I remember Eve wanted me to read Carlyle's *French Revolution* and I couldn't, it was too hard for me, too many difficult words."

"Surprise, surprise," said Sean.

"She was cross. She grumbled at me and called me a coward for not trying harder. I mean, you have to understand she was hardly ever cross with me and never about things like that. But she was irritable and jumpy that morning. When it got to midday she said she'd made a picnic lunch for me, it was too nice a day to stay in, I should be out in the fresh air. That was unusual too, if there was to be a picnic she always came with me, but not this time. You may wonder how I remember all this, all the details, but the fact is I've thought about that day a lot ever since. I've turned it over and over in my mind."

Bruno's car was parked outside the cottage, where he always left it. That signified one thing to Liza, that he couldn't be far off. If he went to paint more than a mile away he always went in the car. Carrying her picnic, she made her way cautiously toward

Shrove House. This time she wasn't going to let herself come upon him by chance as she had when she went marching confidently through the station. He was nowhere to be seen, he must have gone northward through their wood or down the lane toward the river bridge.

The sun was too hot to walk or sit out in, and in the shade under the trees flies swarmed. She let herself into Shrove, into its silent rooms that were as cool in summer as they were warm in winter, replaced *Kim* on the library shelves and took down *Stalky and Co.* For the next four hours she sat watching television.

On those days when she had been out for a long time she always had to brace herself before going home and confronting him again. It had got worse as she knew him more thoroughly, not better, and on the way home she reflected how terrible the future was, filled with days of meeting and being with Bruno, or else—and she hardly knew if this would be worse—going away to the school of his choosing. And still she would see him, for her weekends and holidays would be spent in the "monstrosity," exiled from Shrove.

His car was gone. Her heart leapt up, then dipped again. Of course it most likely only meant he and Eve had driven off somewhere and would return in time for supper. She went despondently into the house. Eve was at home and alone, preparing a chicken to roast, mixing the stuffing, and setting the giblets on to boil.

"Where's he gone?" She no longer used his name when speaking of him.

Eve's face showed nothing, neither happiness nor sadness, it was blank, her large brown eyes empty. "He's gone. Gone for good. He's left us."

At once Liza was enormously happy, bubbling over with delight, with joy. Some precocious sense of what was fitting restrained her from crowing or cheering. She said nothing, she just looked at Eve. Her mother set down the spoon she was holding, rinsed her hands under the tap, dried them, and put her arms around Liza, hugging her tight.

That evening they read Shakespeare together. Liza took Macbeth's part and Eve Lady Macbeth. As Eve predicted, there was a lot of the scene where the wife urges the husband to murder the old king that Liza couldn't understand, but Eve didn't get cross when Liza spoke sentences wrong or put incorrect stresses on certain words. Afterward, they played a tape of Mozart's *Sinfonia Concertante* and then had a French conversation, all things they hadn't been able to do when Bruno was there.

Liza was so happy that she should have slept soundly that night but she didn't. She fancied she heard all sorts of sounds, creaking boards and thumps and something heavy being dragged down the stairs. It could all have been in dreams, it was impossible to know. For instance, she had no reason to believe Eve didn't come to bed until four or five in the morning, only a feeling or intuition that she hadn't. It wasn't as if she had been into the other bedroom to look. The car she thought she heard at one point was probably farther away than she believed, not passing the gatehouse door but a hundred yards away in the lane.

She said nothing about it in the morning, for she and Eve had never been in the habit of telling each other their dreams. Nothing could be more boring, Eve sometimes said, than other people's dreams. But later, while her mother was up at Shrove, cleaning the house in her role as Mrs. Cooper, Liza went into the little castle that Bruno had used as a studio.

His easel was there and his two boxes of paints as well as innumerable extra tubes of color, the names of which fascinated her, though she had never cared to show her interest in front of him. Rose madder tint, light viridian, Chinese white, burnt umber. How strange of him to have gone without his painting things. Even stranger that he hadn't cleaned the brushes he always complained were so expensive, but left them dipped in an inch of turpentine in a jam jar. Pictures, finished, half-finished, blank canvases, rested against the wall. Her own portrait was there.

It was not for a long time that she connected the paint rags in the little castle with Bruno's departure. Then, during that morning visit, they were just rags, a rather larger than usual pile of them filling up nearly half the floor space. A much larger than usual pile, in fact. Old skirts of Eve's torn into strips, a sheet that went on her own bed until she put her toe through a hole in it, a ragged towel.

Another odd thing about the paint rags, which didn't particularly register at the time but remained in her memory, was the color of the paint on them. One had a streak of sap green on the edge of it and another looked as if it had mopped up a spill of Prussian blue, but for the most part they were stained reddish-brown—and not just stained, coated in that color.

Liza tried to decide what color it might be. Not crimson or scarlet lake or vermilion, it wasn't bright enough for that. Too dark for rose madder tint and not dark or dull enough for Vandyke brown. Light sienna? Burnt sienna? Either was possible but that didn't explain why Bruno had used so much of it.

Did the mess in here and the stack of canvases mean he was coming back? She looked for his clothes in Eve's wardrobe, the leather jacket, the check shirts, the sweatshirt with UNIVERSITY OF CALIFORNIA, BERKELEY mysteriously printed on it. Everything was gone. Sometimes he had left his gold earrings on Eve's dressing table, but these too had gone with him. The awful possibility that, having gone, he might still tell tales of Eve to the Tobiases or to education authorities brought her down from euphoria into the depths again.

She had to ask.

"He won't be telling anyone anything," Eve said. "Believe me. I promise."

A letter came addressed to him and Eve opened it. He had asked her to do that, she said. Inside the envelope was a note from an estate agent who wrote that he would have phoned but it appeared that Mr. Drummond and Mrs. Beck were not in the directory. Was Mr. Drummond still interested in making an offer for The Conifers? The name, for some reason, made Eve laugh a lot.

She wrote a letter to the estate agent but Liza didn't see what she had said. They went out together to post it, up the lane to the main road where there was a little old post box with VR on it for Victoria Regina, which meant it had been there for a hundred years.

The month was July and Liza was eleven and a half. The good weather lasted for only a short time, it rained and grew cold and Eve and Liza stayed in, doing more lessons than they had for months. Liza could write French composition now and recite from memory Keats's "Ode to a Grecian Urn."

Because it was so wet, the Tobiases didn't come down as they had said they would, and in August Jonathan Tobias came alone. Liza noticed he had some gray in his hair. Perhaps because Victoria wasn't with him, he spent more time at their house than he had done for years. Liza couldn't help overhearing some of the things that were said, for Jonathan seemed to think that when a person was reading they were deaf to everything.

Victoria, he said, was in Greece with friends. To Liza, Greece was a place full of gray stone temples with colonnades and marble statues and where gods lived in the rivers and trees. It hardly accorded with her ideas to hear that Victoria and her friends found beaches there to sunbathe on and big hotels to stay in, the kind of thing, Jonathan said, that they preferred over Shrove or Ullswater.

Sometimes, aware that she had looked up from her book, he would lean closer to Eve and speak in a whisper. Wishy-wishy-wishy, the way she remembered Heather murmuring. And Eve nodded and looked sympathetic and whispered something back. It troubled Liza that Jonathan seemed to think Bruno was only temporarily away, for this made his departure seem less than permanent.

"I can't help being envious, Eve," he said one sunny afternoon.

The summer had come back and they were all having tea in the garden, under the cherry tree. The bird cherries were ripening to yellow and red and there was scarlet blossom on Eve's runner beans. The courgette plants had flowers shaped like yellow lilies and the gooseberries were dark red beads, but beads that grew hair on their crimson skins.

"Of *me?*" said Eve. "Envious of me?"

"You've got someone you can be happy with. You're in a good relationship."

Liza waited for Eve to deny it or even tell him not to say "relationship." She didn't. She gave Jonathan a mysterious sidelong glance, her eyes half-closed.

"I don't want you to envy me," she said. "I'd rather you were jealous."

There was silence. At last Jonathan said, "Of him?"

"Why not? How do you think I have felt about Victoria?"

Eve got up then and carried the tea things into the house. Instead of following her, Jonathan sat there on the grass, looking glum. He pulled a daisy out of the lawn and picked the petals off. Liza thought he was getting to look old. The freshness had gone out of his face and there were lines across his forehead. His eyes had once been of the most piercing clear blue, but the color was muddied like a blue china bowl with dirty water in it.

She expected him to stay to supper and perhaps for the night. Where Bruno had been, beside Eve in bed, he would be found in the morning. But he didn't even stay to eat with them and was gone by seven. The next day Liza thought Eve seemed particularly pleased and happy and she connected this with the appearance of Jonathan at their door at nine in the morning, calling in to say good-bye on his way back to London.

Sean said, "This is five years ago you're talking about, right?"

She nodded. They were in bed now, snuggled close together for warmth under the two quilts. Sean had bought a second one he'd seen in a closing-down sale. The caravan got bitterly cold at night, but if they kept a heater burning, the condensation was streaming down the walls by morning and their pillows felt damp. Liza, her head on his shoulder, his arms tightly around her, thought of those warm dry weeks, her bedroom with the windows wide open at night, lessons, lessons, lessons, every day in the garden, and Eve saying, "You see, if you went to a so-called proper school you'd be on holiday now, you wouldn't be learning anything but just running wild."

"Wasn't that around about the time of the big storm? What they called the hurricane? I remember because it was when I'd just got to be sixteen. I'd got my first job and I had to get up at five. I was in our kitchen at home, making myself a cup of tea, and the oak tree next door blew over and came through the roof.

It was only a lean-to, our kitchen, and the roof broke like an eggshell. Lucky I was quick off the mark, I got out just in time. It must have been like September."

"It was October. October the fifteenth."

"What a memory! I reckon you had a lot of trees come down at Shrove. Is that how you remember?"

The Day of the Hurricane, the last day she ever gave a name to.

"You're not to hurry me, Sean. I'll get to that soon. We got the hurricane very badly at Shrove. We were one of the worst-hit places, and you'll see why I remember it, the precise date and everything. But there was something else happened first."

The outbuildings at Shrove House were seldom used. They had been stables once and there was a coach house. The stables were built in the same architectural style as the house, of small red bricks with white facings, a pediment over the central building, and above it a clock tower on which the clock face was blue and the clock hands gold. The weathervane on the tower was a running fox with brush extended.

Mr. Frost kept his lawnmowers, the big one he rode on and the small one with which he did around the flowerbeds, in the section of stable to the left of the coach house. Other garden tools were kept in there as well as a ladder and an industrial vacuum cleaner. As far as Liza knew, no one had ever kept cars in the stables. Perhaps they might have done so when old Mr. Tobias was alive, but Jonathan always left his car standing out in the courtyard in front of the stables, and visitors left their cars there too. The stables were really useless, no one went into them, and they remained standing, Liza had heard Jonathan say, only because they were pretty and also a listed building. That meant they were of historic value and must never be pulled down.

She had never been inside them, though she had once seen Mr. Frost come riding out of the section by the coach house on the little tractor that pulled the mower. She came to search them as a last resort.

It was years since she had needed the library steps to climb up to the picture frame for the key to the television room. At nearly twelve she was almost as tall as Eve, would be much taller by the time she was grown-up. Eve, in any case, had long ceased to bother to hide the key or even take it out of the lock. She must have decided Liza was too old now to be seduced by the charms of television, too mature to be intrigued by locked rooms, or thoroughly conditioned in the discipline of a sequestered life. These days she even pushed the vacuum cleaner about in that room in Liza's presence and seemed to take it as quite natural her daughter never asked what the box with the screen on it was.

When she needed the steps but couldn't find them it was for quite another purpose, their primary purpose. *The Confessions of an English Opium Eater* was on the top shelf, far out of reach. The book would have been out of Jonathan's reach and he was six feet three. Although she knew that it was all of two years since she had put the steps back in the library, that she had several times used them in the library since then, she still went to look behind the long curtains in the morning room.

Returning to the library, she saw why they had been replaced. The new ones were up in the dark corner, farthest from the windows, wooden ones this time, perhaps of dark oak, and almost invisible against the dark oak floor where the carpet ended. They were not really steps at all but more like a piece of a staircase consisting of three stairs. Jonathan must have brought them with him when he came in August. Liza could see without attempting to move them that even when she stood on the top stair she wasn't going to be high enough to reach that shelf.

She started to search the house for the missing steps. Eve said she wasn't old enough yet for De Quincey, she wouldn't understand the *Confessions,* there would be plenty of time for her to read it when she was older. And Liza hadn't even wanted it that much when she first came into the library. The title had drawn her to it, for it seemed to have something to do with those drugs she heard about on television. But she wanted it now. She wanted it because she couldn't have it, she couldn't reach it, it was up there in its faded blue binding with the faded gilt flowers on its spine, smugly sitting where it had sat undisturbed for years, for perhaps a hundred years.

The steps wouldn't be in any of the bedrooms but she searched them anyway. She found clothes that must be Victoria's in the wardrobe of what she had always thought the nicest bedroom, a big, light room that looked across the water meadows to the river. A skirt hung there and a pair of jeans and the green silk shirt she had been wearing the first time Liza ever saw her. There were also an embroidered white cotton nightdress and a matching dressing gown. It looked as if Victoria had been sleeping in that room while Jonathan slept in the big room at the front. The steps weren't in there either, or in any of the cupboards, or downstairs in any of the rooms that gathered around the kitchen, the boot room and the pantry, the washing room, the larder, and the storeroom.

Liza went outside to the stables. She could hear the drone of Mr. Frost's mower from the bit of lawn behind the shrubberies. The stables were never locked. There were no locks on the doors, though the coach house had a padlock fastening together the handles on each of its double doors. For some reason, she left looking in the section where the mower had been till last, which was strange because it was the obvious place. Except for the one where the tools were kept, the stables were all quite empty. She couldn't open the coach house doors, only peer through the cracks in them. They were old doors with quite a big split between two of the boards. She could just make out a car inside.

The steps were propped up against the wall between where the tractor had been and where the small mower stood. Liza took them into the house, carried them into the library, and climbed up to get *The Confessions of an English Opium Eater*. It was while she was coming down with the book in her hand that the significance of a car in the coach house where no car had been before fully struck her.

Mr. Frost was now in sight, wheeling around the big lawn on his tractor, wearing gloves and ear muffs. He didn't see her. She replaced the steps, then thought better of it, carried them out again and propped them up in front of the locked doors. High up under the pediment were two small windows.

Liza climbed the steps to the top. That brought her just high enough to see over one of the windowsills. The car stood in the middle of the coach house floor with plenty of space around it. Even so, she couldn't see the name of the make, but she could see the registration plates with the letter at the end of the number instead of the beginning. It wasn't too dark to make out the color, a deep brown, the burnt sienna of Bruno's paintbox. Bruno was gone, but this was Bruno's car, the Lancia car Bruno's mother had had for ten years and only driven seven thousand miles.

The sound of the mower approaching made her look around. Mr. Frost got off his tractor to open the stable. He never talked much, he wasn't the kind of grown-up to ask what she was doing.

"Mind you don't fall," he said.

Going home, carrying the book, she had thought of that night after Bruno had left, how she had slept so uneasily and dreamed so much she couldn't tell in the morning what had been dream and what real. The car she had heard—that had been Bruno's car. She had heard Eve driving Bruno's car up here to hide it in the coach house.

Sean was asleep.

Liza wondered how long he had been asleep, at what point in her narrative he had ceased to listen. Scheherazade. Did the king or sultan or whatever he was fall asleep while she told her stories? Was that in fact the reason she never reached the end of each tale? Because her husband fell asleep first?

Sean was snoring lightly. She pushed him over onto his side so that his back was toward her. Another thing she wondered about was if the sultan and Scheherazade made love before she started on the story or in the middle or what? They must have done that, that was the point of his marrying all those women, wasn't it? There was nothing about it in the book she had read. There wouldn't be, she thought, people cut things out of versions meant for children. Even for children who'd seen what she had seen.

Invisible in the dark, she smiled to herself at Sean's squeamishness. She hadn't told him about the smell of those stained rags or, to spare him, about the red paint fingerprints on the stone floor of the little castle. Up in the vaulted ceiling among the beams a spider had caught the death's-head moth in its dusty web. Sean wouldn't have wanted to hear about that, either, the rare moth long dead among the dusty threads, but the skull pattern on its back still palely gleaming.

fifteen

A disused airfield near the place where the caravan was parked provided them with somewhere for Liza to have her driving lessons. With Sean in the suicide seat—his words—she drove up and down the old runways and learned how to do a three-point turn on the flat area outside a dilapidated hangar.

"You'll pass your test first go," Sean said.

As November began, Liza began to think more and more about Eve and about her trial, which was surely due. She regretted now that when she had the chance she hadn't learned more about crimes and justice and courts. Eve would have known, Eve could have told her.

For instance, would they have it here in the city, which had once been the place the train started from? Or would it be far away in London at what she thought might be called Newgate? I must go to London sometime, she thought to herself. It's absurd never having been to London, even Sean's been to London. She ought to start buying newspapers, but she didn't know which one would be best. Already she had seen enough of them to know that the little ones with the tall headlines would only print the most sensational or sexy parts of a trial while the big ones with pictures of politicians might not print it at all. Television might have it on only once and that maybe on the evening Sean was watching his football.

Life wasn't easy in the caravan. If you wanted to be warm you also got wet. Sean got hold of a tarpaulin from a farmer who had used it to protect a haystack from heavy rain and they spread it right over the caravan. That helped, but it also made it dark. All their water had to be fetched from the stream and boiled. It was impossible to wash clothes and bed linen, which had to be taken to the one launderette still remaining within a ten-mile radius. They used two inches of water in a bowl and tried to wash themselves all over in that.

Liza had got very good at sneaking baths at Mrs. Spurdell's, quite often managing to have one while Mrs. Spurdell was actually in the house, waiting till she was on the phone—she spent hours on the phone talking to her daughter or her friends—and taking two minutes in the tub before giving the bathroom a thorough clean. Even so, Mrs. Spurdell had once or twice remarked on the quantity of water she had heard gurgling down the plughole.

At the school half-term, when Mr. Spurdell had also been in

the house, bathing was impossible, the risk was too great. His study was upstairs next door to the bathroom and he was usually in the study, or liable to go in there. On that late October day, a Monday, she arrived at Aspen Close determined on having a bath. Mrs. Spurdell would be out for an hour, having her hair done. Liza had overheard her making the appointment. She was therefore dismayed to find Mr. Spurdell at home, apparently recovering from the flu, which had struck him down on the previous Friday afternoon while he was reading, according to his wife, Spenser's *Faerie Queene* with the A-Levels English form.

He wasn't up but she had no reason to believe he was asleep. Mrs. Spurdell said he would probably get up later and come down in his dressing gown. Then, if she was still at the hairdresser's, Liza could make him a cup of tea. Mrs. Spurdell put on her new Burberry. She tied a plastic rain hood around her head, not because it was raining, it wasn't, but to make sure she had it with her to protect her set on the way home.

Liza thought she would have to do what she had advised Sean to do. Knowing nothing of hotels, she just the same understood that they must have a great many bathrooms. The Duke's Head, which she passed on her way to Aspen Close, must have more bathrooms than any private house. If Sean didn't want to pay for the swimming pool or the showers, why didn't he just walk into the Duke's Head, march upstairs as if he was a guest there, find a bathroom, and have a bath? Who would know? He'd have to make sure to take a towel with him, of course. He could put a folded towel inside his jacket and take a plastic bag to put it in after it got damp.

It was stealing hot water, Sean said, it was dishonest. He was quite shocked. Stay dirty then, said Liza. She wouldn't think twice about doing it, in fact she'd probably do it on her way to meet him after work. Realizing that she couldn't because she had no towel made her feel cross and she thumped her way into the study, dragging the vacuum cleaner behind her.

Mr. Spurdell had acquired two new books since she was last in there. Liza cared very little about Mrs. Spurdell having a new Burberry or her hair done or unlimited hot water or Mr. Spurdell driving a six-month-old BMW, but she did envy them the books. She resented them for the books, it made her hate Mr. Spurdell especially, though in many ways he seemed nicer than his wife. She sometimes saw him on Friday afternoons returning home just before she was due to leave. The new books he had got were a *Life of Dickens* and *The Collected Short Stories of Saki.*

What wouldn't she give to read that *Life of Dickens*! She could never afford it, she wouldn't even be able to afford it when it came out in paperback. Quickly she forgot all about Mr. Spurdell. She ceased to listen for him. The Dickens in its brown-and-gold jacket was in her hands, she was sitting at the desk reading the introduction, when he came quietly into the room. It was only because of the little dry cough he gave that she knew he was there. She jumped up, clutching the book.

He was a small man, as thin as Mrs. Spurdell was fat. Liza had sometimes thought they were like Jack Sprat and his wife, he able to eat no fat and she no lean. He looked old, an old man who should have retired by now, his jowls melting into a withered neck, his head bald but for a white fringe around the back. Over striped pajamas he wore a brown tweed dressing gown with a cord around the waist tied in a neat bow.

His genial smile brought her immense relief. She wouldn't have to go back to Sean now and tell him she'd got the sack.

Relief became indignation when he said, still smiling, apologizing as if to an ignorant child, that it was a pity there were so few pictures in that book.

"I don't want pictures," Liza said and she knew her tone was surly.

Up went his white tufts of eyebrows. "How old are you?" he said.

After she had spoken the truth she remembered too late the lie she had told his wife. "I'm nearly seventeen."

"Yes, I would have guessed about that. Some of my pupils are your age, only they prefer to be called students." He held out his hand for the book and she gave it to him. "Thank you. I haven't read it yet." Without knowing in the least how she could tell, she fancied this was the way teachers behaved. Bossy. Commanding. Imparting information. As she thought this, he imparted some. "Dickens was a great English writer, some would say the greatest. Have you read any of his books at school?"

"I don't go to school," she said, and added, "anymore. I don't go anymore." What did he think, that she took days off school to come and work for his wife? "But I've read Dickens. I've read *Bleak House* and *David Copperfield* and *Oliver Twist* and *Nicholas Nickleby* and *A Tale of Two Cities.*"

His evident astonishment gave her a lot of pleasure. She thought he'd ask her why she left school so young, she was prepared for almost anything, but not for him to point to the several volumes of Dickens he had in paperback and ask her if she had read *Our Mutual Friend.*

"I told you the ones I've read," she said but not this time in the surly voice.

"Well, you're a surprising young lady. Not quite what you seem, is that right?"

Liza thought this was truer than he knew. She changed the

subject, asked him if he would like her to make him tea, and when he said he would, preceded him downstairs.

Mrs. Spurdell was back before the kettle had boiled, recounting to her husband some long tale of how the hairdresser had read their daughter's name in a magazine, as the author of a letter to the editor about family law. The hairdresser—"who was really quite an intelligent girl, considering"—had cut out the letter but forgotten to bring it. She would bring it next time. Philippa was so modest she hadn't said a word about it. She hadn't mentioned it to her father, had she?

While this was going on, Liza went back upstairs. She finished the study, she made the bed Mr. Spurdell had recently vacated, and ran the vacuum cleaner across the carpet. By then it was time to leave. Mrs. Spurdell was paying her, fishing about in a jar on the windowsill for a five-pound note and claiming to have mistaken a ten-pee piece for a fifty-pee, when her husband came back into the kitchen and handed Liza *Our Mutual Friend* and *The Old Curiosity Shop.*

"I should like them back sometime but there's no hurry."

"You'd better write your name on the flyleaf, dear," said Mrs. Spurdell. She laughed reminiscently. "Do you remember how Jane used to write inside *her* books: 'This book was stolen from Jane Spurdell'?"

It was extremely rude but Liza didn't care. Having something new to read was wonderful. She'd been spinning out the *Life of Mary Wollstonecraft,* making it last, which was an irritating way to have to read something. Mr. Spurdell giving her *Our Mutual Friend* was rather interesting, a sort of coincidence, because that was the book she'd tried to read when she gave up on *The Confessions of an English Opium Eater.* Eve had been right about that, she wasn't old enough for it, and she hadn't been old enough for *Our Mutual Friend,* either, but she would be now.

She'd started to read it that same evening, when she got back from finding Bruno's car in the Shrove coach house. It was a strange thing but she'd never really considered telling Eve what she'd found or asking her why the car was there. She thought she knew why and then she wasn't sure if she did or not. It might only mean that Bruno was coming back, that for some reason he had gone without his car and Eve was storing it for him, he hadn't gone for good. Eve had said he had, but Liza no longer entirely trusted her to tell the truth.

After concentrating on it for all of an hour, she had abandoned the De Quincey and attempted *Our Mutual Friend.* Perhaps she was tired because she hadn't been able to cope with more than the first page. She still lay awake a long time, wondering about the car and what might have happened to Bruno. Nobody had ever known where Bruno was except his mother and now she was dead. His wife hadn't known and neither had his wife's friend the dentist. The estate agent had but Eve had written to him.

That was the night she dreamed Bruno was with them still but about to leave. His silky brown hair was tied back with a piece of ribbon so that you could clearly see the two gold rings in his ear. And his face had even more than usual that angelic look, like a saint in a painting, that so belied the rough speech that sometimes came from that cherubic mouth. She didn't see him leave in the dream. Eve told her he had gone, and later she heard a gun being fired. She was walking in the wood and she heard shots behind her. But this was all in the dream, not in life. On the actual night after Eve said Bruno had gone she had heard no shots, she had heard nothing but a heavy object dragged downstairs and a car being driven away.

Where had the car been all day? Bruno couldn't have gone away in it or it wouldn't have been there for Eve to drive up to Shrove in the nighttime. But it wasn't there, it hadn't been outside when Liza came home. So had Eve hidden it somewhere? Liza realized she could have hidden it almost anywhere, behind the birch tree copse or under the overhanging branches of a hedge, she could have hidden it a few yards from the gatehouse and Liza wouldn't have seen.

Watching a football match that was coming from somewhere in Germany, Sean didn't for a while try to stop her reading. He no more expected her to watch football than she expected him to read Dickens. They had a bottle of wine the supermarket had on sale, the week's special offer.

Rain lashed the tarpaulin that covered the caravan. A howling gale blew the rain in savage spurts against the uncovered parts of the windows so hard it sounded as if they must break. The caravan rocked and shivered.

Liza and Sean sat close together with one of their quilts wrapped around their legs. While Liza read about Eugene Wrayburn, Sean watched the German team soundly beat the English one. He switched off with a sigh and, having first put his arm around her, began to comb her hair. It was a cunning move on his part, he knew the sensuous pleasure she took in it, stretching like a cat and extending her neck as the comb passed slowly through the curtain of smooth dark hair.

He said softly, "What had happened to him, Bruno, I mean?"

Liza closed her book. "I don't know. I mean, I didn't know then. I found out later." She considered. "You'll have to wait till I come to the hurricane."

"Okay, then what about those Tobiases? They split up, didn't they?"

"Not until the following year. But I never saw Victoria again. Jonathan wrote to Eve and told her he was living at Ullswater and Victoria was living in the London house, and soon after that Victoria left altogether. I think she went off with someone."

"So your mum started hoping again?"

"Yes. But that was a way off. I don't know what she felt about the divorce—they got divorced two years later—she never showed me her feelings about that. Somehow I think she understood she'd played it all wrong before."

"She should have made herself harder to get," said Sean.

"Or easier. If she'd gone with him to all those places he wanted her to go to, even to London sometimes, if she'd done that I don't think he'd have ever taken up with Victoria. Eve was prettier than Victoria and cleverer and he'd known her since forever. She had all the advantages. Except that she'd never go away from Shrove, not even for a weekend." She looked up at him. "Should I have made myself harder to get, Sean? I was easy, wasn't I? I just jumped into your arms."

"Oh, you." He laughed and, putting the comb down, hugged her in his arms. "You was a real little innocent, you didn't know no better."

"Was I? Shall I tell you about the hurricane?"

"Wait a minute, I'll fill up your glass. There's one thing I want to know first. Didn't no one come looking for Bruno?"

"Who was there to look? If his mother had still been alive it might have been different. If he'd said he wanted to buy that house. If he'd been to a lawyer or whatever it is you have to do when you buy a house. If the sale of his mother's house hadn't gone through and he'd still been waiting for the money. If he'd still been living in those rooms over the greengrocer's. But as it was, nobody knew where he'd lived and no one needed to get in touch with him."

"It gives you the creeps when you come to think of it."

"I went back into the little castle and everything of his was gone, the paintings, the canvases, the paints, and that pile of rags. It was all gone and the place had been scrubbed out. Even the ceiling, she'd cleaned the ceiling and got rid of the spider's web with the moth in it."

"Those rags, what was it you thought was on them?" Sean spoke in a low voice, tentatively. "You never thought that was paint, did you?"

"I did then. Now I think it was blood."

Sean was silent, his face grim. After a moment or two he said, "Tell about the hurricane, then."

"There's one other thing first. That picture Bruno painted of me, it turned up on our living room wall. One morning I came downstairs and there it was. Eve had taken away the Shrove at sunset picture and put the one of me there instead."

"What did she do that for?"

"I don't know. It didn't look like me, but I suppose she liked it. I'll come to the hurricane now."

As if to encourage her, the wind slapped another burst of rain against the window behind them. The caravan rattled. It hadn't rained that night, the Night of the Storm, the Hurricane, the Great Gale. The storm had been dry, an arid tempest that came up out of the Atlantic, bearing salt on its back. Salt lay in drifts on the windows of Shrove the next day, white as frost, dry crystals the wind had sucked off the sea.

"All the leaves were still on the trees," she said, "that was the worst of it. If the branches had been bare the gale wouldn't have been able to pull the trees over, but they were still in full leaf, leaves don't really fall till November, and they made the treetops like great sails."

"Was you at the gatehouse, you and your mum?"

"When weren't we there? We never went anywhere."

She would have slept through it, enormous though the noise of it was. A heavy sleeper, at the age of eleven she would have slept through bombs falling. Eve woke her up. Eve, who was frightened of nothing, was frightened of this. She woke her up for companionship, for someone to be with, not to be alone while the world was torn to pieces around her.

It was just after four in the morning. Pitch dark and the wind roaring up the valley like an invisible train, a ghost train. The real train that had once run along the valley had never sounded as loud as this. They still had electricity when she came downstairs, rubbing her eyes, peering about her, but the lights went out as she entered the living room. Somewhere out there the wind had brought the power lines down.

"What is it? What's happening?"

Eve said she didn't know, she'd never heard wind like this. Not in this country. We didn't have hurricanes.

"Perhaps it's not a hurricane," Liza said. "Perhaps it's the end of the world. The Apocalypse. Or a nuclear bomb. Someone's dropped a nuclear bomb."

Eve, putting candles into jam jars, said how did she know about things like that? How did she know about the Apocalypse? Who had told her about nuclear bombs? *The television,* thought Liza. She didn't answer.

"Of course it's not a bomb," said Eve.

The candle flames guttered as the windows rattled. Something of the wind penetrated even in here. The curtains bellied out and flattened again against the glass. Eve tried the radio before she remembered that electricity worked that too. For the same reason she couldn't make tea. The nearest gas was five miles away. Liza thought how isolated they were, the nearest house in that village where Bruno had nearly bought a house two miles distant. It was like being marooned on an island in the midst of a rough sea.

She looked out of the window, the glass shuddering against her face. It was still too dark to see much beyond the tendrils of creeper that cloaked the gatehouse till the leaves fell. These streamed out in the wind like blown hair, pulling a black curtain across the window. An enormous crash from somewhere not too far distant drove her back into the middle of the room.

"Come away," said Eve.

Roof tiles clattered off one by one, three of them, each making a sharp crack as it fell and smashed on the stones. The wind was both constant and sporadic. All the time it blew at a steady rate, but it came in gusts too, each one thunderous, tearing through trees and leafy branches, between tree trunks, among bushes, each gust blowing itself out on a howl and a final crash. The earth shook and the ground heaved.

"The trees," said Eve, and then, "the trees."

Her face was white. She put her hands over her ears, then brought them down and clasped them, wringing them. Dismayed, Liza watched her pace the room. This was Shrove where it was happening, Shrove which meant more to her than anything in this world or out of it. These were Shrove trees and at each nearby or distant crash Eve winced. Once she put her hand over her mouth as if to stop herself crying out.

At about six it started to get light. Dawn had been a yellow bar across the eastern horizon. Liza crept out into the kitchen to look at it, for Eve wouldn't let her go upstairs. The wind abated not at all with the pale spreading of light but seemed to take new life from it, roaring and tossing and circling with a shrill whistling sound. A single leafy branch spun in the air and crashed to the ground. The walls of the gatehouse shuddered. The windows rattled. Liza watched the darkness recede from the sky, the livid streak fade, the gray color whiten, and a mass of high, clotted, scurrying cloud reveal itself.

The cherry tree lay across the garden, its branches and dense foliage spread over the lawn, the flowerbeds, Eve's kitchen garden, its roots pointing dark brown, thready fingers into the air. As she watched, the whistling wind, the invisible engine, struck the ash that marked the edge of the lane and the giant tree shuddered. It seemed to hold itself suspended before a quivering convulsed it and it toppled over out of Liza's sight, leaving a sudden white space where all her life had stood this strong, stout, leaf-crowned barrier. She gasped, putting her hand up to her lips.

"Come away," said Eve. "Don't look."

It wasn't until the afternoon that the gale blew itself out. Eve had tried to go outside before that but the wind had beaten her back. Broken branches and twigs, dying leaves, covered the front garden and the lane. One of the Shrove gates had come loose from its fastenings and slammed shut, tendrils of solanum trapped between its iron curlicues.

Liza had never seen her mother in such a tragic mood. She was unhappier than she had been when she heard of Jonathan Tobias's marriage. She was worse than unhappy, she was distraught. The sight of the fallen cherry tree made her weep and she kept crying out that it wasn't real, it couldn't be true.

"I can't believe it, I can't believe it. What's happening? What's happened to our climate? This is madness."

From the gatehouse they couldn't see much. The balsam still stood, though stripped of one of its limbs, but fallen trees blocked their view on all sides. It was as if the gatehouse had been surrounded by a barricade of broken tree trunks and branches, as if the wind, invested with purposefulness and malice, had built it up to hem them in. They were in the midst of a fortification of wind-hewn timber. Liza could see that they would have to climb over logs and scramble through leafy boughs to get out the front gate. Eventually they emerged together at three in the afternoon, clambering over the balsam's huge bough, which blocked their way.

Liza felt very small and alone but she would have considered herself too old to take Eve's hand if Eve hadn't taken hers first. Hand in hand, they stumbled toward the gateway of Shrove. Inside the park, devastation lay on both sides of them, ruined trees and shrubs in heaps where they had fallen, havoc as if man-made, Eve whispered, like pictures she had seen of countryside after battles. Tree stumps stood with shredded trunks pointing skyward. A bird's nest, a huge structure of thick twigs and woven reeds, had been torn from some once-high treetop and lay in their path.

"Paradise destroyed," Eve said.

Two of the great cedars had gone. The limes were down, most of the ancient trees, only the slender supple birches and the little pyramidal hornbeams remaining. Laying waste the park, the wind had spared the house, which stood staring calmly at them, its glazed eyes all intact, its roof unscathed. All that was changed was that a stone vase had tumbled off a pillar at the foot of the steps.

A pale sun, weak and watery, though no rain had fallen, gleamed like a puddle of silver among the soft drifting clouds. Beyond the gardens, beyond the water meadows, a waste of felled willows and splintered poplars, beyond the shining ribbon of the river, the high hills showed hollow places in their woods, holes in the fabric of tree cover as if scissors had ripped rents in cloth.

The air was scented with sap from the ripped leaves and salt from the distant sea. All was silent, the birds silent, but for a plover making its unearthly cry as it wheeled above them.

"Eve was in an awful state," Liza said to Sean. "She was like someone bereaved. Well, like I imagine someone bereaved would be. You know you read in books about people tearing out their hair. She almost did that. I found her sitting in our living room clutching handfuls of her hair. She moaned and cried and threw herself about as if she was in pain. I didn't know what to do, I'd never seen her like that.

"I wonder if she'd have been half as bad if it wasn't trees that had been destroyed but me. That was when I began to get the feeling Shrove was more important to her than I was. It frightened me and I didn't know what to do.

"There wasn't anyone I could turn to, you see. There wasn't anyone. Well, the milkman came and he was useless. Now the trains didn't run anymore he could only talk about the weather and I'd had enough of weather for a lifetime. Mr. Frost came to see if there was anything he could do. I said, you could get her a doctor and I think he thought I was crazy. What's she got wrong with her, then, he said, and I couldn't answer him, I knew he'd think Eve was mad or I was. No one's phone was working, he said, and it might be a week before we got our electricity back. I was left alone with her and I felt helpless. I was only eleven.

"She calmed down a bit next day. She lay on the sofa. We couldn't cook anything but we'd got bread and cheese and fruit. I went up to Shrove and found a packet of a dozen candles. I found a Calor gas burner we could boil a kettle and an egg on, though it took hours. She fell asleep in the afternoon and I went up into the wood, the bit we called our wood.

"I don't know why I went really. It didn't upset me the way it had her, but I'd seen enough fallen trees and destruction to last me forever. But I still went up there. Maybe I thought that if somehow the wind hadn't done much damage there, if for some reason it had escaped, that would be something to tell her and cheer her up.

"Afterward I wished I hadn't gone. I wished I'd stayed at home with her. It caused me such a lot of worry."

"What d'you mean?" Sean asked.

"You'll see. It was what I found there," she said. "Of course it didn't matter in the end."

~

As soon as she came close to the wood, to what had been the wood, she knew her hope had been forlorn. From a distance you couldn't see what lay beyond the outer circle of trees, she and Eve hadn't been able to see when they walked up the lane on the previous day, for the oaks and chestnuts on the perimeter remained standing. Like a whirlwind the gale had bored its way in through the outer ring and once inside behaved like a maddened animal, spinning in circles and destroying every vulnerable thing in its orbit.

Not quite everything, she saw as she came carefully between the standing oaks. A few young trees still stood. Here and there a giant had resisted the onslaught while one or two mature trees leaned at an angle, their final collapse delayed. But between them lay devastation.

The leaves on the tumbled limbs and branches were still fresh. They were still as if growing from twigs that proceeded from branches that grew from a living, rooted trunk. A sea of leaves lay before her. There was no wind now, only a little breeze, a joke of nature playing with destruction, that fluttered all the leaves, scalloped oak and pointed cherry, five-fingered chestnut and oval beech. The leaf sea was a dark quivering green from which protruded here and there an upturned root like a fin, or a broken trunk like the funnel of a wrecked ship. It reminded her of the sea after a storm in a picture in the library at Shrove, for the real sea she had never seen.

For a while she stood there, just looking. Then she waded into the sea of green. Once she began, the image ceased to hold, the comparison was wrong. This was not a matter of striding through water, but of clambering across a rough terrain. Where once had been paths and clearings were broken wood and torn brambles, concealed stumps to trip her up and shattered logs to block her way.

Yesterday she would have been incredulous if anyone had told her she might not find her way through the wood. But so it was. Everything was different. The wind had laid it waste and made a nearly impenetrable wilderness where yesterday morning had stood the ranks of trees and between them, in the depths, had stretched aisles of mysterious green shade. All was havoc now and all was curiously the same. Was it here, for instance, that the great isolated beech had stood, spreading its branches in an arc so huge as to form a circle of deep shade with a radius of fifty yards in which no grass or plant could grow? Or was it here that the larches had been, conifers leafless in the winter but green with new needles in the spring? She couldn't tell, but when she found the beech, felled and prone, its vast trunk gray as a wet seal, its wrenched-out roots clotted with earth and stones, when she saw that she could have cried like Eve.

Struggling onward, climbing over fallen trunks and pushing

aside sheaths of thick foliage, she made her way aimlessly, hardly knowing what she was seeking. Somewhere it hadn't happened? A region of the wood miraculously untouched?

There was just one place. But this only because no trees had stood in the clearing she came to. She had an idea where she was now, in the very heart of the ruined wood, its center, where once a ring of cherry trees and field maples had encircled a grassy space. On the tree stump in the middle of that grass she had sometimes picnicked.

She moved toward it now and sat down on the broad, flat, smooth stump. She looked about her, aware for the first time of the silence. No birds sang. There had always been birds in the wood but at the hurricane's assault they had departed.

The maples and cherries were mostly fallen but some still stood, the biggest and oldest leaning at a steep angle. She wondered if it would be possible to save those half-fallen trees, if there was some way of hauling them up and holding them. Who would do it? Who was there to care? She got up and made her way to the half-toppled cherry, put her hands on its trunk. It felt firm, as steady as an upright, growing tree.

There was nothing to do now but go back, to try to find her way back through the welter of broken branches. She ducked under an overhanging limb of maple, looked down and recoiled, jumping backward and hitting her head. She scarcely felt the pain. Her breath indrawn sharply, she put her hand up over her mouth, though she had no inclination to cry out.

Almost at her feet, *at* her feet until she had retreated that step or two, lay a long bundle of sacking. She could see it was a sack, of the kind Eve said they used to put potatoes in and of which there was a pile in the stable at Shrove, though it was stiff with earth and gravel. And it wasn't just a sack, it was a bundle with something inside it. A length of string, now quite black, had been tied around the top and another length around the bottom.

No, not the top and the bottom, Liza found herself saying, not that but the head and the feet. She came a little closer, not frightened but awed. It had made her flinch and jump back at first; now she was curious. Whatever this was, the storm had unearthed it, tearing up a tree root and heaving it out of its burying place.

Its burying place . . . She was conscious of the smell now. It was a smell she had never smelled before. Strange, then, that she knew it was of something rotten, something that decayed, reminding her—yes, she knew what it was—of long ago, when Heidi and Rudi used to come. One of them had buried a meaty bone and later, perhaps weeks later, Eve while gardening had dug it up, stinking, maggoty, as green as jade, a beautiful color really. . . .

She knelt down. She held her breath, somehow knowing she must hold her breath. There was a tear in the sacking at the top of the bundle just above the string. She picked at it, making the hole bigger. It split open quite suddenly and a flood of soft brown, silky hair spilled out. It spilled into her hands, thick and slippery. The hair came off in her hands and she was holding it. She stumbled away and was sick among the broken branches.

s i x t e e n

"IT was Bruno?" Sean said.

She nodded.

"You poor kid. A kid might never get over something like that."

She wished he wouldn't say "somefink" but there was nothing to be done about it.

"Well, I did. I got over it. I didn't even dream about it. It's a funny thing, you know, but you can't help being sick. It's not what your mind does, it's your body. I was curious, I really wanted to know, I suppose you could say I was *interested.* I knew it was Bruno's hair, I knew it was Bruno dead in there, and I hadn't liked Bruno, I'd hated him, I was glad he was dead, but I threw up just the same. Weird, isn't it?"

He didn't understand. "You must have been shattered to bits. You didn't know what you was doing."

Useless to persist. She gave up trying. "I didn't know what to do next. There wasn't anything I could do but go back home and leave that thing lying there for anyone to find."

"Let's get this straight," said Sean. "She'd killed him, right? She's real bad news, your mum, isn't she? She'd killed him like she killed the man the dogs went for?"

"Oh, yes, she'd killed him. I don't know how. I never said anything about it to her. I was only eleven but I knew she'd killed him and—well, there didn't seem anything to say, if you know what I mean."

He didn't know. She could tell that. "She was in a state, anyway. She was depressed, in a real black depression, for quite a long time. I wasn't going to tell her a thing like that, not something that would worry her as well."

"There must have been someone you could tell. Tobias, like, or the old chap—Frost was his name? No one'd have expected you to get the police, not at your age, but hopefully they'd have done that for you. Didn't you never think of that?"

It was dark in the caravan. She looked at him in the dark and made out his puzzled expression. "She's my *mother,*" she said quietly. He didn't respond, and when she said how it had worked out for the best, how the body was concealed once more, he hardly reacted. "She killed him because he threatened everything," Liza said. "He was going to part her and me and make us leave Shrove."

"Okay. No need to get excited." Sean hesitated. "How did she do it?"

"I don't know. I didn't hear any shots that day he disappeared, but I wouldn't have so far away. You remember that blood on the rags in the little castle? I think she may have used a knife."

He had gone a little pale. "Wasn't you scared of being with her? I mean, she could have turned on you."

"Oh, no." Liza laughed. "I was like the bird that lived inside the crocodile's mouth, I was safe whoever else wasn't."

"I wish you hadn't told me, not that about the sack and the hair. I shan't get no sleep."

"I shall," said Liza, and she was asleep very quickly, her arm around his waist and her forehead pressed between his shoulder blades. If he lay awake, haunted by what she'd told him, she was oblivious of it.

Cautiousness made her rather quiet next morning. She boiled the water for their tea and her perfunctory face-washing in silence. It was perhaps unwise to go into too many details with him. She had told him rather too much on the previous night but now she would be more careful. That remark of his about the police she hadn't liked. Eve had been arrested, had no doubt appeared in one court, was somewhere in a prison, but still there must be many things they didn't know and need not know.

It wasn't one of her days at Mrs. Spurdell's, but still, "I'll come into town with you," she said. It was almost the first thing she'd said that morning. She took the spare set of car keys with her.

For the first time she went all the way into the Superway car park with him, noting where he put the car. He went off into the store and she, having bought a pair of bath towels at Marks and Spencer, wandered casually into the Duke's Head, where she encountered no one in the front hall or on the stairs.

There was no soap in the bathroom. She should have thought of that but how was she to know? She took a bath just the same, enjoying a prolonged soak in the hot water, free from any anxiety about Mrs. Spurdell returning unexpectedly, and dried herself on both of the thick fleecy towels. On her way out a man in a suit and tie asked her if she needed help. Liza said she was looking for Mrs. Cooper. She didn't know many names, having come across so few people, and had to fall back on those from fiction or, as in this case, the name of Eve's invented cleaner.

"Is she staying in the hotel?"

Liza said she was expected today or tomorrow. The man looked in his book and said she'd made a mistake but cast no suspicious glances at the Marks and Spencer's carrier full of wet towels. He didn't seem at all cross or anxious for her to go and as he talked to her about the fictitious Mrs. Cooper, speculating as to where this woman might be staying or how a member of his staff could have made an error, Liza was aware that the way he looked at her and the way he spoke were full of admiration. As Sean would put it, he fancied her.

From Sean alone had she experienced this, had accepted it without thinking others might share his feelings. Now she was beginning to understand desiring her wasn't some idiosyncracy of his but might even be common. She felt her power.

"Don't hesitate to come back if we can help you at all," the man said as she left.

At the rear of Superway she got into the car and started the engine. She drove around the town, teaching herself things Sean hadn't been able to teach her on the airfield. How to start on a hill, for instance, and how to stop in a hurry. He would have been cross because she hadn't got a license or insurance, but that didn't matter because she wasn't going to tell him.

After returning the car, she had to wait nearly an hour for the bus to get her back and then there was a mile-long walk from the bus stop in the rain.

The days that followed her discovery of Bruno's body remained very fresh in her mind. They were dark days, there was no electricity and they lit log fires to keep themselves warm. Because Eve did almost nothing, sat staring at the wall or hid herself in bed, Liza did her best to clear up the front garden, moving all but the biggest and heaviest branches. She went up to Shrove every day on her own, fetching back useful things from the kitchens, firelighters and nightlights, stone hot-water bottles, tinned food, coffee and sugar. It was stealing, she now supposed, though she hadn't thought of that at the time.

One afternoon she went up to watch television. She hadn't associated the television with the electricity supply but she did when she switched it on and nothing happened. It occurred to her to try the phone, though she had never used a phone, but that too seemed dead and stayed silent no matter how many of the buttons she pressed.

She and Eve had no idea of what might be happening in the outside world. That, she now understood, was what Eve had always wanted, to be isolated, to be cut off from all that lay beyond Shrove. But she had hardly wanted it to this extent. Liza suddenly thought of the radio in Bruno's car. That didn't work off the main electricity, somehow it worked off the car itself, perhaps by some means from the engine.

Bruno's radio would tell them what the hurricane had done, if the whole world was devastated, if the electricity had gone for good, if all the phones had been destroyed. But it was no good thinking of that. She wouldn't know how to start the engine or turn the radio on and, even if she could find out, the car was locked away in the stable and the key hidden somewhere.

The next day it no longer mattered, for the electricity men came to mend the lines. Their van went past the gatehouse, bumping over broken twigs and dead leaves. Later, when she went out, she came upon them up on the high poles, restringing cables, and one of them, thinking perhaps that she came from Shrove itself, called out to her that her TV antenna was broken. The storm had torn it from the roof and it was hanging over one of the chimneys.

Liza didn't know what he meant. She had never heard of a TV antenna. To her the complicated grid thing that looked like one of the shelves from their oven was just something you saw on roofs, probably a kind of weather vane. After the men had gone and the lights and heating came on again, she went up to Shrove to watch television.

This time it came on but not properly. The picture ran about all over the place, it rolled over as if someone were turning a handle inside it, lines formed, or the screen looked like a piece of coarsely woven gray material. You couldn't see the people's faces clearly and their voices sounded as if they all had colds.

It was a long time before Liza made the connection between the failure of the television and the broken oven shelf on the roof. She thought it had simply gone wrong. It was old and it had gone wrong. She felt helpless, knowing there was nothing she could do without telling Eve. Her viewing afternoons were over. Jonathan never watched television, this set had been his grandfather's and he certainly wouldn't get a new one or have the antenna mended.

She walked sadly back to the gatehouse. Watching Eve, who hardly spoke, who went through the motions of getting their supper while her thoughts were far away, Liza decided that her mother had no more cause for grief than she had, who had lost just as much, who had lost her only friend.

She had grown up a lot in the weeks that followed the hurricane. It was as if she aged three or four years. She began to know all sorts of things, she was sure, that people don't usually know at eleven. For instance, how to be alone with a woman nearly mad with misery and grief, while feeling—yes, she'd felt it even then—that somehow it was wrong to care so much about a *thing,* a place, a piece of land, a house. If she cared in the same way about the television set, she was only a child while Eve was grown up. It only made her pity her mother the more. She had to look after her, be kind, not trouble her, encourage her in the only thing that distracted her: giving lessons, imparting knowledge. Liza sometimes worked at her textbooks from early morning until late in the evening just to keep Eve's mind off the destruction and the mess out there.

The other thing that helped this fast growing up was her anxiety over Bruno's body. Eve had buried it in the first place because she wanted it hidden, because if it was found she might be in serious trouble. Liza had some inkling of the kind of trouble from reading the Victorian novelists. *Oliver Twist* was her handbook and so was *The Woman in White.* Did they still hang murderers? She couldn't ask Eve. And what did hanging actually mean? What bit of you was hung up? She knew a lot more about beheading. From reading about the French Revolution and Mary Queen of Scots and the wives of Henry VIII, she knew quite a lot about chopping off heads.

Would they hang Eve? She was really frightened when she thought of that, she was a child again, more like five than eleven, afraid of bad men coming and taking her mummy away. Like Eve and the spoiled woods, she wanted to hide herself and pretend it wasn't real. Besides, if she asked Eve about hanging it might make her think she had something more to worry about. Liza didn't ask. She and Eve worked at English literature and history and Latin from morning till night.

Until the day came when Eve didn't get up at all. She lay in bed with her face turned to the wall. Liza went out for the first time for days. It was the last day of October, the thirty-first, Halloween, a dry gray breezy morning.

The ruined wood looked different because all the leaves had died. They hadn't turned brown like the leaves on the remaining living trees, but still green, had dried up and curled and shriveled. As she pushed her way through the wreckage the dead leaves crackled. From the depths a pheasant gave its rattling cry and above her in the single standing tree she heard doves cooing. The birds had come back.

Her heart was in her mouth (as she had read) or perhaps she was only starting to feel sick again as she came to the clearing where the flat, smooth stump stood. But there was no fear of being sick this time or of smelling the smell of maggoty bone, for the bundle had gone.

She had a moment of absolute panic, of wanting to run and not knowing where to run to. Someone had come and found Bruno and taken him away. Then she saw what had happened. The body in the sack was still there, was somewhere down there, *inside* there. The leaning cherry tree had fallen and hidden it. The cherry tree she had clasped in her hands to test how stable it was had not been stable at all, had fallen next time the wind blew, and its broad solid trunk dropped on top of the bundle, driving it back into its grave.

Liza examined the place carefully. There wasn't a sign of that bundle unless you knew what to look for, unless you detected the corner of a sack protruding from where the lowest branch grew out of the cherry trunk. She tried pushing it under but it wouldn't go, so she dragged across branches and fetched armfuls of twigs, piling them up to conceal what remained of Bruno.

No one could find it now until men came to clear the wood. She hadn't thought of that at the time, she had simply been relieved, had believed it hidden forever, but no more than a few days after this a lot of workmen came in a lorry with chainsaws and axes. Jonathan came too. The men began by clearing the gatehouse garden and then they started work on the fallen and damaged trees in Shrove park.

That worried Liza a lot. She was sure they would move into the wood and begin shifting the logs and broken trees. For a whole day she worried about it until Jonathan—who sat for hours in the cottage with Eve, the two of them sighing and shaking their heads over what the hurricane had done—remarked in passing that the "little" wood was to be the last place to be cleared. It might be two years before they began to clear the "little" wood.

Eve got up for Jonathan and pulled herself together. She washed her hair and braided it on the back of her head, she put on her tight black top and her blue and purple skirt and smiled and made herself beautiful for Jonathan.

He came and he did what Liza hadn't seen him do for years, put his arms around Eve and kissed her. When Eve sent her away and said to write her history essay upstairs—she called it her "homework" as if all her lessons weren't done at home—Liza listened outside the door. She heard Eve tell Jonathan it was half-term. Perhaps it was. In that case what she said wasn't really untrue. Of course, that depended on what you meant by a lie. It was a lie if by lying you meant intending to deceive. Eve certainly intended to deceive Jonathan into thinking Liza went to school.

They talked for a long time about the hurricane damage. Both knew a lot of statistics about this being the first hurricane in

England for so many hundred years and about so many million trees being destroyed. They talked about the Great Storm of 1703. It was all rather boring. After she'd heard the bit about delaying till last the clearing of the wood where Bruno's body lay, Liza decided to go upstairs and start writing about the rise of Napoleon Bonaparte. At that moment Jonathan changed the subject and told Eve quite abruptly that Victoria had left him for a lover and the two of them were living in Caracas. There was no hope of a reconciliation, this was what the court called "irretrievable breakdown."

Just as Eve began to say something Liza thought might be interesting there came a great thudding at the front door.

Eve said in a theatrical way, "What fresh hell is this?" and then explained with a laugh that someone called Dorothy Parker had said it first.

The person at the door was only one of the workmen looking for Jonathan to ask about some tree or other, whether to chop it down or leave it as it was, a torn-in-half tree. Liza went upstairs and, not being sure whether Caracas was the capital of Venezuela or Ecuador, looked it up in her atlas.

Jonathan stayed for less than a week. Just one night Liza was almost sure he'd spent in Eve's bedroom. It was a feeling she had, no more, for she hadn't heard them go to bed, had slept soundly all night, and when she came down in the morning there was no sign of him. But she was older, she was beginning to be very aware of things like that.

In January she was twelve.

Next time Liza went to Mrs. Spurdell's it was for one of the afternoon stints, so there was time to put up her hair the way Eve had for special occasions, in a thick braid on the back of her head.

It made her look several years older, she decided. She took with her the books she had borrowed.

Mr. Spurdell seldom got home before she left but he did that day, and he had been in no more than ten minutes when a woman arrived in a red car. Cleaning the bedroom windows, Liza saw her come up the path toward the front door. She was tall and good-looking in a masculine way, with dark hair tied back at the nape of her neck. Her trouser suit was dark gray with pinstripes and her shirt was red silk. But the most attractive thing about her was her warm and intelligent expression that made her look incapable of saying an unpleasant or stupid thing.

Liza waited for the doorbell to ring. Instead she heard the front door open. She must have a key of her own, she thought, and guessed who this was. Jane, who wrote in her books that they had been stolen from her. But she had been much younger then, of course. Jane, the daughter who had something to do with education. Now she could see a resemblance to the photograph.

How could a poor shriveled-up little man like Mr. Spurdell and a fat white-haired creature like his wife have a daughter as nice to look at as this? It was a great mystery. She finished her windows and went downstairs. No one bothered to introduce her, she wasn't surprised about that. Mr. and Mrs. Spurdell just went on talking as if she wasn't there, as if she were a robot cleverly programmed to sweep floors and dust furniture.

Liza said to Mrs. Spurdell that she had finished. Was there anything more she wanted her to do? Mrs. Spurdell said no, there wasn't, and gave her a look as from a feudal lady to a serf, so Liza went into the kitchen and sat at the table, waiting to get her money.

After a moment or two Mr. Spurdell appeared. He saw the books she had brought back on the kitchen table and began to interrogate her about their contents. Who was Miss Gradgrind?

What did Dickens mean by Mrs. Sparsit's Coriolanian nose? What did Mr. Boffin collect? Who was Silas Wegg? Liza was surprised but not disconcerted. She had had plenty of this from Eve and was answering his questions with the enthusiasm of the scholar who thoroughly knows her subject, when the good-looking education woman came into the kitchen.

She raised her eyebrows and gave Liza a wink. "Come off it, Dad, what d'you think you're doing, putting her through an examination? You're lucky she's too polite to tell you where you can put your questions." She held out her hand to Liza and said, "Jane Spurdell. You must excuse my father. He never really leaves school."

"That's all right," she said and, thinking quickly, gave Sean's name. The elder Spurdells had never asked her surname. "Liza Holford."

Mr. Spurdell wasn't at all put out. "This young lady is a dark horse, Jane. I caught her reading my Dickens. I suspect she is on sabbatical, or else she is in our house cleaning for purposes of research. What can they be, I ask myself. Shall we set out to discover her secret?"

"Speak for yourself, Dad," Jane Spurdell said, "and leave me out of it. Her secret, if she has one, is her own affair." She smiled at Liza in a very friendly way. "I say, I do like the way you've done your hair. Is it very difficult?"

Liza was explaining that while it wasn't very difficult to do, it took a long time, you had to allow yourself half an hour, when Mrs. Spurdell arrived with her purse in her left hand and a handful of loose change in the other. Liza could tell she didn't at all like finding her conversing on equal terms with her daughter.

"Perhaps you should have been a hairdresser," she said unpleasantly. "When you've finished the demonstration, I'd like to get through the business of your pay."

Jane Spurdell looked ashamed of her mother, as well she might, Liza thought, and even more embarrassed when she asked for a loan of two pound coins to bring the total up to twelve. Mr. Spurdell had gone upstairs but as she was going he appeared in the hall with paperbacks of *Little Dorrit* and *Vanity Fair*. Liza said nothing about having already read *Vanity Fair*. She was watching, with barely suppressed laughter, Mrs. Spurdell's face as Jane said good-bye and it had been nice to meet her.

In the car, going home, she thought of telling Sean about Jane, how nice-looking she was and how friendly. But she didn't tell him. Without quite knowing why, she sensed he wouldn't like it. He had hated school, alternatively called the teachers power mad and a bunch of snobs. He would think being an educationalist a job for a woman only if she couldn't get a man.

Instead, because he was curious to know, she spoke about the year at Shrove that followed the hurricane. It was strange how much he loved stories. How would he manage if he ever got a girlfriend who couldn't tell him stories? But, of course, he never would get another girlfriend, for they were to be together forever and ever.

"My TV was broken in the storm—well, I thought of it as mine—and I knew I'd never get another. I did lessons all the time instead and gradually Eve got better. It was a lovely summer that year, that was the start of all the lovely summers, the best we'd ever had."

"The greenhouse effect," said Sean.

She was surprised he knew and then angry with herself for being surprised. "Well, maybe," she said. "I wouldn't know. Eve said they had summers like that at the beginning of the century, before the First World War."

"How did she know? She wasn't old enough to know."

Liza shrugged, the way Eve did. "The milkman said, hot

enough for you? He said it every day, he must have picked it up somewhere. The heat didn't stop the men. They worked hard at Shrove, clearing up all the mess, and it didn't look so bad. They'd even planted some new trees in the park and down by the river. The trees did very well because it was like wetlands down there. Even Eve said things weren't as bad as she'd feared and Mr. Frost said every cloud has a silver lining and now with them big old trees gone you could see views you'd never seen before. I think that was the longest sentence I ever heard him speak.

"Jonathan came down to Shrove a lot that year. It was funny really, he never seemed to notice that I was home all the time. I mean, through May and June and July, when everyone else of my age was at school. And in the same sort of way he didn't seem to notice that Mrs. Cooper never came to clean while he was staying at Shrove, though once he was there for nearly two weeks. I suppose he'd had people waiting on him all his life, he took it for granted things got done, cleaning and meals got ready, and his clothes washed. He ate his meals with us, or Eve took them up to him at Shrove. She collected his washing too and washed and ironed it and took it back to him.

"I never heard him say thank-you or even mention it, though perhaps he did when I wasn't there. There were nights I think she spent at Shrove with him, then and at lots of times in the future. If she did, she left the gatehouse after I was asleep and came back very early in the morning. Things were back where they had been before he married Victoria, or she thought they were. She hoped they were.

"They talked for hours about his marriage. They forgot I was there, I didn't have to listen outside the door. She was always asking him about Victoria and the divorce, but I never heard him say a word about Bruno. And all the time Bruno's car was up in his stables and Bruno's dead body was lying in his wood. Rotting in his wood and the worms eating him."

"Liza," said Sean warningly. "Do you mind?"

"Sorry. You *are* squeamish. I don't think Jonathan was interested, I don't think he cared. He was only interested in Jonathan Tobias, and people were important to him only as being useful to Jonathan Tobias. Maybe we're all like that. Are we?"

"I'd put you first, I know that."

"Would you? That's nice. I kept remembering the story she'd told me about old Mr. Tobias and my grandmother and how Eve'd thought then that she and Jonathan were going to get married. It didn't matter about her mother not getting Shrove because she and Jonathan were going to be married. She'd thought like that when I was little and he came down for those three weeks and it was all happening again.

"She thought he'd marry her when he got his divorce. She'd been trying to get him for seventeen years."

s e v e n t e e n

WHEN you're telling someone a serial story you don't say that now you've come to a bit where nothing much happened. It makes your listener not care much about the outcome. Somehow Liza knew this and stopped herself saying it to Sean. Yet, when she was twelve and thirteen, nothing much had happened. Eve had made her work ferociously hard at English and history and languages. She had taught her to sew and to knit and unraveled old sweaters for Liza to knit up again. They had listened to music together, but there had been no drawing or painting, as this perhaps was a reminder of Bruno. Liza missed the television and felt sad on the day the council rubbish collectors came and she saw the old set thrown into the back of the truck.

But nothing of great moment happened. No one came to clear the wood. The British Rail workmen did take up the rails and sleepers where the line had been, but they didn't fill in or block up the tunnel, and the tunnel mouth now yawned like the opening of a cave.

Bruno's car remained locked up in the stable. Once every five or six weeks Liza went to make sure that it was still there. Occasionally, she checked Eve's jewel case to see if the gold ring was still there. It was, it always was. And when Eve wasn't wearing earrings, there were three pairs in the case.

Jonathan came and went. If he talked about Victoria it was only to complain about the amount of money she would expect from him when the divorce went through. Money and property. She would want the Ullswater house and no doubt would get it. He sent a postcard from Zimbabwe and that autumn brought two people with him to Shrove that she had never seen before, a man called David Cosby and his wife, Frances. They came down for the shooting.

"David is Jonathan's cousin," said Eve.

Liza knew about cousins, she had read about them in Victorian novels.

"He can't be his cousin," she objected. "Not if Caroline didn't have brothers or sisters and his father didn't."

"David is his second cousin. He is old Mr. Tobias's nephew's son. He loves Shrove, he loves it nearly as much as I do, I know he wishes it was his."

"If he loves it so much why hasn't he been before?"

"He's been living in Africa for twelve years but now he's come home for good."

David Cosby's face was as dark and shiny a brown as the

paneling in the library at Shrove while his wife's was wrinkled and yellow. The result of the suns of Africa, thought Liza, who had just read *King Solomon's Mines.* They stayed two weeks. This time Eve seemed to be in a rather different position. Liza noticed it without quite being able to say how it was different. Perhaps it was that the three of them at Shrove, unlike Victoria and her friends, didn't treat Eve in any way like a servant. She went up there for dinner three times—Jonathan had caterers to come in and cook the partridges they shot—and left the washing up for Mrs. Cooper to do in the morning.

The funny thing was, of course, that there was no Mrs. Cooper, so Eve had to run up there while they were all out with the guns or in their car and play her pretending-to-be-the-cleaner game. It was a strange thing to do and it made Liza uneasy.

Eve became altogether rather strange in those two uneventful years. Or perhaps she had always been strange and when she was a child Liza hadn't noticed. She had just been Mother. Now, although Liza still knew very few people, she knew more than she ever had before. She could make comparisons. She could begin to question their way of life at the gatehouse, particularly her own. Why did Eve never want to know anyone or go anywhere? Did other people have such a passionate attachment to a place as she had to Shrove? What was the purpose of doing such a lot of lessons, doing them all the time, on Saturdays and Sundays as well, Eve teaching and she learning for hours on end day in and day out? Why?

Eve had stopped going into town. She had found a grocer who would deliver once a week, and what he didn't bring the milkman would. When she did go, a rare once every two or three months, it was to buy books for Liza to learn from, and for another, stranger, reason: to take money out of the bank. Now

Jonathan's checks were sent to the bank by post and the money later drawn out to be hidden at home.

One day, after Eve had come back from town, having paid her only visit there of the entire winter, Liza saw her go into the little castle, carrying a small brown paper parcel. Eve, as far as she knew, had never possessed a handbag. Liza only knew handbags existed because she had seen Victoria and Claire and Frances Cosby carrying them. She saw Eve go into the little castle with the package and come out after a minute or two without it.

Later on, choosing a time when Eve was up at Shrove being Mrs. Cooper, Liza investigated the little castle. It appeared quite empty. There was nothing now to show it had ever been occupied, either by dog or man. She didn't take long to find the loose brick and thence the iron box and the money.

Dozens of notes filled the box, five-, ten-, twenty-, and even fifty-pound notes. She didn't try to count them, she could see there were hundreds of pounds. Besides, she had very little idea of what money was worth. She could have said what five pounds would buy in the time of Anthony Trollope but not what it would buy today, though she suspected a lot less. Eve had never hinted at the amount of money Jonathan gave her. All that Liza knew was that it came in checks. She sent these checks to the bank, brought back the money and hid it here in the wall.

Wasn't that the purpose of a bank, to look after your money? Liza didn't really know. Perhaps everyone behaved like this. Perhaps no one really trusted banks.

But Liza found herself often watching her mother after that, watching her behavior, anxious to see what she would do next. She watched her as once she had listened at doors. There was no listening anymore because Eve never talked to anyone but Liza and occasionally Jonathan on his rare appearances. Sometimes she tried to catch Eve unawares, watch her when she didn't know she was being watched. She would go to bed early, then creep downstairs to watch Eve unobserved from the stairs. But she never saw her do anything except ordinary expected things, reading and listening to music or marking one of Liza's essays or test papers.

She was fourteen before she began asking herself, what will become of me when I grow up? Shall I live here with Eve forever? When she has taught me all the English there is to learn and all the history and French and Latin, what will we do then? What shall I do with all of it?

"Be me," Eve had said, "me as I might have been if I stayed here, happy and innocent and good."

Did she want to be Eve? Did she want to be those things?

That spring, while Jonathan was staying at Shrove on his own, the woodsmen came back to clear the "little" wood.

"Bruno had been dead for nearly three years. I wanted to know how long it took before a body turned into a skeleton but I didn't know how to find out. There weren't any medical books at Shrove or any on forensics. You see, I thought that if he was bones by now, they might not notice so much if they dug him up. I was hoping the sack would have rotted and Bruno just be—well, scattered bones."

"It beats me," said Sean, "the way you can talk about it. A lovely young girl like you, it's weird. You're always the same, like talking about death and stuff that makes other people throw up, you talk about them like they're normal."

She smiled at him. "I suppose it is normal for me. Dead bodies don't upset me. I know I was sick when Bruno's hair came off in my hand but that wasn't *me,* it was a sort of reflex. I expect even doctors do that when they first start."

"You could have been a doctor, d'you know that?"

"I still could," said Liza. "But that's not the point. Maybe other people are taught as children to flinch from death and blood and all that, I mean they're conditioned, but I never was. You've got to remember Eve taught me everything she knew about academic things, but there must be thousands of things children know who lead an ordinary life and go to school that I never heard of. There can't," she said rather proudly, "be many people who've read the whole of Virgil's *Aeneid* in the original and seen two people murdered by the time they're sixteen."

He recoiled a little. The look on his face made her smile again. "Don't worry about it, Sean. It can't be changed, that's the way it is. I'm different from other girls and in some ways I expect I always will be."

"You've got me now," he said. It was something he liked saying and when he said it he always took hold of her hand.

"Yes, I've got you now. Anyway, as I was telling you, the men went up to start working in the wood and I was very anxious. I don't know if Eve was. She was always out and about with Jonathan when she wasn't teaching me. But as it turned out they never found anything. Jonathan had given them instructions to leave some of the logs lying and some dead trees to provide habitats for the wildlife. The cherry log was one they left. It was just chance or luck, whatever you like to call it."

"Luck?" said Sean.

"Luck for Eve, wasn't it? I think she'd been waiting to see what happened. As soon as she knew all was well up there, she got Jonathan to recharge the battery on Bruno's car."

"She did what?"

There hadn't been any real risk. Jonathan hadn't suspected

Bruno was dead. In his eyes, Bruno was just a young healthy man who had been living with Eve, who got tired of her or of whom she got tired, and who moved away. True, he had left his car behind, but Eve had furnished Jonathan with all sorts of reasons for that: it had been his mother's, it was old, where he would be living he had nowhere to park a car. Jonathan was no doubt pleased to be told the car was going at last, Bruno was coming for it, the Shrove stable would be vacated. Recharging the battery on jump leads from his own car engine was a small price to pay for that. Liza didn't know if this was how it was, she told Sean, but it seemed a fair guess.

Eve didn't say a word to Liza about Bruno. It was Liza who overheard her telling Jonathan that Bruno would come for the car tomorrow, the day incidentally that Jonathan himself was going back to London.

"I wondered what she'd do, how she was going to handle it. I even pretended to go out for a long walk in the afternoon to give her a chance to move the car. She did move it and she went off in it, but only to town. She came back an hour later with the boot full of groceries and left the car parked outside the cottage."

"What did she say when you asked when Bruno was coming?"

"I never did ask," said Liza. "She expected me to ask, but I didn't. I knew where Bruno was. I knew he couldn't be coming. I knew his body was up in the wood under the leaves I'd piled around it. We were absolutely silent with each other about it. There was Bruno's car and she was using it—*we* were using it, she drove me to the village once and into town, I had a rash and had to see the doctor—but she never mentioned Bruno and neither did I. Then one day the car wasn't there anymore."

"What d'you mean?"

"She got rid of it. I don't know how or where. But she must

have done. She must have driven it somewhere in the night. I've no idea what happened to it, I don't know about things like that, I don't know how you'd get rid of a car."

"Just leave it parked somewhere, I reckon. Hopefully someone'd nick it." Sean considered. "If the police got it in the end they'd try to find the owner and they could, that'd be easy, they'd do it in seconds on the computer."

Liza said thoughtfully, "The owner was dead. I don't mean Bruno, I mean his mother. It was still in her name, he said so."

"I don't reckon they'd go to the trouble of tracing who the car'd been passed on to and if they tried they wouldn't find him, would they? And they wouldn't search either, not for a man of his age. They'd reason he'd gone off abroad somewhere. Your mum was clever."

"Oh, yes, she was. If they searched for him they never came near us. We never saw a policeman since that one came about Hugh with the beard. When Mr. Frost died it was an ambulance that came, not the police."

Mrs. Spurdell greeted Liza with the news that her daughter Jane had just been appointed Senior Adviser for Secondary Education to the County Council. She was bursting with pride. Since Liza had very little idea what this appointment signified she could only smile and nod. Mrs. Spurdell said it was a team leadership role and payment was on the Soulbury Scale, information that served only to confuse Liza further.

Though she had said nothing about an errand of mercy two days before—and Mrs. Spurdell spoke constantly of her advance plans—she announced that she was on her way out to visit a friend in the hospital. Liza guessed the visit was taking place only because there was exciting news to impart and wondered just how ill the friend was when she saw her employer take some weary-looking grapes from the refrigerator as a gift and transfer them to a clean plastic bag.

As soon as Mrs. Spurdell had gone, Liza had a bath. Then she went into Mr. Spurdell's study to see if he had any new books and spent a happy half hour reading a short story by John Mortimer. It was about courts and barristers and judges and opened to her a whole unknown new world. It also made her think about Eve and wonder when there would be anything in the papers about her. How long must it be before she came to trial?

To save buying one, she always went quickly through Mr. Spurdell's newspaper. As usual, there was nothing. Time to get down to the cleaning, but before she started she looked up Jane Spurdell in the telephone directory. It was the first time she had ever looked up anyone in a phone book but it wasn't hard to do. She was listed twice, not as "Miss" but as Dr. J. A. Spurdell. Liza would never forget the address. By a curious coincidence that might be a good omen of something, the number was the year of her birth and the street name startlingly familiar: 76 Shrove Road.

She'd never forget it but why should she want it? Perhaps it was only that she'd liked her, she liked her better than any woman she'd ever known except Eve. Of course that wasn't difficult, seeing that the other women she'd known were Heather and Victoria and Frances Cosby and Mrs. Spurdell. When you liked people, Liza decided, you wanted to know everything you could about them.

Mrs. Spurdell kept her waiting while she rummaged about in one handbag after another for fifty pee. This made her late and Sean was already there, out on the pavement, when she got to Superway. He had news for her, he was quite excited, but insisted on saving it up until they were in the car on the way home.

"They want me to go on a training course."

"Who's they?"

"Superway. It's a management training course. They're pleased with me, the way I do my work and the way I always get in on time and all that. It's in Scotland, it's a six-month course, and hopefully at the end of it if I'm any good I'd go on to what they call Phase Two."

Liza didn't know what to say. She didn't really understand, so she listened.

"I've never said any of this to you, love. I've never talked about myself much. But I've always reckoned to not being much, if you know what I mean—well, rubbish, to be perfectly honest with you. I was useless at school and I left the day after I was sixteen. I'd been skiving off for months before that. No one ever suggested CSEs to me, I mean it'd have been a laugh. I never even saw myself doing nothing but unskilled laboring work, and that's what I did do. Then Mum got her new fella and they didn't want me, so I moved out. Well, I reckon I've told you all that. I got the car and the van and I took to the road and if I thought about it at all I reckoned I'd be living from one odd job to another until the time come to draw my pension. And now this has come up. It's sort of shook me. It's given me something to think about, I can tell you."

She was moved by him because she hadn't known he could be so articulate. He was so beautiful. It would mean something to her if he could speak and think as handsomely as he looked.

"What will you be?" she said slowly.

"I don't know about 'will.' I said it's given me something to think about. As for what I'd *be*—well, hopefully I'd *be* a manager one day. I'd sort of have my own store, maybe one of them big new ones on an estate."

"We went to one of those, Eve and Bruno and me."

He made a movement as if to brush this aside impatiently. "Yes, you said. I'd have a lot to learn. I'd be an assistant manager first. It'd take awhile. But I'm young, love, and I'm keen."

She wouldn't mind going to Scotland. Now she had begun, she liked traveling about and imagined moving from place to place during the next few years. "Are you going to, then?"

"I told them I'd like to think about it. I said to give me a couple of days."

The caravan was cold and damp. It usually was these evenings when they got home. Liza lit the burners on the oven, the oven itself, opening the door, and started the oil heater. Very soon the condensation began, the water running down the windows and lying in pools. She didn't much mind, as she said to Sean, you didn't have to look at it. So long as she had fish and chips or takeaway, books to read, and a warm bed with Sean to make love with, she didn't care much. Now that she had television and knew she could have it whenever she wanted, she seldom watched it. There was something to be said for being brought up without luxury, without many material possessions. Unlike Eve, she had never wanted Shrove or thought it might be hers.

One gloomy evening rather like this one when Jonathan was in a gloomy mood, she heard him tell her mother he had made his will and was leaving Shrove to David Cosby.

"It should remain in our family," he said like a character in a Victorian novel.

"He's ten years older than you," said Eve.

"His son can have it, then. They're all fond of the place. There's one thing, Victoria won't want it, she won't ask for this place in settlement, she hates it."

Aged fourteen, taller than Eve, looking like a young woman, Liza was developing a woman's understanding. She had begun to ask herself how it could be that Jonathan, who had known Eve since he was a boy, who had been close to her, her lover off and on (and now very probably on again), could have so little comprehension of how she felt about Shrove. He could talk with casual indifference about it to Eve, who loved it better than any person, better, perhaps, Liza sometimes thought, than her own child. He could talk about it to her as if it were just a piece of property, a parcel of land, even a nuisance. And he could talk about leaving it to a cousin whom, until this year, he hadn't seen for twelve years, without its apparently crossing his mind that he might leave it to Eve, as his grandfather had promised to leave it to Eve's mother.

Liza suspected that he too didn't like Shrove much. It was October now and this was only the second time he'd been down this year. His real life was elsewhere, doing things she and Eve knew nothing about. And he knew nothing about what they did. He never asked. It was as if Shrove was something to be packed up in a box when he was away from it and she and Eve puppets to be packed up with it.

Next day he was back again at the gatehouse telling Eve his divorce decree had at last been made absolute and Victoria had "taken him to the cleaners." He was free now. Liza heard him ask Eve if she ever heard from Bruno these days. She said she hadn't and she never would, that was all over and she was free as air. She was as free as he was.

Liza was listening outside the door and Eve and Jonathan were sitting in there in the dusk, the lamps unlit. She heard her mother say that about being free and then she heard the silence. Next morning Jonathan went off to London and thence to France, where his mother was dying.

A postcard with a picture of a French cathedral on it came after about a week to say that Caroline Ellison was dead. Smiling rather unpleasantly, Eve said she supposed he thought a churchy card was suitable for announcing a death while one with mountains or trees on it wouldn't be. Jonathan didn't sound grief-stricken, though it was hard to tell from a postcard. Eve was sure he would come back now, but he didn't and six months later they got a card from him in Penang.

Before that, before the winter started, Liza found Mr. Frost lying dead on the grass beside his tractor.

No one knew how old he was. Eve said very old because his daughter had been only a few years younger than her own mother, who would be seventy if she had lived. For the past few years he had done nothing beyond sitting on the tractor and driving it around the lawns. It was Eve who pulled out the weeds and put the mowings on the compost heap.

It was in early November, an exceptionally dry, sunny November, when Liza found him. He had been giving the grass its last cut before the winter. She was walking up from the river, taking the short cut across the Shrove garden. The sound of the mower had stopped ten minutes before and she thought he must have finished for the day. But the tractor was still there, in the middle of the sunny lawn, yellow leaves of lime and chestnut falling onto the grass, onto the tractor's black leather seat and scarlet bodywork, and onto the body of the old man lying beside it.

At first she didn't know he was dead. She was immensely curious. Her hand on his forehead encountered the coldness of marble. She could see that his veiny blue eyes were dead, they were quite lightless, and there was no breath from his slack mouth or movement of his chest. He no longer looked like a person but rather like one of the statues on the terrace, a prone figure in pale, cold stone.

The strange thought came to her that Eve would bury him. At once, immediately, she knew this was nonsense but she had thought it. She ran to the cottage and Eve came back with her and they went into Shrove House and phoned for an ambulance. They couldn't think what else to do even though they knew he was dead.

Mr. Frost had died of old age. His heart had broken—it had literally broken—with age. And who, now, was to do the Shrove garden?

No one, in the depths of winter. There was nothing to do when the snow came and the frost set hard. On the day Liza became fifteen, the snow fell so thickly and for so long they had to dig their way out of the front door.

But snow seldom lasts for long in England. In February, where it had lain were clumps of snowdrops, and by March the grass was starting to grow, there were catkins on the hazels, and the blackthorn was in bloom. Liza had her lessons in the morning and after lunch Eve went out on the tractor to cut the Shrove grass. The wide stretches of lawn were easy to mow. It wasn't much more than a matter of sitting on the seat and steering, but the edges had to be cut as well and the awkward bits between the new trees. Eve was on her knees pulling out the weeds after sunset, almost until dark.

Liza had never asked her why. She stopped asking questions of her mother after Bruno disappeared. It wasn't a conscious decision on her part not to ask but as if a voice inside her bade her be silent. Asking was dangerous, asking would only do damage, provoke lying, cause embarrassment. Don't ask. So she had never asked, why go on pretending to Jonathan that Mrs. Cooper exists? What harm can it do to you or me if a woman comes here to clean? She had never asked, what did you do with Bruno's car? And now she didn't ask, why are you doing this work in the garden? Why don't you find a successor to Mr. Frost?

Not only was she silent about these things, she also supported Eve in her subterfuges. It seemed natural to do so, it seemed right. For a long time now, when the rare people she saw asked her about school, how she was getting on, if she was on holiday, she had been saying, all right and yes, she was. Jonathan had once asked her, as he was leaving, if Mrs. Cooper was expected next day and Liza had said yes, knowing it would be Eve herself who would clear up at Shrove. She even told Eve he'd asked her. Wasn't she the crocodile bird who warned its host of impending danger?

It was now Eve who performed the tasks that had once been Mr. Frost's. Liza wondered if Jonathan even knew Mr. Frost was dead. Perhaps Eve herself simply kept the checks for his pay that Jonathan sent her. She now had the entire care of Shrove House, its gardens and its grounds in her hands, with Liza helping. Liza hated gardening but she couldn't be there and watch Eve do it all on her own, so she trimmed the edges with the long shears and pushed the little hand mower about, so bored she could have screamed.

Then, around midsummer, Eve found a man to do it. It was a very hot summer, the hottest of Liza's life except the one when she was a six-month-old baby. The grass stopped growing and the sun burned it brown, so there was watering to do instead of mowing. Sometimes Eve was so tired with carrying watering cans and pulling the hosepipe about that she fell asleep on their sofa and Liza had to get the supper. The weeds still grew too. Nothing stopped the nettles growing and the burdock.

Eve said, "I have to keep it going. I have to look after the young trees. It's so beautiful, I can't let it get in a mess. There's not a lovelier place in England. I can't bear to think of it all going to ruin."

Her hands were stained and cracked, the fingers ingrained with dirt, the nails broken. The sun had burned her face dark brown but her nose was peeling. Liza saw threads of gray in her dark hair, which had nothing to do with the sun but perhaps something to do with her hard life. Now that Liza was older she was beginning to see that Eve had made her life hard of her own volition, had made all kinds of difficulties for herself where there might have been ease and pleasantness. But she never asked why.

She did ask, why him? when the old man appeared at the gate saying he'd heard in the village they might be wanting someone to help out at Shrove. From whom had he heard? The postman perhaps, the milkman. Eve was to tell Jonathan he'd heard from Mrs. Cooper. He wasn't quite as old as Mr. Frost, his hair wasn't even gray, but his face was very lined and withered. A hump grew out of his back, which made Liza shrink a little when she saw it. She had always been accustomed to physical beauty or at least conformity. The old man's back was curved as if his spine had been bent into a bow the way you could bend a willow twig. He had strong arms and very large hands.

Eve said, yes, he could come twice a week. She sounded reluctant, grudging, and Liza understood that she had wanted to keep Shrove all to herself. It wasn't just a matter of not having people who might gossip or tell tales about the place, or it wasn't that *anymore.* She wanted exclusive possession of Shrove. If she was going to take Gib on—that was the only name they knew him by—it was because she was worn out, she had hurt her back and had to rest, she could no longer cope alone.

"But why him?" said Liza.

"He lives alone, he's not very bright, he won't try to take over. He can't talk much, didn't you notice?"

Gib had an impediment in his speech that made him hard to understand. He liked riding the mower, he worked hard, and if he couldn't tell a cultivated plant from a weed, he did his best, trimming the edges and sometimes proudly leaving in the midst of smoothly hoed earth a fine specimen of dandelion Eve said he had lovingly nourished up. She went around after he had gone, pulling up the weeds he had nurtured.

Jonathan came in August, while Gib was still with them, and talked a lot about the holiday he was about to take in British Columbia and the Rocky Mountains. He had no wife now and since his divorce he had brought no other woman to Shrove except his cousin's wife, Frances Cosby. But he didn't ask Eve to go with him to Canada. Once or twice Liza thought he came very near to doing this, but he didn't ask her. Perhaps he remembered the rebuff he had received all those years ago when Liza was little, or else he thought she wouldn't be able to leave Liza and they couldn't take Liza because she, of course, was at school.

Would Eve have gone if he'd asked her? Would they somehow have managed about Liza, said she could take time off school? Seeing her mother's sad, almost grim expression after Jonathan had gone, she thought that this time Eve would have said yes.

He didn't ask her but he did, at last, have the bathroom done. It was ten years since he had first promised to do it, but when Liza pointed this out Eve only shrugged and said they must be thankful for small mercies.

Jonathan had gone to the bathroom to wash his hands, only there was no bathroom, there was just the kitchen sink. Perhaps it wasn't pretense when he said he thought a bathroom had been put in years ago, he was sure of it, he thought Victoria had arranged it. Perhaps he really believed that. Eve only smiled and claimed she had forgotten his promises. But the builders came before he had left Shrove, built an annex onto the back of the gatehouse, and turned it into a bathroom.

One of the builders was Matt. They had always wondered what he did, Eve and Liza, and now they knew. He was a bricklayer, like Rainer Beck. The other one was some relation of his, a young man with yellow hair dyed pink at the front. The weather was so hot that Liza lay out in the back garden in the sun after bathing in the river. She had a black swimming costume that had been Eve's. The noise Matt made when he saw her was a whistle on two notes, the meaning of which was lost on Liza, who took no notice of it. She took almost no notice of either of them, for neither was handsome and she already knew that she preferred good-looking people.

The whistle was repeated and Eve came out and told her to cover herself up or come indoors. She explained that Matt and his cousin found Liza attractive, now she was growing up, and that was their low and vulgar way of showing it.

Liza digested this and pondered it for a long time. She wondered why there wasn't anything low and vulgar about the way Jonathan had made a similar sound when he saw Eve all prepared for him and dressed up in a black-and-scarlet skirt and black jumper from the good-as-new shop in town. But perhaps his laughing afterward and kissing Eve made it all right.

Gib was taken ill. The postman who brought Eve the message said he was often ill. He wasn't strong and the jobs he took on never lasted, though he tried, he did his best. By this time it was autumn and the grass at least no longer needed attention. And the rain came at last, day after day of it, until the river rose above its banks and flooded the wetlands, so that the trees stood in water to halfway up their trunks.

They were quite alone, Eve and Liza, in those last months of her sixteenth year. Gib didn't come back and there wasn't, anyway, much to be done in the garden. The oilman came and filled the tank while Eve and Liza were out walking, so they didn't see him, and the postman took to delivering their few letters before either of them was up. As for the milkman, he disappeared and was replaced by a man with red hair who whistled all the time. He told Eve *their* milkman had gone into a home because the dairy had found out about his mental age and said he could no longer work for them.

Jonathan was on the other side of the world, in Hawaii, as they knew from a not-at-all churchy card with a picture of a girl surfing on white waves. A card came from Heather on holiday in Cornwall and another one at Christmas with a note in it saying she'd moved to London and this was her new address.

Once the spring had come, Eve began to fret about the garden. She seldom went to town anymore, but she had to make the occasional visit. She had to go to buy Liza's jeans, her first pair, that Liza had been nagging her about for ages. When Eve came out of the jeans shop she saw an advertisement in the newsagent's window next door.

It said: "Strong man will do indoor and outdoor decorating, clearing sites, general laboring, gardening, and odd jobs." There was a box number, which Eve said meant he came into the shop and collected the replies he'd had. Liza didn't think much more about it because Eve hadn't been able to put a phone number on her reply and had said it would come to nothing, no one wrote letters anymore.

But he must have written and his letter come while Liza was still in bed in the morning because Eve announced one day that she thought she'd found a gardener and not, she hoped, a septuagenarian this time. She probably didn't guess how young he was, either.

"His name is Sean Holford," she said, "and he's coming for an interview on Tuesday."

e i g h t e e n

SEEING her mother's picture in the paper was a shock, worse than seeing what the dogs did, much worse than finding Bruno. She was sitting in Mrs. Spurdell's kitchen waiting for her money and enjoying her own clean scented-soap smell. She had managed a bath and was screwing up her courage to ask Mr. Spurdell if she could borrow his *Morte d'Arthur,* which wasn't a paperback, when he came into the room carrying a newspaper.

He didn't say anything, he looked at her and, when his wife appeared, rummaging for change in two handbags, made her look at the paper too. They both stared at Liza. Then Mr. Spurdell said, "Isn't that an almost uncanny resemblance?"

Mrs. Spurdell said nothing. She was looking rather cross, the way she always did if Liza appeared to be briefly the focus of attention. Shaking his head as if in incredulity, Mr. Spurdell handed Liza the paper, pointing with one finger at a photograph.

Liza's heart began to beat very fast. The picture was of Eve. She stared at it. It showed a much younger Eve and had apparently been taken some years before and as she looked she remembered. Jonathan had taken it. Eve and she had taken the dogs back to Shrove one summer evening and Jonathan had come down the steps and taken a photograph. She should have been in it but she'd been shy and had hidden behind a tree.

The day that picture was taken was the Day of the Nightingale. How it came to be in a newspaper she had no idea.

"You're the spitting image of her, my dear," said Mr. Spurdell. "It struck me as soon as I saw it. Quite amusing, eh? I thought to myself, I'll run downstairs and show this to Liza before she goes. Not that I imagine she'll be overjoyed to find she looks like a murderess, eh?"

They didn't know then, they hadn't guessed. Liza forced herself to smile as she looked up and met his eyes.

"I don't see the likeness myself," Mrs. Spurdell was saying. "That creature, the one in the paper, is quite spectacularly good-looking, criminal or not. If you didn't know you'd take her for a film star."

Liza wanted to scream with laughter, though she knew it was hysteria, it hadn't much to do with amusement. She tried to read what the paper said, but the print swam and bobbed about. The headline she could make out: ALLEGED KILLER BURIED MAN'S BODY. She *must* get hold of this paper.

Mr. Spurdell was already holding out his hand for it. "I suppose, strictly speaking, we shouldn't call her a murderess or a criminal. She is still on trial, she hasn't been found guilty yet. Can I have my paper, please, my dear?"

Even if he thought it odd, she must have that paper. Knowing her voice must sound hoarse, she said, "Could I—do you think I could keep it?"

He gave his indulgent humoring laugh, a laugh she sometimes thought, seeking words for it, heavy with patronage and patriarchy. "And how am I to do my crossword puzzle?"

The problem was solved by Mrs. Spurdell's snatching the paper out of her hand and thrusting into it—for once in the form of one note and two coins—the twelve pounds for her four hours' work. Liza got up and left without another word, without even a good-bye. She had forgotten all about the *Morte d'Arthur.*

The nearest newsagent had no morning papers left. The next one was closed. On some previous occasion in Aspen Close she had heard Mr. Spurdell talking about the evening paper that used to be on sale but which had ceased to exist some months before. By the time she met Sean she was nearly distraught, pouring it all out to him in an incoherent stream.

Sean was always good in a crisis. He liked comforting her, keeping calm, showing his manly strength. He liked her weak and vulnerable. Tomorrow they would buy the newspapers, they would buy all the newspapers. Hadn't Mr. Spurdell said the trial wasn't over? It would have been going on again today. They would watch the television, every news there was.

When they got home he made tea for her. He hugged her and said not to worry, she had him, he would do all the worrying for her, leave it to him, and he began kissing her and stroking her. That led of course to making love and they were in bed for an hour, consequently missing the six o'clock news.

At nine there was nothing about Eve and nothing at ten.

Sean, who had seen hundreds of television programs and videos about murders and police investigations, said this might be because it wasn't a sensational enough case. It wasn't a child or a young girl who had been murdered or something that had attracted a lot of public attention when it happened.

"I just wish I knew more about it," said Liza, who was a lot calmer by now. "I wish I knew about the law."

"You can't know about everything."

"I'd like to be a lawyer. One day I'll *be* a lawyer."

Sean laughed. "Dream on, love. The other day you was going to be a doctor."

She was in a fever of anticipation when they drove into town the next morning. It wasn't one of her days in Aspen Close and she would either have to pass a solitary day wandering about the marketplace and spend hard-earned cash on the cinema or else go home on the bus. But she couldn't wait till Sean came home before seeing the papers.

They bought three, all so-called quality newspapers, but the story was almost identical in each of them. This time there was no picture of Eve. In the first one, which Liza read feverishly, still sitting in the car, the headline was: GATEHOUSE MURDER PREMEDITATED, SAYS QC.

The account was very long, filling nearly half a page. Try as she would, Liza couldn't take in more than the first two paragraphs.

"I don't understand it, Sean. I don't know what it means. It says she's been charged with the murder of Trevor Hughes. Who's Trevor Hughes? I've never heard of him."

"You better read it all. Read all three of them. Look, love, I've got to go or I'll be late. I wouldn't want to be late, not at this juncture. You can stay here in the car, no one'll see you."

She sat in the car in the Superway's underground car park

and read the accounts in all the papers. None of them had a word about the murders Liza knew Eve had committed. All the accounts were about this Trevor Hughes, a sales representative, aged thirty-one, who had been missing from home for twelve years. It appeared that he had quarreled with his wife and, instead of leaving for a holiday with her as they had planned, had gone off on his own.

Mrs. Eileen Hughes said she had identified her husband from his watch and his wedding ring, which had his name and hers inside it. A dentist had identified him by his teeth. How did they do that? Liza wondered. If she enquired of Sean he would ask if she wanted to be a dentist as well and tell her to dream on.

They had found shotgun pellets buried with the man. Buried in the wood? But surely only Bruno was up there. Now they were talking about this man being buried as well. It didn't seem as if Eve had said anything in the court or anyone had said anything on her behalf. But it was going on again today. At the end of the article it said the trial continues.

Liza felt bewildered. She wanted desperately to know, she wished there was someone she could ask, but the only person she could think of was Mr. Spurdell. Reading the newspaper accounts, she had been afraid of coming on her own name but she hadn't, her name wasn't mentioned. Would it be mentioned tomorrow?

She passed a tedious yet anxious day mooning about the town. The admiring manager was off today, so it wasn't even interesting taking a clandestine bath in the Duke's Head. She bought three paperback books, spending two-thirds of the twenty-four pounds she had earned that week. Sean would be cross. She sensed already that Sean was going to expect her to be pleased if her mother got sent to prison for years and years. How long would it be anyway? At least they'd stopped hanging people.

In the afternoon, after having a hamburger and a sundae in McDonald's, she went to the cinema and saw *Howards End.* Why had she never read any E. M. Forster? Because he was born too late to be in the Shrove library, she thought rather bitterly. Next week she'd buy *A Passage to India,* that was by him she was sure, and anything else he'd written. It took considerable strength of will to make herself leave the cinema and not sit there and watch the program all the way through again.

Sean was waiting. He was sure the trial would be on TV tonight. They switched on at six and again at nine and ten, but it wasn't on. Liza said, "I've been thinking. I know who Trevor Hughes was. He was the man with the beard. It says here he went missing twelve years ago and that was twelve years ago. I was four. I thought the policeman who came called him Hugh. D'you remember I said Hugh? But it wasn't, it was Trevor Hughes."

"The man the dogs went for," said Sean. "The one she shot."

"They must have searched the gatehouse and found the ring with the initials and the date inside. But why him?"

"It's a mystery," said Sean. "Like you say, why pick him? Why not the others?"

"I don't know. I don't know anything. I feel so ignorant." Liza thrust her hands through her hair and looked at him mutinously. "We can't go to the police, there's no one we can ask. It's beyond me, it's driving me mad."

When he saw the new books, Sean didn't say a word. She realized that she couldn't always predict how he would react. He was kind, he was good to her. She thought of the men in the books she'd read and the book she was reading now, she remembered Trevor Hughes and Bruno and Jonathan and thought she was lucky to have Sean. Once or twice she repeated it to convince herself, she was lucky to have Sean.

Quite a long time had passed after Eve told Jonathan the new gardener's name before Liza met him. She first saw him on the day he started, but didn't let him see her. It was mid-March and cold, she had been out for a long aimless walk and was coming back, her boots sinking into the marshy ground above the river. That winter she had been taking more and more of these walks, she had been growing increasingly frustrated with solitude, with sameness, with never seeing another face but Eve's. Lessons had become repetitive and she sensed that Eve had taught her almost all she knew. All that was left now was to write more essays about Shakespeare, examine more pieces of eighteenth-century prose, translate more de Maupassant, and do more Latin unseens. She had read all the books in the Shrove library she would ever want to read. Television was almost forgotten, what it had been like, why she had enjoyed it.

Was the whole of life going to be like this? Sean had asked her later on why she hadn't run away. He hadn't understood the extent of her learning and the depths of her ignorance. At the thought of running away, before she met him, she had felt almost faint with fear. She had never been on a bus or in a train, never bought anything in a shop herself, scarcely been in one, never made a phone call, and most important of all, never had any sort of relationship with a contemporary.

So she went for long walks, sometimes to the isolated villages, there to gaze at a village shop or the notice board inside a church porch, to read a bus timetable or stand outside a school and watch the children come out. She was teaching herself about the world Eve had kept from her. Once, anticipating Sean's question, she had even said, I could run away. But the very words, unspoken except in her mind, had terrified her. She saw herself standing in an empty street at night with no idea where to go, how to find food or a place to sleep. She imagined herself not running away but running *home*, throwing herself pathetically into Eve's arms.

But what was going to become of her? She often imagined the future and in the blackest way. She saw herself old, thirty or more, and Eve a really old woman, the two of them going on just the same, everything the same except that the new trees had grown tall with thick trunks and spreading crowns. Would she become the Shrove gardener when Eve was too old to do the work? Or the successor to Mrs. Cooper? She would be sent to town with the shopping basket and list, to cross the bridge and wait for the bus.

She saw herself crossing the marketplace, avoiding with fear the jostling teenagers, let out like effervescent water from an opened bottle. Stepping into the road to avoid them, keeping her eyes downcast like a nun she had seen in a picture. Afraid to speak to anyone but shopkeepers, and then only to ask in a whisper for what she wanted.

Thinking this way, she came dispiritedly up among those trees that were still saplings and saw someone in the Shrove garden. He was a long way off and for a moment she thought he must be Jonathan. But Jonathan wouldn't be clipping the yew hedge. Jonathan never did anything, he never pulled out a weed or plucked a dead head from a rose.

The man was working on the hedge with a pair of hand clippers. It must be the new gardener. She was still too far away from him to see much, but even from a hundred yards off she could tell he was young. Not young as Jonathan or Bruno were, but really young, the same sort of age as herself. She had never thought of hiding from Mr. Frost or Gib, but she was suddenly urgently sure that this man mustn't see her. He mustn't be allowed to see her casually approaching him.

It was easy to avoid his eye, a matter of keeping to the trees and, when the garden was reached, making her way toward the house. Why she was behaving so covertly she didn't ask herself, for she couldn't have replied.

She approached stealthily, careful not to step on a twig or, when she reached the path, let her feet make a sound on the gravel. Now he was no farther away from her than the length of their sitting room in the gatehouse. She looked at him between the branches and the dull pointed leaves of evergreens. He had finished the hedge and was lifting armfuls of clippings into a wheelbarrow, a tall, straight young man, a boy, with broad shoulders and narrow hips. His hair was raven black. She thought of it like that because that was the way the poets wrote. His face was turned away from her. She thought she might shriek with disappointment if she didn't see his face. But at the same time she knew she'd make no sound whatever he did, wherever he went.

Had she made a sound? She wasn't aware of it, unless her breathing itself had become noisy. There must have been something to make him turn from the barrow he was about to wheel away and look in her direction.

He couldn't see her. She could tell that. She stared. He was absolutely beautiful. His face was a pale olive color but with a flush on the cheeks, and his eyes were a dark bright blue. She saw a perfect nose and perfect lips and thought of the stars in those old films she had seen and of engravings of statues in ancient books and portraits by Titian.

His hands were long and brown. Once she had admired Jonathan's hands but no longer. This man had stars in his eyes and his gaze showed that he dreamed of wonderful things. The gods she read about lived in groves like this, half-concealed by leaves.

Because he couldn't see her and could now hear nothing, he shrugged a little and began wheeling the barrow away. He should have had a spear and a winged chariot but all he had were shears and a wheelbarrow. Liza didn't mind. She didn't even mind him going and she didn't want him to come back. In a strange way she had had as much as she could take for the present. An unexpected energy filled her and she ran all the way home, arriving breathless and throwing herself down on the sofa.

In a voice as casual as she could make it, she said to Eve, "Which days does the new gardener come?"

"Mondays, Wednesdays, and Fridays. Why?"

"Nothing. I just wondered."

The following afternoon she went to Shrove and searched for a picture he might resemble. She had done that when Bruno came, but this was different. That had been for the satisfaction of curiosity, this was an act of worship. Upstairs, next to the painting of Sodom and Gomorrah, was a portrait of a young man in black silk and silver lace. Eve called it "indifferent eighteenth-century two-a-penny stuff," but Liza had always liked it and now she gazed in wonder. Their new gardener in elegant fancy dress made her shiver, but pleasurably.

The next day was Friday and she watched for his car from Eve's bedroom window. It was a big old car, dark blue with patches of rust on the bodywork, and if she hadn't known a car had to have a driver she'd have thought it was moving along by its own volition. Rain fell all day on Monday, so he couldn't come, and it was Wednesday before she had a glimpse of him. His car was parked on the gravel by the coach house. She let herself into the house, went upstairs and into the bedroom with the fine views, the one Victoria had used and where she had left her clothes in the wardrobe. It made her jump to see him just outside the window, almost directly below her.

Clematis climbed across the garden front of Shrove House. He was on the steps, the old ones that used to be in the library, tying the clematis vines to the trellis. If he had turned his head to the right and lifted it a little he would have seen her. Any noise she might make wouldn't attract his attention today. He was wearing a headset and had a Walkman attached to the belt of his jeans.

In the week that had gone by she had sometimes wondered if she was remembering him as more beautiful than he actually was. Now she saw that he was even more beautiful than she remembered. Why did she care so much? She was dreadfully bewildered by it all. Was it just because he was the first person of her own age she had ever known? But she didn't know him.

He looked around suddenly and saw her. She was seized with shyness, with shame almost, and felt the blood rush into her face and burn her cheeks. He put up one hand in a salute and grinned. This made her retreat at once and run out of the bedroom. There was a mirror in a gilt frame hanging on the wall halfway down the stairs. Although she had never done this before, she stopped on the staircase and looked at herself in this mirror.

She thought she was—well, very pretty. Better than that perhaps. Nice eyes, big and dark, a full mouth, good skin, Eve always said, and lots of long dark hair. But—did all girls look like this? She need not be quite so naive. In the town she had seen others, but how could she judge? The old television images had grown vague and misty now. Why, anyway, did it matter? She continued to stare at herself, as if contemplating a great mystery.

For a moment or two, for five minutes perhaps, she had forgotten the boy on the steps. Narcissistically, she communed with herself, studying her smooth face and soft pink lips, the slim body and full breasts. How would she look in a dress like Caroline's? Red silk, low-cut. That almost made her laugh. She was wearing blue jeans, a black sweater with a polo neck, and Eve's old brown parka.

Because she knew he was in the back garden, she let herself out of the front door without a thought. She didn't peer from a window first but came straight out. And there he was, standing on the paving, studying the climbing hydrangea that clustered all across the front of Shrove House.

She stood quite still, staring at him, not knowing what to do, without a word to say.

He smiled. "Hi, there."

Something tied her tongue.

"D'you live here?"

She must speak. This time she wasn't blushing. She fancied she had gone pale.

"I saw you at the window, so I thought maybe you lived here. But the lady said no one did. At any rate you're not a ghost."

That should have made her laugh but she couldn't laugh. She found her tongue but not her poise. "That was my mother said that. We live at the Lodge."

"Out in the sticks, isn't it? It could give you the creeps."

Eve would hate him for "the creeps." "The sticks" she failed altogether to understand. "I have to go," she said. "I'm late."

"See you, then."

She didn't dare run. Guessing he was watching her, she walked down the drive, through the park, certain his eyes were on her. But when she looked back he was gone. His car passed her almost before she was aware of it and there he was waving to her. She was too confused to wave back.

At the gatehouse she read *Romeo and Juliet*. "Would that I were a glove upon that hand / That I might touch that cheek." Her future, the loneliness and the sameness, the oddities of Eve, all were forgotten. His was a face "to lose youth for / To occupy age with the dream of . . ." She turned to poetry, for she had no other comparisons and no other standards.

Talking to Eve, she longed to speak his name but was afraid to. Once she had uttered it, she wanted to talk about him all the time, yet she knew nothing about him.

"Where does Sean live?"

"In a caravan somewhere. What possible interest can it have for you?"

"I wanted to know where Gib lived." It was true. Let Eve believe that, knowing so few people, she was more interested in those she did know than others who had led different lives might be.

"Where does Sean keep his caravan?" This time she need not have used his name but she did use it.

"How should I know? Oh, yes, he said down by the old station. Have you been talking to him?"

Liza looked at her between the eyes and said, "No."

This was the place where she had been so frightened. She had come through the station, carefree, enjoying the day, happy in the sunlight, and had seen Bruno sitting there with his painting things, in his lifted hand a brush loaded with gamboge. He had frightened her with his naked hatred.

"You've never told me why you came that day," Sean said. "D'you know, it was seven months ago. We've known each other seven months. What made you come?"

"I wanted to see where you lived. The way I felt, you want to know everything about a person, where they live, what they eat and drink, what they like doing, the way they are when they're alone. You want to see them against different backgrounds." She thought about it. "Against every possible background. You want to see how they'll be in the rain and what they do when the sun shines on them. How they comb their hair and fill a kettle and wash their hands and drink a glass of water. You want to see how they go about doing all the ordinary things."

Sean was nodding earnestly. "That's right, that's it. You're a clever girl, love, you sort of know it all."

That made her impatient. She waved him away. "I didn't mean to see you. I certainly didn't mean you to see me. I just meant to see where you lived and—well, creep away."

"But I saw you and I come out."

She said reflectively, as if talking of other people, another couple. "It was love at first sight."

"Right on. That's what it was."

"I wasn't hard to get. I didn't keep you guessing. I went into the caravan with you and when you asked if I'd got anyone, I didn't know what you meant. I said I'd got my mother. You tried again, you said, was I seeing anyone? It was hopeless. You had to ask me if I had a boyfriend. Then you said, would I come for a walk with you, and I knew it was all right because that's what people said in all those Victorian novels I'd read.'

"And the rest," said Sean, "like they say, is history."

"You must get the newspapers today. I won't be going in till the afternoon. I'm going to ask Mr. Spurdell to explain it to me. I mean, explain why Trevor Hughes."

"And what you going to do if he twigs?"

"If he guesses, d'you mean? He won't."

Later, when she had finished her work, and she made sure she finished in good time, she went along the passage and tapped on

Mr. Spurdell's study door. He had come in about a half hour before and gone straight up there.

He was wearing his half-glasses, gold-rimmed, and they made him look older and more scholarly than ever.

"If you haven't done my room, you'd better leave it," he said.

It angered her rather that he hadn't even noticed. She had taken particular care over the study, dusting his books and putting them back meticulously in the correct order.

"May I ask you something?"

"That rather depends on what it is. *What* is it?"

She plunged straight into the middle of things. "If someone murdered three people, A, B, and C, and the police knew about C, why would she—I mean he or she—be accused in court of murdering A only?"

"Is this some crime thriller you're reading?"

Easier to say it was, though she was doubtful as to what he meant. "Yes."

He loved explaining, he loved answering questions. She knew he did and that was why she had been so sure he wouldn't suspect anything. Anyway, he was far more interested in instructing than in her.

"It seems probable that though the police know about C, they cannot prove he or she murdered him. The same may apply to B. He or she is indicted for the murder of A because they are certain that is something they can prove in such a way as to make a case stand up in court. There, does that help you find whodunit?"

"Why not accuse—indict—the person with killing A *and* C?"

"Ah, well, they don't do that. You see, if your putative murderer were to be found not guilty by a jury and acquitted, the police could come back with C—or for that matter B—and bring him into court all over again on this different charge. If they charged him with both and he was acquitted, they would have lost all hope of punishing him."

It was always "he" and "him," as if nothing ever happened to women and they did nothing. "I see," she said, and then, "Where would he—she—be while they were waiting to come into court?"

He began talking about something called the Criminal Justices Act 1991, a legal measure to do with sentencing and keeping people in prison, but when he got to the point of the Act just being implemented "now, while I speak, Liza," his phone began to ring. She turned to go but he motioned to her to stay while he picked up the phone.

"Hallo, Jane, my dear," she heard him say, "and what can I do for you?"

The conversation wasn't a long one. She felt that she would have liked to send some message to Jane Spurdell, something like her good wishes, but of course she couldn't do that. Replacing the receiver, Mr. Spurdell said, "I thought you might like to borrow another book." He added rather severely, "Something worthwhile."

This was perhaps a reference to what he believed she was reading at the moment. She took her opportunity.

"How long do they send a murderer to prison for?" Since her introduction to newspapers, she had heard, she thought, of quite short sentences for killing people. "I mean, does it vary according to how they've done it or why?"

"If someone is convicted of murder in this country, the mandatory sentence is imprisonment for life."

She grew cold. "Always?" she said, and he thought she didn't know what "mandatory" meant.

"The word signifies something of the nature of a command. Something mandatory is something which must be. We don't have degrees of murder here, though they do in the United States. If it was manslaughter, now, the sentence might be quite short."

The term meant nothing to her. It would look suspicious if she kept on questioning him. He had picked two Hardy novels in paperback off his shelves. She hadn't read them, she thanked him, and went downstairs to get her money.

n i n e t e e n

THAT day Eve had been in the witness box.

Liza was astonished to read that she admitted killing Trevor Hughes. Yet she had pleaded not guilty. Perhaps you could explain that when you understood her counsel was trying to get the charge changed from murder to that word Mr. Spurdell had used: "manslaughter." Sean seemed to know all about it.

Today there was a photograph of Trevor Hughes, a faceless man, his features buried in that thick, fair beard. Eve said she had killed him because he tried to rape her. She was quite alone in the house, there was no one living nearer than a mile away. She got away from him, ran into the house to get her gun, and shot him in self-defense.

Prosecuting counsel questioned her very closely. You could imagine there was a lot more than appeared in the paper. He asked her why she had a loaded shotgun in the house? Why did she not lock herself in the house and phone for help? She said she had no phone and he made much of a woman being nervous enough to have a loaded gun at hand but no phone. When she knew he was dead, why had she not phoned for help from Shrove House, where there was a phone? Why had she concealed the death by burying the man's body?

Before she had given her evidence someone called Matthew Edwards gave his. They didn't put things in order in the newspaper but arranged them in the most sensational way. It took Liza a moment to realize this was Matt, and reading what he had said took her back to that early morning long ago when she'd looked out of the window and seen him releasing the dogs from the little castle.

He told the court of the freshly dug earth he had seen and the dogs running about sniffing it and how Eve hadn't been able to answer when he asked if they'd been burying bones. Liza remembered it all. Eve hadn't answered, she'd just asked him if he knew what time it was and told him the time in an icy voice, six-thirty in the morning.

The trial would end next day. That meant this day, today. It would be over by now. Counsel for the Defense made a speech in which he spoke of Eva Beck's hard life. She had more cause than most women to fear rape, for she had already suffered it.

Liza stopped reading for a moment. She could feel the thudding of her own heartbeats. Unconsciously, she had covered the paper with her hand as if there was no one behind her, as if Sean wasn't there, reading it over her shoulder.

"You'll have to read it, love," Sean said gently.

"I know."

"Want me to read it to you? Shall I read it first and then read it to you?"

She shook her head and forced herself to take her hand away. The uncompromising words seemed blacker than the rest of the account, the paper whiter.

At the age of twenty-one, returning to Oxford from Heathrow, where she had been seeing a friend off on a flight to Rio, Eve Beck had hitched a lift from a truck driver. Two other men had been in the truck. It was driven to a lay-by where all three men raped her. As a result she had been very ill and had undergone prolonged psychiatric treatment. The rape had made her into a recluse who wanted nothing more from life than to be left alone and do her job as caretaker of the Shrove estate.

The society of other people she had eschewed and was virtually unknown in the nearby village. She had been living with a grown-up daughter who had since left home.

Liza sat very still and silent when she had finished reading. All her questions were answered. She could feel Sean's eyes on her. Presently he laid his hand on her shoulder and, when she didn't reject him, put his arm around her.

After a moment or two she said quietly, "Ever since I was about twelve, which was as soon as I could have ideas about it really, I've believed I was Jonathan Tobias's child. I didn't like it much, I'd stopped liking him much, but at least it meant I had a father."

"He still could have been."

"No. She never told me all that stuff, that in the paper, but she did say she hadn't seen Jonathan for two weeks before she went to see him off for America. One of those men in the truck was my father. There are three men about somewhere, they might be in the town here, or driving a lorry that we've passed on the road, and one of them's my father." She looked at him and away from him. "I expect I'll get used to it."

She could see Sean didn't know what to say. She made an effort. "It's mostly not true, what they said. She killed people because they threatened her living at Shrove. She killed them because they tried to stop her having what she wanted. No one's said anything about the way she loves Shrove. And as for me, I'm just the grown-up daughter who's left home."

He put his arms around her.

Grown up. Sean had asked her about that. Not the first time they met at the caravan or the second, but soon. She had gone for a walk with him, as promised, telling Eve she was spending the evening in Shrove library, there were books there she wanted that were too heavy to carry home. After the walk they sat in the caravan. He had a beer and she had a Coke.

That was when she started telling him how she'd lived, isolated, almost without society, in the little world of Shrove. "How old are you?" he'd asked, admitting she looked a year or two older than she was but still afraid she might say she was only fifteen.

That first time he didn't even kiss her. Two evenings later it was too hot to walk far, a close, humid, throbbing dusk, and they had flung themselves down in the long seed-headed grass by the maple hedge. She had looked at his face, six inches from her own, through the pale reedy stems. There was a scent of hay and of dryness. The feathery seedheads scattered brown dusty pollen on his hair. He parted the thin strands of grass and put his mouth on hers and kissed her.

She couldn't help herself, she had no control. Her arms were around his neck, she was clutching his hair in her hands, kissing him back with passion, putting everything she had read about love and desire into those kisses. It was he who restrained them, who jumped up and pulled her to her feet and began asking her if she was sure, did she know what she was doing, if they were going "all the way" she must be sure.

It wasn't possible for her to think about it. When she tried to think, all that happened was that she saw images of Sean and felt his kisses, growing hot and weak, growing wet in an unanticipated way that no instruction or reading had led her to expect. She tried to think calmly and reason it out but her mind became a screen of Sean pictures, Sean-and-herself-together pictures, her body shuddered with longing, and she got no further about being sure or knowing what she was doing than she had in the meadow. It came down to this: when next she saw him she would do everything and anything he wanted and everything she wanted, but if she never saw him again she would die.

She read *Romeo and Juliet* again but it no longer seemed to be about what she was feeling. On Monday evening it was raining, so they met in the caravan and made love as soon as they met, falling upon each other in a breathless joyful ecstasy.

It seemed a long time ago now.

Sean switched on the television and they watched the news. For the first time, so far as they knew, it contained something about Eve. They had to wait until almost the last item. The last was about attempts to put an end to bullfighting in Spain, but before that the newscaster announced laconically that Eva Beck, the killer in the Gatehouse Murder case, had been found guilty and sent to prison for life.

Sean held her, he kept his arm around her all night, hugging her tightly when she awoke whimpering. But still he didn't understand how she felt. She no longer had any identity. With Eve's denial—for whatever good purpose—she had ceased to be anyone, and, with the revelations of Eve's history, had been made worse than fatherless.

No words could be found to express what she felt. She had nothing to say to Sean, so she spoke about the everyday mundane things, what they would eat for supper, what food items he should bring back from the store. It was clear that he was relieved not to talk about Eve or the trial or Liza's own new vulnerability, and it pained her, it angered her. Once or twice, during their disturbed night, he had told her she must put "all that" behind her.

Just as he was leaving she surprised him by saying she was coming too.

"It's not your day for Mrs. S., is it?"

She shook her head. He must think she was coming into town because she didn't want to pass this day alone in the caravan. She sat beside him, saying how nice the weather was, a wonderful sunny day for the start of December. In just over a month's time she would be seventeen, but he didn't know when her birthday was, though he might have guessed. When they were first together they hadn't talked much. It had been all lovemaking and the aftermath of lovemaking and its renewal.

Anxious as ever not to be one minute late, he hurried into the store. The car keys were in his pocket, but she had brought the spare set. A map he never used, his sense of direction was so good, was tucked into the back of the glove compartment. She studied it, left it lying unfolded on the passenger seat.

They couldn't do much to her if they caught her driving without a license or insurance. The way she was feeling today she didn't much care what anyone did to her. It no longer mattered if they caught her and found out who she was, because she was no one, she had no identity. She was just the grown-up daughter who had since left home.

She drove past where the caravan was and out onto the big road. The world seemed entirely different here and had seemed so for the past three months, but for all that it was only about twenty miles from where she was going. Passing a garage, she glanced at the gas gauge. It was all right. The tank was nearly full. She began to wonder how she would feel when she came to the bridge and saw the river with the water meadows beyond and the house floating, as it seemed, above the white mists that lay low on the flat land, when she saw the domain that was the only place she had ever known until a mere ninety days ago.

But when the time came she experienced no startling reaction. It was a brisk breezy day without mist. The sun shone with a sharp winter brightness. Shrove House had never appeared so brilliantly unveiled. From halfway across the bridge, half a mile distant, she could pick out the dark spindly etching the clematis made on the rear walls and the features on the faces of the stone women in the alcoves.

The sun flashed sharply off the window from which she had watched Sean the second time she had seen him. She drove up the lane. Someone had been hedging along here, had mercilessly ripped back the high hawthorns. The gatehouse appeared suddenly, as it always did when the bend was passed. It looked the same as ever and the gateway to Shrove was the same except that the gates, for the first time that she could remember, were shut. The gates that, except on the day after the storm, had always stood folded back like permanently open shutters at a window were so firmly closed that the park could only be seen through their elaborate iron scrollwork and the curlicued letters: SHROVE HOUSE.

She walked up the garden path to the gatehouse. Her key she had always kept. She pushed it into the lock and opened the front door. Inside it was icy cold and smelling of damp. The smell was the stench of hollows in the roots of trees where fungus rotted.

The kitchen was dim and dark because the blind was pulled down. Raising it a little, she looked out, and then she let the string go and the blind spring up to its roller with a crack, she was so shocked by what she saw. The back garden, which had been neat with Eve's vegetable beds and flower borders, with the new tree planted to replace the fallen cherry, the small lawn, all of it was a wilderness of thin straggly weeds. These had not sprung up among the untended cultivated plants but were weeds growing on dug earth. The whole garden had been turned over with spades.

For a moment she couldn't imagine what had happened. Had someone else lived here temporarily, dug the garden and then departed? Had some new and zealous gardener taken over and left again?

Then she remembered what the paper had said about Eve burying the body of Trevor Hughes. Somewhere out there it must be that she had buried him, where Matt said the dogs had sniffed the earth. The police had excavated here, looking for more perhaps, looking for a graveyard. Their spades had made this wilderness. She thought of the numberless times they had sat out in the garden under the cherry tree, the work Eve had done, hoeing, planting, harvesting, but it affected her very little. It troubled her no more than walking in a cemetery.

She pulled the blind down once more and turned her attention to the interior of the gatehouse. Having been away from it for so long, she saw these rooms with new eyes, eyes educated enough by variety to find them strange: the vaulted ceilings, the pointed Gothic windows, the dark woodwork. It seemed remarkable now that she had lived here all her life, or as long as she could remember.

This room, the living room, was not as it had been when she left it. Of course, she couldn't tell how soon Eve had gone after her own departure. But she wouldn't have left it like this, the pictures crooked, the ornaments on the mantelpiece in the wrong order, the hearth rug out of alignment. It struck Liza that she had no idea who owned this furniture. Was it Eve's or did it belong in the lodge? Had it been there when Eve and she first came? The sofa had never stood quite like that, pushed flat against the wall. Someone had searched this room. The police had searched it. She had seen this sort of thing in a detective serial on television.

There was something missing from the room. A picture. A pale rectangle on the wall showed where it had once hung, her own portrait, the picture Bruno had painted of her.

It had never, in her opinion, looked much like her. The colors were too strong and her features too big. But Eve had liked it. Perhaps Eve had been allowed to take it with her, had it with her now, would keep it through those long years. The idea was comforting.

Had the police also searched the little castle?

The green studded door was still unlocked. If they had searched, surely they would have locked it after them. Liza loosened the brick at the foot of the wall between the lancet windows, pulled it out and found the iron box. The money was still there. She took the box with its contents.

Back in the gatehouse she went upstairs. She looked into Eve's bedroom, neat as a pin, desolate. The jewel case was there in the drawer, but it was empty. No gold wedding ring, of course, she had expected that, but no earrings, either, or jade necklace or brooches. She wondered what had become of them.

From the cupboard in her own bedroom she took her warm quilted coat, the two skirts Eve had made her, the red-and-blue sweater Eve had knitted.

The curtains were drawn in here, for no good reason that she could see. She drew them back and looked across the ruined gatehouse garden to the grounds of Shrove. It gave her a little shock to see David Cosby walking across the grass between the young trees. He had a dog with him, a red-and-white spaniel. Once she was sure he wasn't looking in this direction, she drew the curtains again.

His walk was taking him nowhere near the little wood. Liza put the metal box and the clothes into the boot of the car and locked it. She wondered if she dared leave it there for the ten minutes it would take her to do what she had to do and decided she must.

The sun still shone with unseasonable brightness. It was so late in the year that the shadows were long, even at noon. The ground was dry for early December, under her feet softly crackling strata, layer upon layer of them, of fallen leaves. She made her way into the little wood, not wanting to go but aware that she had to. This was as important a mission as the quest for the iron box of money.

Much of the clearing operations she had witnessed but not this replanting. It was unexpected, an unforeseen act. New trees with the deer and rabbit guards on their thin trunks stood everywhere in carefully planned groups. She took heart from the sight of the two dead larches left to stand as a feeding place for woodpeckers and the broken poplar that had put out new branches.

The cherry log lay where it had lain from the time of its fall, or she thought it lay like that. How could she be sure? It was deep now in dead leaves, awash with them almost, with a tide of brown beech leaves that hid two-thirds of the log. But all those leaves had fallen since October. . . .

She squatted down and began burrowing into the leaves with her hands. The relief at the feel of sacking against her fingers was so great she almost laughed aloud. Wedged beneath the log, the bundle was still in place, winter after winter was burying it deeper. Leaves would turn to leaf mold and leaf mold to earth. One day the log itself would be buried as the level of the ground gradually and very slowly rose, while Bruno slept on, undisturbed.

There were no policemen standing by the car taking notes, no David Cosby with his young inquisitive dog. She got into the driving seat and drove down the lane, over the bridge, and took the road to the village where Bruno had wanted to take Eve to live. There, in the village shop, she bought a pack of ham sandwiches, a can of Coke, and a Bounty bar for her lunch. It amused her a little that she had found buying these things in this shop so easy, she who had never dared go in there in former days.

But before that she investigated the contents of the iron box.

The previous time she had looked into the box, and helped herself from it, she had had very little idea of the value of money, what was a lot and what wasn't much. It was different now. She had lived a lifetime of experience in three months, had earned money and knew what things cost. Sitting in the driving seat in a secluded spot by the churchyard wall, she opened the box and counted the notes.

They amounted to something over a thousand pounds: to be precise, a thousand and seventy-five. Liza could hardly believe it. She must have made a mistake. But she counted again and again she reached the figure of a thousand and seventy-five. The money lay heavily on her, not on her hands, but like a burden on her back. She shook herself and tried to see it differently, as a blessing. No longer daring to leave it in the car, she carried the thousand pounds stuffed in her pockets as she went over to the shop. Because there was so much of it she felt she could afford a ham sandwich instead of cheese.

The car restored to the Superway car park, she wandered about the town, afraid to steal a bath at the Duke's Head in case she got caught and they found all that money on her. There wasn't time to go to the cinema. Instead she went to the bookshop, acquiring undreamed-of marvels, among them *The Divine Comedy* in translation, Ovid's *Metamorphoses* in the original *and* translation, before telling herself she must be careful with the money, she must be prudent. They needed that money, she and Sean.

All the same, she postponed telling him about it. Later would do, another day would do. Nor did she show him the new books. She had been to Shrove, she said, she had fetched her clothes. All he was concerned about was her driving the car uninsured and without a license. He was rather angry about that. She hadn't dreamed, when first she knew him, that he would turn out so law-abiding.

The first hint of it she'd had was when the man who owned the land beside the old station discovered that the caravan was parked there and told him to move on. Liza, remembering that day when she had stood with the demonstrators and the last train had come down the line, said he need not move more than a dozen yards. If he parked it by the platform he would be on British Rail land and they never came near the place, they wouldn't find out. Sean wouldn't do it. He said he knew he was wrong being on that man's land without permission, he wasn't sticking his neck out again. He'd move over the bridge and up through the fields and woods to Ring Common, where anyone could be.

It was four or five miles away. Of course he went on coming to Shrove to do the garden. Liza never spoke to him while he was on the mower or doing the edges or weeding, it amused her to walk past him with a casual "hi" or even a shy "hallo" if Eve was with her, remembering their lovemaking of the previous evening. How had she known that her association with Sean wouldn't be acceptable to Eve? That Eve and she were Capulets and Sean a Montague? Instinctively, she had known it, and had kept their love an absolute secret.

At the same time it brought her enormous pleasure to watch him about the grounds of Shrove when he had no idea she was watching him. Observing his handsomeness and his grace, she liked to remember and to anticipate. She even enjoyed the pleasure-pain of needing to go up to him and touch him, kiss him and have him touch her, needing it passionately but still making herself resist.

One day she saw a man talking to him. It was a shock to realize that the man was Matt. The past couple of times Jonathan had been at Shrove he had brought Matt with him. It was a long time since they had seen Jonathan, she and Eve, though weeks rather than months. The years when he had scarcely come at all were gone by. He had been at Shrove in April and now it was June. Matt was talking to Sean about something or other, pointing at this and that in what seemed to Liza a hectoring way before going back to the house.

"What was he saying to you that day?" she asked Sean five months later. "Matt. When you had to stop the tractor and take off your visor?"

"I don't know. What does it matter? I reckon it was only to boss me about. Maybe it was to cut the tops off the lilacs, prune the lilacs. I never knew you was supposed to do that."

"We didn't know Jonathan was coming. He didn't warn us, but he often didn't. I told Eve I'd seen him. I knew she'd want me to do that so that she could get dressed up and wash her hair before he came. That was the evening he first started talking about the money he'd lost. He didn't mind me being there, he talked about it in front of me. He was what they call a Name at Lloyd's. D'you know what that means?"

"Sort of. I saw about it in the papers. They were a sort of insurance company, only very big and sort of important, and something happened so they had to fork out more than they'd got."

"It was to do with that Alaskan oil spill, that was the start of it. And they had more claims that they could—I think 'meet' is the word. Instead of making money, all the people who were Names found they had to pay money. Jonathan was one. He said he didn't know how much it would be yet but he thought a lot, and luckily he had the house in France to sell that had been Caroline's. He looked very miserable. But, you know, we didn't take it very seriously, Eve and I. Or Eve didn't. I wasn't interested. She was interested, she was interested in everything that concerned him, but even she didn't believe he was having a job finding money. She was so used to the Tobiases and the Ellisons having so much of it. They were the kind of people, she said to me, who'd say they were poor when they were down to their last million."

Sean shrugged. He put his arm around Liza. "Feeling a bit better, are you, love? About you-know-what?"

She knew what. The revelation in the paper. Eve's past life. "I'm all right. Only I'd like to go and see her."

"Your mum?"

"Not yet. Maybe after Christmas. I'll find out where she is, where they've put her, and then I'll go and see her."

"You're amazing, you really are. After what she done? After she murdered three blokes? After the way she brought you up? She's bad news, love."

"She never did me a bit of harm," said Liza. "She's my mother. You can understand why she killed those men. I can understand it. There was one place in the world she had a sanctuary, there was one kind of life she could live and stay, well, not mad, and they all wanted to take it away from her, one after the other."

"Not Trevor Hughes."

"Yes, he did. In a way. Jonathan had said she was there to see how she got on, but she knew he meant how it suited *him*. She was on *trial*. It wouldn't have suited him if his dogs had had to be destroyed because she'd set them on someone.

"And Bruno was going to make her leave unless she sent *me* away. You can understand why she killed them, she didn't have a choice. They'd got her in a corner and she acted like an animal would. And now I've read what happened to her before I was born, I know she was getting her revenge too, she was taking vengeance on three men for what three men had done to her."

"Not the same men," Sean objected.

"Oh, of *course* not. Don't you understand anything?" Immediately, she was remorseful. "I'm sorry. I'll tell you about the last one, shall I?"

He shrugged, then said a rather sullen, "Yes."

"I'll tell you about how she shot him."

t w e n t y

THIS would be the last of Scheherazade's stories, she said. Not a thousand and one nights but nearer a hundred. Three and a half months of nights to tell a life in.

"When did I run away, Sean?"

"It was August. No, it wasn't, it was September the first."

She began counting on her fingers. "That was something I never learned. I never learned much arithmetic. I make it a hundred and one nights tomorrow."

"Is that right?"

They were coming home from work on the following day, the hundredth day. Liza had carried the money with her to

Aspen Close, she dared not leave it in the caravan. Stopping work at lunchtime, she had walked around the town until she found a shop to sell her a money belt. In the public lavatory in the marketplace she packed all the notes into the belt and put it on over her jeans. She was so slim the belt looked smart, not cumbersome.

She still hadn't said anything about the money to Sean and he believed that all she had fetched from the lodge were her clothes. Glad of the quilted coat, she rubbed her cold hands together. The heater in the car worked only fitfully.

"I'd got to June, hadn't I?" she said. "It was when Jonathan first started going on about money. He'd brought Matt with him."

"He was always coming out in the garden telling me how to do my job," Sean grumbled.

"Did he? I didn't know that. Matt was a builder up in Cumbria but his business had failed. If it wasn't for him, Eve wouldn't be in prison. He hated us. I think it was because he'd once thought Eve beautiful but he disgusted *her.*"

Sean nodded. "That'd be it. She treated him like dirt."

"If it wasn't for him, the police wouldn't have suspected anything and Eve would still be at the gatehouse and so would I."

"I ought to thank him then, hadn't I?"

She smiled. "Jonathan sort of took him under his wing. Matt was getting married or he wanted to get married and Jonathan had some idea of getting him a place to live near Shrove and having him manage the grounds. While he was there he went out every night shooting rabbits by the car headlights. There was all this banging of guns night after night and the lights blazing over the fields. I hated it, I never liked Matt."

"Them little devils have to be kept down, love. I never seen so many rabbits as there was last summer. And pigeons, they tear the crops to bits."

"When he stayed at Shrove he slept in a room over the coach house. There are seventeen bedrooms at Shrove, but he had to sleep out there. He had to use the outside lavatory behind the stables and wash under the tap that was there for watering the horses."

Sean said seriously, "Tobias couldn't have him in the house, not a servant. Matt wouldn't have expected it."

Liza gave him a look. She shook her head a little at him, but he had his eye on the road. "Jonathan told Eve you were just a temporary measure. Those were his words. He was going to give you the sack at the end of the summer, at Michaelmas—whenever that is—and have Matt and his wife live over the coach house. He said he'd have things done to it to make it possible to live there. Put in one of his famous bathrooms, I expect."

"He did give me the sack. Well, he got Matt to do it."

"I was in a panic when he first said it. I thought he'd get rid of you and you'd have to go and I'd never see you again."

They had reached the place where the caravan was. Sean put his arms around Liza and hugged her.

"You didn't trust me."

"I don't think I trusted anyone by then, not even Eve."

Inside the caravan they lit the gas and the oil heater. The warmth came quickly, though it was a damp, smelly heat. Sean lit a cigarette, making the atmosphere worse, and opened the bottle of wine he had brought from Superway and began unwrapping the samosas and onion bhajis for their supper. Pulling off her coat, Liza hugged herself inside the comfort of the sweater Eve had made. She talked, drinking her wine.

Eve hadn't liked that idea of Matt and his wife living at

Shrove. Jonathan said it meant she could get rid of Mrs. Cooper, she wouldn't have to handle the wages and the organization, she'd have nothing to do but *be* there and, of course, she'd be in authority over them, they'd have to do as she said. Why can't we go on managing as we are? she wanted to know. It would be easier for her this way, Jonathan said, and besides, he had to find something for Matt, he had a duty to Matt.

Liza knew what her mother was really feeling. By this time she understood most of Eve's deeply emotional attitude toward Shrove. Eve didn't want anyone, anyone at all, coming between her and that house and that land, that domain. She even resented Sean's being there. Mr. Frost had been there before she came, was there when her own mother was, she accepted him like she did the train and the inevitable weekend guests, but Sean was new. Of course, she said none of this to Jonathan, and that night Jonathan stayed at the gatehouse. Liza felt very strange about that because she was deep in a sexual relationship of her own and she understood what went on beyond the wall dividing their bedrooms.

The next day she found Eve standing in front of the mirror, peering closely at her face, plucking out a gray hair. She came up behind Eve, not meaning to do this, not meaning to make the contrast. It all happened by chance that her face was reflected behind Eve's, a yard or so and twenty-two years between.

Eve turned around and said, *"Mater pulchra, filia pulchrior."*

Liza didn't know what to say. She could hardly reply that it was true the mother was beautiful but the daughter more so, or pretend not to understand. A lame "I think you look lovely" was all she could manage. But she wondered what the hectic light in Eve's eye portended and her wild behavior that day and her sudden bursts of too-loud laughter.

As it happened, she overheard what Eve said to Jonathan.

She'd got in the habit of listening at doors. It was a way of trying to save her life. Sometimes, these days, she felt her whole life was in jeopardy. If Matt came, would Eve stay? If she and Eve went, where could they go? If Sean went, what would she do? She would die. As soon as she sensed Eve or Jonathan or both of them wanted her out of the way, she knew they were going to talk secrets she should have been privy to, because it was she most of all that they threatened.

That evening she had been at the caravan with Sean. Well, more than the evening. She had been with him from the time he stopped work at four until nine, when he drove her back to Shrove. Home again at the gatehouse, she thought at first that they had gone out somewhere or to Shrove House.

Jonathan's jacket was hanging over the back of a chair but that meant nothing. She went to her bedroom and looked out of the open window toward the house, expecting to see them walking in the pale red light of the sunset afterglow. But they were much nearer at hand. They were sitting on a rug spread out on the grass in the garden just below her window. Or Eve was sitting, her knees drawn up and her arms wrapped around them, while Jonathan lay on his back, looking up at the thin moon that had appeared in the still-light sky.

They weren't speaking but Liza knew that once they did speak she would be able to hear every word. She crouched on the bed with her chin on the windowsill, thinking about Sean, how he had said to her that evening to come and live with him in the caravan. He had asked her, he had said he missed her too much when she wasn't with him, and what was there to keep her here? She couldn't answer that. She couldn't say, I'm frightened to go.

In a way she wanted to terribly and in another way she didn't want to at all. Yet it was only a couple of years before that she'd been always asking herself what would become of her and how would she ever get away? The silence down there was oppressive. When she was beginning to think she might as well go down there and join them, Eve spoke.

"Jonathan, will you marry me?"

It was a worse silence this time. Anything would have been better than this silence. He was was no longer looking at the moon but at Eve. She said with great bravery—how Liza admired her courage!—"I asked you to marry me. Women can do that, can't they? We were going to be married once, when we were very young. It all went wrong, we both know why, but is it too late to make it right?"

He sounded ashamed, Liza thought. "I'm afraid it is too late, Evie."

Eve made a little sound. She whispered, "Why is it?"

"The time for that's gone by, Evie. I'm sorry but it's just too late."

"But why is it? We're always happy when we're together. Don't I make you happy? Hasn't it always been—good with me?"

"I shan't marry again. I'm better alone and maybe you are too. I'll be frank, I don't want to be married. I've tried it and it didn't work. Victoria and I were all right until we got married. It was then that things started to fall apart. It would be the same with you and me."

"Then I have humiliated myself for nothing," Eve said in a hard voice, but almost at once she had turned back to him and suddenly cast herself upon him, clutching him in her arms and crying, "Jonathan, Jonathan, you know I love you, why won't you stay with me? Why have you kept me like this for all these years? I've waited for you for so long, I've waited forever and still I can't have you. Jonathan, please, please . . ."

Liza couldn't bear any more of it. She jumped off the bed and ran away into Eve's room, the way she had done when she was a child.

"She should have known better than that," said Sean.

"It was ironical, wasn't it? There was I being begged to go and live with you and not daring to and there was she begging Jonathan to marry her and being rejected."

She didn't like his reply, though it was complimentary to herself. "No, well, you're sixteen, aren't you, love? And she's a bit past her sell-by date."

"Jonathan was older than she."

"He's a man. It's different. I bet he didn't stay that night."

She digested the first part of these remarks. This was a point of view she hadn't previously come across and she found it deeply unsatisfactory. "He went back to Shrove about half an hour later, and he and Matt went off the next day. I thought he'd never come back but he did."

"Too right he did and that Matt with him. It was the end of August. Matt come up to me all smiles like he was going to give me a raise. It was ten minutes before I was due to leave and I was using that bit of time to thin out the plums. There was so many plums on that damn tree the branches was breaking. He said like he was my boss, Holford, we shan't need your services after the weekend, thanks very much. It was a Wednesday and he said he wouldn't need my services after the weekend. I said, is that what you call giving a person notice? He went on smiling. Take it or leave it, he says to me, you get paid up to Friday afternoon, and he just walked off."

Liza hadn't seen Sean on that Wednesday evening, so the news of his dismissal reached her secondhand. She was nearly frantic when she heard. They weren't in the lodge but at the house. It was such a rare thing for her and Eve to be asked up to the house when Jonathan was there that she had sensed something awful was going to happen.

Jonathan came to the gatehouse at about four in the afternoon. She and Eve were indoors, it was rather a chilly day for late August, and Jonathan talked to them from the window. He didn't come in. He just said, come up to the house for a drink about six, I've got something to tell you.

Eve was sore. She seemed truculent and sulky. No one but Liza would have guessed that what she was suffering from was simple unhappiness. Tell us what? she asked. He didn't answer. I'll take you both out for a meal afterward, if you like, he said.

Probably Eve was imagining all kinds of dreadful things—though nothing so dreadful as the truth. Jonathan received them in the drawing room, very grand. They sat in one of the groups of crimson-and-gold chairs and sofas that were arranged in each corner of the room around a marble or ormolu table. A good deal of the glory was lost when Matt came shambling in with bottles and glasses on a tray and peanuts in a packet. Matt's hair was down on his shoulders now but it had gone gray and he had grown a big belly, so Liza couldn't imagine what sort of a woman would think of marrying him. She had never seen a drunk person or heard the word Jonathan used and would have thought Matt ill if Eve hadn't explained later.

"How dare you come in here pissed? Put the bloody nuts in a dish and then get out."

Jonathan had been drinking too, she could smell it on his breath when he leaned toward her and asked her if she was allowed a glass of wine.

"I've just had Matt give that young man of yours the push," he said to Eve.

"What young man of mine?"

"The gardener."

"You've sacked him? Why?"

Liza could hear the relief in Eve's voice. She was aghast, but Eve was relieved because she was expecting something worse. So that was all Jonathan had got them up there for, Eve was no doubt thinking, to tell me he's got rid of Sean Holford to make room for Matt and Mrs. Matt, and now he'll be wanting me to get rid of Mrs. Cooper.

And what am I going to do? Liza thought feverishly. *Suppose he's gone, suppose he never comes back, suppose I never see him again?*

"I told you I'd got something to tell you, Eve. It's not that I've fired the gardener. It's not that Matt will be taking over. No one will be taking over. The fact is I'm going to have to sell the house. Shrove House will have to be sold."

Trembling for her mother, Liza turned slowly to look at her. Eve was stone-still. She had gone white and suddenly she looked tremendously old, not thirty-eight but sixty-eight, an old woman with a lined forehead and mouth that has fallen in.

"Don't look like that, Evie," Jonathan said. "D'you think I want to do it? I've no choice. I told you about my financial difficulties. I've got to put more into Lloyd's than I dreamed was possible. It's been a frightful shock to me. But you must know what's happened to the Names, it's been all over the papers day after day—no, I forgot, you don't read the papers. The fact is I've got to find close to a million and I can't do it without selling Shrove. If I get fifty thousand for Mama's house in France I'll be doing well, it's more than I can hope for, thirty's more likely. I've been trying to sell it for two years. Again I was going to say you know what's happened to the property market but, no, I don't suppose you do know. I have to sell Shrove. When I do it will just cover me. I shall just keep my head above water."

Eve was staring at him. This was the first time Liza had ever drunk wine and she was making the most of it. It helped. She held out her glass for more and Jonathan filled it absently.

"For God's sake, Eve, say something." He tried, incredibly, facetiousness. "Say something if it's only good-bye."

Liza saw her make an effort. She saw her suck in her lips and raise her shoulders as if in pain. The voice, when it came, was breathless and thin. "You can sell Ullswater."

"The Ullswater house belongs to Victoria now—remember?"

"Why were you ever such a fool as to marry her?"

"D'you think I haven't asked myself that over and over?"

"Jonathan," said Eve, holding her hands tightly clenched together, "Jonathan, you can't sell Shrove, it's unthinkable, there has to be an alternative." She thought of one. "You can sell the London house."

"And where am I supposed to live?"

Eve, who hadn't taken her eyes off him, seemed to stare even more intently. Not liking the look in her mother's face, the glazed, hardly sane look, Liza shifted uncomfortably in her chair. Eve said, "You can live here."

"No, I can't." Jonathan was growing irritable. "I don't want to live here. Things are bad enough without my having to live in a place I dislike." He sounded like a petulant child. "All right, I know I've never told you I don't like this place, but the fact is I don't, I never have. It's isolated, it's miles from anywhere, and you mayn't have noticed this, but it's damp. Of course it is, stuck in a bloody river valley. Victoria got fibrositis through staying here."

"God damn Victoria to hell," said Eve in a voice to make Liza jump out of her skin.

Jonathan wasn't put out. "All right. Willingly. I wish she was in hell. I'm sure I've suffered from her more than you have, more than you dream of. Never mind her, anyway. I have to sell this house, I have to have the million it'll fetch."

"You won't be able to sell it. Even I know that. I may live out of the world but I've got a radio, I know what goes on. The house market's the worst it's been in my lifetime. You won't find a buyer. Not at the price you're asking you won't."

Jonathan refilled Eve's glass from the dry sherry bottle. She lifted the glass, watching him. For a moment Liza thought she was going to throw the contents of the glass at him but she didn't. Nor did she drink from it.

Jonathan said calmly, "I have. I have found a buyer."

Eve made a little pained sound.

"A hotel chain. They're embarking on a project called Country Heritage Hotels. Shrove will be their flagship, as they call it."

"I don't believe you."

"Come off it, Evie, of course you believe me. Why would I say it if it wasn't true?"

"The deal," said Eve, "the contract, whatever, I don't know about these things—is it settled?"

"Not yet. They've made an approach and I've told my solicitor to tell them a tentative yes. That's as far as we've got. You're the first person I've told."

"I should think so," Eve said scornfully.

"Of course I'd tell you first, Evie."

"What will become of me, of us? Have you thought of that?"

Jonathan began saying he would find her a house. Matt and

his wife would stay at Shrove until it was bought by Country Heritage and then they would have to have a home found for them. His idea was perhaps to find a pair of semidetached cottages. On the other side of the valley possibly, and he named the village where Bruno had nearly bought a house. Property was for sale all over the place and much of it going for a song.

There was no question of abandoning Eve. He hoped she knew his responsibility toward her. Unfortunately for her, the hotel chain wanted the gatehouse for use as their reception. They had specifically stated this in their offer.

Eve said flatly, "I will never leave here."

"That's all very well. I'm afraid you must. Do you think it's pleasant for me having to tell you this? Come to that, d'you think I like selling half my property? My grandfather would turn in his grave, I know that."

"He wouldn't," said Eve. "Not where he is, rotting in hell."

"I don't see the use of talking like that. It doesn't help."

"I will never leave here. They will have to take me away by force if they want me to leave here."

It was a prophecy soon to be fulfilled.

The next day, after a sleepless night, a night when she didn't go to bed at all, Eve went up to Shrove to plead with Jonathan. By that time Liza was already telling the news to Sean, and Sean was urging her to come to him, to leave her mother and Shrove and come and live with him. She was old enough, the law couldn't stop her.

Coming back, she encountered Matt in the stable yard with a fat middle-aged woman in an apron. The presence of his wife didn't stop him eyeing Liza up and down in a lecherous way—

just as he had eyed Eve all those years ago—and telling her she'd grown up into a lovely girl who'd soon have all the boys after her.

Jonathan came back with Eve and they spent the day arguing, Eve alternately pleading and shouting, occasionally weeping. As far as Liza knew, they spent the day like this. At four she went out to meet Sean and didn't get home till nearly ten. Eve didn't say anything, she uttered no word of reproach. Liza could hardly believe her eyes when Jonathan put his arm around Eve, lifted her off the sofa, and led her upstairs to her bedroom, where he closed the door on the pair of them for the rest of the night.

Outside, the usual banging started and the flaring lights as Matt went rabbit-hunting. Liza drew her curtains. She sat on the bed thinking about Sean. He would never come back to Shrove to work. Apple-picking had already begun in the Discovery orchards to the north of here. In less than a week he'd be moving on to earn as much as he could picking apples from dawn till dusk through September. How did two people communicate when neither had a phone? Sean didn't even have a postal address.

He said he'd drive over on Monday and they'd meet in the little wood. Why the little wood? she'd asked and he'd said because it was romantic. He'd also said she'd got to tell him if she was coming. Didn't she love him enough to come?

Secure in her love and companionship now, Sean said, interrupting the story, "I still don't know why you had to keep me on the hook so long."

"I've told you often enough. I was scared. I'd never been away. As far as I could remember, I'd never even slept in any bed but mine at the gatehouse."

He patted the bed they were sitting on. "We never slept much, did we, love?"

"Jonathan was practically living at the gatehouse that weekend," said Liza. "They were all over each other, more than I'd ever seen them. Eve'd never been demonstrative in public. Perhaps I wasn't public, perhaps she didn't care, I don't know. They were hugging and kissing in my presence but for all that, Jonathan could never be got to say he wouldn't sell Shrove. She'd plead and cajole and kiss him and at the end of it he'd just say, 'I've got to sell.' "

Then Eve gave up. On Sunday evening Liza heard her say, "If it must be, it must be."

She reached for Jonathan's hand and held it. Jonathan gave her a look that to Liza, who now knew about such things, seemed full of love.

"We'll find a nice house for you and Liza, you'll still have the countryside, the place itself . . ."

Jonathan stayed the night but left early in the morning before Liza was up. She came downstairs to find Eve seated at the breakfast table, glittery-eyed and galvanic with barely suppressed energy, her hands clasping and unclasping.

"He's going to sell Shrove, he's absolutely determined."

"I know," Liza said.

The tone of Eve's voice changed and became dreamy, reminiscing. "He's asked me to marry him."

"He hasn't!"

"The irony of it, Lizzie, the irony! Of course I said no. No, thanks, I said, you're too late. What's the good of him to me without Shrove?"

It was for Shrove she had wanted him. If he had married her a year ago he could have put Shrove in her name and kept it safe from his creditors. She laughed a little, not hysterically but madder than that, a manic laugh. Still, Liza couldn't believe she had been as abrupt with Jonathan as she implied, for he was back at the lodge in the late morning.

When she heard Eve say she'd go pigeon-shooting with him later, Liza thought the world was turning upside-down faster than she could cope with. Eve never killed birds or animals. Now she was saying the pigeons destroyed the vegetables she grew and would have to be kept down. Jonathan sounded quite happy to teach her to shoot with the four-ten, the gun, Liza thought, she had used to shoot the man with the beard. Only Jonathan, of course, had no idea of that.

Neither of them seemed deflected from their purpose by the fact that in a month or two Shrove would be sold, Eve would have left the gatehouse, and it would hardly matter to her whether the vegetables survived or not.

In the afternoon Liza went up into the little wood to meet Sean. In arranging where to meet she had been careful to arrange this trysting place a good distance from where Bruno's body lay. They made love on a bed of soft dry grass, walled-in by hawthorn bushes. But afterward, holding her in his arms, Sean grew grave. He had to work for his living. He wasn't going on benefit if he could help it. For the next two days he could take a job clearing a house of furniture for a dealer in town, but after that he'd have to move on to where the apples were. He wanted her. Would she come?

He couldn't wait forever, he couldn't really wait beyond Thursday. And after that how would they get in touch with each other?

She hadn't liked that, the fact that he wouldn't wait. In the romantic plays and books she had read, the true lover had been prepared to wait indefinitely, not make conditions and threats. She got him to say that he'd come back here next Saturday, same time, same place. By then she promised she'd have made up her mind. She would have separated herself from her mother and come to him or else she'd be staying. Was it her imagination that he had seemed reluctant? Instead of ardor, her request to him had been met with doubts about whether he could make it, much depended on where he was, he would do his best.

When he had gone and she had watched him go, heading for the place where he had parked the car, far up the lane, when she had seen the last of him as the trees absorbed him, the tears came into her eyes and she started to cry. They were tears of frustration, of impotence and self-pity at her own indecisiveness. Wiping her eyes on the backs of her hands, then rubbing them with her fists like a child, she walked slowly back the way she had come.

It was nearly six, she calculated, the sun still high in the sky but some of its heat departed. Sean and she had been together for three hours but it had seemed no more than three minutes. She was thinking about her dilemma once more, wondering if some middle way could be found, some compromise, whereby she could continue to be here with Eve and keep Sean nearby, when she heard the first shot.

Liza's instinct, whenever there was shooting on the grounds, was to take herself as far away from the neighborhood of those reports as possible, even to cover her ears. Her dread was of actually seeing a bird fall to the ground, bloody and with feathers flying, or a rabbit brought down as it fled for cover. But this time she was not exactly sure where the shot had come from, it was often hard to tell. At any rate, it wasn't in this wood and wouldn't be in their back garden.

She saw Matt first. Although she knew of Jonathan's intention to shoot pigeons, when she caught sight of Matt in the far distance, almost up by Shrove House, she thought it was he who was after the birds. Then she saw Jonathan and Eve standing together between the largest remaining cedar, the blue *atlantica glauca,* and the group of new young trees. They weren't very far from her, no more than a hundred yards, quite near enough for her to see that they had only one gun between them.

Jonathan had been demonstrating something and now he put the shotgun into Eve's hands. Holding it gingerly, she raised the barrel in a clumsy way, with what seemed an effort. He gave her a kindly glance, then adjusted her hands, moving them farther apart. Their shadows had lengthened as the sun sank and now streamed out thin and dark across the leaf-patterned grass. When Jonathan clapped his hands to make the pigeons fly Liza stopped looking, opened the gate, and let herself into the gatehouse garden.

She had forgotten to cover her ears. The gun went off, once, twice, three times. There came a cry no bird could have made, a high-pitched scream quite clearly audible from where she was. She stood still. For a moment a little child again, she saw in her mind's eye the bearded man as he died on the grass in the dusk.

Almost without realizing it, she had put up her hands over her ears. But there was to be no more firing. She took away her hands, she turned around and saw Matt running across the grass, waving his arms.

Between the trees, on the open green that the sun and shadows dappled, Jonathan lay sprawled on his back. Eve had dropped the gun and stood looking down at him, her hands clasped under her chin. Liza ran into the house.

twenty-one

SHE'D shot him," Liza said. "I knew at once it was on purpose. If he was dead he couldn't sell Shrove and it would go to his cousin David Cosby, who loved the place and wouldn't dream of selling it. It was the only way to make sure she got it. Marrying him wouldn't have worked, he'd still have sold it.

"The way she looked at me, I read it all in her face. The trouble was Matt. Who knows what she'd have done if Matt hadn't been there? Pretended to find Jonathan dead that evening or next day and made people believe he'd been out shooting alone? But Matt had seen. I don't mean he'd seen her do it, but he'd seen them together firing at the pigeons.

"Eve said to me, tell the police you saw nothing, tell them you don't even live here, you're just visiting, and then she said, why tell them anything? You don't have to be here. Matt didn't see you. So I went and sat in the little castle and they didn't know I'd been there. I think I knew then that she wanted to handle it all on her own.

"The police knew she had killed Jonathan but they could never prove it wasn't an accident, no one saw it happen, you see. I've been thinking a lot about it since the trial and that's the conclusion I've come to, that once they knew she'd killed Jonathan they remembered Bruno going missing and then they started thinking about the man called Trevor Hughes. They'd actually questioned her about him and she'd denied ever seeing him, but they'd got a record of it, they never forgot. I expect that's what happened.

"When they searched the gatehouse they didn't find Bruno's earrings because she was wearing them. She was wearing them the night before I left so I'm sure she still had them on the next morning. They did find Trevor Hughes's wedding ring with his initials inside and his wife's.

"They must have asked Matt if he knew anything about Trevor Hughes. Or else Matt went to them of his own accord and told them what he remembered that morning when the dogs behaved in that strange way. If she'd killed him they wondered what she'd done with his body and eventually they started digging.

"I'm sure they'd have liked to indict her for shooting Jonathan, but they were afraid she'd be acquitted. And they got nowhere trying to trace Bruno. But when they found Trevor Hughes's bones they found shot among them that came from that four-ten shotgun, that same one Jonathan was using to teach her to shoot pigeons. And they must have found his watch too for his wife to identify. I expect it went on for weeks after they first arrested her. I'd really like to know how they managed that—I mean, did they charge her with murdering Jonathan and then give that up and charge her with manslaughter instead just to hold her? And when did they think they'd got enough evidence to be sure of getting a conviction on the Hughes murder charge?"

Sean was staring at her incredulously. Liza smiled at him. "I told you, I'd like to be a lawyer. I'm interested in the law."

"You're a bright girl. You shouldn't be cleaning for that old woman."

Liza shrugged. It didn't seem important, it was only temporary. She began clearing their takeaway containers off the table. "D'you want a cup of tea?"

"In a minute," he said. "I've got something to tell you first. Now it's my turn. *I've* got something to tell *you.*"

She filled the kettle, lit the gas, and, catching sight of his expression, turned it low. "What, then?"

"I've been accepted for the management course."

As soon as the less than enthusiastic words were out, she regretted them, knew she should have congratulated him. But she had said, "Well, you knew you would be."

A flush darkened his face. "It's not been as straightforward as that. As a matter of fact, it was touch and go. They only took five out of two hundred applicants."

"And you're one of the five? Great."

She must have sounded kind but indifferent, maternally indulgent perhaps. He said, "Listen to me, Liza. Come and sit down."

Her sigh was audible but she sat down next to him.

"The course starts in the New Year but they want me up there next week. It's in Scotland, a place near Glasgow. They wanted to put me in a flat with the other four, that's the way they fix it, but I'll have you with me, so I said I'd see to my own accommodations. I never said caravan, I wasn't telling them all my private affairs."

"Glasgow?" she said. "That'll be a long way from wherever Eve is. But I don't suppose it'd be for long, would it? Didn't you say six months?"

"Liza, hopefully this is only the start. You've not been following me. This is a new way of life. It's great the things they'll do for you once you've shown you're up to the course. For one thing, the idea is to manage one of their stores and they're building new branches all the time. There's one they're putting up now on the M3. Hopefully I could be assistant manager of one of them by this time next year. They'll help you with a mortgage on a flat."

He must have seen she didn't know what he meant. While he explained what a mortgage was, she fidgeted about, suddenly wanting a cup of tea more than anything in the world but not quite liking to get up and make it. He took hold of her hand, imprisoning it.

"It's a great chance for me. It's sort of made me see myself differently, like I'm not the person I reckoned I was, I'm better, I could be my own man, a responsible person with a real career."

Yes, she thought, you even talk better. It's made you articulate, you can suddenly express yourself. Then he shocked her.

"There's something else I want to tell you, love. I want you to marry me, I want us to get married."

It was as much as she could do to speak. *"Married?"*

"I knew it'd be a surprise." He leaned toward her and gave her a quick kiss on the cheek. Fondly he said, "You silly nana, you've gone all red. If it's on account of your mum, I don't mind that. It'll be just the same to me as if you was any other girl with a normal family."

"Sean . . ." she began but it was as if she hadn't interrupted him.

"I'll get paid when I'm training, that's another great thing. Hopefully you won't have to work no more. I wouldn't want my wife going out cleaning anyway. And when the kids start coming you'll want to be at home . . ."

This time she shouted to break the flow. "I'm not yet seventeen years old!"

"That's okay. You have to be over sixteen to get married, not over seventeen. It's seventeen for a driving license."

She burst out laughing. It was too much. Unlike him though this would be, he had to be making some elaborate joke. It was a moment or two before she understood, before she saw from his hurt face that he was deadly serious. "Oh, Sean, don't look like that, don't be so *silly.*"

"Silly!"

"Well, of course it's silly talking about marrying and having children and one of those things, a what-d'you-call-it, a mortgage. We've got our lives to live first. I'm not even grown up really. In the law I can't sign a contract or make a will or anything."

"Shut up about the fucking law, will you?"

She flinched a little, got up and went to the stove. "I want my tea if you don't," she said in a chilly voice, Eve's voice. He was sullen as she had never seen him. Suddenly she realized that she had never crossed him, everything had gone pleasantly for him until this evening, but now the sultan was looking at her head and sharpening his sword.

"I don't mind coming to Scotland for a bit," she said in a

conciliating voice. "I'd quite like somewhere else for a change. We could try it. You might not like the course."

He took his tea without a thank-you. "You'd better listen to me, Liza. Have you thought where you'd be without me? You'd be lost, you'd be nothing. Thanks to the way that bitch brought you up, you wouldn't last five minutes on your own. You don't even know what a mortgage is! You never knew what the Pill was! The best you can do to earn your living is cleaning or picking apples. You don't know nothing except for rubbish out of books. She's crippled you for life, and you're going to need me to get you through it."

It was an echo of Bruno, Bruno's words outside the old station. She brought the teacup to her lips but the tea seemed tasteless.

"I'll be your husband, I'll look after you. There's some as'd say it was a pretty big thing I was doing, considering who and what your mother is. You don't reckon I'd rather live in this clapped-out old van than in a decent flat, do you? It'd be okay sharing with those guys, but I've a responsibility to you, I know that, and I'll be taking the car and the van up to Glasgow on Friday. I won't say I'll be taking them anyway, whether you come or not, because you'll have to come, you don't have no choice."

"Of course I have a choice."

"No, you don't. It's like this, you have to come with me just because you can't be left here with no place to live, no family, no friends, and—you have to face it, love—no skills. The truth is you're more like six than sixteen. It's not your fault but that's the way it is."

She said nothing. Taking her silence for acquiescence, he turned on the television. She thought he looked pleased with himself. The look on his face was Bruno's when he thought he had persuaded Eve to move into that house with him. After a little while he opened a can of beer and began to drink from the can. He must have been aware of her eyes on him, for he turned around, grinned, and made the thumbs-up sign, intended no doubt to reassure. She picked up the book Mr. Spurdell had lent her, *First Steps in English Law,* and found the place she had reached in it the day before.

That was the first broken night she had had since she shared a bed with Sean and almost the first that they hadn't made love. She lay awake, thinking how much she had loved him and wondering how that could have changed. How could you feel so passionately for a person and then, suddenly, not care anymore at all? A few words, a gross gesture, an insensitive assumption, and it was all gone. Had it been like that for Eve and Bruno?

She was out all day on Saturday, roaming the fields by herself, but on Sunday it rained and she lay in bed, reading. When she refused to get up and tidy the place, shake out the mats, help him fetch water, he accused her of sulking. They both went to work in the morning and met as usual at five. It was dark, pitch dark, when they reached the caravan, and there was no water. They had forgotten to fetch the water before they left. Liza took the bucket and a torch.

It struck her as somehow silly that it was pouring with rain yet they had no water. She held the bucket under the pipe that protruded from the hillside, filled it, and made her way back, once nearly falling on the slippery mud.

Once in the caravan she opened a can of Coke. She was washing her hands at the sink before she saw what he had done to the books. She glanced into the living area as she reached for the towel. A piece of book jacket, a torn-off triangle, red lettering on a black background, lay on the table. It brought a constriction to her throat. They had no wastebasket, only a plastic sack under the sink. The sight of its contents made her feel rather dizzy.

Sean wasn't looking at her, he was watching television, a can of beer beside him, a lighted cigarette in his left hand. She had the feeling he was consciously not looking at her, forcing his eyes to fix on the screen.

Easier than rummaging in that sack was to see what he had done by examining the books that remained. Mary Wollstonecraft was gone and *The Divine Comedy* and the *Metamorphoses. Middlemarch* was gone. With bile rising into her mouth, she saw that he had spared *First Steps in English Law* and the two Hardy novels. Those belonged to Mr. Spurdell and he knew it. Sean was always law-abiding. He wouldn't destroy "other people's" property. She didn't count as other people, she was his.

She walked across and switched off the television. He jumped up, and for a moment she thought he would hit her. But she had misjudged him there. Sean wouldn't hit a woman.

"Why?" she said, the single word.

"Come on, love, you know why. You've got to put all that behind you, that life. You've left the place, she's gone, you're out in the real world now. Them books, they was just a way of hiding yourself from real life. Hopefully you're not going to need them in the future. We've got our whole future before us. Isn't that what you said yourself?"

Had she? Not in that context, she was sure. He was triumphant, he was in charge. She felt as angry as she now guessed Eve must sometimes have felt.

"They were *my* books."

"They was *ours,* love. We've been through that before. Okay, so you bought them with the money you earned. How would you like it if I said that Coke you're drinking was mine because it was my money paid for it? It's the same thing."

It was illogical and Eve had taught her to be logical, to be reasonable. Eve must have felt like this when Bruno pretended to have a social conscience to cloak his need to possess her utterly. She must have felt like this when, after seventeen years of striving and repudiation, of hope and humiliation and desertion, Jonathan had at last asked her to marry him.

Liza was impotent, she had nothing to say, she could only imagine how he would twist what she said. She set their food out, she made tea, she put the television on again and was rewarded by his seizing her hand and squeezing it in his own. Together they watched an episode in a Hollywood miniseries. Or Sean watched it while she fixed her eyes on the screen and took her mind elsewhere.

She could clean a house and fetch water from a spring and read books but it was true what he said, in other ways she was more like six than sixteen. She couldn't manage on her own. Even if she worked eight hours a day for Mrs. Spurdell or someone like Mrs. Spurdell, she would still only earn £120 a week, and she doubted if she *could* do eight hours' housework a day. Where would she live? How would she afford anything?

Was there anyone in the world who would pay her to translate Latin into English for them? She knew nothing about it but that she doubted. Besides, she knew from investigating in Mr. Spurdell's study that you had to have certificates and things, diplomas, degrees, before people would employ you to do things which weren't housework or putting packets on a shelf in a supermarket.

She had nowhere to live. Jonathan Tobias might have helped her about that but he was dead. She had no father, only one of three men who knew nothing of her existence. Eve didn't seem to care for her. Eve didn't know where she was or what had happened to her, but perhaps, in Eve's position, she wouldn't care, either. Or Eve might care very much, might be in an agony of anxiety, when she found out, as she must have, that Liza had never got to Heather's. But no one had come looking for her, no one had put pieces in the paper about her or on the television. Liza knew there was no one to look after her but Sean. There was only Sean.

He held her hand. Soon he had his arm around her. She was full of cold dislike for him, which she somehow knew would have warmed into simple irritation after a night's sleep. If he would leave her alone. If he would leave her to come to terms with it in her own way. She had to, after all. She had to make the best of it because without him she was useless and helpless.

Only he wouldn't leave her alone. He must have been able to tell how hostile she was to him, he must have sensed her reluctance to be touched by him and understood something by the way she took his hand off her leg when he began running it up and down her thigh. They would have to share a bed, she was resigned to that, but when she realized he intended making love she spoke a firm, "No!" And then, "No, please, I don't want to."

But making love wasn't at all what happened. She had asked him once if he would ever force her and he had treated the question as ludicrous. But he took no notice when she told him she didn't want him, she didn't want to do it. He silenced her by clamping his mouth over hers. He held her hands down, tried to force her thighs apart with his knee, and when that didn't work, with his foot. To justify himself, he pretended she was playing coy and laughed into her mouth as he thrust like a dog in the street, as he shoved his penis hard inside her, held her arms stretched out the width of the bed, pinioning her.

She was powerless. It hurt, as it had never hurt even the first time. When it was over and he was whispering to her that he knew she had really enjoyed it, he could always tell if a girl liked it, she thought of Eve and Trevor Hughes. Eve had had a pair of dogs to call, but she had nothing.

He fell asleep immediately. She cried in silence. It was weak and foolish, she was a baby to do it, but she couldn't stop.

Eve would never have tolerated such treatment. Eve never permitted persecution. Not since what had happened on the way back from the airport. Her own suffering was nothing like as terrible, but bad enough, a foretaste of a possible future. Eve had revenged herself on three men for what three men had done to her. That was why she had done those things, for vengeance more than for fear or safety or gain. More for vengeance than for Shrove.

Was this then what her own life would be? Making love when she wanted to and also making love when she didn't want to. Or doing *that* when she didn't want to. After what had happened, she thought she would never want to again. She remembered the day of Jonathan Tobias's wedding and how Eve had used the occasion as an opportunity for a lesson, as she so often did. She had taught Liza about marriage and marriage customs but had said nothing of having to do what a man wanted when you didn't want to, of men getting their way because they were stronger, of working for them and waiting on them and submitting to their right to tell you what to do.

Perhaps she hadn't because Liza had been only a child then. It was a lifetime ago and she was a child no longer. But once more she was in a position where she couldn't run away. And it was worse than last time when all she needed was courage. Now she had nowhere to run to.

One other thing Eve had done for her, though, apart from teaching her so many of the things Sean said were useless, and that was to teach her to rough it. Life had never been soft. They made their own pleasures with the minimum of aid, without toys, television, videos, CD players, external amusements. Eventually, after years, they had got their bathroom. The gatehouse had an old fridge and an even older oven, but there was no heating upstairs, no down quilts or electric blankets of the kind she'd seen at Spurdells', no new clothes—those jeans and the padded coat were the only things she possessed not made by Eve or from the Oxfam shop—they'd had none of that takeaway or processed food she'd got used to with Sean but never really trusted. They'd made their own bread at the gatehouse, grown their own vegetables, made their own jam and even cream cheese. Everywhere they went they'd had to walk once Bruno was gone.

Her mother had given her a kind of endurance, a sort of toughness, but what use was that in the world of Spurdells and Superway? You didn't need to be tough, you needed certificates and diplomas, families and relations, a roof over your head and means of transport, you needed skills and money. Well, she had a thousand pounds.

She could see the money belt on the table where he had thrown it when he stripped her. If he knew about the money, he would want it. Once he wanted it, he would take it. He would say that what was hers was theirs and therefore his. She got up, washed all traces of him off her body, pulled on leggings and the blue-and-red sweater for warmth and, curling the money belt up as tightly as she could, thrust it inside one of her boots.

Keeping as far from him as she could, on the far edge of the bed, she went to sleep.

t w e n t y - t w o

PROUDLY showing Liza her box of decorations that had all come from Harrods, Mrs. Spurdell said it was too early to dress the tree yet. But there was no point in deferring the purchase of it until later when the best would be gone. Philippa and her children were coming for Christmas. Jane was coming. Having once told Liza Philippa's Christian name, Mrs. Spurdell had since then always referred to her as Mrs. Page while Jane was "my younger daughter."

It was the first Christmas tree Liza had ever seen. Indeed, it was the first she had ever heard of and the rationale for uprooting a fir tree, winding tinsel strings around it, and hanging glass balls on the branches was beyond her understanding. As for Christian customs, Eve had taught her no more about Christianity than she had about Buddhism, Judaism, and Islam.

She could hear Mr. Spurdell moving about in his study upstairs. His school had broken up for Christmas. With the two of them in the house she had no chance of a bath. She scrubbed out the tub and put caustic down the lavatory pan. While she was cleaning the basin it occurred to her to look in the medicine cabinet. There, among the denture-cleaning tablets, the vapor rub, and the corn solvent, she found a cylindrical container labeled: MRS. M. SPURDELL, SODIUM AMYTAL, ONE TO BE TAKEN AT NIGHT. Of its properties she knew nothing except that it evidently made you sleep. She put the container in her pocket.

If she didn't have her money in her hand before she gave notice, she thought it quite likely Mrs. Spurdell would refuse to pay her. While she pushed the vacuum cleaner up and down the passage, she worked out various strategies. Determined to be honest and not to prevaricate, she knocked on the study door.

"Do you want to come in here, Liza?" Mr. Spurdell put his head out. "I won't be a minute."

"I'll do the study last if you like," she said. "I've brought all your books back."

"That's a good girl. You're welcome to more. I've no objection to lending my dear old friends to a sensible person who knows how to take care of them. A good book, you know, Liza, 'is the precious lifeblood of a master spirit.' "

"Yes," said Liza, "but I don't want to borrow anymore. Can I ask you something?"

No doubt, he expected her to ask who said that about a good book but she already knew it was Milton and knew too, which was very likely more than he did, that it came from *Areopag-*

itica. He was all smiling invitation to having his brains picked.

"How can you find out where someone's in prison?"

"I beg your pardon?" The smile was swiftly gone.

Now for the honesty. "My mother has gone to prison and I want to know where she is."

"Your mother? Good heavens. This isn't a game, is it, Liza? You're being serious?"

She was weary with him. "I only want to know who to write to or who to phone and find out where they've put her. I want to write to her, I want to go and see her."

"Good heavens. You've really given me quite a shock." He took a step forward, glanced over the banisters, and spoke in a lowered voice, "Don't give Mrs. Spurdell a hint of this."

"Why would I tell *her*?" Liza made an impatient gesture with her hands. "Is there a place I could phone? An office, I mean, a police headquarters of some kind?" She was vaguely remembering American police serials.

"Oh, dear, I suppose it would be the Home Office."

"What's the Home Office?"

Questions that were requests for information always pleased him. Prefacing his explanation with a "You don't know what the Home Office is?" he proceeded to a little lecture on the police, prisons, immigration, and ministries of the interior. Liza took in what she needed.

She drew breath and braced herself. Sean's words came back to her, about being more like six than sixteen, about being helpless. "Please, may I use your phone? And may I look in the phone directory first?"

He was no longer the benevolent pedagogue, twinkling as he imparted knowledge. A frown appeared and a petulant tightening of the mouth. "No, I'm afraid you couldn't. No to both. I can't have that sort of thing going on here. Besides, this is the most expensive time. Have you any idea what it would cost to phone to London at eleven o'clock in the morning?"

"I'll pay."

"No, I'm sorry. It's not only the money. This isn't the kind of thing Mrs. Spurdell and I should wish to be involved in. I'm sorry but no, certainly not."

She gave a little bob of the head and immediately switched on the vacuum cleaner once more. When the bedrooms were done, she came back to the study and found him gone. Quickly she looked for Home Office in the phone book. Several numbers were listed. She wrote down three of them, knowing she didn't want Immigration or Nationality or Telecommunications.

The house was clean and tidy, her time up. It seemed harder than it had ever been to extract twelve pounds from Mrs. Spurdell, the last pound coming in the shape of fifteen separate coins. Liza thanked her and said she was leaving, she wouldn't be coming anymore. Mrs. Spurdell affected not to believe her ears. When she was convinced, she asked rhetorically how she was supposed to manage over Christmas. Liza said nothing but pocketed the money and put on her coat.

"I think you're very ungrateful," said Mrs. Spurdell, "and very foolish, considering how hard jobs are to come by."

She began shouting for her husband, presumably to come and stop Liza from leaving. Liza walked out of the front door and shut it behind her. All the way down Aspen Close she expected to have to run because one of them was pursuing her but nothing like that happened. If the manager who admired her had been on duty in the Duke's Head she would have asked him if she might use his phone, but there was a woman in reception. While she was occupied at the computer, Liza walked upstairs and had a bath.

Not waiting for Sean but going home on the bus, it occurred to her as she climbed to the front seat on the top, that for a six-year-old—like the milkman with a child's mental age?—she hadn't done badly. Surely she had been resourceful? She had acquired a soporific drug, discovered how to find her mother, had even found the phone number, had given in her notice, had a bath, and lacking a towel, dried herself on the hotel bathroom curtains.

Would she have done better if she'd grown up in a London street and been to boarding school?

Sean had finished at Superway. He had unpacked his last carton of cornflakes and last can of tomatoes. A little wary of her still but no longer sullen, he described how the manager had shaken hands with him and wished him well.

"Does anyone know about me?" Liza asked him. "I mean, the people at your work? Do they know you've got a girlfriend who lives with you and who I am and all that?"

"No, they don't. I keep my private affairs to myself. So far as they know, I'm all on my own."

"Will you drive to Scotland?"

"'Course I'll drive. What you got in mind? First-class train tickets and a stopover in a luxury hotel? You've got a lot to learn about money, love."

He began fretting about a new law that had come in, excluding caravans from all land except where the owner's express permission was given. The sooner they were gone the better. Would the law in Scotland be different? He'd heard it sometimes was. Liza knew more about it than he did, she had read it up in Mr. Spurdell's newspaper. For instance, she knew that if your caravan was turned off a piece of land and you weren't allowed to park it anywhere else, the local authority was bound to house you. It might not be a real house or a flat, it might be only a room, even a hotel room, but it would be *somewhere.* She wasn't going to say any of this to Sean and risk a sneer about her cleverness and her aspirations.

All the time they had been there she had kept the caravan very clean. Cleanliness was ingrained in her, Eve had seen to that, and she could no more have left her home dirty than she could have failed to wash herself. For all that, it was a poor place, everything about it shabby, worn, scraped, scuffed, chipped, broken, cracked, and makeshift-mended. But the gatehouse had been shabby too. Would she want anything like the "monstrosity" Bruno had picked or the Spurdells' house, she who had been spoiled for choice by Shrove?

The caravan and the car, a home and a means of transport. With those, life would be possible, some kind of future would be possible. She watched Sean speculatively. Spartan living wasn't all that Eve had taught her.

No one had known where Bruno was and no one had cared except an easily fobbed-off estate agent. Trevor Hughes had had an estranged wife, glad to see the back of him. No one knew Sean wasn't alone. Her existence, her presence in his life, all this he had kept secret. He had left Superway and at this branch they would think no more about him, no doubt he was already forgotten.

At the Glasgow end they would expect him to turn up for the course on Monday. If he didn't come they wouldn't set in motion a police alert but conclude that he had changed his mind. She knew little about life, but the experiences she had had were of a peculiar nature. Few could look back on a similar history. She knew from experience, from the disappearance of Trevor Hughes and Bruno Drummond, that the police do little about searching for missing men in their particular circumstances. In this case it was unlikely an absent man would even be reported missing.

Sean's mother had long since lost interest in him. His brothers and sisters were scattered in distant places, long out of touch. The chain-smoking grandfather was too ancient to bother. The people he called his friends were pub acquaintances and caravan-site neighbors like Kevin.

While Sean watched television, she looked at herself long in the glass, the cracked piece of mirror ten inches by six that was all she and Sean had to see their faces in. It had seemed to her that Eve had never changed. The woman she had run away from a hundred days and nights ago was in her eyes the same woman, looking just the same, as the mother who had brought her to Shrove when she was three, not older or heavier or less fresh. Yet now as she looked at her own face it was a youthful Eve that she saw, different from the Eve of the present, an Eve she had forgotten but who came back to her as herself. As Jonathan had once said, as Bruno had said, she was a clone of that Eve, fatherless, her mother's double, her mother all over again.

With her mother's methods, with her mother's instincts. What would Eve have done? Not put up with it. Never yielded. Eve would have argued, remonstrated, reasoned—as she had—and when all that was to no avail, when they wouldn't agree or see her point of view, appeared to give in and conciliate them.

Retreating to the kitchen where he couldn't see her, she reread the instructions on the label of the sodium amytal carton. One would evidently send him to sleep. Two, surely, would put him into a deep sleep. And while he slept? He had often reproached her for not being squeamish enough, for an ability to confront violence and blood and death.

She had never been taught a horror of these things. If she was horrified by any of violent death's aspects it was at her own weakness in vomiting when she found Bruno's body. Eve had taught her to be a perfectionist, to be good at everything she did. She would do this well, cleanly, efficiently, and without remorse.

"What time do we start in the morning?" she asked him.

"First thing. Hopefully we can be on our way by eight."

"At least it's stopped raining."

"The weather forecast says an area of high pressure's coming. It's going to get cold, cold and bright."

"Shouldn't you put the towing bar on tonight?"

"Christ," he said. "I forgot."

She doubted if she could do it herself. In the past, when he had done it, she hadn't bothered to watch him. This evening, of course, she watched him all the time, studying what he did, assessing him in every possible situation, as she had done in those early days when she was in love with him.

Perhaps, at sixteen, you were never in love with the same person for long. It was violent, it was intense, but of short duration. Did teachers like Mr. Spurdell, or people like Eve, ever ask if Juliet would have gone on being in love with Romeo?

Sean worked by the light of a Tilley lamp and a rechargeable battery torch. Wrapped in the thick padded coat, she sat on the caravan steps in the quiet and the darkness, appreciating for the first time how silent it was here and how remote. Like Shrove. This place had the advantages of Shrove. Not a single light was visible, not an isolated pinpoint in any direction across the miles of hills and meadowland. The black land rolled away to meet the nearly black sky. If she strained her ears the gentle chatter of the stream was just audible.

Above her now the stars were coming out, Charles's Wain pale and spread out and Orion bright and strong. The white planet, still and clear, was Venus. The air had that glittery feel to it, as of unseen frost in the atmosphere. Metal clinking against metal occasionally broke the silence as Sean worked, that and the soft ghostly cries of owls in the invisible trees.

She hooked her thumbs inside the money belt, feeling its thickness. How was it she knew that if she let Sean live and went up north with him he would sooner or later find out about that money and demand it himself? She did know. She could even create the scene in her mind with her telling him it was hers, hers by right of her mother, and Sean saying she wasn't fit to have charge of money, he'd look after it and put it toward the home they'd buy.

He finished coupling the car to the caravan. They went back inside and he washed his hands. It was late, past eleven, and as he kept saying, they had to get up early.

"Don't you worry, I'll wake you," he said. "You know what you are, sleep like the dead. I don't reckon you'd ever wake up without me to give you a shake."

She didn't argue. Her dissenting role was past and now she was all acquiescence. Eve had given in to Bruno over the house and to Jonathan over the sale of Shrove. Perhaps she had murmured, "Yes, all right," to Trevor Hughes before she bit his hand. You gave in, you smiled and said a sweet, "You win." You lulled them into believing theirs was the victory.

"Wake me up at seven and I'll make you tea."

It wasn't unusual for her to say that, she often said and did it. He never had a hot drink at night, always had one in the morning. She put the pill container behind the sugar basin, opened the drawer where they kept cutlery, their blunt knives and forks with bent tines, and checked that the one sharp knife was there, the carver. It was good to be the kind of person who didn't flinch from weapons or the consequences of using them.

He was already in bed. Her throat felt dry and her stomach muscles tightened as they had on the previous night and the night before. On neither of those nights had he touched her. Last evening he hadn't even kissed her. But she was afraid just the same, of his strength and her own weakness, knowing now something she'd never realized and would once have refused to believe: that a woman, however young and vigorous, is powerless against a determined man.

When she came to bed and switched off the light she fancied she could feel his eyes on her in the darkness. Gradually, as always happened, she became accustomed to the absence of light, and the darkness ceased to be absolute, became gray rather than black. The moon had risen out there, or half a moon to give so pale a light. It trickled thinly around the window blinds.

His eyes were on her and his lips tentatively touched her cheek. He must have felt her immediate tension for he sighed softly. An enormous relief relaxed her body as he rolled over on his side away from her. She withdrew to the side of the bed, to put as many inches as she could between herself and him.

She would sleep now and in the morning she would kill him.

twenty-three

DREAMING, she was herself and not herself. She was Eve, too. She looked down at her hands and they were Eve's hands, smaller than hers, the nails longer. A shrinking had reduced her to Eve's height.

Yet she was in the caravan where Eve had never been. She knew she was dreaming and that somehow, by taking thought, by a process of concentration, she could be herself again. It was dark. She could just make out the shape of Sean lying in bed and a hump in the bedclothes beside him as if another body lay there, *her* body. She had come out of her body the way the Ancient Egyptians believed the Ka did. But it felt solid, her hand tingled when she drew a nail across the palm. It was no longer Eve, for Eve had come in and was standing at the foot of the bed.

They looked at each other in silence. Eve's hands were chained, she had come out of prison, and Liza knew—though not how she knew—that she must go back there. In spite of the chains, painfully, with a great effort, Eve reached up and took the gun down from the caravan wall. There was no gun there but she reached up and took it down. A little moonlight gleamed on the metal. Long ago, years and years ago, Liza had known that her mother took the gun down from the wall but she had never seen her do it.

Eve came up to her, holding the gun in her manacled hands. She did not speak, yet her message communicated itself to Liza. It would be easy. Only the first time was hard. Sleep would still be possible and peace of mind and contentment. Long days of forgetfulness would pass. Eve smiled. She began to whisper confidingly how she had wrapped herself in a sheet, taken a kitchen knife, and crept upstairs to the sleeping Bruno.

Liza cried out then. She reached for Sean, for the bed, for the body of herself and entered it again, her body growing around her, waking as she woke. And then she was up, huddled and crouching in a far corner. The moon still shone and its greenish light still infiltrated the caravan, seeping between window frames and blinds. It was icy cold.

Gradually full wakefulness returned. The cold brought it back. Strangely, the dream had been quite warm. She fumbled around in the half dark, first for Mrs. Spurdell's pill container, then for the sweater Eve had knitted. As she pulled it over her head, the dreadful feeling came to her that once her eyes were uncovered again she would see Eve standing there, chained, smiling, advising.

She opened her eyes. They were alone, she and Sean. It

struck her as very strange, almost unbelievable, that she had meant to kill him.

More cold would come in but still she opened the caravan door. The steps glittered with frost. She prised the top off the pill carton and threw the pills into the long wet grass in the ditch. The frost burned her bare feet and when she was back inside again sharp pains shot through them.

Despair seemed to have been waiting for her in the caravan. It was there in the cold darkness and the smell of bodies and stale food. The world hadn't fallen apart when Eve told her to go. It was falling apart now, one staunch rock after another tumbling and landsliding, Eve, Sean, herself. Soon the ground beneath her feet would founder and split and swallow her up. She gave a little cry and in an agony of grief and loneliness, flung herself face-downward on the bed, breaking into sobs.

Sean woke up and put the light on. He didn't ask what was the matter but lifted her up in his arms, held his arms tightly around her, and pulled her close to him, burrowing them both under the covers. Murmuring that her hands were frozen, he squeezed them between their bodies, against his warm body.

"Don't cry, sweetheart."

"I can't help it, I can't stop."

"Yes, you can. You will in a minute. I know why you're crying."

"You don't, you can't." Because I can't kill you, because I'll never kill anyone, because I'm not Eve.

"I do know, Liza. It's because of what I done the other night, isn't it? It seemed funny at the time, like a joke, and then I got to remembering what you'd said to me when we first done it, back in the summer, like I'd never make you if you didn't want to, and I'd said I never would. I've been ashamed of myself. I've hated myself."

"Have you?" she whispered. "Have you really?"

"I didn't know how to say it. I was like embarrassed. In the light, in the daytime, I don't know, I couldn't say it. I'm not like you, I can't express myself like you. I've felt that too, maybe you never knew it but I have, you being like superior to me in everything."

"I'm not, I'm really not."

"It's so bloody cold in here I'm going to light the gas. I don't reckon we'll sleep no more. It's nearly six."

Wiping her wet face on the sheet, she watched him get up, wrap himself in the clothes that lay about, and then put a match to the open oven. Her eyes hurt with crying and she felt a little sick.

What he said next surprised her so much she sat bolt upright in bed.

"You don't want to come with me, do you?"

"What?"

He got back into bed and pulled her down under the bedclothes. He hugged her and held her head in the hollow of his shoulder. His hands were always warm. That hadn't really registered with her before, or she had taken it for granted. She remembered the sunny summer days and how she had watched him, that first time, from among the trees at Shrove and his puzzled look as he stared unseeing at her, aware as people mysteriously are of being observed.

He said it again, "You don't want to come with me," but not this time in the form of a question.

Shaking her head under the bedclothes, she realized that the movement indicated nothing to him and she whispered a small, "No."

"Is it because I—I forced myself on you?"

"No."

"I'd never do it again. I've learned my lesson."

"It's not because of that."

"No, I know." He sighed. She felt his chest move with the sigh and was aware of his heart beating under her cheek. "It's because we're not like the same kind of people," he said. "I'm an ordinary—well, I'm working class and you're—you may have been brought up in that cracked way but you're—you're light-years above me."

"No, no, Sean. No."

"You only got to listen to the way we talk. I know I get words wrong and I get grammar wrong. Hopefully that'll change when I get into management. I might say you could teach me, but that wouldn't work. In a funny sort of way, I knew it wouldn't work when it first started last summer, only I wouldn't admit it even to myself. I suppose I was in love—well, I know I was. I'd never been in love before."

"Nor I."

"No, I reckon you never had the chance. I had but I never was. Not till you. Only, love, how'll you make out on your own?"

"I'll manage."

"I do love you, Liza. It wasn't just for sex. I loved you from the first moment I saw you."

She put up her face to him and felt for his mouth with her mouth. The touch of his lips and the feel of his tongue on hers quickened her thawing body. She felt the quick familiar ripple of desire. He sighed with pleasure and relief. They made love half-clothed, buried under the piled covers, his hands warm and hers still icy, while the blue gas flared and the water from condensation flowed down the windows.

It was eight when they woke up, much later than he had intended. She was making tea, wearing her padded coat, when he said, "I'll tell you what I'll do, I'll leave you the van."

She turned around. "The caravan?"

He thought she was correcting him again. "Okay, teacher, the *cara*van. Always got to be right, haven't you? Always know best. That's what you'd better be, not a doctor or a lawyer, but a teacher."

"Did you really mean you'd leave me the caravan?"

"Sure I did. Look at it this way, I was going to take the van on account of you, but if you're not coming it'd be better for me to share with those guys, it'd be easier."

"You could sell it."

"What, this old wreck? Who'd buy it?"

Her hesitation lasted only a moment. "I've got some money," she said. "I found it when I went to Shrove. It was Eve's but she'd have wanted me to have it."

"You never said. Why didn't you tell me?"

"Because I'm horrible—or I thought you were. Don't be cross *now.* It's a lot, it's more than a thousand pounds."

She was ashamed because she'd thought he'd grab the money as soon as he got the chance and here he was shaking his head. "I always said I'd not live off my girlfriend and I won't. Even"—he smiled a bit ruefully—"if you're not my girlfriend no more. You'll need it, love, whatever you do. I'd get in touch with that Heather if I was you. Hopefully, she's been wondering what you've been up to. It'll be a relief to her. And then maybe you and her can go together to see your mum."

Liza gave him his tea. "I'll tell you what I'm going to do, Sean. I'm going to cook us a big breakfast of eggs and bacon and fried potatoes and fried bread and if it stinks out the caravan, who cares?"

"We'll meet again one day, won't we?" he said as he started on his first egg. "You never know, we might both be different."

"Of course we'll meet again."

She knew they never would. Whatever became of him, she would be different beyond recognition.

"You'll need someone to look after you." He fretted a bit as he packed his bags. They were Superway plastic carriers, the only luggage he had. Guilt over her made him fret. "You'll get hold of Heather, won't you? That money you've got, it's not all that much. I'll tell you what, I'll drive you into town, it's on my way. You can phone her from there."

"All right."

"I'll feel easier, love."

Instead of hating the new situation, he was relieved. Just a bit. She could tell that, she could see it in his eyes. Tomorrow it would be more than a bit, it would be overwhelming. He wouldn't be able to believe his luck. As it was, now, he was forcing himself to put up a big pretense of being sad.

"I'll worry about you."

"Write down where you'll be," she said, "and I'll write to you and tell you what's happened to me. I promise."

He gave her a sidelong look. "Don't put in too many long words."

The two phone boxes in the marketplace were both empty. Sean parked in front of them. He felt in his jacket pocket and gave her all the change he had: coins to phone Heather and coins to phone the Home Office. There were enough of them to last even if people at the other end kept her waiting while they went off to find someone. First, he said, she must get on to directory enquiries for Heather's number. She'd got the address still, hadn't she?

"But maybe you'd better come with me, after all, love. Just

for a week or two, until we've found someplace for you to go, until you're sure of this Heather."

She shook her head. "You've left the van behind, remember? You've left me the van."

That he was grateful for her use of his term she could see in his eyes. They seemed full of love, as they had been in those early days, at apple-picking time, in the warm sunny fields. She put up her face and kissed him, a long soft passionless kiss. It troubled her, and always would, that she had thought of killing him. Even if she hadn't really been serious, even if it was a fantasy created out of stress and memory, it would always be there. More than anything else, it would be responsible for making any further love or companionship or even contiguity between them impossible.

"Drive off," she said. "Don't wave. I'll be okay. Good luck."

But she watched the car go, she couldn't help herself. And he did wave. He did a funny thing, he blew her a kiss. She was left in the cold marketplace, on the pavement, with shoppers all around her.

The phone boxes weren't empty anymore. A woman had gone into one of them and a boy into the other. She sat down on the low brick wall built around a flower bed, an empty flower bed, the earth thinly sprinkled with frost. It didn't matter to her how many people went into those phone boxes, if a queue of fifty formed, if someone went in and vandalized them like they'd done to the one outside Superway, pulled the phones off the wall, it wouldn't matter to her because she didn't mean to phone anyone. What she had to do now was think of how to find out where a certain street was.

She thought about it. If she didn't fix her mind on something practical it would fill up with fear, with the realization of her utter aloneness. Sooner or later she was going to have to confront that, but not now. A picture of herself as a silly little ignorant girl sitting on a brick wall weeping rose before her eyes and she resolved not to let it become real. She would go into a shop and ask.

They didn't know. The shop was full of small objects Liza thought were called souvenirs, brooches and key rings and little boxes, fluffy animals and plastic dolls and china mugs, that she couldn't believe anyone would want to possess. The people who worked there all came from outside the town. You could get a street plan, one of them said. How do I, she asked, and if they looked at her strangely, they nevertheless said, a paper shop, yes, that's the best place, there's one three doors along.

And there was. And they had a street plan. They didn't seem to think it was a funny thing to ask for. It was a long way away, her destination, two miles she calculated from the rough scale.

On the way she passed street people who had been out all night on the pavement or in doorways if they were lucky. It brought back to her what Sean had said about "poor buggers sleeping rough." Would she be one of them? It was a possibility. A thousand pounds wasn't the fortune she had thought it when she first took the iron box. It didn't seem much when you could pay a twentieth part of it for that pair of shoes she saw in a shop window she passed.

The shops stopped soon after that and there came a place with a red fire engine half out of its door. Seeing one like it on television made identification possible. Next door was a big imposing building with a blue lamp over the door and a notice board on either side of the entrance. The blue lamp, like the one on the car, told her what it was before she read the County Police sign.

She stopped and stared at the poster on the notice board. The strange thing was that she recognized the painting in it as Bruno's before she knew it for her own portrait. The big features, the strong colors that had never been her features and colors. No one passing would know it for her. If anyone came by they would never connect the brown-and-yellow daub on the poster with the girl who stood looking at it.

No doubt, it was the best the police could do. It was all they had. Probably they had never before come upon a missing person who had never had her photograph taken. The poster said: HAVE YOU SEEN THIS GIRL? It said she was missing, gave her name and age, her height and weight and the color of her hair, that anyone knowing her whereabouts should be in touch with them.

Liza turned away. She felt enormously more cheerful, she felt full of hope. Eve hadn't forgotten her, Eve did need her. If no one had found her it was because the only likeness of her that existed was Bruno's strange daub. She began to walk fast along this street of small red houses, all linked together in a long row of roofs and chimneys and tiny gardens, each with its car at the pavement. Warmth began to spread through her and she felt the blood come into her cheeks.

The house she was going to wouldn't look like these, she had decided, but either like Mr. and Mrs. Spurdell's or else like the one Bruno had nearly bought, or a mixture of the two. That sort was beginning to appear now, prim, neat houses each hugging to itself its small, walled piece of land.

The name of the place where she had grown up and the year of her own birth. Shrove Road was on the edge of the town where the country started. Number 76 wasn't at all what she had expected but a house that looked as if left over from some distant past time when there were no other buildings but the church and the manor and the farms. This one had been a small farmhouse, she thought, which even now stood in a big piece of land with trees on it.

She was suddenly afraid. Of no one being at home, of her assumptions and assessments being all wrong, of walking back again to the bus stop past the street people. The bell by the front door didn't chime like the one in Aspen Close or toll like the bell on the door at Shrove. It buzzed. She took her finger away as if the insect that made the buzzing had stung it, then, more confidently, pressed again.

Jane Spurdell didn't recognize her. Liza could tell that and, inspired, she grasped a handful of her hair and pulled it to the back of her head.

"I know. It's Liza. Wait a minute, Liza Holford."

"Yes."

"Come in. You must be cold." A glance outside had told her Liza had come on foot. From where? "I'm miles from anywhere."

"I'm used to being miles from anywhere," Liza said, and that was the start of telling her. Not all, not a hundred nights of life story, just the essentials and an outline of her present state.

Jane Spurdell made coffee. They sat in her living room, which was a mess, but a nice mess with books on shelves and piled on tables and even on the floor.

"I want to study the law but I've a long way to go, I know that. I've got to get"—she couldn't remember the names of the examinations—"oh, GC Levels or something. And I want to find my mother and go and see her. I've got a thousand pounds and a caravan to live in."

"The law sounds a good idea. Why not?" Jane Spurdell said. "You can use my phone if you want to phone your mother." She looked a little wary. "I'm not sure about the caravan, I mean if you came to ask me if you could park it here, I'd have to think about that one."

"No, I've got it on a place where they'll make me move and when I can't they'll move me and find me somewhere to live. They have to." Liza finished her coffee. She was warm now and feeling strong. "I came to ask you one thing I know you can do for me."

"Yes?"

Liza didn't want to face it that for a moment she had sounded like her father. She said in a rush, "Please, can you arrange for me to go to school?"

It was relief that Jane felt. Liza could tell that. Whatever she had expected it hadn't been that. She had anticipated begging, requests for money, time, attention—even, perhaps, affection.

"Yes, of course I can," she said, relief beaming in her smile. "Nothing easier. It's not difficult. You can start somewhere in January. I only wish more people were like you. Is that all?"

Liza gave a great sigh. She was going to be all right and she wasn't going to burst into tears of relief or make confessions. A good time was beginning and she was going to think of that and be a Stoic.

"That's all I want. To go to school." She held out her cup. "And please may I have another cup of coffee?"